BOOK ONE

THE IMMORTAL INVESTIGATION

MICHAEL CRONK

To Kit
For liking a humble short story I wrote in 2015
and encouraging me for years to turn it into a real book.
You are the essence of music and the colour of starlight.

Contents

Chapter 1

"I've got a date tomorrow night!"

Jason had barely opened the apartment door and already his roommate was up in his face, talking to him, and completely blocking the entryway.

The nerve of some people.

"Good for you," Jason drawled and gestured at the door.

"She's really something," his roommate went on in a flurry of energy, oblivious to Jason's mood. "She lives at Maristow House. You know the big mansion out of town? That's hers! Ka-ching, am I right?" Jason gave up and simply barged his way inside. "Anyway, she's a vampire so she's super shy. But she's *really* good looking—"

"Peter," Jason said, his voice snapping more than he intended. Peter recoiled back. "I just worked a ten-hour shift on a Saturday. Can you please wait until I'm drinking?"

"Oh, yeah sure buddy," Peter said and he suddenly thrust a beer bottle at Jason. The glass was cold and the lid was already off, and Peter even presented it with a broad, charming smile. *That was fast. Where did he pull that from?* Still, Jason couldn't be mad at his roommate. The guy was so naturally handsome he was hard to dislike. Peter could be a supermodel, with his tall and lean body, soft features, blue eyes and gorgeous smile. Not that he was Jason's type at all, not with that relentless self-confidence.

Jason grumbled as he took the beer bottle. "Thanks." Yet the rim had not even reached his mouth before Peter started talking again.

"Her name's Silvana."

Jason groaned as he stepped inside the apartment and kicked off his boots. There was no escaping this conversation now.

"We met at university, and we've been chatting online all week. She wants to hang out tomorrow night."

"That's great," Jason started, then trailed off, glancing around at their small living area. "You uh… do much studying today?"

Peter snorted derisively. "Oh yeah. Loads."

"Right. I just assumed you were too busy studying to do any cleaning."

The apartment was covered in clutter. Textbooks, backpacks, empty beer bottles and dishes littered every cushion of the couch. There was even a milk bottle sitting on the bench with a puddle of condensation around it. The apartment was already such a small space it could barely fit a two-seater dining table, and the kitchen–that was more of a kitchenette–struggled to fit even one person amongst its cramped cupboards and tight corners.

Jason sighed as he reached for the dishes on the table. Peter cut in quickly. "Whoa dude, I got this. You've been at work all day, so just chill. I'll take care of this."

"Oh," Jason paused, rubbing a calloused hand over his clean-shaven chin. "Well, thanks."

"Couch is all yours."

"Are you sure about that?" Jason pointed to a bowl with soggy half-finished cereal still inside, sitting right in the middle of the central cushion.

Peter appeared, sweeping the bowl up and dusting the couch with his palm. "Your throne awaits, your majesty."

Jason offered a smile as he sat down. *I guess I am a bit uptight. I should get excited for him.*

"What do you have planned for your date?" he asked.

"Well!" Peter buzzed with more energy as he started cleaning. "Nothing fancy. And not just 'cause I'm a student and therefore destitute." He laughed at his own joke. "I'll pick her up from her house, take her into town for dinner. And yes, pay for both meals. I know she's shy, so I figure a simple dinner date will give her the chance to open up."

"And after dinner?"

"I take her home again like a gentleman."

"So just dinner? Seems like a short date. What if it goes well?"

"Then I take her home even earlier, ey?" Peter winked dramatically, the movement making him drop a spoon off the top of the tower of plates he carried, and the whole thing wobbled menacingly when he tried to catch it mid-fall.

Jason shook his head. "Seriously, mate, you're not gonna push for sex on the first date, right? You'll blow your chances."

"That's not all that's gonna blow." Peter winked again and his broad smile made a dimple pop on one cheek.

Jason stared at him. "And it's creepy."

"All right fine! She was wearing one of those superhero t-shirts, so maybe we can see a superhero movie afterwards."

"Better."

"You should come with us."

Jason blinked. "What?"

"Well… here's the thing. It's not actually, officially, technically, a date. It's more us two just hanging out. She said I could bring someone, if I wanted."

"No."

"Jason, you could do with some fun."

"I could also do with some rest. I just worked a six-day week. I have Sunday off, then I'm back at the station Monday to Friday. All I want is sleep."

"That's my point. All you do is work." Peter dragged a chair over and sat down in front of the couch, facing Jason directly. "Jase, we've been friends for a long time."

"I wouldn't say friends…"

"Shut up," Peter said casually, and Jason chuckled. "You've always worked hard, and never played. You don't have that many friends."

"But I like that. I'm happy this way, really."

"Come on. You haven't dated anyone in… how long?"

Jason grimaced.

"You only ever leave this apartment to work, workout, or when I drag your ass outside to make you socialise. What if I marry Silvana and move into that big mansion of hers? Will you ever leave this place again?"

Jason frowned. "Is Silvana bringing anyone?"

"Probably not. She's shy, remember?" Peter slapped him on the shoulder. "Come on, man. Be my chaperone."

"All right," Jason said and held up his hands defensively before Peter could launch into his next ridiculous argument. "I'll come and watch you date a girl. That doesn't sound awkward at all."

Peter grinned. "Good call." He stood up and moved back towards the kitchen. "Besides, I could use a police escort. She is a vampire, after all."

Jason blinked. Then he blinked again, before turning to stare at Peter's back. *He really did just say vampire. I thought I misheard him the first time. What is he…*

"Oh," Jason muttered. "Cause she's shy. She's *like* a vampire. I get it." He shook his head and took another swig of beer, before realising he'd somehow already finished the bottle. *Damn.* He stood up. "I'm gonna take a shower."

He took off his tie and unbuttoned his police shirt. Underneath, his chest was firm without being particularly buff, and his arms had the faint outline of muscle. Jason had always kept himself fit and focused more on cardio than bulk. But he didn't have Peter's natural looks. Jason's hard, angular face made him look like he was always scowling, which seemed to make others nervous.

"Wait," Jason called, his mind finally catching up. "You're not trying to help me socialise. You just want me to *drive you!*"

Peter spun around, his hand pressed to his chest in mock outrage. "What? How dare you, good sir." Jason glared at him, and with his shirt off, he knew he cast an intimidating figure. "Fine. I need a lift. But I *am* doing you a favour. Hell, I'm doing the world a favour. Look at you, stud! You'd be a gift to womankind, hell, all of mankind! If only you went out more."

"Don't flatter me," Jason growled, trying to hide his smile.

"All right. I'm killing two birds with one stone. I get a lift, and you get some fun. Happy?"

Jason sighed. He was too tired to argue. "What time do we leave?"

* * *

"Are you sure this is the right address?" Jason growled as he turned the car engine off.

He looked across a lifeless grove filled with twisted skeletons of old trees and mounds of dead leaves at their bases. There was no sign any human had ever been here, no house, not even any tracks. His phone still said, 'you have arrived at your destination,' for all the help that was.

"Yeah. Silvana said you've got to walk over the hill," said Peter confidently, though he was scanning the dead trees as if trying to convince himself.

They climbed out of the car, and the sound of their doors slamming echoed loudly in the empty woods. They met at the front bonnet and paused, scanning the trees in front of them while Jason wondered why he'd let himself get talked into this. He checked his friend and found Peter already staring at him. "What?"

"Thanks for dressing up, by the way," Peter drawled.

"What's wrong with jeans and t-shirt?"

"That's how you dress at home."

"It's practical. And flattering." Jason flexed his shoulders back and squeezed his biceps. Peter rolled his eyes, making Jason smirk. "Well, I think you're overdressed. Button up shirt? With collar and long sleeves? I thought you said this wasn't officially a date."

"This shirt brings out the blue in my eyes." Peter smiled, his perfect teeth and wide mouth created twin dimples in his cheeks. He even batted his eyelashes, as if he knew how gorgeous he was. *Show-off.*

They started walking in unison, their feet crushing down on piles of leaves and snapping dead twigs. The air smelt of damp mulch and beech wood. The last rays of sunlight flickered through the canopy above and cast misshapen shadows on the forest floor.

"There's not even a driveway," Jason said. "Are you sure we're..." he cut off as he glimpsed a blue turret over the rise. He jogged to the top of the crest.

Spread out before him was a huge mansion. It seemed impossible that something so large had been almost invisible just moments ago. The building was two stories high and shaped like a long rectangle. The roof was made of faded blue tiles, and the walls were a grim grey stone. Jason could see the outline of a dozen different rooms through external windows. Yet despite its splendour, the mansion was clearly past its prime. The walls were blackened by exposure, and the colour of the tiles were mismatched and patchy. The diminished beauty made it look old and eerie.

"This is her… 'house'?" Jason said.

"I am *not* paying for dinner," Peter grumbled.

There was no clear path through the forest so they ploughed down the slope, watching every step on their hard trek through deadened foliage and over twisted tree roots. Peter was breathing hard by the time they reached the front door. A great stone archway marked the entrance to the property, guarded by two stone dragon statues on marble pedestals. The doorway was two sturdy wooden panels of old oak timber, chipped and faded by time.

"I see why you wanted a chaperone," Jason said. "This place gives me the creeps."

"Yeah, I thought I'd need protection. But not that kind of protection, ey buddy?" Peter elbowed his ribs. It was only a friendly nudge, but Jason still had to supress the urge to punch him back on reflex.

Peter crossed to the door, found a huge metal clasp and knocked it on the anvil several times. Each bang could be heard echoing inside the mansion halls. Seconds passed as Jason imagined bizarre possibilities of what might happen when the doors opened. There was a clunk of a shifting lock and the door swung inwards with a creak.

A young woman stood framed in the doorway, and Jason was immediately stunned by her beauty. She had very pale skin that contrasted with the piercing brightness of her blue eyes. Her long, dark hair reached the middle of her back and framed her appealing, slender form. Yet despite her clear beauty, she wore casual grey jeans and a loose t-shirt with a picture of cookie-monster in his usual cookie-eating frenzy. Jason frowned in suspicion. The goofy clothes felt like a distraction from…something.

"Hey!" Peter said in a sing-song voice. "Silvana, how you doing?"

Silvana was silent as she looked between Peter and Jason. "You brought someone with you?" she said. Her voice sounded flat, almost like she was disappointed. Or maybe sad?

"I did indeed, m'lady," Peter said with a bow. "This is my chaperone, Jason."

"Hi," Jason said.

Silvana looked between the two men. "But…this was supposed to be a date."

"Oh." Peter trailed off. "I see."

Silvana blinked rapidly. "I'm sorry. I've clearly made a mistake. We don't have to do this." She reached for the door.

"Wait," said Jason as he turned to leave. "I'm sorry too. I don't have to be here. I can just go wait in the car."

"Everyone, just chill." Peter held up a hand. "Sorry about the misunderstanding, Silvana. But Jason is my roommate and I'd like to have him join us. You did say I could bring someone if I wanted."

"But… I was just trying to be polite. I didn't think you'd actually…" Silvana blushed quickly offered a small bow towards Jason. "I'm sorry, I'm being so rude. Please, uh…hello Jason, it's a pleasure to meet you." She held out her hand and offered a smile that failed to hide her fluster.

Jason took her hand, and flinched in surprise. "Oh! Your hands are freezing." He cringed, and quickly shook her hand properly. "I'm sorry. It's good to meet you too. And…sorry, I don't mean to intrude on your date. Peter just…"

"It's fine," Silvana said. "Really, it's my fault."

"Right! Well, before we get started," Peter said, "how about a tour of your beautiful home?"

Silvana's eyes widened. "We really should get going. I'm very hungry."

"Just a quick look," Peter said and stepped around her. Jason reached out to restrain him, but his friend was too quick and entered through the main door. Silvana gave Jason a nervous glance, then chased after Peter, leaving Jason in the doorway with nothing to do but follow.

One step inside and Jason felt like he had travelled back in time. Two suits of medieval knight's armour stood guarding the entrance like sentinels. The walls were made of thick blocks of grey stone that belonged in an old castle and not the 21st century. The furniture had faded colours of orange and brown and smelled of old musk. There were oak tables and oil paintings in golden frames. Everything was covered in a thick layer of dust, and white cobwebs lined the corners of the roof.

Jason remembered the front door was open behind him, and thought it was about to slam itself shut and scare the crap out of him like in some horror movie. He turned around to stop that from happening…

The door was already shut. He hadn't heard a sound.

"Should've brought my firearm," he muttered.

Peter and Silvana could be heard whispering from further down the hall. Jason followed their voices. He passed several archways into other darker rooms, all filled with dusty display cabinets whose contents were covered in shadow. Jason tried not to think about how much they cost. A grand staircase led to the upper floor, and two hallways intersected with one another, leading to the east and west wings of the mansion. Jason heard murmuring ahead. He stepped into the room the voices were coming from and his breath caught in his throat.

It was like Jason had stepped into a large throne room from medieval times. A huge oil painting hung on the wall depicting a battle scene with knights and horses, a grey sky, and muddy ground stained with the blood of the fallen. Elsewhere, stone pillars reached to the ceiling two stories above. There were a dozen lounges in the middle of the room, laced in crimson velvet and entwined with gold patterns of swirls and loops. Jason noted the exits leading further into the house.

There were two other women in the room, staring at Peter. They looked to be in their late thirties, and were no less beautiful than Silvana. One had short black hair that barely reached her chin, with brown eyes and a stern profile. The other had long silver-blonde hair and blue eyes. Both women had the same slender form and pale skin as Silvana, though they dressed in full-length ball gowns that suited their surroundings. Jason noticed a pair of grey goblets they'd left on the table and an open bottle of red wine beside it. They had been drinking before being interrupted.

"Sweetie," said the woman with long silver hair, "I didn't know you were bringing them inside." Her tone was noticeably full of displeasure, and Silvana visible recoiled.

"Sorry, my fault," Peter said. "You have such a beautiful home. I couldn't resist a quick peek inside. Jason!" he called and waved him over, oblivious to the distaste on the older woman's face. "Come here and meet our hosts." He faced the ladies with a smile. "A pleasure to meet you. I am Peter Erikson. Now based on what Silvana's told me, you must be Aunt Emberline," he gestured to the stern looking woman. "And this is Lisbeth, Silvana's…do I say mum?" he pointed to the woman with silver hair.

"We're *both* her aunts," Emberline corrected with a snappish, cold tone.

Peter scrambled to apologise, but Lisbeth spoke over the top of him. "Sweetie, is this what you're wearing?" Again her tone was laced with condescension.

Silvana clutched an arm over her middle. "It's appropriate for going into town. I can't wear a gown."

"I wouldn't expect you to," Emberline said. "But that's a shirt for children, dear. It's a little undignified."

"I think she looks great," Jason blurted out, and instantly found everyone looking at him. *Oh shit.*

"Who are you, again?" Emberline asked, swivelling her disapproving gaze to him.

"Uh…Jason Turner." *Why did I give my last name?* "I'm…Peter's chaperone."

"How quaint," Emberline said. "And a Turner, no less. An old name. It first appeared in England after the Norman conquest. Common for leatherworkers."

Jason's head tilted. "Yes, that's correct. How did you know that?"

"I have an interest in names," she said simply.

Lisbeth hurried over and reached towards him. Jason thought she was going to embrace him and held up his hands to ward her off. But she just wanted to shake his hand. Despite her strained tone, Lisbeth showed significantly more warmth than the other aunt, with a generous smile and gentle manner, though her thin fingers were also bitingly cold. "It's very nice to meet you."

"You have a lovely home," Jason said.

"And what do you do, Jason?" Lisbeth asked. This time her voice was sweet, but her sparkling blue eyes were squinting slightly.

He felt excited at the question. "I'm a policeman. I only started three months ago but I'm going to work my way up to becoming a detective. I'd love to solve crimes for a living."

"Sounds dreadfully scary," Lisbeth said.

Jason grinned. "I know. But I used to watch crime shows with my mum…" He trailed off as he noticed again the wine goblets on the counter and the red stains where lips had pressed on the pewter rims. Everything here would fit in at an antique show.

Lisbeth gave him a polite smile and turned back to Silvana. "You're welcome to have dinner here, you know."

"Thank you, Aunty," Silvana said in a formal tone. "Peter's already picked a restaurant."

Peter looked at Jason and winced. "Well, sure," Peter said. "But your home it so beautiful. And since you're offering…"

"Yes! This home is so often empty," Lisbeth said. "I for one would prefer some laughter in here."

"Let's not intrude," Emberline said, her voice hard as the stone walls. "The young couple have plans for their night. Let's leave them be." Her tone made it sound like she was dismissing everyone in the room. Even Peter took the hint.

Silvana gave her aunts a bow – an actual bow – and backed away towards the exit. Jason didn't move.

"Goodbye Jason," said Lisbeth. "It's been lovely meet—"

"Where did you get the blood?"

All movement in the room stopped. Lisbeth paused in polite surprise. "Whatever do you mean?"

"It was on your breath," Jason said. "Metallic scent. And a slight staining on your teeth. That's not red wine in those glasses over there, is it? Else it wouldn't stain the rims so prominently. It's too thick to be wine. So where did you get it?"

The women looked at each other with flat expressions. Peter was grimacing in discomfort, but Jason held his ground, back straight and shoulders tensed.

"I don't have the patience for your intolerance," Emberline said. "This is our home. We don't have to explain anything to you, young man."

"And what if I came back here with a warrant to search the premises? Would that make you want to explain anything?"

"Jason!" Peter cried. "Could you *not* be such a douche?"

Jason turned to his friend. "It's not safe to be here. They're *drinking* the blood. Like some kind… like, they think they're vampires."

Peter frowned at him. "I already *told* you they were vampires."

Jason blinked. "What?"

"It was the first thing I said," Peter said. "When you came home last night, I said I had a date with a vampire. I was pretty clear."

Jason blinked again. "But…you had just finished telling me that Silvana was shy. You were describing her mannerism. You know, she's a vampire, because she's introverted!"

Peter just rolled his eyes. "You dumbass."

Jason glared angrily at his friend. "Peter," he hissed, "there's no such thing as vampires."

Emberline said in a voice laced in frost, "I assure you, there is indeed such a thing."

Jason looked around the room now, as if for the first time. The incredible beauty of the women, their pale cold skin, and this huge mansion that was far from civilisation. It all made more sense now. Yet the idea was insane. Vampires? That was just a movie monster to scare people, or silly love stories. Jason couldn't believe it.

Then he noticed that he was standing in the middle of the room. The three women were surrounding him. Silvana was blocking the exit.

Jason breathed deeply and watched for signs of movement.

"Peter," Jason said in a calm voice. "Why did you bring me here?"

"I already told you. Silvana said I could bring a friend if I felt nervous," Peter said. "Of course I felt a little nervous. It's not every day you go on a date with a vampire."

Jason growled. "Well, it makes sense now why you wanted me here. You wanted a cop to protect you. That's all I'm here for."

"I'll still pay for your dinner," Peter said.

Jason was ready to punch him, but Silvana cut in. "I'm sorry we surprised you, Jason," she said. "I should have given you a better warning when you arrived. But I'm a little rusty with social cues. My mannerism *are* a bit like a vampire." She gave a polite laugh, but Jason didn't join her. Her smile faded as she turned to Peter. "I just wanted to go out tonight. But we can do this another time."

"No way! I still want to go out," Peter said. "Although…Jason drove us here. So I guess it's up to him."

All eyes turned to Jason expectantly. He cursed inwardly and turned to Lisbeth. "You still haven't answered my question about the blood."

"And she won't," Emberline cut in firmly.

"It's fine," Peter said. "I'll come back tomorrow on my own, and…"

Jason sighed. "Forget it, Peter. I can see you're determined to go through with this, and I have a civic duty. I'll be your bodyguard."

Silvana and Lisbeth clearly relaxed, though Emberline continued staring with a cold, blank expression.

"Thanks Jason," Peter said. "And I promise you and I won't fall in love." Jason pulled a confused face. "You know, as my bodyguard?" He started to sing, "*And I…eeeiii…will always love…*"

"Oh shut up," Jason said as he stormed out of the room, but Silvana gave a polite laugh.

Jason continued storming down the hallway, fuming that Peter could make jokes in a situation like this. When he reached the door he looked up to find the handle. He stopped short.

Lisbeth was already standing in the doorway ahead, holding the front door open for them. Jason had not seen her move. He had not even heard her.

He watched her closely as they approached. "Thanks for agreeing to do this, Jason," Lisbeth said in a sweet voice. "Really. You have no idea how much I appreciate it."

He nodded and said nothing in reply.

"Have a good time, sweetie," she said to Silvana. Jason didn't take his eyes off her until they'd left the house and Lisbeth closed the door behind them.

Chapter 2

"Table for two, sir?"

"Three, actually," Jason replied and held up his hand to get her attention.

The young waitress startled, and Jason swore her eyes squinted jealously at Silvana for a moment. "Right this way," she said.

The restaurant was full of people on a busy Sunday night. At least, as full as a restaurant in a small town was ever likely to get. The room was well-lit, with plain white walls and a few modest artworks on the wall, yet overall a dull décor. Jason noted about forty patrons of various ages talking in subdued voices and behaving responsibly. His real focus was on Silvana. He didn't know how safe it was for a vampire, real or otherwise, to be in a restaurant full of people, but he was holding himself responsible for whatever she did.

Peter obviously felt no such concern. He rushed over to pull Silvana's seat out for her. She blushed as she sat and thanked him. Peter took a seat next to her, leaving Jason to sit on the opposite side of the four-seater table, facing them both.

"Well, this is nice," Peter said. "I heard they do steak sandwiches here." He looked at Silvana. "Uh…you do eat, right?"

"Yes."

"Of course. Silly question." He picked up a menu. "Order whatever you like. Dinner's on me."

Jason grinned. "So, steak and more steak?"

"Shut it, Jase."

Silvana started reading the menu and the table went quiet as Peter seemed to run out of things to say. They all studied their menus far more than necessary, considering there were limited options. Jason cleared his throat and tried to start a conversation. "Silvana, what do you do?"

She looked up, almost like she was surprised to find him there. She gave a forced smile that Jason took as her trying to be polite even though she didn't really want to talk to him. "I'm about to start studying medicine."

"Oh." Jason nodded. "You must be smart."

He nearly slapped his forehead in embarrassment. *You must be smart? Nice job, dumbass.* Peter was shaking his head at him. A part of Jason wanted to shout, *this is why I don't socialise!*

But Silvana gave an awkward smile. "It's not that big a deal. I've studied medicine before. It's just that so much has changed recently, and I've haven't had much practice in the real world, so I need a refresher."

"Wait," Jason held up his hand. "You've studied medicine…before?"

"Well, yes. Mortals have made huge advancements in medicine in the last decade. Unless you're working every day as a doctor, everything you've learned becomes obsolete quite quickly."

"The last decade? So ten years ago?" Jason gave a laugh. "Aren't you about twenty-one, maybe twenty-two years old?"

Silvana's face went still. "Not exactly."

Peter gave a laugh. "I bet they still amputated broken limbs back when you first studied!"

Silvana rolled her eyes. "It wasn't that bad. At least they stopped prescribing opium and arsenic, like they did in the Victorian era."

"I'm sorry, the what now?" Jason asked. He stared at Silvana. "How old are you?" he whispered.

Silvana's face was a cold mask, yet her fingers twitched in discomfort.

"Hey mate," Peter said with a grin, "for your next topic of conversation, just stick to the weather, yeah?"

But Jason didn't back down. He kept staring at Silvana, as she stared back with those eyes of blue ice.

"Hi everyone!" said the waiter as he appeared at the table. "Having a good time?"

"Thank you, yes," Silvana said stiltedly, like it was a rehearsed line, "One steak sandwich, and a caramel shake please."

"Nice!" Peter gave her a winning smile. "I'll have the same thing, but swap the shake for a beer." Then everyone looked at Jason expectantly.

"Same thing, with lemonade."

The waiter seemed to sense the tension and disappeared quickly. Peter started talking about his own studies and happily monologued for a few minutes. It was a solid distraction, and just what was needed for an easy-going first date. But Jason couldn't help notice Silvana had dodged his question about her age and was continuing to avoid his gaze.

"Business is simultaneously the most useful, *and* the most useless degree," Peter said with a laugh. "Everyone in my course thinks they're going to be a CEO after this. But it never happens. You just know a lot about how businesses work in theory. Actually starting or running one is completely different."

"Interesting," Silvana said, in a polite and obviously insincere tone. Peter sensed it too and trailed off. Silvana seemed to regret killing the conversation, so she asked, "Have you two been friends long?"

"Since school," Peter said with a nod to Jason. "We went through high school together, here in Plymouth. I moved away to London for a few years. Thought I was gonna make it big acting on West End." He rolled his eyes and made a sound that was half chuckle, half groan. "When I came back to start studying for a real job, Jason was looking for a roommate."

"We hadn't seen each other in years," Jason added. "Then we jumped all the way up to moving in together."

"Sounds like a challenge," Silvana said, the barest hint of a smile quirking her lips.

"You have no idea."

Peter laughed. "I'm a delight and you know it."

"And Jason, do you have a special girl in your life?" Silvana asked.

Jason grumbled and fidgeted with his cutlery. "Uh…no."

"Jason's permanently single," Peter drawled with a wink. "I think he's celibate."

"I am not. I'm just…focusing on my career for now."

"But it's being a while," Peter said. "How long since you last dated someone, even casually?"

Jason tried and failed to keep the scowl off his face. "I don't do casual. I have to feel comfortable with someone before I become attracted to them. Unless I really like them, I'm happier on my own."

"I can't imagine," Peter joked.

"That sounds beautiful," Silvana said. "You prefer deeper connections, or none at all."

"Yeah. Exactly."

The waiter returned with their food, and Silvana spoke up. "Excuse me. Can I get a bottle of red wine and three glasses?"

"Of course," the waiter said.

Peter stammered. "Uh, a whole bottle is pretty expensive. I wasn't planning…"

"No, it's my shout," Silvana cut in. "I haven't been out since…well, it's been a while. I really needed this. Thank you both." The bottle arrived a moment later, and Peter was the first to help himself to it. Silvana poured a glass and handed it to Jason.

"Thanks," he replied.

He took the stem of the glass and his fingertips brushed up against her cold skin.

They ate in silence for a minute. The quiet chatter of other diners was a pleasant background noise, and the steak sandwich was surprisingly tender with a hint of rosemary pairing well with the red wine. Yet Jason couldn't relax. He kept staring at Silvana out of the corner of his eye. Finally the question burst out of him.

"You don't really believe you're a vampire, do you?"

Peter groaned.

"I don't go around advertising it," Silvana said, an edge to her voice. "We live in secret for our protection and yours."

"So it's a secret society kind of thing?" Jason asked. "Is it a cult? Where everyone drinks blood in a circle?"

Silvana's lip twisted. "What do you want? Proof?"

Jason shrugged. "Sure. Show me proof." He took a sip from his wine glass.

She was looking right at him when suddenly her eyes changed. The blue iris turned pure black and the white of her eyes seemed to fill up with crimson, like a drop of blood that had fallen into liquid. Within a second both her eyeballs were filled with dark red.

A glass shattered. Jason felt a sting in his right hand, and realised he'd squeezed so tight he'd broken the glass of wine he'd been drinking. He quickly checked his hand for glass fragments, noticing a few small shards cutting into the soft flesh of his palm. It wasn't too bad. A single drop of blood oozed from broken skin.

Jason flinched. He was across the table from a vampire. *Bleeding*.

He looked up. Silvana's red eyes were staring intently at his hand. She breathed sharply. Her eyes were wide.

Silvana darted forward, and Jason leapt up from the table, knocking his chair back and nearly falling over it.

But she had only reached for his injured hand. Her gesture had been tender.

Peter let out a snort. "Smooth, mate."

The waiter came back and started making a fuss over the broken bits of glass. Another staff member came over to clean up the fragments.

Silvana was still watching him closely. Her eyes were back to their usual blue and white. He hadn't seen them change again. "Jason, are you ok? I have a bandage in my purse." Silvana reached into her handbag and pulled out a bandage, anti-bacterial cleaner, and a water bottle. "Here, sit," she said, pointing to his chair as she walked around the table. Jason hesitated at her offer, so she clutched his wrist with her cold hand and guided him back to his chair, ignoring his objections. With a sudden tenderness, she rinsed off his hand with water, cleaned the cuts with her ointment, and wrapped it up securely with the bandage.

"You know," she said wryly, "when I said I needed real-world practice at medicine, I didn't mean right this second. But I appreciate the gesture." She gave a full smile that lit up her face.

Jason studied her. Silvana's eyes shone with sincerity, like a deep sadness was hidden there behind the smiles and laughter. The cool touch of her hand soothed Jason's pain. He found himself unable to speak.

"Great job, bodyguard," Peter joked. "Good thing my date can protect you."

"It's my pleasure," Silvana said. "Really."

All thoughts of those red eyes were pushed from Jason's mind. All he could think about was how his immature friend had ever attracted such a woman.

* * *

The three of them stepped outside the restaurant an hour later. Jason's hand was wrapped in a pristine white bandage, the cuts barely causing him pain. He hadn't asked any follow up questions about vampires for the remainder of their meal. Instead he merely continued to watch Silvana from the corner of his eye as she laughed at the ridiculous comments Peter made about his studies.

It was night in the town of Plymouth, England. A salty breeze was blowing in from the seafront, so cold it felt like prickling needles on Jason's face. A small scattering of people were moving around the streets. It was a quiet evening in an already quiet town, and the yellow light from streetlamps were too weak to properly light up the walkways.

"Anyone else want to go for a walk by the water?" Peter asked.

"Isn't it cold enough already?" Jason asked.

"Not if we cuddle."

"Sure. And what will Silvana do?"

Peter snorted. "Silvana, don't you have resistance to the cold?"

"Something like that," Silvana said. "A walk would be nice." Peter reached his hand out to her. She paused, before taking it in hers and walking alongside him. Jason began to follow behind like a dutiful bodyguard. He watched them sceptically.

Something was up with Silvana, and it was more than just red eyes. She'd acted disappointed when Jason showed up at the front door, as if she wanted the date to be more serious than it was. Yet she seemed withdrawn from Peter as well. *Maybe she's in two minds about this date.* Or maybe she was hiding something.

Jason looked up to see a trio of strangers walking towards them on the footpath ahead. He tensed with automatic distrust of other people.

Peter guided Silvana to the side to let the other group pass. Jason kept his head down. The three strangers sounded like teenagers, laughing and speaking in loud voices. They passed without any interaction, and Jason felt a tension leave him.

"Whoa, hang on!"

One of the teenagers called out. Jason spun around into a defensive pose.

"Don't I know you?" said one of the boys, pointing at Silvana.

There were two young men, both wearing shorts and polo shirts. One had bright blond hair with a long fringe, the other had his hair trimmed short in a buzz cut. Both were lean and fit.

"I'm sure you don't," Silvana said and turned to leave.

"No, I'm sure I do. I recognise your scent." He leaned closer and whispered, "Vampire, am I right?"

Jason froze in place. It seemed impossible. *How could he have possibly known? Surely he couldn't smell her? Unless...* he looked at the young man again. He had pale skin and wore no jacket in the freezing cold. Was this another vampire?

"Sir, I am enjoying a walk with my friends," Silvana said. "I bid you a good night."

"Hang on," the blond man said, his thick London accent drawing out every syllable in crisp diction. "Don't walk off in the middle of a conversation. That's rude."

The two boys had a young woman with them, and she was in a stunning red cocktail dress. *On a Sunday night, of all things.* Her wavy brown hair fell over the sides of her stunning face, giving her the look of an Instagram model.

Clearly, the two teenage boys are acting out to impress this girl. I must avoid challenging them or they'll try to compete with me. Jason braced himself for a confrontation. He kept himself standing between the trio and Silvana.

"She said she doesn't know you, mate," Jason said. "Now have a good night."

The man with the buzz cut put his arm around the man with blond fringe. "Don't be rude to my sweetheart," he said, then planted a kiss on the blond man's cheek.

Well, I called that wrong.

"Yeah," the blond man said. "I have half a mind to teach you how to behave politely. I'm not scared of a mortal."

"Mortal?" Jason wondered.

"Just tell us which house you're from," the buzz cut man said. He inhaled sharply through his nose. "Wait, both you men are mortals? Interesting. She must be hunting for a new partner. Or two partners!"

"It's none of your business," Silvana snapped.

"Oh, she's a feisty one," said the woman in the cocktail dress. Her accent was a thick cockney that rarely showed up in Plymouth. "Just tell us your 'ouse, baby. We're only curious."

"Please leave us alone!" Silvana cried. Her loud voice echoed in the street, and Jason looked around to see if anyone was witnessing this. Yet the walkway was deserted.

"So defensive," said the blond man. "Why don't you want to tell us?" He laughed. "Oh, is it because your house has fallen so far? Tell me, are these mortals even from another house? Or are you dating all the way at the bottom of the barrel?"

Silvana's eyes filled with red.

The buzz cut man crouched low and sneered at her. His eyes turned red as well.

Jesus Christ...

"Just tell us the name of your house," said the blond man. "It doesn't have to get violent. You're probably too weak to take us on, aren't you?"

"Try me," Silvana hissed.

That was it. Jason knew he had to act. He steeled himself, stepped forward and spoke with the voice of command. He vaguely noticed Peter holding his hands up and shouting, "Now wait just…" but Jason already had the mental momentum built up.

"Officer Turner, Plymouth Police. You will stand down now, or I will place you under arrest."

His voice rang out over the boardwalk just as a howl of wind whistled through the nearby buildings. He had delivered the line perfectly, yet all three of the teenagers look at him with open disgust and fury, and he knew he had just challenged the wrong people.

"Damn straight!" Peter shouted. "Now get the fuck out of here."

The tension broke, and suddenly all three of them started to back away. "Alright geez," said the blond man. "Just trying to have a conversation." They turned back down the street and moved on without another word.

"That's right, bitch," Peter called after them. "Keep walking."

Jason grinned. "Nice job, man."

Peter looked at him, and for a second his eyes seemed annoyed. But his face relaxed a moment later. It had just been the remnants of his confrontation. "Damn, Jase, you're one scary dude!"

"Oh…god, I'm sorry. I didn't mean…"

Peter laughed and slapped him on the shoulder. "Don't worry, mate. You scared the right people. You ok, Silvana?"

She had retreated a few steps, her dark hair falling over her face. "I'm sorry," she whispered. "I shouldn't have let them rile me up like that. I don't know what came over me."

"It's ok," Peter said. "Those guys were jerks anyway."

Silvana looked up at Jason and offered a smile that failed to hide the pain written over her face. "Thank you for standing up to them."

Jason caught again the look of annoyance that flashed across Peter's face. "Peter did it too. It was a team effort."

"Oh right!" Silvana winced. "I'm sorry. Thank you, Peter."

"Ah, don't even start. It was all Jason. Good thing I brought you with us, chaperone. You did a great job." But it was clear to Jason, he was putting on a brave smile. Jason had accidentally showed him up in front of his date. He needed to be careful not to do that again. This was Peter's date, not his.

"If anyone's a bit shaken," Jason said, "I'm happy to shout a round of beers."

"Hey! This guy saves the day again!" Peter said with a cheer.

* * *

The trio returned to the mansion carpark well after midnight. Jason's one round of beers had turned into three, plus a few extra for Peter who was thrilled to no longer be the one paying. Jason had remained sober enough to drive.

"We have to walk you to your door," Peter slurred.

Silvana gave a nervous laugh. "I assure you, I am perfectly safe. I don't need protection."

Peter smirked. "As thrilled as I am to hear you say that, I still say you can never have too much protection," Peter said with a wink at Silvana. She didn't react.

"I have work in the morning," Jason said flatly.

"I'm sure there'll still be crime in Plymouth either way," Peter laughed. Jason kept his mouth closed.

They walked down the hill towards the mansion. The two men struggled in the dark with the uneven slope, but Silvana seemed to float across the uneven ground and reached the front door well before them.

"I think we should come inside for a moment, just to say hello again to your aunts," Peter said.

"They might already be asleep," Silvana said as she placed a hand on the ornate door handle, positioning herself between the men and the entrance.

"I'm sure they won't bite."

"I'm not so sure," Jason deadpanned. Silvana flinched ever so slightly, and he grimaced. "Sorry. I just meant your Aunt Emberline didn't seem like our biggest fan."

"She's no one's biggest fan," Silvana mumbled.

Peter just chuckled. "I'm sure I can win her over," he said and stepped around Silvana to pull open the front door with a squeak. She grimaced, but followed him without complaint.

The couple entered the mansion, but Jason lingered in the entrance for a moment. The hallway was in total darkness now, and the harmless furniture that had looked so exquisite in the light now cast heavy shadows that took on bizarre shapes. Everything about the scene put Jason on edge. Yet he couldn't leave Peter alone, so he stepped inside and closed the door.

A figure stood beside him. He gasped as he looked up.

It was just the suit of armour by the door. Jason growled under his breath. He rushed through the hallway, constantly checking around corners and moving as quietly as he could.

He found everyone in the same lounge room as before. It looked as if Lisbeth and Emberline had not even moved. There were still pewter goblets on the table, though almost empty of their contents. The room was lit by a single candle. Jason wondered if this place even had electricity.

"Welcome back, Jason," Lisbeth said. "We were just telling Peter that you two are welcome to stay the night—"

"No," Jason said immediately. Then he remembered to be civil, and added, "We wouldn't want to intrude. It's quite late, and I have work in the morning."

"Nonsense," Lisbeth said sweetly. "We have so much room here. Our guest rooms are hardly ever used. And Peter looks a little worse for wear." They noticed him swaying on his feet yet trying to keep steady.

Jason maintained a straight face, and spoke slowly and calmly. "I appreciate the offer, but I can get Peter home safely."

"Well speak for yourself," Peter said. "I would *love* to stay."

"You really don't have to," Silvana said. "We can see each other tomorrow, if you like.

"Oh tonight will be fine."

"We'll be in separate rooms the whole time," Silvana said pointedly. Peter merely shrugged.

"Peter!" Jason said in a harsh whisper, trying to keep his friendly smile fixed on his face. "Come on, buddy. I drove you here, and I want to go home."

"Dude, I'll just grab a taxi tomorrow."

Jason looked around the room as feelings of anxiousness settled in. He did his best to stay calm and pleasant, but he could feel Emberline watching him with that cold glare. "Please excuse us for one moment," he said and dragged Peter from the room. They crossed the hallway, into another dark room with high-back leather chairs and an unlit fireplace.

"What's your problem?" Peter demanded.

Jason turned to his friend, and without a word, cuffed him on the side of the head.

"Ow!"

"What the hell are you doing?"

Peter rubbed his temple. "Silvana wants me to stay the night, man. What do you think I'm doing?"

"You do not want to sleep in this house. That blood in their glasses could be from the last guy they invited to stay."

Peter smirked. "That's bull. This is all because you want Silvana."

Jason hissed, "No, it's because they think they're fucking *vampires*. Or maybe they are? I don't know, I saw two people tonight with blood-red eyes. That was fucking weird! But I don't know what else they're capable of. All I know is I want my blood to stay inside my body. And yours too. Come on, Peter, sober up. Think clearly."

"You're just jealous of my sex appeal. Silvana is *so* into me. Accept it."

Jason blinked in surprise. His annoyance began to flare towards his roommate. "You're a colossal idiot. And you know what? You can stay here tonight and die. I've chaperoned you to dinner, like we agreed, but I never agreed to stay the night at Dracula's castle! I'm getting the hell out of here." Jason spun on his heel and walked out of the room. He returned to the three women with the intention of politely wishing them a good night.

Emberline was lounging on her chair, sipping the dregs from her glass. There was blood on her lips, until she licked them clean and inhaled sharply as she savoured the taste. There was something animalistic about it, like a hunter savouring a fresh kill.

"We'd be happy to stay the night," Jason blurted, and swore to himself. "I just need to get a change of clothes from my car first."

"Wonderful," Lisbeth said. "I'll show you to your room when you get back."

Silvana offered him a sweet smile. There was still that sad look in her eye. *Is that pity?* Jason smiled back as if nothing was wrong.

Then he went back out to his car and grabbed his police belt, armed with handcuffs, pepper-spray, and his police-issued Glock 17 handgun. No matter what happened tonight, he would be ready for it.

Chapter 3

Jason lay awake on a four-poster bed in a room all on his own. He refused to let himself sleep even for a second, instead keeping his ears primed for any sounds of movement. And there were plenty of those in the dead of night. The wind whistled through the tree branches outside, rattling the window frame and creating strange creaks of the house settling. Timber floorboards groaned and shifted in the cold English air.

And footsteps, slapping against the stone floor, just outside in the hallway.

Jason didn't hesitate. He silently rolled out of bed and moved to the door as the footsteps approached his room. Jason braced himself up against the wall and waited, alert and ready. The sound stopped at his door. Nothing happened for several long seconds. Then the handle rattled, and the door swung open. A dark figure stepped inside.

With one motion, Jason tripped the intruder and shoulder-slammed them into the ground.

"Geez love, you're pretty keen!"

Jason slackened his grip. "Peter?"

His friend recoiled. "Jason?"

The two men moved back and stood. They looked at each other in the dark, only able to see each other's silhouette. "What are you doing here?" Jason whispered.

"What are *you* doing here?" Peter replied.

"This is my room."

"Oh…" Peter groaned. "Oh damn! I thought this was Silvana's room. Was wondering why you were here. My bad." Peter quickly gave his friend a pat on the shoulder and stepped out, closing the door behind him and leaving Jason shaking his head.

He crossed the room, lay back down in bed, and tried his best not to imagine what Peter was up to now.

It was beginning to irk him that Peter was making so much headway with Silvana. Peter wasn't exactly a bad guy. *Just childish. And selfish.* Meanwhile Silvana was intelligent, capable, kind, gorgeous…Jason stopped that line of thought. The two were dating each other. It was no business of his whether or not she was out of Peter's league. It was her choice.

Not that I'm jealous, he thought to himself. After all, Silvana thought she was a vampire. Or maybe she really was a vampire. Jason remembered those red eyes. But real vampire or not, she was dangerous. Her aunts had refused to explain where the blood was coming from. He couldn't trust Silvana, no matter how beautiful and brilliant and… he stopped himself again.

Yet she always seemed just a little sad, in a way that tugged on Jason's heartstrings. He wondered what he could do to help her. Maybe there was some way to break through that polite shell surrounding her.

The sound of footsteps came from the hallway again. Jason rolled his eyes. It had only been a few minutes, so Peter was probably still wandering the halls looking for Silvana's room. The pattering of feet came closer to Jason's room. He almost expected Peter to stumble in again and start…

Jason sat up straight. The footsteps were coming from down the hall in the opposite direction Peter had gone. The person out there could not be Peter.

Was someone following him?

Jason moved to wait beside the door again and listened closely. Someone walked past his bedroom, but this time they moved on and continued down the hallway. Jason couldn't figure out who it was. The three women moved too softly to be making those heavier thuds. Was there someone else in the house? Jason steadied himself, and quietly slipped out of his room without letting the door creak. He followed the footsteps down the hallway while glancing over his shoulder every few seconds in case someone else appeared behind him.

Ahead, a figure moved around the corner and out of sight. Jason followed them with light, stealthy steps. He reached the end of the hallway and listened. The person's footsteps were just a few paces ahead. Jason turned the corner and saw a large shape, bigger than anyone Jason had seen so far in the house. He stepped out from behind his cover.

Lights flashed on. Jason was momentarily blinded as the hallway was suddenly lit up. He blinked several times to clear his vision.

In front of him was a huge man, a stranger, middle aged with a thick beard and shaggy clothes. He had one hand on the light switch. In his other hand he held a gun. A small handgun, held confidently, and aimed at Jason.

Gun! Quick! Defuse the situation!

Jason stayed calm. He slowly raised both his hands and stepped into the middle of the hallway, where he stayed perfectly still.

"My name's Jason. I'm not going to hurt you."

The large man was shaking slightly, his eyes wide with terror. They looked at each other for a long moment. Jason tried to relax and to stop imagining the gun going off.

"You're...human?" the man whispered.

Jason frowned but nodded slowly. "Of course."

The man tilted his handgun to the side. "Are you a prisoner?"

"I'm a guest."

"Ah…That's what they'd tell you," the man whispered and slowly lowered the gun. "I'm Alex Bishop. You were…Jason?"

He nodded.

"You probably don't realise this, Jason," Alex said. "But your hosts are not what they say they are." He glanced over his shoulder and whispered even softer. "They're vampires."

"I heard."

Alex looked incredulous. "You know? Then why are you here?"

"Let me ask you a question, Alex," Jason whispered. "What are you doing here, and why do you have a gun?"

Alex scowled darkly. "I'm just a concerned citizen. Do you know what these monsters have done? They've sucked the blood from hundreds of people. Slaughtered whole families. Do you know how many lives I'll save?"

Save? If you do what, exactly? Jason breathed in deeply. "Is that true? They've murdered people?"

"Of course it's true. Their very existence depends on it."

"So you're planning to shoot them in their sleep?"

"While their defences are down." Alex shrugged, his hand secure on the gun. "It's the only way. Otherwise they'd tear me apart. Do you know how powerful they are? They can throw trucks. Stop moving trains. This is our only chance. Can you show me where they're sleeping?"

Jason paused for a long moment. Could he condemn three people to die simply because they were vampires? Wasn't it his job to protect the community? He looked Alex up and down, and noted his confidence with his weapon. He thought about the women he'd met tonight, their secrets, and the blood in their goblets that they refused to explain.

"They're down this hallway," Jason whispered.

The two men shared a nod of understanding. Alex turned on his heel and switched off the light.

Instantly Jason moved. He reached into the back of his belt and pulled out the Glock 17 he'd fetched from his car. He jammed the nozzle into Alex's back.

"Police. Don't move," Jason whispered.

Alex flinched. He slowly turned his head to look over his shoulder. His face was totally covered in darkness. "What are you doing?"

"Upholding the law," Jason whispered. "Now hold still." Jason reached over Alex's shoulder, took the gun out of his hand and stashed it in his own belt. "Good. Now I will walk you to the door—"

Alex dropped his shoulder and launched himself at Jason. For a brief instant, Jason had a clear shot at the assailants' head. He was a policeman. He could fire the gun. It was self-defence…

But he let the gun fall from his hands.

Jason was hammered in the chest. Alex pinned him against the wall, grabbed him around the middle and squeezed the breath out of his lungs. The fight was almost silent except for the slightest scuffle of feet and strained breathing. They were invisible in the dark corridor.

Alex's grip was overwhelming. His strength was too much to combat directly and he was slowly reaching for the gun in Jason's belt. Desperate, Jason twisted his core to loosen the big man's grip, and Alex let out a gasp as Jason's hand now clutched at his face, pushing it away. There was a grimace of pain and a short cry that echoed awkwardly in the silent hall.

Alex lashed out for Jason's groin, but the cop dodged the grab and used the big man's momentum to wrap his arm around his neck. They moved in front of a window and the moonlight cast their shadows along the walls like ghostly spectators. Jason stepped around Alex so that he was behind the bigger man, pulling on his neck, and using his legs to trip him. Jason held his opponent down in a chokehold. Alex thumped his feet once on the stone ground. Then twice, and the bangs echoed loudly through the mansion. Jason finally forced him all the way to the floor and pinned him with his knee. Then with his free hand, grabbed the gun from his belt and stuck it against Alex's temple.

"That's enough!" Jason hissed. Alex's face was covered in darkness, but Jason still sensed the burning rage that seemed to ripple off the man's body in undulating waves.

The intruder relaxed his body. Jason quickly let go and moved a few steps back, keeping his gun trained. He bent to pick up his own discarded Glock, and aimed the weapon that was more familiar to him. Alex coughed softly a few times and breathed heavily. He got to his feet.

"Now walk to the fucking door," Jason growled.

Alex obeyed. Slowly, the intruder moved back through the hallway and down the stairs. Jason stayed a few steps behind with his gun raised. They made no sound as they went through the main corridor, walking over the stone floors until they reached the main door. Alex opened it, then stopped short in the doorway, his gigantic frame filling the space.

"You and I could have stopped them," he said. "Two men with guns. Do you know how many lives you've just killed by your choice?"

"I know three lives were just saved," Jason said.

"They're not alive, you idiot. They're undead monsters. They deserve to die!"

Jason's hand started shaking. He clenched his jaw, and flexed his grip on the gun handle. "Shut up," he whispered.

Alex turned around and glared back at him. "What kind of man are you? A real man would fight against monsters."

Jason felt the heat rising in his blood. "Shut up."

"We should have killed those bloody whores. Put a gun to the bitch's head, and pulled the goddamn-"

A gunshot went off.

Alex went silent. Jason was panting heavily as a single wisp of white smoke came from the nozzle of his Glock. It was aimed above Alex's head, the bullet flying into the woods outside and disappearing into the night.

"Get the fuck out of here," Jason spat in a hoarse whisper.

Alex's eyes were wide now. He held up both hands, and stepped silently out into the night. The door swung shut behind him.

Jason breathed out slowly in relief. He rubbed the spot on his chest that Alex had hit. His heart was racing. *Why the hell did I shoot at him like that? Stupid. Childish.* He'd have to report this incident and he knew he would get in trouble for that gunshot. But that was tomorrow's problem. For now, he could rest easily knowing he saved three innocent women from being slaughtered in their sleep. He gave a small sigh as he lowered his gun and turned around.

The three vampires were standing in front of him.

Jason let out a wordless cry. Emberline, Lisbeth and Silvana were wearing long white silk gowns that wavered behind them. Their pale faces shone in the darkness. Their eyes were black, the irises fully expanded. Jason was panting heavily and tried to stay calm.

"You don't think we're monsters?" Emberline whispered.

Jason shook his head, even as he forced down a wild urge to raise his gun at them. Emberline took a long step towards him, so that he was within reach of her cold hands. She whispered again.

"Are you sure?"

A chill crept over Jason's whole body. He wondered if he had made a terrible mistake.

"Well… maybe. I'm not sure what you are," he said with a shaky voice. "But I don't think you're a demon."

Emberline smiled widely, showing all her teeth, seeming every bit the predator. "That doesn't make me an angel."

"I suppose not. Maybe it just makes you human."

"Not exactly," she said coyly.

"Yes, exactly," Jason said, growing in confidence. "You're no more or less than any other person, not matter what else you are. My duty is to protect people. Including you."

The policeman and the vampire stared at each other intently. Jason still considered if he could raise his gun in time.

Yet Emberline stepped back and gave a smile. "Thank you, Jason." Her face showed genuine admiration, and Jason relaxed slightly.

"Right. Uh…sorry about the gunshot. I didn't mean to wake you."

"You didn't," Lisbeth said. "We heard the silent alarm. We had it installed for this very reason. Protection from people like that."

Jason frowned. "This happens often?"

All three women wore pained expressions. "More often than you'd think," Emberline said. "Mortals hate us, just for being what we are. Isn't that why you brought your gun into our home?"

Jason's mouth fell open. *God, I brought a gun into someone's house. I even had the urge to point it at them.* He quickly tucked his Glock back in his holster. "I'm sorry," he said.

"Don't be," Lisbeth said. "You just stopped a gunman in our house. We were worried you were going to join him, but you fought to help us. You're a good man."

"Whoa, what's happening here?"

Peter staggered into the hallway with wide bleary eyes. "No wonder all the bedrooms are empty."

Silvana smiled at him. "Jason just captured an intruder." Peter swung around, staring at Jason in drunken confusion, his mouth slack and open.

"Yes, how can we repay you?" Lisbeth said.

Jason didn't hesitate. "Tell me the truth. Where do you get the blood?" He saw their unhappy expressions and shrugged. "I'm sorry. But I need to know."

The women shared a look, and Jason wondered if he'd caused a problem, but Silvana held up her hands. "It's alright, I'll tell him," she said, though it looked like it pained her. She stared at Jason with a nervous tremble.

"The blood comes from our husbands," she said.

Jason blinked. "Husbands?"

"Wait, you have a husband?" Peter cried.

"No, that's not…" Silvana stopped with a wince. "My aunts each have a husband. My uncles. They each volunteer their blood so that we can live. Just a litre each month, that's all we need."

Lisbeth nodded, her eyes glittering in the moonlight. "It's a sign of their love."

"Where are your husbands now?" Jason asked, and Silvana looked upset again.

"They stayed away tonight, so they wouldn't intimidate…Peter."

It all fell in place for Jason. The goblets of blood, the standoff behaviour of the women, even why Silvana was disappointed that Peter brought a chaperone. "Tonight wasn't just a casual date. It was an audition. You're looking for a husband."

Peter's eyes went wide.

Silvana nodded. "Yes," she said. She struggled to speak, and as the words came out, tears filled her eyes. "Arthur, my husband, passed away just a few weeks ago. We'd been together for fifty-seven years. Now, I need…" she trailed off. "I don't want to rush anything. But I am dying. By Imperium law, vampires can only take blood from a spouse. So if I don't marry soon, I will only live another five weeks at the most."

That's why she looks so sad. She just lost a husband. Yet she already has to move on to survive...

"Wait," Jason cried, interrupting his own thoughts. "You were married for fifty-seven years?"

She nodded.

"You really are immortal?"

"I am."

Jason nodded, not quite able to fathom this. "And you want...Peter?"

"No," Silvana said firmly.

Peter offered a strained laugh and raised his hands. "I'm sorry I didn't catch the maniac wondering the halls. I'll catch the next one, I swear."

Silvana glared at him. "You tried to sneak into my room at night, despite my every indication that it was unwanted."

"Oh." Peter stared at the floor.

Silvana moved towards Jason. She stood only a hand span away, staring up at him, and Jason finally realised her intentions.

"Jason, you are so kind. You're loyal enough to stay here for Peter's sake. And you're very, very brave. I'm so sorry to be this forward but..." Silvana struggled with the words, until she just blurted out in a jumble, "...you'd make an incredible husband."

Jason was at a loss for words. A flurry of emotions rushed through him, too many to process all at once. He could feel everyone watching him. Silvana gave a half-hearted smile. "I know it's a bit soon for a proposal. I really, really didn't want it to go like this. But you deserve the truth. So...how about it? Will you marry me?"

Jason breathed in deeply a few times to steady himself before he answered.

"How about...we go on another date first?"

Silvana smiled. "I would like that."

Chapter 4

The back of Jason's eyes were throbbing, like someone had tied little weights to his lids. Going out on a Sunday night had been a bad idea.

Then again, it wasn't as bad an idea as staying the night in a vampire's mansion, fighting off a gunman, and receiving a marriage proposal. *Dear God, what the hell happened last night?* His only comfort was he'd been able to avoid speaking with Peter. His roommate was still asleep in Silvana's mansion that morning and when Jason had tried to wake him, he just muttered, "I'll catch a taxi." So Jason left him there. Still, he was only delaying an awkward conversation.

Jason stashed his gear in his work locker and double checked himself in the mirror. The belt was tight, his tie was tighter, the uniform was ironed and pressed to perfection and shined a bright blue. His handgun, pepper spray and handcuffs were stashed at his belt. He straightened his badge though it didn't need straightening. Overall he looked professional and physically imposing. No one would notice the one day of unshaved facial hair and the tiredness in his bones.

The police precinct was relatively quiet, even for a Monday morning. The holding cells were empty and only a few officers had crowded around the coffee maker, waiting for that bitter and cheap office coffee to drip into the pot. Jason checked the desks. All were vacant.

None of the detectives had shown up on time. Again.

"Turner!" a voice called out.

A middle-aged man waved him over to the kitchen and Jason joined the other cops there.

"Morning, Douglas," he said. "Everyone."

Douglas was a chubby guy with a round face and a pronounced double-chin. There was a hardness to his features though, like the extra weight was really the weight of the world and not just comfortable living. Douglas always had a glimmer in his eye and smile lines that deepened every year.

"Hey rookie. How was your weekend?"

"I went on a date."

"Oh, a date?" Officer Martin perked up with interest.

Martin was a middle-aged woman – Carol Martin – and Jason always found it awkward calling her by her last name. She was tall and slim with bright blue eyes and a short crop of brunette hair that was regularly dyed to hide the greys.

"Bout time you had a date, Turner," she said. "I'm sure the ladies have been lining up."

Jason rolled his eyes. "Technically I was just the chaperone."

"Seriously?" Douglas asked. "You pulling my leg? You actually escorted someone else?"

Martin smirked. "I could see you as an escort. A male escort."

Jason turned to her. "Hey, this is a workplace." The group laughed at him, thinking he had been joking. He didn't bother trying to explain and started pouring himself a black coffee. "I really was a chaperone. My roommate was meeting someone and he wanted a second opinion."

"Sounds uncomfortable," said Wilson, the fourth and final officer there. He was shorter than average and had a more traditional 'dad-bod'. Wilson was a husband and father of two girls, and that summed up his entire personality. Jason didn't mind the guy, really. It's just that every conversation with him would last about five seconds before he started a monologue about his family.

"It reminds me of when my wife and I tried a double date, before we got married. Course we didn't have kids back then…"

Right on schedule.

"So how was the date?" Douglas cut in and Wilson shot him a dirty look.

"It was uncomfortable," he said. "My mate was a bit of a dick and it really turned the girl off."

"Are you sure she didn't just have eyes for you instead?" Martin asked with a wink.

"Well she did propose to me at the end of the night, so…"

Everyone laughed, again thinking he was joking. Jason grumbled under his breath.

"The *woman* proposed?" Douglas laughed. "She sounds progressive, mate. Exactly your type. Tell me you said yes?" And he laughed again.

"Let's see the ring!" Martin cried.

"When I proposed to my wife," Wilson began…

"*Officers!*" a woman's voice rang out like a cracking whip and all chatter ceased. A woman was crossing the bullpen and gestured to the side rooms. "Meeting in the briefing room," she announced.

"Captain, we're all here," Douglas said. "Why don't we just…"

The captain stared at him across the room, with a straight, flat expression.

"Sorry Ma'am," Douglas said and lowered his eyes.

Everyone sniggered as they left the kitchen and took their coffees into the briefing room. The area was lined with desks and chairs and held enough space for forty people. Currently, there were seats set up for only seven. Jason sat in the front row, his back straight and hands clasped on the desk.

Captain Aisha Kader walked into the briefing room, a woman in her late forties, or maybe fifties. Jason dared not ask. Her curly brown hair was worn short and framed dark brown eyes filled with fierce intelligence. She always looked like she was reading Jason's mind and was not happy about what she found there. Kader had slightly darker skin, suggesting a Middle-Eastern heritage. (Again, Jason dared not ask).

"What's the news, boss?" Douglas asked, leaning back in his chair and making it creak.

"Don't call me boss," Captain Kader said. "And sit up straight. This isn't fucking preschool."

"Jesus…" Douglas complained, yet sat up as requested.

Kader shuffled some papers on the pulpit in front of her. "We had four more reports overnight of motorbikes revving in suburban areas. Once again, they're appearing between one and two a.m.. We can assume it's the same culprits we've heard for the last three weeks. I want us to increase patrols. Douglas and Turner, you'll be moving through Crownhill to King's Tamerton. Martin and Wilson, you're covering Devonport to Cattedown."

"Patrols, Captain?" Jason asked. "These bikies aren't going to be active during the day. They're probably still asleep."

Kader frowned at him. "Good job, *Detective* Turner," she drawled. "I think you've nearly solved your first crime."

A few chuckles sounded around the room, but they were tinged with a nervousness.

"I mean no disrespect, Captain," Jason said. "I just wonder if night patrols wouldn't have more luck. I mean, what are we even looking for?"

"Motorbikes, Detective Turner," Kader said. "I thought you could have figured out that much on your own." More nervous chuckles.

"Sorry, ma'am," Jason said flatly.

He tried to sit back, showing through his body language that he was giving up the question. But the captain either didn't see it, or didn't care.

"This precinct doesn't need any more detectives right now, Officer Turner." *Clearly,* he thought, and wanted to point to the detectives' empty desks. "Especially ones that are only three months out of the academy. If you want to be seriously considered for the role, you'll need to prove you can work with the team and follow orders. Understood?"

Jason nodded, trying not to let his annoyance show. "Yes, ma'am."

"And you don't need to show off how insightful you are every five seconds. I've been a cop for over twenty years, Turner. I know the benefit of day patrols."

"Yes ma'am."

"Good." Kader picked up her papers. "Douglas, report in at ten, two, and four. Martin, report on the off hours. Dismissed!"

"Captain," Martin called. She rushed to the front and spoke in a whisper, where only Jason and the captain could hear, "Aisha, I was thinking Jason and I would make a better team…"

"Officer *Turner,*" the captain cut in, "has already been assigned, *Martin.*"

Martin whispered lower, "But Turner won't talk about his child's bowel movements for the next eight fucking hours!"

Kader broke into a smile. *She never smiles at me,* Jason thought. "Sorry, Carol. How about I shout you lunch sometime to make up for it?"

"There'd better be wine."

Jason turned as a large heavy hand slapped him on the shoulder. "Come on, son," Douglas said warmly. "A day on patrol means McDonalds!"

"What are you? Six years old?" Jason said with a laugh.

"My two-year-old hates McDonalds…" Wilson started.

Douglas quickly dragged Jason out of the room, Martin glaring at them until they were out of sight.

Chapter 5

"I don't understand the captain," Jason said, between mouthfuls of his bacon and egg muffin. "I treat her with respect. I obey her every order. I'm extremely courteous. But she mocks me every chance she gets."

"It's not that bad," Douglas said with food still in his mouth. The sloshing and lip-smacking sounds made Jason want to stab out his own ears. "This happens every time a precinct gets a new recruit. It's just part of being a rookie."

"Mate, I know how hazing works. This doesn't feel like hazing."

Jason stared out the window of the parked car on a grey, cloudy day. Only a few people were walking around town at late morning, and nearly all of them were elderly. Everyone else had already reached their destination for the day. Plymouth may be classified as a city on the maps, but it was a small town in reality.

"It feels like I did something to set her off," Jason said. "But I don't know what it was. It's not like I treated her poorly."

Douglas burped, and Jason rubbed the bridge of his nose. "Well maybe it's not about you," the big man said. "She's just trying to establish herself. You gotta remember, Kader's a woman working in a man's field. She's gotta be extra tough to demand respect, you know?"

Jason blinked. "That's rather progressive of you, Dougy. Am I rubbing off on you?"

"Nah, it's me daughter."

"Oh?"

"Yeah, the Mrs says she thinks Tracey is gay. Or bisexual or whatever. Ever since she says it, I've started seeing signs of it everywhere, you know? So I'm trying to learn more about that stuff, in case Tracey ever wants to tell me about it. It's important I react well, you know?"

"Doug, that's really awesome," Jason said, a genuine smile on his face. "Don't worry, you'll be fine. That is, if you say, 'I love you', and don't use the term, 'bisexual or whatever'."

Douglas chuckled as he wiped his mouth, started up the car again, and drove down the streets. Jason wound up the window to cut off the flow of seaside air, too cold for a moving vehicle.

"The captain's just letting you know she's in charge," Douglas said. "Don't take it personally."

"Maybe," Jason said. "But I think the detective thing might have pissed her off too. You hear how she calls me 'detective' sarcastically? It's cause I told her I wanted to be a detective one day. She's mocked me for it every day since. But I just wanted to let her know my career goals."

"That there's a rookie error, rookie," Douglas said as he steered around a corner. "You basically told your new boss you wanted to leave as soon as possible. Like you think you're too good for this place."

"Oh...I didn't realise."

"What you gotta do is show you care about this job too, and you're not just using it to get to the next one. Don't act like you're too good for policework."

They drove in silence for a few minutes. Jason checked the time. Only 10:33 a.m., and they had already covered their entire patrol area once. They'd probably repeat it another three or four times during their shift. It seemed like a total waste of time to Jason, to patrol during the day for hooligans that only came out at night. But then, there wasn't exactly a lot of work on for the Plymouth police at the moment. The Home Office had been cutting their budget for the last decade. Every year, they justified it by saying crime was down. In reality, crime was down because the police didn't have the manpower to handle all the crimes that occurred. Fewer crimes were properly dealt with and reported.

Jason sighed. They didn't have these small-town problems in London. There, detectives solved real crimes instead of chasing up noise complaints. Maybe he'd get to London one day and be a big, important detective, solving murders and cracking impossible cases. Something his mum would have been proud of.

"I forgot to ask you something," Jason said, and Douglas grunted to show he was listening. "I had a bit of an incident last night. There was a man…at the girl's house I went on that date with. He was acting aggressively. Turns out he had a gun, so I disarmed him to be on the safe side and let him go…"

"What?!" Douglas shouted, then had to steer the car back onto the road. Jason swore and gripped the door handle. "You encountered an armed assailant? And you didn't *arrest* him?"

"The defendant didn't want to press any charges," Jason said. Inside he thought, *Crap, this might be a bigger problem than I realised.*

"Doesn't matter," Douglas said. "You still needed to bring him downtown and take a statement. An aggressive man with a gun sounds like he should have a profile on record. What did you do with the gun?"

Jason winced. "It's in my locker. That's why I brought this up. I was gonna ask you what to do with it."

"Jesus fucking Christ, rookie. As screw-ups go, this is a pretty big screw-up. I gotta tell the captain."

Jason cried out, "But I stopped the guy! That's a big deal!"

"Sure, kid. But you didn't follow procedure. Now we need to find that girl you dated and take a statement. Hopefully, we can still find this man before he does something else stupid."

"Wait," Jason said. "Look, please don't tell the captain. She's mad at me enough as it is. And do we have to interview Silvana? It's just... I have another date with her tonight. It'd be weird if I investigated her."

Douglas gave a loud, huffy groan. "Look, that doesn't matter. We need to find this gunman, Turner, so we have to speak to whoever this guy interacted with."

"He told me his name. Alex Bishop."

Douglas sighed. "I don't like keeping secrets from the captain, kid. We really should follow protocol..." he sighed again, deeper this time. "Tell you what, since you've got a date with the lady, we'll go see her tomorrow for her statement. Maybe then, she'll actually be happy to see you, hey? But we have to find this Bishop guy right away. Look him up, will you? We'll see what he says about last night and maybe, just maybe, it won't be necessary to tell the captain."

Jason was already typing the name into the database. The police car had a touchscreen on the dashboard for entering in names and licences while on patrol, though the upload was painfully slow. He found Alex Bishop and recognised his ID, then pulled up the address.

"Roborough."

"Ah," Douglas said. "That's only 10 minutes from our patrol. Bloody lucky, rookie. We can see this punk and hopefully avoid the captain finding out."

"Thanks, Douglas. I owe you one, man."

"Damn right. Gotta say, I'm surprised at you, Turner. You're usually such a stickler for the rules. You can't count on me covering for you next time, ok?"

"I know. I'm sorry. I just…got a little stupid in front of this girl."

"Oh yeah?" Douglas suddenly had a huge grin on his face and a spark in his eye. "Tell me about her. Silvia, right?"

"Silvana. Yeah, she was really something else. Really smart, you know?"

"You don't have to be a feminist here. How was the body?"

"Dude!" A brief pause. "She's got a freaking amazing body." Douglas cheered happily. "And she's really funny. Very quick witted. But I'm a little worried about her family."

"Oh yeah?"

"She lives with her two aunts…"

"Two aunts? Not her two mums, hey?" Douglas chuckled again.

"Just aunts." *I think.* "They're both pressuring her to find a man. But she only just uh…got out of a long-term relationship. She says she wants to date me but I feel like she's not actually ready for it, and it's just her family pressuring her, you know?"

Douglas hummed. "Are they catholic, or something? Cause they might just be very traditional."

"Yeah. I think it's safe to say they're traditional."

"Well families are always tricky. Word of advice; don't make her choose between you and the family. That never goes well."

"Yeah…"

They reached a small suburban lot, filled with old townhouses made from eighteenth century brick and stone. "What do we know about Bishop?"

Jason read through the file. "Alex Bishop, forty-five years old. Divorced. His ex has custody of the two kids."

"Ouch. Any history of violence?"

"Nothing official. The divorce was for 'irreconcilable differences'."

"Well that's just PC for 'couldn't fucking stand each other'."

Jason chuckled. "Bishop works for Plymouth shipping. No criminal record other than a few driving offences."

"Strange. Sounds like a normal guy. Wouldn't expect him to be swinging a gun around."

They reached the address and parked outside a plain old townhouse just like the hundreds of others in the area. The homes were small, lower socio-economic, and suitable only for people who lived alone. Several gardens out front had died and turned into brown patches of dirt and dumping grounds for beer bottles and chip packets. Jason felt sad and lonely just being here.

Douglas took point on the job. He buzzed the icon on the front door. "Mr Bishop?" he called. He waited a half a minute, buzzing twice more, but no answer. "He might not be home. If that's the case, we'll need a warrant."

"We could go to his workplace on the docks," Jason said.

"Not without getting approval from the captain. Sorry rookie, looks like…"

The front door suddenly opened, and a short, middle-aged Indian man came out. "Oh, can I help you, officers?" he said.

"We're just looking for someone who lives here, nothing serious," Douglas said. "Are you the owner?"

"Yes, I'm Ricky Babu, sir. I thought you were here for the noise last night."

Jason blinked. "Some kind of disturbance? Was it motorbikes?"

"What? No, the gunshot."

"Gunshot?" Douglas blurted.

Mr Babu smiled, trying to hide his discomfort. "Oh last night, around 3 a.m. I heard a bang from the room upstairs. Sounded like a gunshot. I was going to call the police this morning. A tenant must have called first."

"Wait, you heard gunshots in the middle of the night and you didn't call the police straight away?" Jason asked.

Babu gave a nervous smile and ran a hand through his thinning hair. "Oh, I didn't hear any other noises. It was quiet after that. I wasn't even sure it was real. I knocked on the door for the upstairs room this morning, but I think the tenant had already gone to work."

Douglas cut in, "Who lives in the upstairs room?"

"Oh, uh…Mr Bishop, I think."

Jason and Douglas exchanged a look. "Can you let us into his room?"

"Oh sure, sure, I have a key. Follow me."

Mr Babu stepped into a side office and searched through several cupboard doors, muttering under his breath. Jason whispered, "Does he seem nervous to you?"

"Like a sinner on judgement day."

The owner returned. "Follow me. Oh, the elevator's getting repaired, so it's just up the stairs. Not far."

Douglas swore under his breath.

Two flights of stairs later, they stood in a plain hallway with two apartment doors on either end. "Who lives in the other apartment?"

"No one. Can't find anyone." Mr Babu fumbled with the keys, and opened the door to Alex Bishop's home.

Jason recognised the smell at once. It reminded him of the scent from Silvana's house and the two goblets he'd seen Lisbeth and Emberline drinking from. The smell of acid and metal.

"Jesus," Douglas said and drew his firearm. Jason copied him, and gestured for Babu to remain behind. Douglas took point, calling out, "Mr Alex Bishop? You in here? This is the Plymouth police department. We just want to ask you some questions."

Douglas led the way into the kitchenette. The floor was littered with beer bottles and rubbish bags that had been stacked by the door and forgotten. Unwashed dishes cluttered the kitchen and clothes were discarded in the middle of the room. The smell was coming from the bedroom. Douglas took position at the door, and Jason moved to cover him. He kept his hands on his weapon, despite wanting to cover his nose for the smell. The senior officer turned the handle, and the door opened with a squeak. Douglas took one step inside, then flinched back, his face white.

"Sweet Jesus…"

Jason went through the door without waiting.

Alex Bishop was lying on the floor, dressed in the same clothes Jason had seen him in the night before. Red stains marked the carpet all around him, covering a two metre area in the shape of a puddle. His skin was ghastly pale from a severe loss of blood.

And yet, there was no blood anywhere. Just red stains on the carpet. It was as if all the blood had been…removed.

Like someone bled him dry, then didn't let a single drop go to waste.

Jason mumbled, "My God…"

Chapter 6

Silvana woke with an ache behind her eyes. It felt like a vacuum cleaner was somehow in her brain, yanking her skull inwards. She sat up in bed, hoping that adjusting her position would alleviate the pain. Nothing changed. Sighing, she clutched her head and tried to breathe through the discomfort as she stepped into her ensuite to prepare for the day.

She dressed in her blue ball gown and tied the corset at her side, though she had to pull the strings tighter than normal before it clung to her stomach correctly. She was definitely thinning. She knew she should join the family for breakfast, but as she raised her hands to her hair and began to brush, all the energy drained from her limbs. The thought of brushing her hair now felt impossibly hard.

Silvana stumbled across her bedroom and sat down at her desk. An artist notepad sat on an angled easel and she flicked through delicate pages until she found a vague pencilled sketch of a woman, fit and curvaceous to an almost impossible level, dressed in a superhero costume. Silvana smiled, picked up her colours, and began to fill in the gaps.

There came a knock on her bedroom door. Silvana noticed the little hand on her silver clock was already pointing at ten. *Where did the hour go?* She leapt to her feet and closed her notepad. "Come in."

Aunt Lisbeth poked her head through the door. Her hair was done up in an elaborate half bun even though she was spending the day at home. "Sweetheart, you weren't at breakfast. Is something wrong?"

"Just tired, Aunty."

"I'd better check, just to be sure." She opened the door fully, and Silvana saw the med kit in her aunt's hands.

"Aunty, that's not necessary. We already know what it's going to show."

"I beg to differ," Emberline said, appearing in the doorway. Her short hair was tied up in a perfect vertical column from the top of her head. "You should treat this situation with its due severity."

Silvana bit back her reply. "Yes, Aunty."

Lisbeth sat on the bed and patted the mattress next to her. Silvana bowed as she approached and sat exactly where she was told to sit. Her aunty strapped a blood pressure test onto Silvana's arm and began to inflate it. "Are you experiencing any light-headedness, dizziness, or feelings of fainting?"

"Just light-headedness."

"Can you describe your symptoms?"

"Yes. Exactly like they were yesterday."

"Silvana," Lisbeth chided.

She resisted the urge to sigh. "Low energy, feelings of fatigue, an ache behind the eyes. Basically your classic vampire thirst."

"It's been five weeks since your last drink, Silvana," Emberline said, crossing the room and standing next to Silvana, looming over her. "This is not 'classic' vampire thirst. Your body has gone beyond the limits of what it can sustain. It is beginning to starve. You'll be lucky to survive another three weeks."

"I'll last four weeks at least, Aunty."

"Oh really?" Emberline drawled. "I suppose you must be getting blood from somewhere we don't know about. Perhaps prowling the countryside preying on helpless mortals?"

Silvana blinked. "Why would you say that?"

"Well you seem to think you'll last four more weeks. You must be breaking the law and stealing blood from mortals if that's the case."

"Aunty!" Silvana cried in horror. "That's abominable! Please don't joke about that. I'm just saying that based on my blood pressure, I still have four weeks left."

Emberline's face was a mask of ice. "Don't forget. You'll be bedridden and unconscious for much of those final weeks. Which means you have two weeks maximum to court this mortal and marry him."

Silvana bowed her head. "I understand."

Lisbeth gave a polite sigh to lower the tension as she deflated the strap on Silvana's arm. "Seventy over forty. That's too low, Silvana. It should be ninety over sixty minimum."

"It's still within acceptable range. It's not dangerous yet."

"But it will be!" Emberline snapped, pressing her thin lips together. Silvana tried to tilt away from her, yet she was trapped on the bed between both aunts.

Lisbeth cut in again. "Any blurred vision? Lack of concentration? Shallow breathing?"

"Not yet."

"Well, you still shouldn't skip breakfast. You need to have lots of red meat and foods that are high in sugar."

"I know, Aunty."

"What did you have for dinner last night at the restaurant?"

"Steak sandwich and a caramel thick shake."

"Hmm. Well don't enjoy it too much. As soon as you're on blood again, you'll need to clean up that diet. It'll ruin your figure, you know."

Silvana wanted to scream. *Is nothing I do good enough?* Instead she looked towards her closed notepad and remembered the sketch she'd been working on and imagined what she would add to it next. She felt her mood begin to calm.

"Let's talk about your disastrous date last night," Emberline said.

Silvana inhaled sharply. "Excuse me? What was disastrous about it?"

"You dumped Peter and proposed to his roommate, Jason. And he turned you down."

"He did not turn me down!"

Silvana froze. She had lost control of her voice and made it far louder than appropriate. "I'm sorry, Aunty. I just meant Jason and I have a date tonight."

"You're starting all over again. You just spent two weeks wooing Peter, then turned him down in one night. Now you have to start that whole process from the beginning. You don't have time to waste. He needs to make a decision imminently."

"I can't rush him. He's not from any of the immortal houses. This is all weird to him."

Emberline scowled. "Then you should have courted someone from within the houses like I told you too. A marriage to an unconnected mortal gains us nothing. His name is Turner, for God's sake! He might as well go around proclaiming himself a peasant."

Lisbeth nodded along eagerly. "Emberline is right, sweetheart. You still have time to contact Arthur's family. I'm sure his younger cousin…"

"Absolutely not."

"Then we'll speak to my cousins, the Glucksbergs," Lisbeth said. "They're familiar with vampire needs. We could have a husband for you by the end of the week."

"They'd only offer their oldest mortal, someone near at the point of death. In a few years, I'll be here again. I'd rather make the most of this time."

Emberline huffed, "This family could benefit from a marriage alliance. Why are you so stubborn about courting an outsider? Why are you risking your life for this?"

Silvana had enough. She moved off the bed to escape her aunts and went to stand by her desk, tracing a finger along the wooden frame. Another wave of ache appeared behind her eyes and she found herself unable to care about the conversation.

"Is this about Arthur?" Lisbeth said.

Silvana clenched her hand into a fist, then forced it to relax. "It has nothing to do with Arthur."

"Oh sweetheart." Lisbeth appeared at her side and wrapped an arm around her shoulders. But rather than feeling comforted, Silvana felt suffocated.

"I'm sorry if we seem insensitive. Your husband just died. It must seem cruel that you must remarry so quickly. It's natural to feel sad about losing Arthur."

Silvana shut her eyes. Everything her aunt said felt wrong. How could she tell them the truth?

I'm not sad about it at all.

"Trust us," Emberline said, her tone softer as she stood at Silvana's other side. "We've gone through this more times than you. The best thing to do is find your next partner. You will process your emotions in time but just do it from within the safety of another marriage, when you're not also dying of thirst. One problem at a time."

"Yes, Aunty."

Lisbeth clapped her on the shoulder. "That's my girl."

Silvana couldn't believe it. They thought they had just fixed the way she felt, as quickly as that. How could she tell them about any of the thoughts going on in her head? All the emotion, and rage, and despair? Still, it was easier to just go along with them. It was too hard to put her feelings into words, and they never listened anyway.

"So what are your plans for this boy, Jason?" Emberline asked. She stood closer now and Silvana could see each of the individual flecks of brown in her eyes.

"Yes. How are you going to court him?" Lisbeth asked, packing away her medical kit.

Silvana knew she had to answer quickly and firmly, else they would start talking over the top of her with advice. Her words came out in a rush. "I'll start by getting to know more about him, and sharing more about myself—"

"You can't share too much!" Lisbeth cut in. Silvana nearly shouted at her, but held her tongue instead, knowing it would get her nowhere. "He is still an outsider. You know the law. You can share about yourself, but not about our world."

"Tell him about vampires," Emberline said, "but no more than that."

"Yes. We would hate for him to marry you because he thinks he'll become immortal."

"And don't sleep with him."

"Aunty!"

"I mean it. Wait until he is committed, lest he abandon you after."

"Yes. Seduce him if you must," Lisbeth said, "but give no satisfaction until he is yours."

Silvana kept her face free of emotions like a pristine mask. Her voice was flat when she replied. "Yes, Aunties."

"And don't talk about Arthur," Emberline said. "It's bad form."

"And don't tell him anything about our family name. He doesn't need to know anything about that.

"Yes, Aunty."

Lisbeth smiled. "Good. Now why don't you come join us for a late breakfast? We have eggs and fruits for protein and sugar."

"Thank you," she said, and let her aunts lead her out of her room.

She glanced back at her notepad. Maybe she'd get back to it later today.

59

Chapter 7

I t took nearly three hours to turn Alex Bishop's apartment into a crime scene. It had been several months since the last murder – or even a major crime – in Plymouth and every member of the emergency services was slow to respond. Though Jason suspected the detectives were still getting out of bed.

He spent those three hours waiting outside the door in the hallway. Captain Kader had given strict instructions; "Don't piss all over the evidence, *Detective* Turner. Touch nothing until the real detectives get there." He was set on guard duty while Douglas went out to the car to do radio correspondence. The forensic team showed up to do a sweep through the apartment, but denied Jason's request to watch and learn.

Giving him three hours with nothing to do except think.

Alex Bishop had shown up at a family home, armed and intending to commit murder. Jason wanted to smack himself in the head. He should have arrested the man. He'd only let Alex go because he was trying to avoid more violence.

You let him go because you were considering shooting him.

Jason pushed the thought away. It didn't matter now. Alex was dead, and Jason had missed his chance to put the man somewhere safer. Now he'd been completely drained of blood.

The real question was; which vampire killed him? Lisbeth, Ember-line, or Silvana?

Was it possible some other vampire had made a move? Surely there were more than three in the whole world. There was that teenage boy last night with the red eyes. Maybe someone had killed Alex to incriminate the three women. But it was extremely unlikely. The first rule of an investigation, the most obvious motive is usually the correct one. That meant one or more of the vampires had followed Alex home, murdered him and drained him.

Maybe Alex was right to fear the vampires. Maybe I was wrong to spare them.

He pushed that thought away too. He was not going to feel guilty for sparing someone's life. That was just dumb. But he had to think about this logically. The likely suspect was Silvana. He knew she was thirsty for blood, since her supply had run out. He should come clean to the captain and bring Silvana in for questioning. He couldn't tell them she was a vampire or they'd think he was crazy, but he could explain about the break in. It would be enough to start an investigation. Besides, he didn't owe Silvana anything.

Yet, he was definitely attracted to her. At least, he thought he was. Maybe that wasn't real, and it was just some vampire trick. He had no idea what she was capable of...

He made up his mind. He would tell the detectives everything, except for mentioning vampirism. They probably wouldn't believe that anyway. He hated the idea of exposing the three women to the police, but if they were innocent, they'd have nothing to worry about.

When the two detectives finally showed up, he was ready to cooperate. They entered the crime scene, and Jason swore he could hear the WHO playing in the background.

The lead detective was a clean-shaven and fit man in his mid-forties. Detective Lynch was quite literally tall, dark, and handsome.

Third-generation British Jamaican, he had a lean face and a masculine jawline, plus he had the highest arrest numbers in the city. He was also effortlessly charming in a way Jason would have killed to be able to mimic.

Lynch's companion was a shorter Caucasian woman, with shoulder-length hair and a trimmed fringe. Detective Cole had pouty lips and high cheek bones and looked like the kind of woman who would ask for the manager.

"Officer." Detective Lynch paused in front of Jason and the crime scene door, his large frame filling the hallway. "You the one who found this place?"

"That's correct, sir. Jason Turner, sir."

"Ah, Turner," Cole jeered. "The rookie who wants to make detective."

Jason managed to hide his wince. "I was hoping I could shadow you both on this case. Just watch, listen, learn…"

"You want to help? You can fetch me coffee," Cole jabbed a thumb to the stairs behind her.

Jason looked down at the coffee cup already in her hand. He decided not to mention it and instead, smiled to hide the pain. "Sure. How do you take yours?"

She softened. "I don't actually need a refill yet."

"Just let me know when."

Lynch rolled his eyes, unimpressed by the whole discussion. "Don't know why you'd want to be a detective anyway. Beat cops catch more criminals in this town."

"Hardly criminals. Most of my arrests are for drunk and disorderly."

Lynch looked like he'd just stepped in something unpleasant. "Come on, rookie. I'll show you just how shit detective work is. It's too late for me, but maybe we can still save your soul."

"That's encouraging."

"It wasn't supposed to be."

Lynch led the way with Cole following close behind, shaking her head. Jason tried to hide his excited smile, but it was quite impossible. *It's finally happening! I'm working with real detectives! After the captain sent me on fucking patrol!*

The crime scene was filled with the three members of a forensic squad, all wearing white hazmat suits, blue gloves, with their faces covered in masks. Yellow plaques with numbers were placed next to any object that was out of place, and in Alex's messy apartment, it applied to just about everything.

"Tommy, what have you got for me?" Lynch said, walking over to a figure in white.

Tommy looked down and read off his notebook. "No signs of forced entry. No signs of a struggle. Victim had a single gunshot wound to the rear of the head. Murder weapon not found on the scene. It's unclear how the assailant left."

Lynch grunted. "You sure there was an assailant?"

Tommy shrugged. "Gunshot to the back of the head. If it was suicide, he'd just point it at his forehead. You can't reach around that far."

"Oh sure you can. I reach around all the time." He grinned. "For my boyfriend."

"Fuckin' hell," Cole groaned.

Lynch gave a dark chuckle. "Find some hard evidence of an assailant. The head thing won't hold up in court on its own." He gestured to the bedroom. "Vic's in here?" Tommy nodded, and Lynch left without another word. Jason noted that the forensic team had already done a sweep of the bedroom and the body, and were now looking elsewhere in the apartment while the detectives took their turn. He followed them.

The bedroom still held Alex's body, but now with more numbered plaques. Lynch crouched, while Jason stood in the corner, careful to stay out of the way.

"He's lying on his back," Lynch said. "How the hell was he shot in the back of the head?"

"He's been moved," Cole said. "Look at the blood splatter." She pointed to the markers. "The assailant must have already been in the room waiting. Victim enters, sees someone in the corner, turns to run, bang. Bullet to the back of the head."

"Ok, but why move him here?" Lynch said, pointing to Alex's body in the middle of the room, still laying limp and cold. "He's a big guy. Would have been a lot of effort just to move him."

"Look at all the blood marks." Cole pointed to the faded ring around the body. She called out, "Hey Tommy! You didn't clean up the blood?"

"It was like that when we got here."

"Any idea how the perp cleaned it?"

"No idea, boss lady. Couldn't find any smells or residue of cleaning products. I'll do some more tests and let you know."

Cole shrugged and turned back to Alex's body. "It's got to be organised crime. Victim was working for someone, and either screwed up or turned traitor. We should look into his next of kin and any work friends. I bet you the blood was collected to use as a threat to his allies, like sending a finger in the mail."

"Damn, slow down, Nicky," Lynch said in a flat voice. "This is the first job we've had in weeks, and I could use the overtime."

"Excuse me," Jason asked. "Why did you call her Nicky?"

Lynch snickered. "Her name is Cole, so one time I called her Nicole. Which was shortened to Nicky."

"He only does it to piss me off," Cole said.

Jason laughed, and both detectives suddenly turned serious. "Got something to add, rookie?" Lynch asked.

"No, detective."

"Good," Cole said and held out her coffee cup without even a glance in Jason's direction. "Cappuccino. Two sugars, four shots."

He glared at the cup, but took it without complaint.

"And don't get me that Starbucks shit. I drink real English coffee, got it?"

"Oh you're doing a coffee run?" Tommy yelled from the living area.

Soon everyone else was placing orders, and Jason was typing all five separate requests into his phone. Finally, he went outside to borrow the police car from Douglas.

"Oi, where you off to?"

"Coffee run."

"Then get me a double-choc mocha!"

Jason growled, yet added it to the list. As he was typing, a message popped up on his phone.

Hi Jason. We still on for dinner tonight? Regards, Silvana.

It made his heart leap in excitement, and his anger at being turned into an assistant was quickly forgotten. But he immediately crushed that excitement down. Silvana might be a suspect. He had to be careful.

He messaged back, *Sure. Looking forward to it.* He winced. It sounded too formal, so he added, *Cause I'm hungry already. ;)* He hit send and chuckled at himself for half a second, before feeling incredibly awkward and desperately wishing he could un-send the message.

"Damn it, man, get it together."

* * *

Forty minutes later, Jason returned to the crime scene with two trays of coffees. It felt surreal calling out orders, then literally stepping over a dead body to hand them out.

"So," he asked in his most casual voice. "What did I miss?"

Lynch was typing on his phone while standing in the kitchen. He spoke without looking up. "Interviewed the owner and the two residents. Same story. Heard the gunshot and ignored it. No other clues." He chuckled and looked up at Jason, flashing a brilliant smile. "Cole should have made you stay for that. Three boring, predictable conversations with members of the general public that offered nothing useful and wasted a lot of time. That's ninety percent of detective work right there."

Jason grinned back. "Sorry I missed it."

Lynch went back to his phone. Everyone else was in the bedroom with the body, and Jason found himself preparing to ask the real question on his mind.

"You ever seen that before? Someone bled dry?"

"Nah…"

"Cause you know what my first thought was?"

"Mmm?"

Jason felt awkward but said it with a laugh. "A vampire."

"Nah, mate. People are just fucking weird, you know? Lot of freaks out there. That's always the reason for this sort of bizarre stuff."

"Oh yeah? So you've never seen anything that would be…" Jason trailed off, embarrassed about what he was about to say, but Lynch seemed to come alert.

"What?" he asked curiously.

Jason tried to give a harmless shrug. "Supernatural."

Lynch paused, and Jason started to brace himself for another hazing, but Lynch only seemed thoughtful.

"Yeah, definitely," the detective said. "Few years back there was a murder down by the water. Young girl, just over eighteen. Pretty thing, so straight away you know it's gonna be some creepy motherfucker who killed her. And we found the creepiest fucking guy I've ever seen. You know the type. Early twenties, handsome as Hemsworth, and absolutely full of himself. The kind of guy they make crime documentaries about. So I interview this guy and he's giving me all the red flags. This guy is properly psychopathic, right? He was chauvinistic towards Cole, and aggressive to me like he's tryna be the alpha dog. Definitely some white supremacy bullshit too."

Lynch stopped to sip his coffee and cleared his throat. "Thing is, he had an air tight alibi. He was at a party on the other side of town, nowhere near the vic. But this is where it gets weird, yeah?"

He leaned in and whispered. "We found CCTV footage from outside the club this party was at. This guy goes into the building an hour before the murder and doesn't come out. Exactly five minutes after the murder happened, this creep appeared *outside* the building, walking from the direction the murder occurred. He re-enters the party even though everyone there was sure they never saw him leave."

Jason blinked. "So he left the party in secret, committed murder, and came back without anyone seeing him."

Lynch shook his head. "That's the thing. The murder was ten kilometres away. He couldn't have covered that distance in five minutes. The math just doesn't add up. Even if he had a motorbike, he'd be driving through the densest part of the city and he'd have to be doing a hundred and twenty kilometres at least."

"So it's like he had superhuman speed?"

"Exactly. Now I know it's him, right? Detective's instinct. But there's nothing to tie him to the crime. I even tried to trick a confession out of him, but it didn't work. I had to let him go. So I un-cuffed him in the precinct, and I was so pissed about it that I marched right out of the building. And you know what happened next?"

"Yeah?"

"This kid appears in front of me on the street outside."

Jason frowned. "He got there before you?"

"Shit yeah. I have no idea how he could have done it. But he did. And it's like he did it deliberately just to mess with me. To prove he could have done that ten kilometre run. To show me he knew that I knew, and we both knew there was nothing I could do."

"Jesus," Jason said. He felt the urge to look over his shoulder and make sure no one was watching him, waiting to jump out of the shadows. "But you don't think he was supernatural?"

Lynch laughed and waved his coffee around. "Course not, mate. We must have had the wrong guy. He probably committed some other crime and that's why he seemed so guilty. And he caught me on the street cause I obviously lost track of time during my fit of rage. It's just that in the heat of the moment, and the stress of it all, you get caught up thinking it's real." He pointed at the bedroom. "That's all that happened here. You got to keep a clear head in this job. Don't lose sight of the facts."

Jason nodded. "What happened to that guy?"

"Nothing. We got a profile on him now. All we can do is book his ass next time he fucks up." He sighed. "Never did find that girl's killer, though. That one still pisses me off."

They stood in silence for a moment as Lynch went back to his phone. Jason felt his heartbeat racing. He knew in his gut that the young man had committed the murder. He had some supernatural power that the police weren't aware of. He must have been a vampire, or something similar.

My God, how often does this happen?

He had to speak to Silvana, and find out more about her. He had to redefine what was possible and what wasn't. He had to know what else could be out there.

Jason checked his phone. Silvana had texted back.

All right, no entrees. We'll go straight to mains. ;)

He rolled his eyes even as he smiled. *She is trying so hard not to come on strong. Maybe this will be a nice night after all.*

"Officer Turner?"

He looked up. Detective Cole had re-entered the room, yet her eyes were squinted in suspicion and her voice cracked like a whip. "What's this about you knowing the victim?"

The mood in the room changed at once, like a blanket of snow had landed on every occupant. Officer Douglas was standing in the doorway and he gave Jason an apologetic half smile.

Jason stammered. "Oh…uh…" He felt Lynch's eyes on his back, watching him closely with his hands near his belt. Jason scrambled to explain, "I met him on a date." He stammered, "I mean, with another person. I was on a date with someone else, and he approached us…"

"The victim?" Cole snapped.

"Yes, the victim approached us…" Jason trailed off with a grimace. "I suppose it looks bad that I'm flustered, doesn't it?"

"Officer Turner," Lynch said, "I'm going to need you to come down to the station with us and answer a few questions."

Jason sighed. "Yeah, that makes sense."

"*After* you drop your firearm," Cole said, her hand on the handle of her gun, the holster unstrapped.

Jason felt his heart pounding as he realised the danger he was in. He held one trembling hand high as he unhooked his entire holster and placed it on the counter next to him, then he stepped away with his hands held up.

Lynch grabbed him by the shoulder and pushed him towards the door. "This looks bad, rookie," he muttered in Jason's ear. "You knew the victim, then asked to shadow me? Well here's a detective tip for you. That right there is what we call 'suspicious behaviour'."

Chapter 8

"So you were just in the wrong place at the wrong time?" Cole sneered. "Do you know how often we hear that excuse?"

"Well, actually," Jason said, trying not to fidget with the handcuffs that held him to the table, "considering Alex was threatening three women with a gun, and I stopped him, I'd say I was in the right place at the right time." He couldn't help a smug grin. "And considering how rare murders are in this town, I'd say you *don't* hear that excuse very often."

Cole pressed her lips together.

"Hey, wise-ass," Lynch snapped, leaning forward in his chair. "You're in enough trouble already. Don't piss my partner off any further."

Jason lost his grin immediately. He had to admit, Lynch was intimidating as hell when he wanted to be. The slightest rise in his voice made Jason feel like a two year old who'd painted the walls with sticky handprints. The interrogation room was cramped and dimly lit, and Lynch's dark skin made him partially blend in with shadows, giving him a strange ghostly presence.

The detectives were clearly aware of this effect. Cole was doing most of the work pressing for details, and Lynch just loomed like a hammer above an anvil. It was less good cop, bad cop, and more professional cop and scary cop. Their team dynamic was flawless.

"Sorry, sir," Jason said. "Look, I had every intention of telling you two everything the first chance I got, but I didn't know when to bring it up. I'm still a rookie, and this is the first time I've worked with detectives."

"So that's your new excuse? You're a rookie?" Cole snapped.

"It's not a great excuse, but that's the truth."

"If we'd heard it from you first, we might have understood. But the fact that your partner had to come clean for you seems to suggest you were hiding something."

Ah, Douglas. Can't say I blame you, mate.

"And watching the detectives who are investigating the crime you're suspected in doesn't look good either," Lynch said in a gravelly drawl.

"I know. But I've told you everything now. There's nothing else I can say."

The detectives glanced at each other with cold, flat expressions. Jason knew they were putting pressure on him now. He just had to wait it out.

Cole finally sighed. "Tell me the names of the people you were with last night."

"Fine. Emberline, Lisbeth, and Silvana. I don't know their last names, but they live up at that mansion on the north side. I think it's called Maristow House." Cole raised an eyebrow, as if impressed. "I visited last night with my friend, Peter Erikson."

"Erikson?" Lynch asked with a frown. "And what's your relationship with him?"

"He's my roommate."

"You're roommates with Peter Erikson?" Lynch said coyly.

"He's not my boyfriend, if that's what you mean. We went to school together. He came back to town a few months ago and we were both looking for a new place. He invited me to meet Silvana, as a chaperone on their date."

Lynch and Cole exchanged a glance. Their faces had no expression, but somehow they understood each other. Jason prepared to explain the whole chaperone dynamic.

"Well that's all from us," Cole said. Jason blinked in surprise, but said nothing. "Although," Cole said, "there's someone else who wants to speak with you."

Jason gulped. He had a good idea who they meant.

The detectives left the room, and Cole paused to hold the door open for Captain Kader. She stepped past the detectives with a nod, straightened her shirt and scowled at him in silence.

"Hi Captain," Jason said with a resigned tone. "Were you listening? Or should I explain from the top?"

"Don't bother."

Kader stood opposite him, knocking the chairs aside. She loomed over him now with a hard expression. *Maybe Douglas is right, and she needs to prove who's in charge.*

"Are you fucking stupid?" she asked in a quiet, flat voice.

"I might be," Jason replied. She didn't say anything for some time. He didn't look up at her as he couldn't bear to make eye contact.

The captain sat down and her tone was soft when she spoke. "I know you didn't do it. And the detectives know too," she said. "But they've got to do this by the book. You don't get special treatment cause you're a cop. In fact, they'll probably drill you harder than if you were a regular guy."

"I understand."

"It's a funny thing about being a public servant. Corruption and incompetence often look identical and have the same results. I don't believe you are corrupt. But incompetence can be just as deadly."

"Yes, ma'am."

"I just have one question." She leaned forward, her face hardening into a frown. "Why'd you let that man go last night? That was a serious lapse in judgement."

"I didn't know what was going to happen to him."

"Obviously, *detective*," she drawled. "But you had grounds to arrest him. In fact, you had an *obligation* to arrest him. Why didn't you?"

Jason felt the words weighing down his tongue. He knew the answer immediately. But to actually say it out loud…he'd never done that before. Still, he didn't have a choice. The captain was his superior and she deserved the truth.

"I don't like violent men, captain. In fact, I *hate* them." He spat the word with all the venom he could muster. "Alex Bishop and I fought hand to hand. When I finally had my gun on him, he started saying horrible things about those women, and …" he winced. He couldn't look his captain in the eye as he said it. "…I wanted to shoot him. I even fired a warning shot. That's why I let him go. I wasn't in control."

The captain was quiet. The pause made the tension in his chest become unbearable. He waited for her to yell and demand his badge.

Instead, she whispered, "I read your file, Turner. I understand."

He blinked at her. "You do?"

"Of course. I divorced my husband for a similar reason. I hate violent men." The captain suddenly smiled and looked *bashful*, of all things. "Truth be told, I expected you to be a bit like that yourself. A lot of men learn violence and repeat the pattern. But I understand now. You're actually more like me. Violence has made you hate violence."

"Exactly!" he burst out. "Cause I know what it's like to be on the receiving end. Why would I ever want to do that to another human being?"

For the first time since he joined this precinct, Kader gave him a real, genuine smile, and Jason couldn't help but smile back.

"You're a good kid, Turner. However," she lost the smile and her tone hardened, "that's still no excuse for letting Mr Bishop go last night. You need to get that knee-jerk reaction of yours under control.

The best thing you can do when you encounter a violent man is make him face justice. When you wear that uniform, you have the power to stop men like that. Don't waste that power."

He nodded. "I won't, captain. I promise."

"Good. Now moving on," Kader reached forward to unlock the handcuffs around Jason's wrists. "It's important that you stay far away from this case. No more shadowing the detectives. In fact, just stay away from them altogether. I'll have to keep you on patrols for the next fortnight or so, unless the case is solved first."

"That's fine. Thank you, Captain." He was disappointed that he wouldn't join in more of the case, but considering his screw up with Bishop, this was the best he could hope for.

"I'll ask them to include you on their next case, once this one calms down." Her eyes glimmered. "I know I mock you about the detective thing – and that's not going to change – but you might actually make a good detective one day."

Jason felt his throat tighten. He swallowed and had to blink a few times to keep his eyes clear.

"So don't throw that away by being too eager. Don't take shortcuts. Don't get stupid. Do the hard work and take the time to do it right, so that when you can become a detective, you're ready for it."

"Yes, captain." He paused. "You should know something else."

"Oh?"

"That girl I told the detectives about. Silvana. I'm seeing her again tonight. But I can cancel that if you think it's a good idea."

Kader blinked at him. "Are you literally asking my permission to go on a date?"

"Well…yeah, kind of!" He shrugged. "I got in trouble for not coming forward with information, so I want to be open about this. I assume Lynch and Cole are going to that mansion this afternoon to continue their investigation, right? So I don't want to get in the way."

The captain shook her head. "No, it's fine. Date the girl. But make sure you see her *after* the detectives have come and gone. And don't talk to her about the case. Just keep it professional."

"Yes, captain. Thank you, captain."

Chapter 9

Jason arrived at the manor well after dark. This time, he'd dressed up slightly. His shirt had a collar. It even had buttons.

Tonight, the leafless trees looked like skeletons in the moonlight. The wind through the woods made everything rustle around him as if the grounds were filled with crouching animals, watching him from within the dark.

Jason hurried over the hill to the mansion's entrance. He banged the door knocker four times, and waited.

A man answered the door. He appeared to be in his sixties, bald and thin, with narrow eyes and thick bushy eyebrows that gave his face an angry scowl. "Yes?" he said.

"Oh…I'm Jason. I'm here to see Silvana. You must be one of the husbands…"

"The police were here today," the man snapped. He spoke with crisp diction, like upper-class London. "They interrogated my wife. Do you realise how dangerous this is for her? You know what she is, you zounderkite."

Zounderkite? Jason held up his hands. "Ok, that had nothing to do with me. Your intruder last night was murdered, so there is an investigation. That's pretty standard proced—"

"That's exactly my point!" the man snapped louder this time. "We had an intruder! Don't you think we suffered enough invasion of privacy?"

Jason gave a warm smile. "You must be Emberline's husband."

The man's eyes widened. "What the hell is that supposed to mean?"

Yep. Guessed correctly.

"Sir, I'm just an officer. I have no control over the detectives and their investigation. In fact, I've been ordered to have nothing to do with it. If you have a formal complaint, you'll have to contact my superiors at the precinct."

The old man scowled at him. "You have no idea what my wife is capable of, young man. What I am capable of."

"Is that a threat?" Jason cut in. "Are you threatening me, sir?"

"Oh, it's more than that." The man leaned in so close that Jason could smell his aftershave and whispered, "I'm from an old family. Older than this country. You have no idea what I could do to you, beardsplitter."

Older than this country? Beardsplitter?

Jason didn't understand the insult. Yet something about the way this man made his claim convinced Jason it was true. *Who the fuck is this guy?*

"Jason!"

Silvana appeared and her beauty made Jason's breath catch in his throat. She was glancing at the man nervously. Jason felt his heart lurch at the sight of her piercing blue eyes. She wore blue jeans, and a grey Spiderman t-shirt that was snug against her chest. She smoothly stepped between the two men.

"Jason, this is my Uncle Phillip."

"Oh we've met. He's made quite an impression."

Phillip glared at him silently, chin pointed up.

"Did you want to come inside?" Silvana asked.

"Um…I'm not sure if that's a good idea. Is everyone angry with me after…"

"No, of course not," Silvana took his arm with her cold hands and pulled him inside, gently nudging Phillip aside. "No one blames you for the police visiting. We were sad to hear about what happened to that man. You know we never wanted that, right? Even if he did come into our home, we'd never do anything like that."

Jason nodded. "I'm sure." Silvana was staring at him with those bright blue eyes, and he felt all thoughts fading from his mind. He blurted, "But I'm not allowed to talk about the case."

"How convenient," Phillip interjected. "He's done nothing but avoid taking responsibility since he got here."

"Phillip, please," Silvana said gently before Jason could get a word out. "Jason is my guest. Please speak to him with civility."

But Phillip simply clenched his jaw as he turned and walked away without another word.

"I'm sorry for Phillip," Silvana said.

"That's ok. Thank you for defending me." He knew he was grinning like a schoolboy but he couldn't help it.

Silvana blushed. "It was nothing." She cleared her throat, "So, uh…how did Peter take the news?" She squeezed her eyes shut as if regretting the words.

"I actually haven't seen him yet. He was asleep this morning, and still at university when I came home from work." He still had to have *that* conversation at some point and wasn't looking forward to it.

"Oh. I thought he left with you?"

"No, he said he was catching a taxi."

"Ok. Uh…you're not mad about…"

"No. I mean, it was surprising. But understandable."

She gave a nervous laugh, then fell silent. They stood in the doorway about a metre apart, hands at the sides and not speaking. Jason noticed again the two decorative suits of armour and considered asking about them, but didn't know what to say. He squirmed slightly.

"Are you hungry?" he asked. "Sorry, dumb question." He winced and fell silent again.

"Would you like a tour of the mansion?" she asked. "Oh, unless you're hungry?"

"No," he blurted out, then winced again. "I mean, thank you, but I'm not actually that hungry. I haven't worked out today. Usually I work out after my shift ends and that…um, gives me an appetite."

"Would you like to work out?"

He paused, unsure exactly what she was suggesting. "Um, no that's ok. I was happy to come here tonight instead of my usual…"

"We have a gym."

He blinked. "A gym?"

She flashed a gorgeous smile that made his breath freeze in his chest. "We have a gym. I use it all the time. We can work out together if you like?"

"I…really? That sounds amazing!" He laughed with disbelief. "Are you sure you're ok with it?"

"Honestly, I work out alone most days, so I could use someone to spot me."

Jason stammered a moment more, but he couldn't help himself. "I've got my gym gear in the car!" he cried and raced back up the hill.

* * *

Ten minutes later, Jason was dressed in loose shorts and a plain grey t-shirt and carried a blue towel over his shoulder. His water bottle was tucked under his arm.

The gym room had everything he could have hoped for. Weight

racks, squat racks, barbells, and a range of cardio machines. This was literally his dream home. *Perks if you do marry her.* But he ignored that thought. He wasn't going to rush into anything…

"Ok, I'm all set," Silvana said.

Jason turned to look at her.

She wore tight-fitting black leggings that clung to her thighs and hips, accentuating her slight curves to make them stand out. Her bright blue sports top exposed her midriff and the faint line of cleavage beneath her clavicle. She'd pulled her hair up into a high ponytail that swished with every movement. The sweet scent of jasmine and sweat wafted past his nose.

Sweet Jesus…

"Oh!" she cried, jolting him out of his daze. "I'm sorry for staring at you." He hadn't even noticed her staring. She gave a nervous laugh. "It's just been a while…I mean! Not like that! Oh god…" Her face was bright red. "I meant that Arthur was seventy two when he passed and…" she cut off. "I'm so sorry, I shouldn't." Then she blurted out in a near-shout, "So where would you like to start?!"

She was clearly upset about her late husband. Jason wanted to help. He wanted to reach for her, hold her close and keep her safe and maybe take in the scent of her long, dark hair…

God what is happening to me? She's still a suspect in a murder. Keep it professional.

"I usually stretch, then do something high cardio to start."

"Sounds good," she said in that too-cheerful voice.

She rolled out a yoga mat, sat down, and reached for her toes. Jason sat a respectful distance away and copied her. He'd done a bit of work on his flexibility and was a little smug when he could touch his toes easily. He glanced over to see if she was watching him.

Silvana was hugging her legs. Her face was pressed against her thigh, with her legs and back straight.

Whoa...

She looked at him. "Are you going to start?"

He grinned. "This is my best."

"Oh! I'm sorry," she said and came out of her stretch. "I didn't mean to be rude."

"No, it's ok. I thought you were trash talking. It was funny."

"Ok. Thank you."

He reached one arm over his head and bent to the side. "Before we start, I'm curious about something."

"Yes?"

"I've seen movies with vampires in them…"

"Oh yeah. Where they sparkle in the sun."

"God no. I watched the movies where they burst into flames in the sun."

"Oh that's much better," she said dryly.

He chuckled. "I was just wondering what you can do?"

She changed position, cupping her feet together and bending forward. "Well, the movies are a bit exaggerated. Mortals have always been a bit superstitious. Vampires are just slightly above-average humans. We're not superhuman. More like Olympic athletes."

"Ah," Jason said as he stretched to the other side. "So it's more like you're in peak physical condition?"

"Yeah. Have you heard of Captain America?"

Jason blinked. "What?"

"He's a superhero…

"Of course I've heard of Captain America! I've seen all seven films starring Chris Evans."

"Eight films," she corrected, then blushed. "You're forgetting his cameo in Homecoming."

"WHAT?!" he cried with a laugh. "Of course, your Spiderman t-shirt. You're a big superhero fan."

Silvana blushed even more. "The point is vampires are a lot like the captain. Peak human condition. We could maybe hold back a small helicopter but we're not strong enough to Hulk-smash a building, or throw cars."

"I see."

"You know, you're in pretty good shape yourself. You're probably just as strong as I am."

He frowned at her. "Are you just saying that so I don't feel emasculated?"

"No, of course not."

"Uh-huh."

They finished stretching, and Jason hopped up and down on his toes. "Alright! I was thinking a quick one K run would do for a warm up."

"Awesome."

They stepped up to a pair of treadmills and started them up at a brisk walking pace. Jason frowned. "I thought you said you worked out alone, but there are two treadmills side by side…"

"In case anyone wanted to join me."

"Oh, right. Like your husband?" Jason nearly slapped himself for saying it.

Silvana gave a sad sigh. "I tried to convince him but Arthur never really exercised…"

"Oh…" He wanted to change topics and considered asking about the other people in her family, but thought it best to avoid that topic altogether. Desperate, he increased the treadmill speed to a jog. Silvana copied him, still silent. "So, you like Captain America?" He could hear how corny it sounded.

"Oh yeah. I've read all his comics since issue one. I even have a collection."

"A collection?"

"Hey, this is just our first date. You have to earn the right to see the collection."

He laughed, and noticed how she smiled and relaxed her shoulders when he was laughing. It took him a while to get his breath back while jogging, yet Silvana seemed fine. So he increased the speed on the treadmill into a steady sprint. She immediately matched it.

"Wait, *since* issue one?" he asked breathlessly. "Didn't the first Captain America come out in the 40s?"

"March 1941," she said proudly.

"So…is that how old you are?"

Silvana went silent and ran while looking straight ahead. "You know it's rude to ask a lady about her age," she said with a playful tone.

"I know. I'm sorry, but… I would like to know."

He waited. Each footstep was a loud thud, making the lack of speech more noticeable for it. He almost apologised and told her to forget the question.

"I was about ten," she said. "When I read the first issue."

"Ten," he repeated. "So, that would make you about ninety years old."

"Ninety-one," she said.

"Ninety-one?" He couldn't quite picture it. "But you said you practiced medicine in the Victorian era?"

"My teachers did. It was only a generation or two earlier, for mortals."

Mortals? Jason ran without speaking. He was huffing with each breath, whereas she was silent. Suddenly she started panting and Jason had the distinct feeling that she was putting it on, just to make him feel better.

"Well you're in great shape for your age," he said as he slowed his treadmill down. "I can't keep up."

"Really?" She flinched. "Sorry, that was rude of me. Uh…weights?"

Jason nodded and stepped off the treadmill. They moved to a rack with a barbell already loaded. He checked the numbers.

"A hundred and fifty kilos," he said wryly. "Is that how much you normally bench press?"

"Uh…I don't know who left it like that."

He threw his towel on the ground. "Ok Silvana, what's going on?"

A wave of panic flushed over her face. "What do you mean?"

"How strong are you?" He held up his hands in an appeasing gesture. "I can see you're avoiding the issue but it's ok. I want to know."

Silvana had frozen in place. "It's no big deal. You don't have to worry about it."

Jason wanted to insist on the issue but stopped himself. Silvana was fidgeting with her hands and avoiding his gaze. This wasn't nervousness. This was *fear*. Why would she be scared? She was looking for a husband to make a long term commitment. So why hide strength? Why not impress him with everything she had? Did it have to do with being ninety one years old?

Unless…

"Silvana," he asked in a polite tone. "How old are your aunts?" She looked uncertain, so he tried to smile to put her at ease. "Just approximately. They must be older than you, right?"

She gave a half smile. "They're somewhere over two hundred. They've never told me exactly."

"Of course," he said. "So they have some pretty old-fashioned values, don't they? About how men and women should interact."

"You can say that again. They're very old fashioned," she said with a laugh.

"So they probably think a man should be the strong one who's always in charge, while the woman should be submissive and manage the household."

Silvana stared at him with wide eyes. "Please, Jason," she said in a whimper. "I didn't mean any disrespect. If we got married, you'd still be the one in charge, Jason. I mean Arthur was much weaker physically, but he was still in charge. I'm sorry, I shouldn't keep bringing him up."

Jason held up his hands. "Silvana, it's ok." She flinched at his words. "Look. I actually don't believe that sort of thing. I wouldn't want to be in charge of you anyway. I think you need to be equals in a relationship."

She sniffed sharply. "Oh Arthur would have hated to hear you say that. He had very strong opinions about this…" she cut off again, and held a hand to her face. "God, what is wrong with me? I don't know why I keep mentioning him." She was suddenly blinking rapidly and turning away.

Jason felt tense. This Arthur must have shared the same old-fashioned values as Silvana's family. Had Silvana been oppressed all her life? If so, then maybe she was just dating Jason because she felt pressured to.

And if that was the case, how could he tell who she really was? If she was only letting herself be what her family expected of her?

"I have a request," he said, and tried to give his most light-hearted smile. "If you're up to it."

"Ok. Anything," she said.

"I was hoping you could show me how much weight you can lift."

She hesitated, the uncertainty clear in her shifting eyes. "I don't know… is that what you want?"

He grinned. "I'll go first. See if you can beat this." He laid down on the rack with the one hundred and fifty kilogram weights and gripped the bar. "You better spot me."

Silvana came to stand beside him, her black leggings were near his face…*Don't look!* He focused on the barbell. He had lifted weights close to this amount but his personal best was one hundred and ten.

Maybe, if he really pushed himself…

He gripped the bar, squared his shoulder blades directly underneath him, inhaled, then pushed with all he had.

The bar lifted off the rack…by one centimetre.

Then he dropped it back down.

"Oh shit!" he cried with a laugh. "I have no chance of lifting that!"

"You got it off the rack! That's amazing!" Silvana cheered.

He sat up and shook his head. "You're just saying that to spare my feelings."

"No, really. Most men couldn't do that much."

"I bet you could," he said with a flat tone. Silvana still looked nervous, so he cheered her on. "Come on, I want to see how strong you are. Can you do it?"

"Well, yes, but…"

"I find strong women very attractive."

Jason felt a little guilty for the manipulation. But it worked. Her face lit up as she took his spot on the bench. Jason manoeuvred around the bar and stood behind her to spot.

"Ok girl, when you're read—"

The barbell went straight off the rack. She held it over her chest then lowered it all the way down, and all the way back up again, before she racked it with ease.

Jason's mouth hung wide open. His hands were still ready in the support position and had frozen there uselessly.

Silvana sat up and upon seeing his expression, immediately looked away. "I'm sorry, I shouldn't have done that. You were being so nice, and I got…"

"That. Was. Amazing!" Jason roared.

The smile that lit up Silvana's face was almost childlike. "You really mean it?" she laughed.

"You made that look easy!" he cried. "Incredible. Is that the most you can do, or can you go further?"

"Maybe a little further," she said, blushing. Yet she suddenly clutched her head and her mouth hung opened in a pained expression.

Jason leapt to her side. "Are you ok?" he cried.

"Mmm," she nodded, but her eyes were squeezed shut. She was clearly trying to hide how much pain she was in. "I'm just very thirsty. I haven't had as much blood as I need. I feel...dizzy."

"Silvana," he whispered. "I'm so sorry. I didn't even consider that. I shouldn't have pushed you."

"No, no, it's ok." She smiled sweetly. "But I think I should stop there."

"Of course. God, I feel terrible. I didn't even think of your condition."

She clutched his hand, a look of tenderness on her face. "It was worth it," she said. "I'm just going to rest. But you can still work out! I'm happy to watch. In fact...I'd be more than happy."

He raised an eyebrow. "Oh?" She wore a coy smile. "Well, thank you. But I think we should have dinner. Food will make you feel better, right?"

"It will."

"Then let's get you some food." Jason offered her a hand to pull her up. When she stood, they were only centimetres apart. She kept her grip on his hand. His breath caught again at the sight of her, up close, her scent of faint sweat flooding his senses.

"I really enjoyed that," she said, looking directly into his eyes. "It was nice to be strong for a change."

He studied her a moment, then shook his head. "For a change? Silvana, you're always strong. Aren't you? You don't have to hide it around me."

The look she gave him then – her eyes filled with wonder and sadness, and her mouth slightly open – made Jason wish that he could be all of that for her. More than anything, he wanted to be the one to help her believe in herself.

But he let go of her hand.

"So, where do you want to grab dinner?" he asked.

He saw a flicker of disappointment on her face. Then she forced a smile. "Wherever you like. I really don't mind."

Chapter 10

Jason drove them towards the town centre. There was a particular restaurant he had in mind, Henry's Manor, where he could find fancy food at cheap prices. *And burgers. Tasty, tasty burgers.*

Silvana was dressed in her jeans and Spiderman t-shirt again, concealed under a thick jumper. She had gone silent when they reached the car. Normally Jason loved silence, especially since he started partnering with Douglas who talked non-stop about nothing. But this seemed like a tense silence. Silvana was thinking, though about what, Jason had no idea. He tried to force down his own insecurity and let her take her time.

Until he couldn't stand the silence.

"So, I was wondering something," Jason asked. "How come no one knows that vampires are real?"

"Ah yes. Why are we hidden?"

"Yeah."

Silvana pressed her lips together. "It's complicated."

"Cause there are many reasons?"

"No. Cause I'm not really supposed to talk about it."

"Oh."

"There are…laws about telling people. You're not from an immortal family, so I can't share anything with you. But the law also says because I'm courting you, I can tell you about vampires. Does that make sense?"

"Yeah ok. Please, just tell me what you can. Don't break any laws for me."

Jason felt the twinge of guilt in his stomach. She was trusting him with some of her biggest secrets, but he was only on his first date. He had no idea if they had a future together. Was he using their potential relationship to trick her out of information? Yet it was too important a chance to miss. Detective Lynch had already suspected a supernatural murderer. Who knows how often that sort of thing happened? Jason had to know what was out there.

So, he let Silvana speak. And didn't stop her.

"We have a ruling government called the Immortal Imperium," Silvana said. "They oversee every house and every head of state. Every immortal must answer to them."

"Wait," Jason cut in. "Every immortal? Not just every vampire?"

"Oh…"

"So you mean…there are other immortals, not just vampires?"

Silvana put a hand over her mouth. "I'm sorry, I shouldn't have said that. But yes, there are others."

"Like what? You mean all those monsters in the night time, all those urban myths and fairy tales we were told as children, they're all real?"

"Some are real. You have to remember that most of those myths are clouded by fear and superstition. Mortals are very prejudiced against our kind, so they tend to exaggerate. I mean, come on! I don't burst into flames in the sunlight, do I?"

Jason chuckled. "Come to think of it, I've never actually seen you outside during the day."

She didn't return his laugh. "Well, I don't."

"Oh. Ok."

"And I don't need to murder hundreds of people every time I feed.

I just need one litre of blood each month. It's not even that much."

"And you don't throw cars at people."

"Exactly."

Jason frowned in thought. "So, are you truly...immortal?"

Silvana smiled. "Not as you might think. We don't live forever. We just live a lot longer than mortals. I know the word immortal means undying in the mortal dictionary. But for us it really means 'long-lived'."

"How long-lived?"

"Most immortal species have a maximum lifespan of under one thousand years."

"One thousand?" Jason gasped. "But... you said you were ninety-one!"

"I *am* ninety-one. By immortal standards, I'm still a child."

"Oh...wait, you said *most* immortal species. Do some live longer than a thousand?"

"Damn!" Silvana cried. "I shouldn't have said species." She shook her head. "No, one thousand is the max. The oldest immortal on record was nine hundred and ninety eight. No one's ever gotten past the one thousand year limit. However, some immortal species have a shorter lifespan. Sometimes two hundred years, sometimes five hundred. They're still a part of our community."

Jason shook his head. "That's incredible. How do these people live for so long without getting noticed?"

"Sometimes they do. You ever heard of Methuselah?"

"From the bible? Wasn't he the oldest man ever?"

"Nine hundred and sixty-nine years. Most of Adam and Eve's descendants were immortals who lived over nine hundred years. Some of our immortal theologians believe that Adam and Eve were not the first humans, but the first immortals."

"Ah. And the tree of knowledge of good and evil was like, a

radioactive spider?"

She chuckled. "Oh, I like that! But the tree was probably more of a metaphor for them getting their powers."

"Interesting…"

They reached their destination. Henry's Manor; a 16th-century stone building with an updated modern sign spelling the name in cursive English. They parked on the street outside, and Silvana took his hand in her cold grip as they walked in. Jason found himself gripping back.

The inside was filled with modern furniture and a flashy new bar that stood out pleasantly against the old building background. The place was nearly empty on a Monday night, yet the TV mounted on the wall blared a replay of the day's football match, and several patrons talked in louder-than-necessary voices.

Jason chose a seat in the back corner, away from anyone else, Jason read the menu for a minute in silence without actually processing a single word. He could feel Silvana's tension coming off her in waves as she waited for him to speak.

"Your Uncle Philip," he said on impulse. "What's his last name?"

Silvana frowned at him. "Clarke. That's my whole family's last name."

"Right. Then what did he mean, saying he's from a family older than this country?"

Silvana pressed her lips together. "He shouldn't have said that."

"I just ask because those three teenagers from last night were talking about your 'house'? They seemed real determined to know which one you belonged to."

"Jason, I…" she tugged at her jacket sleeve. "I'd really prefer to not talk about it, if that's ok."

"Oh. Ok sure." He decided not to push it.

They fell back into silence. Jason's mind was racing with questions about immortal species and houses. He tried to think of something else to say, yet all he could think of now were prying questions about her family and her 'house'.

"You actually listened to me," Silvana said.

"What?"

It took him a moment to realise the irony of what he'd said. "Sorry. Yes I was listening to you. I just meant, what do you mean?" He winced. *Smooth, dude.*

She gave a bashful smile. "I told you I didn't want to talk about something, and you accepted it straight away. I was prepared for a big fight about it."

"A big fight? Why would you expect me to fight you?"

"Not you. I mean…" she trailed off, like it was hard for her to speak. "My late husband, Arthur. Anytime I asked for something it turned into a fight. Mostly I ended up letting him have things his way."

"That's terrible." Silvana gave a small nod. "Well, I'm not like that. I guess you could say that my mother taught me to respect women. So I'll always try to respect you the way you deserve."

Silvana gave a grim laugh. Jason couldn't believe that was her reaction. He'd expected a little more gratitude. *Not that she should have to be grateful for basic respect, but still!*

"I'm sorry for laughing," Silvana said. "It's just…Arthur would have hated to hear you say that."

"I see," Jason said. "If you don't mind me asking, is your whole family like that?"

"Not all of them. My Uncle Nicholas is really sweet. It's just that… they don't really listen to me. They still talk like I'm a child, because by their standards, I am. And they're always pushing me to do what *they* want, not what I want."

"Like getting married really quickly?" he said derisively.

"Hey," Silvana replied, an edge in her tone. "I want that too.

Marriage is important to me."

"Ok, sorry."

"Cause you know, mortals can be very cruel towards vampires. Marriage is how we prove that we're safe to be around, by marrying a mortal and being a good spouse."

"Ok, fine! I get it already."

"What's that supposed to mean?"

Jason felt himself getting defensive. He tried to take a breath to calm down, but it ended up sounding like an exasperated sigh. "I don't mean to attack your beliefs. I just think that…marriage is not always good for everyone."

She clenched her jaw, and Jason realised he had said the wrong thing. "I don't think that's true at all. My marriages taught me to show respect, to my husband, my family, and my community. I conduct myself with the highest honour. I make an amazing wife."

Jason stared back at her. For the first time since he'd met Silvana, there had been real fire in her voice and all traces of her usual timidness was gone. He had to tread carefully. "I'm sure you do. I'm sure you make your family very happy. But what I want to know is, are you happy?"

She went quiet. Her mouth fell open, but no words came out.

"I'm sorry," Jason said. "You just said your husband used to get his way most of the time. Sounds like you were unhappy."

"He was my husband. I did my duty as a wife, just like I would for you."

"So if we got married, you would obey everything I said?" Jason thought it was a devastating truth bomb, but her reply shocked him.

"Yes," Silvana said, as if it were obvious.

Jason couldn't help it. He wanted to be polite, but his opinions burst from him without any tact. "I think couples should be equal. No leader, no follower. Just equals. Any time a relationship has a leader, they will always turn into an abuser."

"Are you calling my husband an abuser?"

That surprised him. She was triggered by that word. *He probably was, but maybe she's not ready to confront that just yet.*

"I wasn't saying that. I just don't think it matters what your gender is. The husband shouldn't automatically be the leader, and the wife shouldn't be the follower. Society should not decide what roles people take."

Silvana turned her head to look away from him. "Sometimes society doesn't give people a choice," she said softly.

Jason stopped. He'd been so full of righteous indignation he hadn't noticed that something was bothering her. He lowered his voice. "Silvana, did you ever get a choice? Did you ever marry for love?"

Silvana looked at him with a sad smile. "I'm trying to now."

All the breath was knocked out of him. "You...love..."

"No! Not yet. I mean...that is to say, I'm not in love with you already, Jason. I'm just saying that this is the first time I've tried to have a marriage of love and not just marry to make connections for my family. This is all new to me."

Jason just sat there silently. She was trying to make a choice for herself, perhaps her first choice ever in nine decades of life. She was putting so much on the line, and it largely depended on him. He couldn't even consider the level of commitment she was talking about.

"Please," she said. "Can we talk about something else? Damn, how come a waiter hasn't come over yet?"

"I think you go to the counter to order."

"Oh."

They trailed off again. Silvana wasn't talking either, and soon the silence grew between them into a widening gulf. Jason couldn't think of anything personal to say, so he just asked, "I have another question.

This government body. What did you call it?"

"The Immortal Imperium," she said.

Did she sound sceptical?

"Yeah. Do they have a police force? Do they catch criminals and such?"

She frowned. "The Imperium have their own set of laws. They don't exactly overlap with mortal laws, but yeah, you can bet they enforce them. Their punishments are harsher than mortal justice, and they rarely show mercy."

Jason shivered as a chill ran up the back of his neck and the room seemed to grow silent. "Do they use…torture?"

She nodded. "Tortures from the Middle Ages. After all, that was within our lifetime for many of us."

"Damn." He thought for a moment. "So their laws don't match ours exactly. Then what does it mean if someone commits a crime, and the Imperium doesn't act?" Silvana stared at him, and her eyes grew so cold that he shifted in his chair. "What?" he asked.

"Jason, please," she said, her voice suddenly desperate. "I don't feel like talking about this anymore."

"Oh. I'm sorry, Silvana. I was just…"

"No. I've already been interrogated once today." Her tone was sharp and cold like jagged ice. "I came here to court you. Not to account for my whereabouts in the last twenty-four hours."

"I'm not interrogating you," Jason said. "I just don't know about any of this 'immortal' stuff."

"Oh really? Cause you sound like a policeman gathering information."

Jason sat back. She was right. That was exactly what he was doing. *Damn, she is perceptive.*

"Ok, you're right," he said. "I sometimes find it hard to stop being a police officer. I love my work and I really want to become a detective one day. So I'm always asking questions."

"Are you sure?" Silvana asked. "It just seems like you feel very strongly about this."

She was right again. Obviously his emotions were slipping through, so there was no point denying it anymore. She deserved the truth.

"I know I'm not supposed to talk about this. My captain will be furious with me…" Silvana only stared at him, waiting. "Today I found a man who had been murdered. His blood had been drained. And damn it, that *scares* me!"

He felt his heartrate start skyrocketing. *Oh God, why am I getting so worked up about this?* He quickly looked away, breathed deeply, and steadied himself. "I don't like knowing that there are things out there that I don't understand. I feel unsafe." He gave a bleak laugh. "Look at me. I'm a grown man who's scared of monsters! I hate to admit it, but I'm terrified of them."

A dab of moisture had formed in his eye, and he blinked it back.

"I'm sorry," Silvana whispered. "This is my fault."

"What? No, this isn't your fault at all."

"This is why I tried to hide my strength. I didn't want to scare you."

Jason frowned. "That had nothing to do with you," he said. "Silvana…I'm not scared of *you*."

"You just said you're scared of monsters…"

He saw it then. The shame in her eyes, the self-loathing written all over her face. *Oh my god.*

"Silvana, I didn't mean you. I…I meant…"

"It's ok, I don't blame you, Jason. I never should have tried to court a mortal from outside the community. You were always going to hate me."

"No, I don't hate you!"

"It's fine," Silvana said and stood up abruptly, her chair squeaking loudly. "I'm so sorry I dragged you into this. I'll find my own way home."

"Silvana," Jason cried, but she marched away from him without another word.

Chapter 11

Jason followed her out to the street. "Silvana?" he cried out. Several bypasses stared, but he ignored them and called out again, "Silvana, wait. Please." She showed no signs of stopping, or even having heard him. Her long black hair bounced wildly and waved as she marched to the street corner, heading away from his car. He jogged to catch up. "Silvana, where are you going?"

"Home," she said curtly.

"Well at least let me drive you."

"I don't need to be driven!" she hissed in a harsh whisper. "I'm a monster, remember? I can run there in the same time it would take to drive."

Jason stumbled over a loose cobblestone, cursing under his breath before turning back to Silvana. "Really? That's…actually really cool. I had no idea you were that fast—"

She talked over the top of him. "Jason!" she spun around, her eyes wide. "What do you want from me?"

"I…what?"

Jason had to pull up short to avoid walking into her. She had stopped at an empty street corner under the light of an old lantern and whirled to face him. Silvana stared, her eyes unwavering as she waited for an answer, yet the silence only grew between them.

"I don't understand," Jason said.

She gave an exasperated cry. "Everything I do is wrong. I don't know what you want me to be!"

"I…" he frowned. "I just want you to be yourself."

"How can you say that? You're terrified of me! How can you ever love something you're terrified of?"

"Love?" Jason balked.

Silvana's eyes widened. Her lip quivered, then she spun around and started running at incredible speed into the shadows of the city streets.

"Wait, Silvana!" He ran after her but she was swiftly getting further away. *Oh my god, she's fast!* Jason threw aside all inhibition and sprinted at top speed. He was a fit man and the fastest in his class at the academy. Yet even at his best, he was falling further behind Silvana. So he tried calling to her again. "Silvana, wait!"

Someone moved in front of him. He had no time to slow down, and he ploughed into a pair of strangers.

Jason hit them hard. Yet instead of bowling them over, Jason *bounced off them.*

He fell backwards onto his rear. The two strangers were standing over him, completely unaffected.

What?

"Why hello!" a young man said. "Look, it's our lovely old friend. And he knows our dear Silvana."

"Could be a different Silvana," said the second man.

"Oh, sure. Such a common name after all." The first man spoke with a crisp Londoner accent, like the aristocrats in movies. *Surely that's not his real voice?* "This guy doesn't look like anything special. So what's he doing chasing Silvana down a street at night time?"

"He's a perv, then, isn't he?" said a young girl, appearing beside the two men. "What kind of gentleman chases a lady like that?"

Jason finally stopped seeing stars long enough to study the trio. His mouth dropped open.

"It's you!"

The three teenagers from the night before stood over him now. The blond man with the long fringe, and his partner with the buzz cut loomed above him. The beautiful young woman stood behind, arms crossed and sneering. Once again, the men were dressed in smart casual jeans and polo shirts, and the woman wore a hot-pink cocktail dress in high heels.

"I'm so sorry about that," Jason said. "I didn't see you." He started to stand up.

A foot hit him in the chest. Jason went back down on his back, clutching his rib cage and wheezing for breath.

"Stay down, game!" the blond man shouted. The trio laughed, and Jason felt his blood run cold. They had become violent so quickly. This was dangerous. Three young people, possibly immortals with powers he couldn't understand, all drunk with confidence. This had suddenly become a life and death situation. People died in exchanges like this all the time. The streets were quiet. He was in the middle of a small town, yet somehow no one was around. He looked ahead, but Silvana was long gone by now.

"Oh, get this," the woman said. "He's hoping Silvana will come rescue him. Isn't that pathetic?"

Jason strained to speak, "Silvana's my date."

"Oh, so you think you *own* her, then?" said the woman. "You think she belongs to you, and not the other way around, game?"

"What do you keep saying? Game? What are you talking about? I'm not playing a game!"

The blond man knelt towards him, and his eyes were filled with pure joy. It seemed chillingly inappropriate.

"You're not playing a game, my friend," he said. "You *are* game."

Like hunting. Game is what you call the animal you hunt.

"You're all immortals," Jason said.

"Oh very clever!" the blond said with a laugh. "But it still won't save you."

Save me? Jason looked between them and saw the same malicious glint on the blond man's face.

"We can't actually hurt him," said the man with the buzz cut. "We'd get in trouble."

"But he doesn't know that," said the woman.

"He might."

"Hey!" Jason called. "Stop talking about me like I'm not here." They glared at him. "It's impolite," he added weakly.

"Let's see what he knows," said the blond man, crouching to lean over Jason and smiling handsomely. "Maybe he knows enough to live, and maybe he doesn't. Let's see." He clapped his hands together with a grin, then stood up and posed with his hands on his hips. "Tell me, mortal. What am I?"

Jason steadied his movements. He needed to act confident, even as he lay on the ground. Any sign of weakness always encouraged violent people.

"You must be a vampire," he said boldly.

All three of them laughed.

"What?" said the blond man. "You think *I'm* a vampire? With my flush, full cheeks? I should be insulted."

Cheeks? Jason frowned. Then he saw it. The blond had full colour in his face. There was none of the paleness that showed in Silvana and her aunts.

He looked at the man with the buzz cut and noticed it now. Less blood in the skin. It was a faint clue, yet obvious if you knew what you were looking for.

"He's the vampire." Jason pointed at buzz cut.

"Correct," said the blond, and the buzz man looked smug. "But that hardly counts. You saw his red eyes last night. And we're not asking about him. We're talking about me." He grinned. "What am I?"

"I don't know. A werewolf?"

"Oof!" He held his hand over his heart and cried out like he was in pain. "That one hurts. Does this game have no respect?"

"I don't think he knows what you are," said the woman. "Maybe he's never heard of your type. The word isn't on his mind."

"Give him a hint," said the vampire.

"Fine. Here's one clue, and it's the only one you're getting. Last chance."

The blond man stared at Jason, and suddenly his eyes…*changed*. The colour shifted, and the iris expanded until there was a thick black dot surrounded by a sea of liquid gold.

"How…" Jason cried, and the man laughed. He blinked once, and his eyes returned to normal. Jason tried to remember all the supernatural creatures he'd heard rumours about over the years. He tried a guess. "You're a…a…a shapeshifter? A changeling?"

The blond man sneered. "That's a foul word. Changeling? How dare you? It'd be like if I called you motherfucker."

"He's a metamorph," the woman instructed.

"Don't tell him that!" said the blond metamorph. "He was supposed to guess."

"He was close enough," said the woman.

The vampire grinned. "The more civilised word is skinwalker."

"Alright, a skinwalker and a vampire," Jason said. "And what about you?"

The woman looked at Jason with a sly grin. "You may have guessed what Gerald is. But you won't get me, sweetie."

"A telepath."

The trio blinked. "What?" the woman cried.

"You said the word wasn't on my mind," said Jason. "Sounds like a mind-reader to me."

The vampire laughed. "He got you, Kate."

"Shut up, Ryan!" she hissed back.

Jason sat up slightly, propping himself up on his hands. "So is that it? I guessed what you are, so you'll stop harassing me in the street?"

The metamorph – Gerald – tsked and shook his head. "I do not like the tone you're using, game. We are here to protect our people from monsters like you."

"I wasn't going to hurt Silvana. I promise you that," Jason said.

"Oh really?" said Kate. "Cause I think you're lying. I think you were planning to hurt her."

"What? That's not true."

"I can read your mind, you idiot. I know you were planning to hurt her."

"I wasn't!" Jason insisted, then stopped short.

He *had* been thinking that. He was planning to hurt her, just not physically. Somehow in his mind, he had already decided to end their courtship. She was too much trouble, too old fashioned, and too much under the control of her family. He felt racked with guilt for it because without him, she wouldn't get the blood she needed. So in a way, he was planning to hurt her. *Oh shit...*

"Oh shit is right!" Kate said, and Jason felt his blood freeze in his veins. "That's right, I heard that. And that." She let out a burst of laughter, and Jason blushed. "Oh look at that! He panicked because he knows I can read his thoughts, and now he's trying so hard not to think about oral sex. But look! He's thinking about *performing* oral sex, not receiving."

"What a little bitch," Gerald said.

"Is that what you want?" Kate said, standing over him so he could nearly see up her dress. "You want to munch on me? You want this pussy?" She grabbed at her crotch, winking down at Jason.

"Stop it!" Jason shouted.

"But I can't stop. I see everything that comes into your mind. All your dark secrets are exposed to me." She frowned, and her beautiful face became sharp and twisted. "And here it comes. You're thinking of… daddy!" She spoke in a baby's voice. "Aww, are you 'oping ee will come save you from the bwig bwad wolf?"

Gerald laughed as his entire face shifted into the head of a wolf. Grey fur covered his face and triangular ears and his long snout was full of a carnivores' teeth. He let out a real, genuine wolf's howl. A second later, Gerald's human head and blond hair returned. He laughed at the look on Jason's face.

"No, wait," Kate said, studying Jason intently.

"Stop it! Get out of my head!" he roared.

"You don't want daddy to save you. No…you're thinking of him because…we *remind* you of him!" Kate cooed softly and leaned right into his face. "Aww, did daddy used to scare you? Was he mean to the poor wittle—"

Jason punched her in the face.

It wasn't at full strength since he was sitting down, but it was enough to knock her off her feet.

The trio were stunned, and Jason used the chance to launch to his feet, take aim, and deliver his most powerful frontal kick at Gerald's chest. His heel connected hard with the metamorph's ribcage.

Gerald staggered backwards…for one step. He merely blinked at Jason in surprise. The kick hadn't done half the damage he'd expected.

"Oh shit," Jason muttered.

The telepath may have been as physically strong as a regular human, but the metamorph was certainly much more powerful.

The vampire moved. He was as fast as a professional boxer. He came at Jason's flank, and before he could even respond, the vampire jabbed him twice under the ribcage.

Jason staggered back with a cry of pain. The metamorph approached from the front and swung his fist. Jason held up his arm to block but at the last second, the metamorph's arm grew to twice its thickness, sprouted black fur, and formed into the thick padded hand of a gorilla. It batted aside Jason's defence and slugged him in the jaw.

He staggered, yet somehow stayed on his feet. He danced backwards to put some distance between the two men, but the vampire closed in again. Jason knew he couldn't match them in strength. He couldn't outrun them, judging by Silvana's speed. And he had no way to defend himself.

So he launched forward to surprise them.

He crouched down and threw a low punch, using his legs, torso and shoulder to put maximum strength into it. The blow hit the vampire in the stomach hard enough to make him pause. Jason moved to uppercut with his left fist. The vampire saw him coming and smoothly dodged. *Not enough damage!* Jason roared in frustration. Something blurred in the corner of his eye.

Gerald shifted, and suddenly he stood before Jason as a three-metre tall, hulking white polar bear. Jason stumbled back, his entire body filled with a primal fear.

"Holy fucking—"

A massive white paw with curled claws swiped at him. Jason fell back. The claw missed him by an inch. The bear lopped forward – a sheer white wall of mass – and a single paw pinned Jason down at the shin. He screamed as the pressure made pain race up all the way into his hips and spine. The shin might be broken. Jason looked up into the bear's snout and giant black eyes.

"You arsehole!" a woman cried, and Kate appeared next to him with a bloodied nose.

Jason barely had time to turn before she swung back and kicked him in the side of the head with her high heel.

It was an awkward blow that didn't quite land, but it hurt like hell. Jason squirmed underneath the polar bear and held up his hands to protect his head. Kate kicked again, and again. She wasn't strong even by human standards but with Jason on the ground, his head exposed, it would be easy for her to kick him to death from this angle.

He looked at the bear, and cried out wordlessly in terror when he saw Gerald's human face, sitting flat against the bear's head, watching him and smiling.

"You didn't get far, game," Gerald said. Another kick hit the side of Jason's head, and his vision blurred. He could see the vampire's feet just behind him, blocking his escape. He tried to squirm out from under the bear paw, but it was useless. Gerald was too strong. Kate kicked him in the jaw again, sending pain ricocheting through his head. If he didn't do something fast, he was going to die here.

"You should have shown better respect for your superiors," Gerald sneered. "We are your higher predators. We are your kings and queens, created by God to rule over you."

Jason held his arm high to guard his face, so Kate struck his shoulder repeatedly until he felt his bones ache and he was gritting his teeth in pain.

Gerald sneered as he spoke. "And God said, 'Let him have dominion over the fish of the sea,'" *Kick.* "'And over the birds of the air,'" *Kick.* "'And over the beasts of the earth.' Do you get it, mortal? Our dominion is a divine right!"

Desperate, Jason punched at Gerald's human face. The blow connected and the metamorph cried out in obvious pain. Jason couldn't hide his smile.

"Argh, bastard!" Gerald's face morphed back into the bear's snout and roared with deafening fury. His beady black eyes fixed on Jason and with a loud snarl, the bear's jaws opened wide, revealing so many spikey teeth.

"STOP!"

A high-pitch voice screamed, and suddenly Silvana was there, standing between Jason and the jaws of the massive bear.

"Leave him alone!" she screamed. "He is my guest! Do you hear me? Jason is my guest and comes under my protection according to Imperium law!"

Jason was panting heavily. His mind was disorientated from the pain, but he could sense the trio around him growing still.

"If you kill him, your families will be required to pay mine restitution," Silvana said. "In fact, I should insist you pay one right now, just for injuring him! Now back off!"

The pressure on Jason's leg vanished, and he let out a pained groan in relief. He collapsed, yet was surprised to land in cold, thin arms that wrapped around his shoulders and pulled him close. Silvana nuzzled him and her black hair fell partially across his face. He breathed in her scent. *Lavender shampoo and crushed autumn leaves...*

"Silvana, we found this man chasing you down the street," Ryan said, his voice more charming now. "We thought you were in danger, so we intervened."

"But he attacked us," Gerald said. "He punched Kate right in the face, unprovoked."

"I find that hard to believe," Silvana said. "You harassed me last night. Now you pretend like you're my rescuers? I'm more inclined to think Kate was reading his mind without permission and he defended himself from being violated."

"He's a piece of shit!" Kate shrieked.

The two men turned to her sharply and held up their hands to calm her down. She ignored them. There was blood running from her nose.

"He has violent urges all the time. He wants to murder you and your whole family."

"Kate, stop it!" Gerald hissed. He turned to face Silvana. "You can't prove anything. Let this go. Believe me, we had the best intentions, and things didn't go as planned. That's all."

"Don't listen to him, Silvana," Jason muttered. "You can kick his ass."

He could barely lift his head for the pain throbbing. He couldn't see anyone's expressions. He could only hear Gerald's cold laughter.

"See, Silvana? He's the violent one."

"Shut up!" Jason snapped but his voice sounded weak.

"I'll forget this happened," Silvana said. "But you need to leave right now. And God help you if this happens again once I've found a husband."

"Oooh, scary!" Kate mocked her.

Jason still couldn't look up, but he heard the sounds of their footsteps moving away. He listened until they had passed out of hearing range.

Silvana crouched over him. "Hold still, Jason. I'm going to take care of you."

"Thank you," he muttered weakly. "It's not too bad, overall. I should be able to stand."

"Not so fast. Just stay down until I've checked everything."

Silvana examined his eyes, head, chest, and limbs. Jason slowly felt his dizziness subside as time passed. He chuckled.

"I thought you'd appreciate another chance to practice medicine. You can thank me later."

She smirked at him. "Very cute," she drawled and sat up. "Well, you're lucky. No broken bones. But you'll have some nasty bruises on your forearms, shoulder, left leg, and head. Do you want to go to the hospital?"

Jason thought of the captain, and the detectives who were already suspicious of his activity. "I'd prefer not. But do you think it's necessary?"

"Men…" Silvana sighed. "No, it's fine. But you're coming back to my place so I can patch you up properly. I'll get you some ice packs to limit the bruising."

Jason groaned. "You're not going to carry me, are you? Aren't you… weak from hunger?"

"I'll be driving your car. Come on, I'll help you walk back—"

A sudden loud noise cut her off. Jason jolted in fear, thinking it was some enormous beast, before he recognised the sounds of man-made engines. A moment later, three motorbikes pulled out onto the main street, all of them revving at top volume, before they shot off into the night. The sounds of their howling could be heard for a full minute after they sped out of sight.

"Well," Jason drawled. "Now we know who's been revving motorbikes at night. The captain will be thrilled."

Chapter 12

Jason managed to walk back to his car, leaning on Silvana for support. His body was tender and sore from each blow, yet overall not as bad as he had expected. It was his shin that felt especially tender and his throbbing head that gave him concern. The world seemed to spin around him. Still, he didn't let himself groan in front of Silvana.

He slumped into the passenger seat of his humble brown Hyundai. Silvana started up the car and drove without a problem, so Jason leaned back and shut his eyes.

"Hey, stay awake," Silvana said. "I'm worried you might have a concussion."

"Don't worry. I definitely do."

"Are you feeling nauseous? Blurred vision? Headache?"

"Definitely headache, but that might have been the kicks in the head."

Silvana gave a soft harrumph. "You can keep your eyes closed if you like. But don't fall asleep, or you'll roll around the car and bang your head."

"Got it."

The motion of the car pulled him from one side to another. The pain started to ease further and his mind was beginning to clear. He started to process what had just happened.

"So…" he said, making his tone light. "I just saw a guy shapeshift into a polar bear. That was pretty wild." Silence. He kept his eyes shut. "He even had a human face at one point. That's gonna live in my mind forever. Feel like I can see it now with my eyes shut."

"Like Frodo."

"Hmm?" Jason frowned. "Like Frodo?"

"Yeah, at the end of the third one. 'I can see him with my waking eyes'. That part."

"Huh. Yeah exactly." He took a long breath. His head throbbed, and he waited for it to settle down. "That girl could read my mind. It was really…" his voice lost all pleasantness. "It was horrible. You were right to call it a violation. She told me she could see my darkest secrets, and immediately, I started thinking about them."

"It's a telepath trick. They can only read your surface thoughts. You know, what you're thinking about while in their presence. They can't see your memories or knowledge unless it's on the front of your mind. They have to trick you into thinking about them first."

"So she claimed she could see my darkest secrets, in order to get me thinking about them…that's cruel."

"I know. I'm sorry. They should never have done that."

Jason forced the cheer back into his voice. "In all that craziness, I have one very important question."

"Just the one?" Silvana mocked.

"Why'd you come back for me?"

Silvana was quiet. Jason kept his eyes closed and let the silence grow between them. He gave her space to think it through.

"You want me to be myself, right? You want the real me?"

"Yeah," he said.

"All right. Well, my first instinct is to tell you I heard the sounds of the fight, or that I wanted to come back and talk through our argument. But if I'm being my honest self…" she paused, as if waiting for him to confirm. When he didn't say anything she eventually said, "…I still need to marry someone so I can drink their blood. I came back because I felt hungry and weak after trying to run away and it reminded me that I don't have many other options."

Jason felt an initial stab of disappointment, and then wondered why he felt that. Had he been hoping she came back because she cared about him? Hadn't he already decided not to continue the courtship? So what did he really feel for her?

"Well, I admire you for telling me the truth," he said.

"Even though it makes me sound like a monster?" she said. Her tone was clearly passive aggressive.

"Silvana, I owe you an apology."

Jason finally opened his eyes. They were already outside the town, and only the car's headlights gave light now. He could see the outline of Silvana's face in the glow, her skin luminous. The outside woods were pitch black and every tree limb took on deformed shapes as it flew by.

"I expressed myself poorly, in the restaurant. I was telling the truth when I said I'm terrified of monsters. But I wasn't referring to vampires or any other immortals." He frowned. "Well, I wasn't at the time. Gerald may have changed that for me."

"That's fair. Skinwalkers scare everyone. That's where the werewolf myth comes from, you know."

"Huh. That explains why he hated being called a werewolf." Jason chuckled. "But what I meant to say was…I think human beings can be monsters too. I've seen people do horrible things. They weren't vampires or skinwalkers. But they were still monsters."

His chest tightened, and not from the bruises. It was hard to get the words out. "After I met you, I started to realise that there were people out there with powers and abilities I don't understand. And it scared me. Because what if someone like that was a monster?" He took a heavy breath. "What if they were evil, just like human beings can be, but they had the power to do so much more damage?"

"So…" Silvana spoke up before he could go on. "You weren't saying you were scared of me?"

"No," Jason said clearly. "I mean, you're different to most people. And I admit, I'm a little cautious around you because I don't really know you yet. But I'm not scared of you."

"Oh." Silvana let out a sound of relief. "God, I got so upset! I thought you were afraid of me because I lifted the heavy weight in my gym. After you specifically told me to lift it! I thought, 'what kind of twisted psychopath does he have to be, to force me to show my strength, then blame me when he gets scared of it'?"

Jason blinked. "Twisted psychopath?"

"Sorry, that's just what I was thinking."

He chuckled to show he wasn't offended. He saw her relax at the sound. "I truly think it's cool that you're strong. But it scares me that other people are that strong too. It scares me that there may be murderers running around and there's no way for cops to catch them because they're committing crimes with powers that should be impossible. There's no way to get evidence against them. It's… terrifying."

"Yeah, that makes sense." Silvana made a whimpering sound. "You poor thing. You were thinking about how scary an evil immortal would be, then you run into a skinwalker, of all things." Silvana shook her head, her face screwed up in discomfort. "That must have been awful for you, facing your worst fears."

"It wasn't great."

"Maybe I should have been more forthcoming on information. I could have warned you." She sighed. "I know it's against Imperium law and that I'm only meant to tell you everything when we're married.

Sorry, *if* we marry…" she grimaced. "Right now, I could get in trouble for telling you about skinwalkers, for example. But it's an unfair rule. You were attacked tonight just for being near me. You should have been warned."

"No, it's ok. I don't want to get you in trouble. Don't break any laws on my behalf."

"You're such a police officer." They both laughed slightly, but there was nervousness between them. "Alright. I can tell you one thing about the immortals without getting in trouble. All species are either physically enhanced, or mentally."

Jason thought about that. "So vampires and metamorphs would be physical, and the telepaths are mental."

"That's right. The physical species are stronger and faster, but we also look different to mortals. We stand out, with red eyes or shapeshifting. Whereas most mental species blend in with mortals. They have no differences, no scent. Quite undetectable." She gave a pained expression. "The mentally enhanced immortals rule the rest of us. The Imperium are all mentally enhanced."

Jason had wanted to ask more. But he also didn't want her to catch him acting as an investigator again. At least now he had a somewhat better idea of what to expect.

He was also enjoying Silvana's company. She was smart, and well spoken. In fact, he finally noticed how she was acting differently. Less timid, and more confident. *This must be more like herself. Who she really is.* He felt like he was speaking with an equal. It was exciting.

Yet he still felt hesitant, thinking of the investigation into Alex Bishop's murder. He considered her a suspect. Here she was opening up about her true feelings, while he was keeping secret his suspicions of her.

"I've been meaning to ask you something," Jason said. "Why do we have to get married?"

Silvana glanced at him as she drove. "Jason, what do you mean? I'm a vampire. I need blood. Any of this sounding familiar?"

"No, I mean why marriage? Why can't you just have my blood right now?"

"Are you seriously asking why I don't murder you right now? Jason…"

"I don't mean murder. Just take my blood. I'll gladly give it to you if it'll save your life."

He could see the confusion on her face and he finally understood. She genuinely had no idea what he was trying to say. The idea was so foreign to her way of thinking. So he explained it simply.

"What if I just give you my blood now, and we don't get married?"

Silvana frowned. "That's crazy. We couldn't do that."

"Why not?"

"That's not how it works for a vampire."

"So, if you drank my blood right now, it wouldn't work? You'd still be hungry?"

"Well…no…but that's not the point."

"Wait," Jason said, his voice growing louder with realisation. "So there's nothing scientifically different about my blood after we get married? There's no physical difference?"

"No…"

"So you could just have anyone's blood, any time you needed it, if you really wanted to."

"No! Jason, it wouldn't be right!"

"But the only thing stopping you is tradition. You only want to get married because of tradition."

"You don't understand," her voice rang out through the car.

Jason realised he'd been pushing too hard. He softened his voice.

"I'm sorry, Silvana. Please, explain it to me. I want to understand."

She glanced at him again, and he made sure he had a serious look on his face. "All right," she said softly. "Vampires have to marry mortals for good reason. Before this, we had a problem with some vampires… overfeeding."

"Is that where they kill the victim? Take all their blood?"

"Yes, but more than that. I'm talking about killing multiple people. We don't need a lot of blood to survive. One litre a month is enough. But the more blood we drink, the stronger we become. Vampires who drink until they are full can do some terrible things."

"Right. So that's when they become the Hulk?" Jason offered, expecting her to enjoy his superhero reference. But she shook her head seriously.

"It's not just physical strength. Imagine if a mortal body-builder used steroids. It would make them stronger, but it wouldn't make them superhuman, right?"

"Right."

"It's not like that for vampires. If a vampire drinks heaps of blood, they don't just become physically stronger." Silvana gave a long pause, her eyes focused on the road, and Jason realised her iris was wider than was natural to help her see in the dark. "They develop evil abilities. Abilities that the Imperium have outlawed. Abilities that truly make them monsters."

Jason whispered, "Like what?"

"We don't know. No one's done it in centuries. The Imperium keeps the information hushed up because they don't want people getting ideas. But there are rumours. Well, more like legends, really. Some claim that an empowered vampire could use mind control."

"Seriously? Like a telepath?"

"No. Telepaths can only read your mind. I've heard that an empowered vampire can have total enslavement over a person. Apparently at full power, they can control thousands of mortals."

"My god…"

"They also have telekinesis. Like in Carrie."

Jason blinked. "Don't you mean like Scarlet Witch?"

"Well, of course. I just picked the more famous example." They shared a laugh. "Vampires at that stage are nearly unstoppable. And they almost always become pure evil. Absolute power corrupts absolutely, and all that. In ancient times, they became known as gods."

"Like Zeus? Thor?"

"More like Hades, Loki, Anubis."

"Jesus! Just from drinking too much blood?" Jason frowned. "How much blood does it take?"

"We don't know. It might require drinking blood from thousands of mortals. But it might only take a few. Again, the Imperium doesn't tell us."

Jason imagined Ryan, the vampire who attacked him on the street, being able to mind control the entire town. He imagined an army facing down the vampire, and Ryan with a wave of his hand sending them all flying.

"God…it's like Akira."

"That's the anime, right? I haven't seen it," Silvana said.

"Guy gets superpowers, goes on a rampage. Nothing can stop him."

"Oh. Like Franklin Richards." Jason blinked at her. "The son of the Fantastic Four couple. He has like super mind powers."

"Yep. Like that." Jason sighed. He hoped by referencing a fictional story, the idea would seem less terrifying. Instead, it only made him feel even more small and powerless. He always wanted to be a police officer and a detective so he could fight the bad guys. Now he just found out that the bad guys might have superpowers. This changed everything.

"That's why it's the law to only take blood from a single mortal spouse. It stops vampires from going bad. It also proves to the other immortal species that we can be trusted."

"Wait, so getting married is not just tradition? It really is an official law?"

"Yes. But it's also more than a law. It's a moral. Something I firmly believe in."

Jason stopped himself from speaking back. Her push for marriage was even more complex than her life and death. Marriage was used to keep the vampires from becoming something like a supervillain. It made sense. But he still hated the thought of it. Marriage and love being used to control people. It felt wrong, even with such high consequences at stake.

"Do you see now why I assumed you were saying I was the monster?" Silvana asked.

"Yes."

"And do you understand why I need to have a husband and obey him? To make sure I never hurt someone. It's like Spiderman. Great power, great responsibility."

Jason clenched his jaw. "I understand why the Imperium put the law in place. But I'm not sure I agree with their methods."

"What? I thought for sure you would agree. You're a policeman. You hate monsters so much. Don't you see the need for the law?"

"Of course I do. But the whole point of the law is to protect people. If the law hurts people, then it should be changed. I worry that forcing people to marry hurts them."

"But what if the law protects people from monsters?"

They reached the outside of Silvana's mansion. She pulled the car towards the usual parking space, just before the hill that blocked the mansion from sight.

Jason sighed. "That's the problem. Monsters break the law all the time."

The car engine stopped, and immediately the sounds of shouting could be heard from outside. The voices of men. The words were muffled, but the tones were angry.

"What's that?" Jason asked.

"Hang on," Silvana said. She circled the car and came to his door to help him stand. "I think we have more intruders tonight."

"Oh great. Speaking of monsters." Jason reached into his glove box and pulled out his service pistol and a pair of handcuffs. "Let's go."

Chapter 13

Torchlights were flickering through the trees as Jason and Silvana reached the top of the hill. Below, a wave of voices were shouting at once. Someone was banging on the mansion's entrance as a single voice broke through the cacophony to scream, "Get out here, you evil bitches!"

Another shouted, "Murderers!"

A large group of people were crowding around the mansion's front door, banging on the wood as if trying to break them open. Jason guessed there were nearly twenty people, mostly males, and many were wielding makeshift weapons like cricket bats, a sledgehammer, and a long crowbar. He scanned for firearms or knives, but couldn't see any. *Doesn't mean they're not there.*

"My family!" Silvana cried and made to sprint down the hill.

"Silvana, no!" Jason shouted and grabbed her by the shoulders. The act of pulling her caused a painful spasm in his shoulder, making him groan in pain. *Oh why did I do that?*

Silvana was immediately checking him over, even as she snapped, "What are you doing? My family is in danger!"

"Those men could be armed. Let me call the police first."

"Don't, Jason. You can't bring the police here. Not again."

"You need them. Those men could have guns. Are you bullet proof?"

"Of course not!" she snapped defensively, and he saw the fear in her eyes. *But she wasn't afraid of the skinwalker. Why is she afraid now? Is it cause they're mortal?*

"All right." He stood up with a groan. "We won't call the police just yet. But let me handle this."

"You? Jason please, let me. I'm not going to fight them. If it goes bad, at least I have enough speed to escape. They'll tear you apart in your current state."

"I have training for this sort of thing. I can control a crowd. If they see a vampire, they might turn murderous."

Silvana frowned at him, worried. "You can't fight them in the state you're in."

"I'm not going to fight. I'm going to negotiate." Jason looked forward towards the group of angry men. "These aren't monsters. They're just frightened people. I can deal with that." He trudged forward.

The shouting voices had risen into a frenzy. "You'll pay for what you did!" yelled the man with the sledgehammer. He had a scruffy beard and ponytail littered with leaves and twigs, and he was hefting his giant metal weapon onto his shoulder ready to swing at the door. Others in the crowd cheered him on as they pointed their torches at the entrance, egging this man on.

"Break it down!"

"Make them face justice!"

"We must save our children!"

No one was looking towards Jason. So he took his Glock 17 from his jeans, held it high, and fired twice.

The loud pops made the whole crowd flinch in unison. People fell to the ground, ducking low and covering their heads. A woman's high-pitch scream came from among the mob. All the angry shouting turned into cries of fear.

"Attention!" Jason roared. "This is the Plymouth police department!"

Dozens of eyes flicked in his direction. The sounds of panic quieted down and Jason puffed out his chest and raised his chin.

"My fellow officers are on their way. They're sending a riot squad and SCO19. Anyone found trespassing when they arrive will be arrested and detained. You have two minutes to disperse, or I will place every single one of you under arrest."

There was a pause. Everyone stood silently, and Jason felt his hopes rise.

"You see!" a man shouted and pushed his way to the front. The speaker was a Caucasian middle aged male, about six foot, bald and plump around the middle. "Do you see, my hunters? Even the law enforcement is on their side! The vampires have control over our government!"

Oh boy. They're crazier than I thought.

"You're all breaking the law," Jason shouted. "I'll protect the occupants of this house, just like I'd protect any of you if you were surrounded by an angry mob."

"He's a slave!" the leader shouted. "The vampires are controlling his mind. We need to get in there and kill them before they kill us! Remember Alex Bishop!" The speaker didn't look that inspiring. Yet everyone there seemed to hang on his words.

Jason flinched. How did they know Alex Bishop? Were these his friends? Or some cult he was involved in?

"No one's killing anyone tonight," Jason yelled. "The police are investigating the death of Alex Bishop. It's too early to say what the cause was. Do not take the law into your own hands."

"We don't have to listen to you," the speaker said. "There's only one of you. If you try to stop us, we could kill you easily."

Jason clenched his gun a little tighter. *My god, he threatened me with murder just like that!* A few people were looking at the speaker with shock, yet they seemed to agree.

"Hey, we're not killing a cop," cried a young Asian man with a long fringe. "We're the good guys here. We're trying to save the world from vampires."

Well, there's one decent person here.

"He's protecting those monsters," the speaker said. "He's clearly their thrall. It's time to wipe those vampires from the world before anyone else is taken."

"Stand down," Jason shouted. He held his gun in two hands pointing at the ground in front of him. The pose was meant to show he was ready to fire at a glance.

Everyone watched the leader as he stared at Jason. He turned to the man with the ponytail and took the sledgehammer out of his hands, holding it in a firm two-handed grip.

"As the good book says, 'Put on the whole armour of God, so you can defend against the devil's tricks.'" The man stepped towards Jason, hefting the sledge hammer up into a striking position. "'For we are not fighting against humans. We are fighting against forces and authorities and against rulers of darkness and powers in the spiritual world.'"

"Funny," Jason said. "You're the second person to quote the bible tonight to justify attacking me. Some good book, am I right?" He let out a laugh.

No one joined him. *Oh shit. I just made a joke out of fear, and now I've lost all control.*

The leader came within three steps of him. He paused, flexing his grip on the hammer's handle and crouched slightly. "Last chance," the man said.

"I was about to say the same thing."

Jason's mind was racing. What would his captain do? Kader was probably going to yell at him either way for not calling for back-up.

He couldn't let Silvana come rescue him, or the mob would lynch her. Should he run? He wouldn't be able to fight back physically in the state he was in.

No. He knew the law. If someone threatened a police officer with violence, the officer was authorized to use necessary force to defend themselves. He was authorized to shoot this man. That's what the captain would want at this point. That was the only way out of this situation.

Could Jason do it? Was he really capable of shooting a person?

I can't be a violent man! I swore I'd never hurt someone like this!

I could just wound him.

No! I won't be that kind of man!

The leader roared and sprang forward, swinging the sledgehammer...

...and Jason lowered his gun and fell backwards.

He hit the ground with his ass. The hammer swung over him harmlessly. Then the leader stepped up to him, brought the hammer around, and lifted it high over his head. The look in his eye was murderous.

"Whoa buddy!" the Asian man ran up behind the speaker and stopped just out of reach. "I think you've made your point. You don't actually have to hurt the guy."

The man growled under his breath, "Well, cop? Are you going to make me do it?"

Shoot him! You have to shoot him now! Damn it Jason, you know it's the right thing to do!

But Jason left the gun at his side.

A blur appeared, and Silvana knocked the man off balance and sent him falling backwards. She stood over Jason, her hair still swinging from the momentum of her speed.

"Don't you dare touch him!" she shrieked, and the ferocity in her

voice chilled Jason. The sound echoed through the woods long after it was made. Her plain jeans and t-shirt couldn't downplay the raw power she exuded.

She's so strong.

The crowd went silent again. But the leader roared from on his back, "Look, one of the vampires! Don't let her get away!"

No one reacted. Jason wondered if they were finally cowed. Then one man took a single step forward, and suddenly everyone was moving towards Silvana.

Maybe she can fight them. She looked back at Jason. Their eyes locked, and hers were visibly trembling. *No. She's afraid.* Jason snatched up his gun and climbed to his feet, ready to make a stand.

A loud bang rang out and everyone went still again as the mansion's front door swung open. The inside was so dark it looked like a portal into pure blackness. A loud clanking sound came from deep within the mansion's walls. The crowd itched back as something moved within the shadows, growing louder and thumping its way towards the light of the torches.

Two figures emerged from the darkness, covered in the steel armour of medieval knights and both holding two-handed longswords.

Jason recognised them. *The suits of armour. They weren't just decoration.*

"Get off our property!" a metallic voice rang from inside the armour, sounding clearly male. "Or we'll hack off your limbs and leave your headless torsos to rot!"

"Don't be afraid!" the leader howled. "Attack!"

One man charged forward with his crowbar. Jason couldn't quite see what happened. All he could tell was that the knight sidestepped the crowbar and swung his sword. A piercing metal clang rang out, followed by a shrill scream of agony.

The crowd suddenly turned and ran. The area cleared within

seconds.

The mob leader was motionless on the ground before Silvana. And one man was left lying on the ground, at the foot of the knight that had struck him down. But Jason didn't feel relieved at all. *Oh my god, is that man dead?*

He leapt to his feet, putting a gentle hand on Silvana's shoulder as he passed and moved straight to the man on the ground, expecting blood and dismemberment.

The man was in one piece. He just had a huge welt on the side of his face, shaped like the flat side of a longsword. The man was awake, but he stared at the sky with a confused expression.

"He'll be alright," said a male voice from inside a metal suit. "But that worthless rantalion is not worth your time."

What? Jason ignored the suit and checked the wounded man's face with his hands. There were no broken bones or cuts, just a big red mark that would later turn into a killer bruise. So Jason left him there and moved towards the leader of the riot.

He was still lying on his back at Silvana's feet, his dark beady eyes staring up at her. Jason grabbed him, rolled him over by force, and locked a set of handcuffs onto his wrists.

"Sir, you're under arrest," he said.

The man swore under his breath over and over, but he didn't address Jason at all. When the man was finally secured, Jason stood and faced Silvana. She was staring at him, her face tense, yet her emotions unreadable. Jason found himself unable to speak. The image of her standing over him, screaming raw defiance, left him in a state of awe. But he saw a hint of tension around her eyes as she watched him, as if worried about his reaction. He tried to reassure her.

"You were incredible."

It came out as a whisper. It was all he could say, yet Silvana seemed to understand. She looked proud of herself for the first time that

Jason had seen.

"Hey, lawman!" a voice shouted. "What are you doing with that assailant?"

Jason looked at the two armoured knights. "You must be Silvana's uncles."

"You must be a detective," the voice jeered as the knights raised their visors.

The lead knight was Phillip, his face looking rugged and old in that too-large helmet. He'd been the one to launch the attack. He glared at Jason now.

The other man was even older. He had a thin, narrow face with sunken cheeks and dozens of wrinkles. His skin had dark spots on it that marked him as far past his prime. Yet he had a thick crown of white hair, and held that two handed sword without any signs of strain.

"We came out here," Phillip growled, "to chase these ruffians off our property. So why have you detained one, zounderkite?"

"I'm placing him under arrest," Jason said. "The police will press charges. It will deter people from threatening you again."

"This is deterrent enough!" Phillip said and shook his sword.

"Stop insulting our ally, Phillip," the other man said in a slightly raspy voice. "This man stood alone against twenty. It's a brave deed to have witnessed." He bowed his head to Jason. "Greetings, friend. I am Nicholas the Third."

The Third? Jason copied the bow, matching the angle. "Uh... Greetings to you also, friend. I am...Officer Jason Turner."

Nicholas grinned back as he placed his sword tip on the ground and leaned on the handle.

"Well, *officer*," Phillip said. "You can take both of these men off our..."

The man who'd been hit with the sword gave a groan as he staggered to his feet. He took one nervous look at Phillip, then cried out in terror and stumbled off into the night as fast as he could go.

"Good riddance," Phillip gave a satisfied grin. "Well, you can take that one." He pointed to the mob leader. "Let him go, or escort him away. I don't care which."

"Don't you want to press charges?" Jason asked. "This guy led an angry mob to your doorstep."

"We could handle them," Phillip growled. "And pressing charges will only bring more people to our property. We just want to be left alone."

Jason shrugged. *Well, I'm a victim too, so I'm pressing charges.*

The mansion door opened again, and the pale, graceful figures of Lisbeth and Emberline emerged, floating out in their evening ball gowns. "Is it safe, my dear?" Emberline asked, with an air of absolute confidence.

"My sword has protected thee, my heart," Phillip replied.

Emberline moved to his side and placed a gentle hand on his shoulder, using a tenderness Jason would not have thought her capable of. Lisbeth moved towards Nicholas and pressed her youthful lips to his weathered face. Nicholas grinned like a teenager being kissed for the first time.

"Oh look at that," Lisbeth said in her sweet voice. "The whole family is here. Have we all met Jason?" Everyone nodded. "And Silvana, dear, welcome back. How was your date?"

Silvana glanced at Jason. They opened their mouths at the same time, and neither spoke. *Damn, we paused too long and now it's awkward.* "It was..." he started.

"...nice," she finished. "We talked a lot."

"Learnt a lot about each other," he added.

He smiled at Silvana, and she returned it with sincerity.

"That's nice," Emberline said, in a tone that suggested it wasn't. "But has he accepted your proposal yet?"

"Aunty!" Silvana cried. "Can we not do this in front of Jason? I told you this morning, he's unfamiliar with our ways. It may take some time."

"You don't exactly have time to spare, Silvana."

"I know, Aunty! I can handle it."

Their voices were growing louder, so Jason blurted out the first thing that came to mind to try to ease the tension.

"I have to ask. Why are the old mortal men protecting the super immortal women? Does anyone else here think that's a little weird?"

He was answered by total silence.

"Oh come on!" he cried, waving his hands around. "I'm a young man in his prime, but Silvana could still beat me up easily. And you lads aren't exactly…you know."

"Do you think you could take us?" Nicholas said with a cheeky grin. He put on a gruff voice, "Do you feel lucky, punk?"

Jason blinked. "Did you just quote Dirty Harry?"

Nicholas's smile broadened. "Indeed. They're my favourite films. I own all of them on VHS," he said proudly.

VHS? Oh my god…

"Our husbands protect us," Lisbeth answered in an overly sweet voice. "Age and strength has nothing to do with it. What's important is the courage of a knight in the face of danger."

"Our honour, piety, and dedication," Nicholas chimed. "The three tenants of the Knight Templar."

Jason's eyes widened. "The what now?"

"Not that *you* would understand, boy," Phillip said. "Judging by that black eye of yours, I don't think you'd know the first thing about protecting a lady."

"Hey, I was fighting a fucking polar bear."

Phillip wasn't impressed. "And after you lost that fight, you failed to protect yourself from this mob too. You were even armed! You had command of the scene. But you failed to take action. Typical zounderkite."

"Ok first of all, what are these words you keep calling me?"

Silvana whispered, "Uncle Phillip's a bit old-fashioned. He uses Victorian era insults."

"Of course he does," Jason whispered back. In a louder voice, "And second, are you saying I should have murdered this man?" He gestured to the mob leader at his feet.

Phillip growled, "I didn't say murder. You saw me strike a fool with the flat of my sword. Yet no one was slain."

Nicholas spoke up in a softer voice, and Jason recognised that the older man was trying to deescalate the situation. "You could have wounded him, Jason. It would have given you back control over the situation. You should have taken action, son."

"Hang on," Jason cried. "You both saw what happened? You were inside, watching, and you didn't intervene when this man tried to murder me with a sledgehammer?"

"You should have protected yourself," Phillip sneered. "Are you not a man?"

"But you intervened for Silvana."

"Silvana is family!" Emberline snapped, her voice cold and commanding. "My husband did his duty and protected her. You are not his responsibility, mortal. And after your performance tonight, I have serious concerns about your ability to protect Silvana."

"Aunty!"

"Silvana doesn't need protecting," Jason said.

Lisbeth held a hand to her breast as if mortified.

Emberline replied, "That's a shameful thing to say."

"Stop, please," Silvana said, coming forward and standing at Jason's side. "Forgive me for saying so, but Jason is right. You should have protected him as well, since he is my guest. The rights of hospitality extend to him when he is on our property."

Phillip's expression soured at Silvana's words, but he stayed quiet.

Silvana pressed on. "Jason was already wounded from an attack by three immortals. I was bringing him back here for medical care and to report the attack to the Imperium. He was in a weakened state, yet he still approached the mob alone to protect me."

"Well he can't come inside now," Phillip said. "He needs to escort this mortal from our property." He gestured at the mob leader, still handcuffed on the ground and sneering at the family in helpless rage. "We've already said enough in front of him. Let us retire for the evening. Silvana, come!"

Phillip turned and led Emberline back towards the doors. Lisbeth and Nicholas followed, the suits of armour clanging loudly as they moved. None of them checked to see if Silvana would obey.

Jason bit his tongue. He hated that they talked down to Silvana. She was probably older than both men, but was still treated like a child. Still, he would only cause more problems if he made a big deal out of it. The older men were right, he still needed to escort the assailant to the police station, and he was bruised and exhausted from his long day.

"Don't worry about the medical treatment," Jason said. "I'll be fine. Can I message you tomorrow?"

Silvana was scowling like she was trying to hold back her emotions. *Wait, is that defiance I see in her eyes?* Jason held his breath, hoping for a glimpse of the real Silvana. But a moment later, she let out a long sigh, and the fight went out of her.

"All right," she said. "But let me get you something first. I have a…energy drink for you."

"Um…no that's fine."

"Trust me. You'll want this." Silvana ran inside the house, overtaking her family.

Lisbeth turned around. "Goodnight, Jason," she called.

"Goodnight," he called back. "Good to meet you, Nicholas the Third."

"The honour was all mine," Nicholas said with a bow, though he could only bend a few centimetres forward.

Phillip and Emberline didn't look back.

A moment later, Silvana re-emerged. She handed him a small glass vial, containing about fifty millilitres of a light blue liquid.

"It's an energy drink," she said, then leaned in to whisper so the mob leader couldn't hear. "It's actually an elixir I bought off an alchemist. It will speed up your body's recovery time. Drink it all now, and your wounds will heal in minutes. You won't even have bruises tomorrow."

She planted a quick kiss on his cheek, then stepped back. "Can you text me when you get home? Just so I know you're safe?"

"Sure," he stammered. She smiled at him once more – looking dazzling – then ran inside, leaving Jason in the dark, in the woods outside a creepy old mansion and alone with a man who had just tried to murder him, holding an 'elixir'.

What have I gotten myself into?

Chapter 14

Jason took his captive back up the hill to his car. The man had his hands cuffed behind him, so Jason sat him in the back seat and opposite the driver. He even put the man's seat belt on, as awkward as it was for both of them, and sat behind the wheel.

The elixir was just a pale blue liquid. It looked like dyed water. What had Silvana promised? That it would speed his recovery? She even mentioned buying it off an alchemist. *Ok, apparently alchemists are a real thing, whatever that means.* Was he supposed to blindly put this strange substance into his body without knowing what it contained? It could be a love potion, binding him to her will. Maybe he could ask the forensic team to run some tests on it. But how could he convince them? What would he say?

I hardly believe it myself, even though I saw a polar bear with a man's face. What the fuck was that?

He put the elixir in his glove box, started up the car, and drove off.

"So what's your name?" Jason said.

"I don't have to tell you anything," the man growled. "And you're supposed to read me my rights. What kind of cop are you, when you don't even read a man his rights? Is that how corrupt you are? First you fuck that vampire whore, and now you arrest an innocent man!"

"All right," Jason sighed. "There's a lot wrong with what you just said. First, I don't need to read you your rights at the time of arrest. That's America. In Britain, the detectives will only advise you of your rights before an interrogation. Also, not that it's your business, but the girl and I had one date, which you interrupted. And of course I arrested an innocent man. Everyone's innocent until proven guilty. Still means you get arrested. But you're hardly innocent, aren't you? Now what's your name?"

The man gave a childish huff. "Well I'm still not telling you anything."

Jason shrugged. "I'll just call you John Doe. So, John Doe, did you know Alex Bishop?"

"Don't you dare say his name!"

"Are you related to him? Or just a friend?"

"I'm a concerned citizen. Because it's very concerning that a man is sucked dry by vampires in our own town and the police cover it up."

"Actually, I'm trying to figure out what happened. You're the one being unhelpful."

"You know who killed him. The vampires! Who else?"

"Oh, I don't know," Jason hummed. "Maybe someone who hates vampires?"

"Piss off."

Jason took a breath. "And those people at the mansion tonight. Were they all friends of Alex Bishop?"

"Is that so surprising? He was a good man with many friends."

Really? Jason remembered Alex breaking into a family home with a gun and planning to murder them all in their sleep. He also remembered the tiny, shitty apartment where Alex lived alone. But he decided not to mention it.

"How do you all know each other?"

John Doe suddenly jerked forward in his seat. Jason flinched and the car swerved on the road. "You're wasting time!" John yelled. He made no further aggressive moves, and Jason calmed himself. "You know the vampires did it. You know what they're capable of. You need to bring them down before they destroy us all."

"Bring them down?" Jason scoffed.

"Don't you know? The vampires are ruling the world!"

"Ok mate."

"They've been ruling the world for centuries! They have a secret government where they control us from the shadows. You know the illuminati? Knights Templar? That was all them!"

"Alright buddy, you're just saying Knights Templar cause you heard Nicholas say it before…"

"He spoke the truth!" John yelled louder. "Think about it. Those vampires are immortal. They never die. So they're richer than you and I could ever be, because of inflation. How do you think they afford that mansion? You don't see any of them working on the docks do you?"

That was actually a good point. Silvana's family had to be wealthy to own such a lavish mansion, even though none of them seemed to work. And being immortal would make it easier to maintain wealth. But this stuff about them ruling the world? Impossible. They were hermits, living on the outskirts of society.

"They have a council," John said. "Some form of government. And *theirs* controls *ours*."

"Really?"

"All of our politicians and leaders may be human, but they're all working for the vampires."

"That's imposs…" Jason stopped.

No. Maybe it wasn't impossible. *I saw a polar bear with a human face. Anything's possible.* He had to have an open mind about this. There was so much he didn't know or understand. He had to at least consider the possibility.

Then it occurred to him. What had Phillip said, the first time they met? *"I'm from an old family. Older than this country. You have no idea what I could do to you."*

And what had the skinwalker Gerald said? *"We are your kings and queens, created by God to rule you."*

Jason shivered. Something was wrong here. John Doe may be a violent man, but he knew something about the immortal world and Jason would be naïve to ignore it.

"What do you know about their government?"

John Doe smiled broadly. "Ooh, that's sparked your interest, hasn't it?" He leaned forward and spoke in an overly dramatic stage whisper. "I heard that the vampires rule by using other people as their puppets. Sometimes their own flesh and blood."

"So family members? Mortal relatives?"

"That's right. I don't know exactly how it works. But some family members become immortal, and others become the leaders of mankind. In the olden days, they used to be the kings and queens of Europe. You know all the royal families were connected to each other, right?"

"Families…" Jason muttered. *Phillip's from an old family. Could John Doe be onto something?*

"Yeah, royals would marry into each other's families all the time. That's how they would forge alliances. But it wasn't just about ruling countries either. It was maintaining supremacy over other vampire houses."

"Ok. But the monarchies all died out."

"Exactly! These days the vampires don't need to worry about kingship. Their representatives go into politics. The vampires fund the election campaigns with their fortunes. Because not just anyone can get elected. You must be able to *afford* the campaigns. And it's not just the politics. It's billionaires. There's less than three thousand people in the world that own most of the world's wealth. But they're just the faces for the money, the representatives. Behind every billionaire is a vampire family!"

"Is it always vampires?"

John blinked at him. "What do you mean?"

"Well, what about the other immortals?"

"There are others?!" John shouted, and Jason immediately regretted his words.

At that moment the police station came into view. Jason was quick to park the car next to the entrance. He stepped around to John's side of the car and pulled him onto his feet.

"Hey, come on man, you need to tell me about the other immortals!" John cried.

Jason ignored him and led him up the stairs towards the station entrance. He swiped his access card to get inside. The building was empty, and the lights were off. Plymouth was too small a town to require 24/7 police presence at the station, but someone would be on call to come in for emergencies.

Jason escorted John into the holding cell and closed the bars behind him. "Come on, officer! Tell me more!"

"Bring your hands towards the bars, and I'll uncuff you."

"Look, I'm sorry I attacked you tonight. I didn't realise you were one of the good cops. I thought you were in their pay. But you're an honest man. I see that now."

"Do you want to keep the cuffs on all night?"

John growled and turned around. Jason reached through the bars, took off the cuffs, and pulled them back through.

"I'm going to write an arrest report," Jason said, "then I'm going home. You can stay here the night. The detectives will question you in the morning."

"What?! You can't leave me here overnight. I'm unprotected!"

Jason moved to his desk and turned on his computer. "I'm going to need your name, date of birth, and address."

"Hey! Listen to me," John shouted. "The vampires will come for me. They'll want revenge because I challenged them. You must stay here and protect me!"

"And you must tell me your name, date of birth, and address."

"No! Not unless you protect me!"

Jason sighed. "Your name."

"Harrison! Timothy Harrison!"

"Ah. Nice to meet you, Tim."

Jason filled out the form. He tried to ignore Mr Harrison's calls for protection. There was no way Jason could stay in the police station all night. *It would seem too suspicious.* He was already going to have a hard time explaining this arrest. Besides, the vampires weren't coming after Harrison. It was a ridiculous notion. And even if they did, they couldn't get through the bars. Even Gerald the metamorph wouldn't be able to break steel bars.

But there *was* a killer out there.

If Harrison was killed, that would be the second person Jason had interacted with right before their murder. Besides that, he had a duty of care to protect this man. Could he really just leave him here?

He finished the form, printed it, and turned off his computer. He turned to face Harrison in his cell. The man was white in the face, as if the blood was already drained. His knuckles were clinging to the cell bars.

"Would you like me to leave the lights on for you?" Jason asked.

* * *

Jason finally got home at midnight. The sounds of Timothy Harrison's angry shouts still rang in his ears. But he had left the prisoner several blankets and left the lights on. Mr Harrison would be fine.

Still, I'm going in early tomorrow. Just in case.

Jason's small apartment was dark and smelt faintly of beer. He flicked on a light and found Peter's bedroom door was wide open and unoccupied. *That's strange. He must be out with friends tonight.* Jason claimed the bathroom to himself and took a long, hot shower, using extra heat to soak his bruises. They would be sore for a few days. He thought of the 'recovery elixir' Silvana had given him still sitting in the glove box of his car and felt guilty for not using it.

Silvana!

He rushed out of the shower and checked his phone. There was a text waiting for him.

"'Hey Jason. Sorry to seem like a nag. I just wanted to check that you got home safely. Is everything ok? Kind Regards, Silvana.'"

He chuckled as he wrote back.

"'Hey. Just got home safely. Sorry for the late reply, it took a while to check that guy into the station. Thanks for a great night!'"

He hit send, and immediately regretted the last part. It would probably sound fake. So he added, *"I mean it. I did enjoy being with you."'*

He hit send, and immediately regretted that too. He was being over-emotional. Hadn't he considered breaking it off at one point? But here he was, reaching out to her again. Maybe, he'd changed his mind? The memory of her standing up to the mob of angry insurgents came to mind, and it made him smile.

She had already texted back.

"'Jason! It's so good to hear you're ok. It's been a weird night, so I was a bit worried. Did the elixir help?'"

He felt a deep stab of guilt. He took a moment to dry off, get dressed, and lay in bed, all the while considering his response. He despised lying, but couldn't bear to tell the truth. So he just replied, *"It was really helpful, thank you. Did you want to see each other again tomorrow night?"*

He hit send…and immediately regretted it again. *Damn, if I see her tomorrow, she'll see I still have bruises!* He started typing…

She had already texted back.

"Yes I would love that!"

"Oh crap," he muttered to himself.

Another message.

"But can I come to your place? Things with my family are a bit tense. I'm so sorry about how they were tonight."

"That's ok. Families can be tense sometimes. You can come here. But I should warn you. My place is no mansion."

"I wouldn't expect it to be. I don't mind. How about I bring some food? I'd be happy to cook."

"Sounds good. Looking forward to it."

He started thinking of other questions he had for her. About her family, their history, and their role in world events. But he was tired. Anything he said now might come out a little too harsh. So he just messaged, *"Really sorry, but I have to sleep now. I'll see you tomorrow."*

"Oh I'm so sorry for keeping you up. I forget that I'm up later than most. (Vampire, and all that). :) Thanks for texting me. Good night Jason!"

He couldn't help the smile on his face.

"Good night, Silvana."

He was still smiling when he fell asleep.

Chapter 15

Jason stumbled through his kitchen, still bleary eyed. Everything ached.

He reached for the jug to make himself a coffee. It wasn't there. He spun around like a drunk man, searching. *There.* It was on the wrong corner of the bench. He set it to boil and opened the cupboard.

Where the hell's my cereal? Damn it, Peter! He stood on his tip toes. The cereal bags had been pushed to the back of the shelf. *Why?*

A moment later he was in his bedroom opening his draws to find a pair of socks, yet all his underclothes looked blurred. He blinked a few times, but nothing changed. He couldn't see anything in the draw. Then he realised the clothes were all strewn together. Nothing was folded. *Peter! What possible reason...* He crossed over to Peter's room, ready to raise some hell.

The room was still empty. It looked like Peter hadn't come home last night. Where could he be? And if he was out, then who the hell had touched all his things?

Jason snapped to attention. *Someone's been in my apartment!*

He grabbed his phone and started a call. He ran to check the front door. Still locked. He checked the door to the outside balcony. Still locked. *How did they get in? Are they still here?*

The phone answered. "Officer Turner?" said a woman's voice.

"Captain!" he cried. "Yes, good morning. I'm at home, and I think someone broke into my apartment. Everything's been moved around like they were searching for something. But both the doors were locked all night. I'm checking the windows now…"

"Hey, hold up a second, Detective. I can solve this one for you."

"Huh?"

Captain Kader was chuckling. "I already caught the culprits. The robbers were none other than Detective Lynch and Detective Cole."

Jason stopped in place. "What?"

"They searched your apartment, genius. They got a warrant yesterday and searched it last night while you were out. You're a suspect in Alex Bishop's murder, remember?"

"Oh…"

"That's right. And you'll recall, a detective with a warrant does not need a person's permission to enter the home. Nor do they need to inform them."

"Right. But if I'm under investigation, shouldn't I be stood down until it's resolved?"

"Asking for the day off?" The captain chuckled again. "See you at the office, Detective." She hung up.

Jason let out a long sigh. If people had been in his home, he would have to let Peter know. It was time to face that conversation. He dialled Peter's phone and started getting ready for work as it rang on and on. It answered just before going to voice mail.

"The fuck?" Peter's groaning voice came on the line, his words slurring together amid heavy breathing.

"Hey Pete, it's Jase. Sorry it's earl—"

"Jase? God you know what fucking time it is? Why aren't you just texting?"

"It's important."

He heard a loud grunt and the ruffling of movement on the

mouthpiece for several seconds before Peter's voice came back, sounding much clearer.

"Yeah sorry for snapping, bro. What's up?"

"I have to give you a heads up. The police searched our apartment."

"Oh shit! You're kidding?"

"I wish."

"What'd you fucking do, ey?"

Jason gave a loud sigh as he started dressing in his police uniform while holding the phone to his ear. "Well actually, I found a dead body."

"Whoa."

"Yeah. But like…I can't tell you everything. Let's just say I screwed up on some police procedure and now I'm a suspect. They came and searched the apartment. So I wanted to warn you that our stuff has been moved around but it wasn't me, yeah?"

"Sure bro. Damn, sorry to hear that. Everything ok at work? I know how much you care about your job."

"It'll smooth over," Jason said the exact second that he tripped on his pants leg and stumbled into the wall. *Shit, that's a bad sign.*

"Ok cool. Well thanks for the heads up."

"That's all right. Uh…" Jason put the phone on the chest of draws so he could get his hand through the sleeves of his shirt. "So look, haven't seen you much."

"Yeah, just hanging with some friends from uni. Went out drinking last night. Good times."

"On a Monday night?"

"Fuck you."

Jason laughed. "Well, I actually wanted to…uh…apologise I guess. For the way things went down with Silvana." Peter was silent, so Jason rushed to fill in the space. "I never expected that. I really wasn't uh…trying to do that."

"I get it, mate," Peter said, yet there was an edge of warning in his voice. "I know that was Silvana's call. And I fucked up by trying to go into her room, and yes, you did warn me. So that's on me."

"Ok well thank you—"

"What I don't understand," Peter went on, "is why you agreed to go out with her."

Jason paused halfway between doing up his buttons. "What?"

"Come on, mate. She was on a date with me first. You should have checked with me before deciding to go out with her. You and I have been friends for years. But you picked her straight away. It's supposed to be bros before hoes."

Jason curled his lip up in disgust. He considered trying to explain the concept of female autonomy and outdated gender roles, but figured Peter wouldn't really go for that. Instead he explained.

"I understand, Pete. It's just that you'd only been on *one* date with her. If you were boyfriend and girlfriend, I would have checked, definitely. It just wasn't that serious yet between you guys. That's all I was thinking."

Peter was quiet again. This time, Jason let him sit in silence and refused to explain any further. He finished dressing and held the phone to his ear.

"Yeah sure," Peter said eventually, a hint of reluctance in his voice. "I guess that's a fair point."

Jason held in a sigh of relief as he moved into the kitchen to start preparing food. "Thanks man."

"So are you still seeing her?"

"Yeah. Saw her last night."

"I see. Well just so you know, I'm interested in trying again."

Jason froze halfway through pouring a coffee. "You are?" he asked.

"Course! She's so hot! So let me know if you strike out, and I'll have another go at the bat."

Jason couldn't think of anything to say and just stood there silently.

"Anyway, bro, I better have a shower. You wouldn't believe what I smell like right now. I might see you tonight, I might not, yeah?"

"Uh…yeah," Jason stammered.

"Later bro!"

* * *

Jason arrived at work an hour before his shift started. He went straight to the holding cell to check on its occupant. Timothy Harrison was still there alive and well, if a little pissed off. A tension in Jason's shoulders that he hadn't even realised was there lifted off him.

"Yes I'm alive," Mr Harrison growled. "No thanks to you. Sleep well last night in your comfy bed?"

"Yes, as a matter of fact. Thank you for asking."

Jason moved towards his desk but was surprised to see he wasn't first to arrive today. A large man sat nearby in the detective's chair. Jason crossed the room.

"Good morning, Detective Lynch," he said in a friendly tone.

Lynch jerked in his seat and suddenly reached up to turn off his computer monitor. Jason only glimpsed a picture of bank statements before they disappeared from the screen. Lynch spun around, and Jason stepped back when he saw the cold stare pointed in his direction. "Can I help you, officer?" Lynch said in a voice that implied he wouldn't help with anything.

Jason wasn't bothered. "Well, since you asked, I was wondering if you knew where I kept the sugar. Couldn't find it anywhere this morning. Thought you might know."

Lynch stared back. "It was up your arse. I'm surprised you couldn't see it, with your head already up there."

"Well. Maybe you should investigate my arse. If you even have the skills to find it."

Lynch said nothing. He just stood up slowly and loomed large enough to cast a shadow over Jason. Lynch crossed his arms and the muscles in his forearm flexed tight and hard.

"Tell me about this man you brought in. Timothy Harrison."

Jason didn't blink at the change in topic, but his eyes shifted nervously towards the holding cell. He could feel Mr Harrison's gaze on his back.

"He was with approximately twenty other people at Maristow House. They blamed the inhabitants for Alex Bishop's death and tried to force entry. I confronted them alone and restrained Mr Harrison. The rest of the mob fled on foot."

"What were you doing there in the first place?"

"I was on a date."

"Escorting your friend again? Erikson?"

"No. Peter wasn't invited. I was dating Silvana myself, not chaperoning anyone."

"Silvana really gets through men."

Jason bit his tongue. It was clearly bait, so he ignored it. "If you're going to interrogate me, should we at least move to the interrogation room?"

Lynch smiled menacingly. "Oh that's a great idea. I'll get my handcuffs. I've got a few hours to kill anyway."

Jason smirked. "So you're into handcuffs?"

"That's enough!"

Captain Kader appeared next to them, half a metre shorter yet just as determined. "You won't be interrogating Officer Turner again," she said in her commander's voice. "He's already filled out an arrest report. You can read his statement there."

"I'm still allowed to interrogate him," Lynch said, his tone respectful but with hint of agitation. "Just to jog his memory. Make sure he didn't leave anything out."

"I left out my opinion of you," said Jason. "Want to hear it?"

"Officer!" Kader snapped. "Wait for me in my office."

"Yes ma'am."

Jason held his head forward and marched to the captain's office without a sideways glance. He heard tense whispers behind him. He ended up sitting in the captain's office for five minutes before she returned. He stood to attention as she sat at her desk. She did not tell him to be at ease.

"Turner...the fuck?"

Oh crap. "Can you be more specific?"

"That should tell you something, Turner. Your captain is mad, and you can't narrow down which of the many reasons is pissing her off."

"But I arrested the intruder this time," he blurted, then regretted it. He sounded like a child seeking his mother's approval.

"That's great, detective. You did your job. But what's the old saying? Something about, 'one good deed does not outweigh a multitude of sins'?"

Jason paused in thought. "I think it's a bible verse, ma'am. And it's love that outweighs the sins."

She shrugged. "I was raised Islamic."

"Anglican," Jason shrugged back.

"Well hallelujah." She sighed. "Turner, when I defended you from the detective just now, you responded by being a snot-nosed little prick. It's just like when my youngest son gets in trouble, and my eldest starts laughing at him. It's bad form."

"Sorry, captain."

"And yes, you did arrest Harrison. But you also left him alone in a police building at night."

"Yeah, but he committed the crime at night. You know criminals, so inconsiderate of office hours."

"Yes, that is their worst crime," she said flatly. "You also approached a group of twenty hostiles without calling for backup. That's the kind of rookie error you rarely get to make twice."

"Yeah…" Jason grimaced. "The owners of the property said they didn't want more police on site. I thought…"

"So?" she snapped. "Citizens don't write the rule book, rookie. You call for backup, and apologise afterwards. An officer needs to call it in any time they enter a dangerous situation. You're lucky that mob only gave you a few bruises."

"Oh…actually these bruises are from a separate incident."

Captain Kader sat back in her chair, crossed her arms, and took a long breath. "Christ, Turner, what now?"

He smiled. "I think I found the bikers causing all those disturbances. I was going to write a report first thing. That's why I'm here early."

Kader pinched the bridge of her nose. "Please tell me you didn't spend your off time doing…vigilante investigation."

"No. They found me, actually." He paused. "And they gave me the bruises. I was gonna put it all in the report…" he trailed off when he saw her expression.

"Turner," she said, "you're not going on patrols today. You're on desk duty. Today, tomorrow, and into the foreseeable future."

He forced himself to breathe deeply before he spoke. "May I ask why?"

"Because you're too full of enthusiasm. You're going to stay where I can keep an eye on you. I don't want you getting into more dangerous situations. The detectives are already out for your blood and I don't want you making it worse."

"Captain…is this about the detectives? Or is this a punishment?"

She studied him in silence, and the brief moment felt like hours.

"It's not a punishment, Turner. This is training. And training often feels like punishment to someone who has suffered a lot in life."

Jason looked away.

"Do the desk duty. Start by writing that report on the bikers who attacked you. I'll ask the other officers if they have any paperwork for you."

"Is that all?"

The captain looked like she wanted to say more, but she simply nodded her head once. Jason regretted the cold tone he'd used on her. He could see she was trying to help. At last, she added, "Dismissed."

He left the office without saying anything else.

Outside, Lynch was on his mobile. He looked up when Jason entered, glaring at him. Then he stood up, grabbed his coat, and left the precinct.

Ass.

Chapter 16

"Desk duty, huh rookie? You are so lucky!"

Douglas was leaning against Jason's desk, and the big man's extra weight folded over the edge. Either he was oblivious of Jason's desire to work, or he just didn't care.

"I would love more desk duty," Douglas went on. "All this running around is going to give me a heart attack. Not from the exercise, mind you. From finding dead bodies. Scared the shit outta me yesterday. I'd rather stay where it's safe."

"It's not exactly detective work," Jason said, not looking up from his typing.

"Uh, where do you think detectives normally work?"

"I mean, I'm doing paperwork. Admin. We should have someone on staff to do this crap for us."

"Really? You think HQ would consider spending a few thousand pounds a year for the Plymouth police to have an admin guru?"

"We could ask nicely."

Douglas chuckled and shifted his weight, bumping the desk and making the screen shake. Jason rolled back in his chair and turned to face him. "Don't mean to be rude, partner, but don't you have somewhere to be?"

"Nah. Captain has us on patrols again today for the motorbikes.

Not exactly high priority." He scratched the two-day stubble on his chin. "So what are you working on?"

Jason tried to stop being so grumpy. He forced a smile. "Writing a report."

"Oh nice. Though I'm a bit surprised you're not practicing your detective skills on yesterday's murder case."

"Can't. I'm under strict orders. The detectives consider me a suspect. I can't be anywhere near that case."

"Oh, right." Douglas ran a hand through his thin hairline. "Sorry I ratted on you, champ. Didn't mean to get you in trouble."

"It's fine, mate."

"It's just too bad! It's not often we get a murder case in Plymouth. Would've been good practice for you."

"Yes, thank you, Douglas," Jason drawled.

"Well, hopefully, there'll be another murder soon, ey?" Douglas grinned and slapped him on the shoulder.

Jason couldn't help it and he grinned back. The guy was charming.

"How's the family?" Jason asked, feeling himself lighten up a little. "Any news on your daughter?"

"Nothing from Tracey yet. But I think we've made some progress. When I got home last night, I told her a little bit about finding that body."

"Uh...why?"

"To open up! Be vulnerable and stuff, you know? Show her that I'm available. It's like if I can share about myself, then she can share about herself. Right?"

Jason frowned. "I guess that makes sense. But was a murder really the right thing to share?"

Douglas stared at him blankly. "Why wouldn't it be?"

"Nevermind. Good job mate."

"Hey guys!" Officer Carol Martin appeared by the desk and

immediately put a hand on Jason's shoulder. "Douglas, you have to switch with me. I can't be on patrol with Wilson again. He kept describing his newborn's diaper explosions!"

"And how is that going to convince me to switch?"

"Prevent human suffering, you ass."

Douglas shrugged. "I wouldn't be preventing it. I'd be experiencing it."

"Don't do this to me…"

"Hey guys!" Wilson called out, as he came to stand in the one centimetre of empty space Jason had left around his desk. Now all three officers were pressed up against him, and Martin still kept her hand on his shoulder.

Wilson had a huge smile on his soft, narrow face. "What's going on? Party at Turner's desk, hey?" He fist-bumped Jason's shoulder. "That reminds me. My wife wants to design invitations for little Katie's first birthday party. The theme is elephants!"

Douglas asked flatly, "Katie…the newborn?"

"Oh, yeah. Can never be too prepared. Their first party sets a precedent of expectations, you know."

"Whose expectations?!" Douglas cried.

"Hey Wilson," Martin said with a bright smile. "Dougy here was suggesting we switch partners for today's patrol…"

"No I was—"

Wilson let out a loud whoop, the kind Jason heard from pre-teen boys and not from grown men in their late thirties, and certainly not in a police precinct.

"Oh, great idea!" Wilson cried. "You know I could really use some advice from a fellow-dad. Making the jump to two kids is so stressful!"

"Oh you have two kids? I didn't realise," Jason mumbled.

"Yeah, Jase. Adam and Katie. Where've you been, man?"

Jason rolled his eyes. "You know guys, I've got a lot of work to do…"

"Actually Captain wanted me to work alone," Douglas said. "There's some additional work she needs done. Sorry to disappoint you, Wilson."

"Don't worry about it. I'll just help with your other work too," Wilson said. "Hey, how soon did you move the second child to their own room? Like, does it *have* to be the same length of time as the first?"

Douglas stared at him flatly. "I only have one child."

"Oh." Wilson frowned. "Well, I guess that makes me the expert parent around here, hey?"

Douglas rested his hand on his belt, next to his firearm.

"Officers?" the captain called, standing in her office doorway. All four officers looked up like deer in the headlights. Kader had her hair back in a short ponytail and was crossing her arms. "Why is everyone crowding around your desk, Officer Turner?"

Jason tried to throw up his hands in bewilderment, but there was no space. And Martin still had her hands on him.

"Captain, I've asked them to leave several times. They won't listen to me."

"Please stop distracting them, Detective."

"Thank you Cap— wait, what?"

Kader had a coy smile. "You heard me. You have a lot of work to do, rookie. Focus up and stop disrupting the others. You're being a bad influence."

Jason growled through his breath. He knew she was joking but he hated being the butt of the joke. Still, he tried to sound chipper when he said, "Sorry, Captain. You heard her, guys. I have work to do."

The captain gave him a friendly nod and went back into her office.

"Oh don't worry about her, sweetie," Martin said and stroked her hand all the way across one shoulder to the other. "We all know you're doing a great job."

"Ok that's enough touching, thanks," Jason said and brushed her hand away. "Can I please get to work?"

Douglas shifted off the desk and stood up, shaking Jason's computer with his movement. "Good luck, kid." He shuffled away, Wilson following at his side, already chatting amiably about kids and the benefits of shared bedrooms versus separate. Martin gave him yet another pat on the shoulder, then left him alone at last.

After a minute, Jason checked around to confirm the room was clear. Detectives Lynch and Cole were offsite again. The captain was in her office. He was finally alone.

He opened the police database and searched: *Gerald.*

The Plymouth police were not exactly prioritised around budget time, so their software was outdated to say the least. The database ran on a program that still used the 2008 version. The whole design felt ancient and the system froze up constantly while in use. Still, it was the best Jason had.

Hundreds of names came up. He refined the search to Plymouth addresses, and found twenty-six people. He started opening them one by one, looking at their faces. It took him some time. The database was sinfully slow today, and he had to open and close each page.

He didn't recognise any of the faces.

Damn. He looked up the name Ryan. There were eighty names in Plymouth. He let out a groan and started clicking through.

Around the fiftieth name, he sat back in his chair and cupped his face in his hands. *What am I doing?* He was searching up immortals. Would they even appear in this database? Were they citizens? He had to test it.

He typed in Silvana.

Three names came up. He found her first time.

"Silvana Clarke. Age twenty-seven. Born in Cardiff. Moved to Plymouth three years ago. Works as an on-call nurse."

Jason blinked. Was this information correct? Aged twenty-seven seemed unlikely. Maybe there was false IDs for immortals. For a moment, Jason wondered if maybe she wasn't really immortal at all. Maybe none of this stuff was real...

No. I saw a polar bear with a human face.

He searched for Silvana's family. All of them had the last name Clarke, like she'd said. That made no sense. How could Phillip and Nicholas share a last name? Emberline and Lisbeth were traditional, so they would have taken their husband's names when they married. So unless they married brothers with the same last name, then the name Clarke was a cover.

"What family are you from, Phillip?" Jason mumbled. "What are you hiding?"

The profiles held no further clues. But now that he had confirmed immortals could appear on the database, he kept searching through the many Ryans in the area. It took nearly an hour because of the slow system, but eventually he exhausted the list. No sign of Ryan, the vampire.

"What was the telepath's name..." he muttered. *Ah yes, Kate. Probably one of the worst names to search for.* Was it short for Katie with an I-E, or Katey with an E-Y? Catherine with a C or Kathryn with a K? There were too many options. Still. He had to try.

If one of the immortals was called Gerald, a rather old name... He searched for Kathryn with a K.

One hundred and thirty names.

"Faaarrrk!" Jason growled. He let out a long sigh. But with no other option coming to mind, he started clicking through.

It took him two hours. But, eventually, he found her.

Kathryn Smith was apparently twenty-three, studied veterinary science, and worked as a part-time nurse at the local vet. *Smarter than I expected. Did I judge her by her accent? Oh, accent prejudice.* She was also the registered owner of a Kawasaki Ninja Carbon, a motorbike valued at thirty thousand pounds.

"Bingo," Jason said. "Now how did you afford such an expensive bike on top of those student loans?"

He looked up the university she attended. Birmingham. His instincts told him there was something there. *Birmingham university...* Then it hit him. He searched for anyone who had studied at Birmingham but also had an address in Plymouth.

Fifteen names. He scrolled through them all until he saw the name Rion Dankworth. *Ha. Dankworth. What a weird name.*

He read it again. Rion, with an i.

Ri-on.

Ryan.

He clicked the name. *It's him!*

Jason had found the vampire. He recognised the buzz cut hairstyle, pale skin and masculine jaw. Rion Dankworth had studied business and was currently unemployed. He also owned an expensive motor-bike. *They all met at university. Maybe I can find this Gerald too...*

Jason looked to the end of the list. But there was no one named Gerald, or any variation of the name. Either his real name was completely different, or he didn't study with the other two.

Still. Two out of three ain't bad.

Jason checked the time. It was nearly eleven and he hadn't finished writing his report on the incident with the three immortals. At least now he was able to include his personal identification of two of the suspects involved. He powered through the report. When he finished, he took a printed copy straight to the captain's office.

As Jason neared her office window, he could see the captain on the phone. He waited outside her door and wondered if it'd be rude to knock. He heard her say, "No, I'm keeping him here."

Jason froze with his knuckle near the doorframe. It felt wrong to eavesdrop, and even more so on his captain. But he continued to listen.

"There's no initial reason to suspect him. There's no connection to this Richard. It would have to be a random violent crime." A pause. "I'm not discounting his history. But there's no criminal record. No precedent. And no catalyst." Another pause. "No, Lynch. Not until you find me hard evidence. I won't authorise it."

There was silence again, then the sound of the phone receiver being placed down. *Sounds like Lynch hung up on her. What was that all about? Were they discussing me? But who's this Richard?*

Jason knocked on the door.

"Come in, rookie."

"Captain," he said with a blank face. "I finished my report."

"Do you want a medal? I'll read it in my own time, thank you. Just put it on the desk." She waved towards an empty tray on the corner of her desk.

"Captain, using the database, I was able to identify two of the suspects who attacked me." She looked up with hard eyes. He hurried to explain, "Their photos match. I only used it for this purpose."

"Oh? And if I check your history, will I find you made any searches relating to the current murder investigation?"

He froze up, his mouth hanging open. "Oh crap…yes, actually. I searched Silvana…the woman I'm seeing."

"Just her?"

"…and her family. But it wasn't about the investigation, I swear."

The captain shook her head. "I'm revoking your use of the database."

Jason was silent. He didn't react at all. Internally he thought, *God, what is with this woman? It's like Jekyll and Hyde.*

"This is just to avoid suspicion with Lynch and Cole. Again, it's not a punishment."

He understood. But it didn't make him feel any better. "Yes,

Captain."

"Is that all you wanted to tell me, officer?"

"Yes ma'am."

"Dismissed."

Jason left the office with his fists clenched. He made his way back to his desk and sat down to spend the rest of the day doing meaningless admin.

Chapter 17

The day had been a disappointment. The detectives released Timothy Harrison without pressing charges, and the captain had asked Jason to let it go. Meanwhile he had wasted a day on the job when he should have been tracking down Kathryn and Rion. Again, the captain had told him that someone else would look into it.

When he tried to leave at the end of the day, his captain asked him to leave his gun in his locker. "Just as a precaution," she said. "I don't want Lynch getting any more obsessed with you."

Jason agreed with a flat, "Yes ma'am."

She reassured him once more that it wasn't a punishment, yet he couldn't help feeling like he was very deliberately being made the enemy here.

At least Silvana had texted him throughout the day. He hadn't had time to reply much but it was comforting to find messages from her waiting for him on his breaks. She'd asked about his journey to becoming a police officer. He was all too happy to share his ambitions of becoming a detective and she seemed interested. It left him feeling giddy.

Jason stopped at the grocery store on the way home to pick up food for Silvana's date. He was so focused on seeing her again when he suddenly looked up to find himself at the store entrance. He stopped in place. *What the hell am I here for?* He hadn't decided on a menu at all. He didn't even know what she liked. He'd been so preoccupied about texting her.

Although…maybe he should text her again. He had to ask about food, after all.

He had a big goofy grin on his face when he opened his phone. There was a message waiting for him.

"Hey dude. What are you up to tonight?"

Jason read it twice. What the hell? What was Silvana referring to? Was he missing something…

It was from Peter. Jason hadn't even noticed the name in his excitement.

Oh great. He really should have told Peter he was bringing someone over. And yet, if Peter was still interested in Silvana, maybe…he shouldn't tell him? Jason let out a groan. He hated lying, even when the situation needed it, but he texted back, *"I'm working overtime tonight. Probably do a gym session too. Won't be home till late."*

Jason felt gross in his stomach. He didn't bother messaging Silvana and instead just threw several types of red meat and spice in his basket and went through the checkout. By then Peter had messaged back.

"Really? I asked Silvana if she wanted to hang out and she said she's busy. You sure you two aren't hanging out? Cause I could chaperone you this time, yeah?"

Jason felt an instant stab of annoyance. He took a deep breath before he replied. *"Sorry, Pete. Maybe she was just being polite."* He left it there, holding back several more savage comebacks. Jason passed through checkout while waiting for another reply from Peter, but none came.

Wait, if Peter was asking out Silvana, then maybe it's because he's free tonight. Does that mean he might be home? So he whipped out his phone and texted, *"What about you, buddy? What are you up to tonight?"*

Jason drove home. Another text from Peter was waiting when he arrived.

"Studying, since apparently there's fuck all else to do. Some uni friends are doing a study group and dinner, so I guess I'll tag along. Apparently they're doing dinner at a pub called 'The West Hoe'. How good is that? You know I can't say no to a good hoe. ;)"

Jason breathed a sigh of relief. *"That's awesome, man. Have a good time. Let me know if the pub is any good."* He put it in his pocket and went upstairs to his home.

The apartment was just as he left it. Everything had been moved out of place by the detectives search. He still checked through the rooms to make sure nothing else had been moved, then he locked the doors and windows, just to be safe. It bugged him that everything was out of order, yet he had to admit that the place still *looked* neat. Silvana wouldn't even notice all the little things.

He started unpacking his food and setting it up to sizzle on the frying pan. Thoughts of work were running circles in his head, and he still seethed with frustration from the captain assigning him useless filler-tasks. He tried to put those thoughts aside, not wanting his work frustrations to put a damper on the date. He started thinking of Silvana.

She was much nicer to think about.

He remembered the way she stood between him and the mob, fists clenched at her side, hair swaying with the momentum of her speed, and screaming in defiance. *God, she was sexy in that moment.*

But also dangerous. She was strong enough to face off against an entire mob. He still didn't know enough about her family, her history, or her involvement with the death of Alex Bishop.

She also seemed so reserved around her family, like she was on her best behaviour and not really being herself. He had seen glimpses of the real her, and he liked what he was seeing. Why was she so different with her family? It could be a part of her traditional views. Her obedient and submissive attitude came from a culture and a past life she had lived long before Jason was born. He tried to be open minded about it, but if he were honest with himself, he hated it with every fibre of his being. He also knew there was so much more to Silvana. Deep down he knew she was capable of breaking the shackles of her past life. He pictured her fighting off the mob again. *Oh yeeeah…*

Maybe that should be his goal tonight. Instead of interrogating her for more information about her history and family, he could find out who the real Silvana was when she wasn't trying to please everyone. What did she really want in life? What made her happy?

Someone knocked on the door, and Jason found himself smiling. He wiped his hands clean, threw a tea-towel over his shoulder for effect, smiled brightly and straightened his posture as he opened the door.

Silvana had arrived, dressed in tight fitting jeans and a t-shirt with an iconic blue police box on the front. She carried a cold bag that looked way too heavy for someone of her stature to carry so easily, and her hair was tied up in a bun. It was the first time Jason had seen it pulled away from her face. It made her features seem more angular. Stronger. Almost battle-ready.

Silvana was smiling and her cheeks were slightly flushed. "You look very handsome," she said.

Jason looked down. He was only wearing jeans and a loose t-shirt. It wasn't flattering. Come to think of it, he hadn't even showered after work. *Damn, I'm a slob.*

"You look amazing," he blurted out.

It was true. Her clothes were tight enough to show her slim waist and the curve of her hips.

Jason realised he was staring. He cleared his throat and felt his cheeks grow warm. "I've got dinner cooking."

"What?" Silvana asked. They looked at each other, and Jason finally noticed the cold bag she carried.

"Oh…you were gonna cook!" He slapped his forehead. "I completely forgot! I'm so sorry."

"Jason, it's alright."

"I swear, this wasn't a passive aggressive act."

"No really, I don't mind. We don't have to eat my food."

"We still can if you like. I mean, if you wanted to cook…"

Silvana gifted him a warm smile. "I'm sure that whatever you're cooking is just as…"

The smoke alarm went off.

"God fucking…" Jason ran into the kitchen and snatched the frying pan off the stove top. He snatched the spatula and flipped the steaks. They made a satisfying loud sizzle as the red side touched the pan, although the top side was lined with black. He set the pan down and grabbed a towel to start waving at the fire alarm to dissipate the smoke.

Silvana was opening one of the windows. Jason gave her a sheepish grin. "I hope you like chargrilled."

"I love chargrilled," she said with total sincerity, and Jason felt all the shame and embarrassment fade away.

Someone banged on the front door. Jason let out a sigh. "Probably one of the neighbours," he said. He stepped out of the kitchen to open the front door. "Sorry, just cooking…"

It was Peter.

"What?" Jason cried.

"Oh hey roomie," Peter said with a grin. He was wearing pink shorts and a Hawaiian shirt with the first two buttons undone, exposing his hairless chest. "Fancy seeing you here."

"I…was just…"

"I thought you were out tonight. You didn't…lie to me did you?"

Jason felt his chest tighten and his breathing grow more difficult. He never lied. How had he let himself be caught out so quickly? He was too flustered to even speak.

"And Silvana!" Peter called, his smile growing even wider. "So nice to see you again. You're not busy tonight, are you?"

Peter stepped around Jason's broad frame and entered the apartment. He stood in the middle of the living space, breathed in deeply and clapped his hands. "That actually smells pretty good. I hope you've got enough for three."

Jason and Silvana exchanged a nervous glance.

"Peter," Silvana said while clenching one of her hands. "Jason and I were having a private dinner tonight, just the two of us."

"That's fine. I'll be your chaperone." Peter winked at her.

Jason was barely holding back his annoyance. His frustration helped him squash down the guilt he felt. "What are you doing here, Peter?" Jason asked as he moved back to the kitchen to fix up the frying pan.

"I live here."

"Yeah, but you were at uni tonight."

"Well, call me crazy, but I was a bit concerned when a got a text message alert saying my home was on fire." He drawled. "What's that saying? Liar, liar, apartment on fire?"

Jason ignored his jibe. "You would have only received that text message a few seconds ago. How'd you get back here so quickly?"

Peter laughed. "I was already coming back to get changed. I'm not going out to dinner in a Hawaiian shirt. It's bloody cold at night."

"Uh-huh."

"But I guess I can cancel those plans. Those guys suck anyway." He offered another charming smile. "So what are you cooking?" Peter tried to step around Jason to get into the kitchen. Jason didn't move. "It smells good, mate. Do you need some help?"

"No."

Peter laughed. "All right, chef, I won't interfere. This will be fun, just the three of us. As I recall, we got along fine last time."

"Look, Peter," Silvana said. "Would you mind giving us the night together, just Jason and I?"

"Oh don't be like that." Peter turned to face her directly. "Look, I feel really bad for how I acted the other night. I just want a chance to smooth things over. How's this; Jason will be chef, and I'll be the waiter."

"It's alright, Peter, we don't need your help," Silvana said with gentle firmness.

"Ok, Jason can do all the work then." Peter laughed on his own. He seemed to notice the mood in the room at last, so he turned to Silvana. "Look, I'm hoping we can still be friends. You're a special girl, Silvana. And even if you don't want to date me anymore, I'd still like to see you from time to time."

Silvana was blinking rapidly. Her shoulders were set high and her eyes flicked towards Jason. So he stepped in and took her hand.

"Another time, Pete," Jason said. "We'll catch a movie together. Just not tonight, ok buddy?"

He patted Peter on the shoulder and gave him a gentle nudge towards the door. Peter's lip twisted like he was about to argue but instead he gave another smile.

"That'd be great, Jase. Maybe next weekend. Isn't there a superhero movie out at the moment?"

"There's always a superhero movie," Jason said.

"All right, sorry for crashing your party. I'll be out of your hair in a second." Peter stepped past them and went into his room without another word. Jason went back to the stovetop and Silvana sat quietly at the table, scrolling through her phone. A few minutes later Peter came out again in long trousers and a jumper. No one acknowledged him, and he took the hint.

"Have a good night," he said, though with a noticeably frosty tone.

"You too," said Silvana.

"Thanks Pete. I appreciate this," Jason said.

Peter didn't say anything else and abruptly the door shut with more force than necessary. They waited until they heard the sound of footsteps moving down the hall.

Jason set a plate down in front of Silvana. "Bon appétit!" he said

"Ah, je suis sûr que je le ferai."

"Of course you speak French."

"Oui!"

The two plates each had a single rump steak with extra chargrill on one side, spiced with black pepper and rosemary, with a side of steamed potatoes and broccoli. It was a modest meal, though Jason did not reveal it was literally the best cooking he was capable of.

"This is genuinely amazing," Silvana said. "I can't thank you enough."

"Thanks. Um…I think it's safe to say you're probably the better cook."

Silvana shrugged. "To be fair, I've had more time to practice. May I pour you some wine?"

"Great idea."

She deftly uncorked the bottle and poured out the red wine with a flourish. For a moment it looked like blood, in Jason's mind. Then he blinked away the image.

"Merci beaucoup," he attempted to say, though his English accent butchered the pronunciation. It only made Silvana smile more.

They ate in silence. Silvana paid him several more compliments on the food, and he thanked her each time, but it never evolved into a conversation. He was furiously trying to think of something to say. Since they weren't talking much, Jason ended up eating most of his meal in a few short minutes. Afterwards, he felt so awkward that he decided to just be direct.

"Can you tell me about yourself?"

Silvana blinked. "Um…what exactly?"

"I'm not sure. Anything?"

She stared at him. "Well, that doesn't give me much to work with." She laughed and it sounded entirely strained. "All right. Well, I speak French."

"Yeah. That's pretty cool." He could've slapped himself. *Pretty cool? Come on, man.* "So are you fluent?"

"Technically, yes. But any French person can tell I'm not a native speaker. There's a wide gap between fluent and native. Do you speak any other languages?"

"I did Spanish in school. Don't remember much."

"Ah. Well, my French is out of date." She shrugged. "I learnt it during the 40s. I speak like an old person. At least with English, I know how to deformalize. I can use more slang, sound more natural. 'Sup!" she grinned and casually took another sip of wine.

"Oh very natural."

"Thanks. It's hard though, because a lot of other immortals still use Shakespearian English. And some of the really old ones speak what's known as 'Middle English'. If I spend too much time in immortal circles, I start sounding weird."

Jason nodded thoughtfully. "Interesting. Do some of them speak Latin?"

She didn't seem impressed like he expected. "Latin died in the sixth century. About four hundred years before the oldest living immortal was born. It's a dead language even for us."

"Right. Sorry." He took another mouthful of wine, and the topic trailed off again.

"I've got to say," Silvana said, "I'm a little disappointed by the bruises on your face."

Jason nearly groaned. He'd forgotten all about the elixir and hadn't tried to cover his bruises better. "Oh…sorry about that. I appreciate you giving me the elixir and all, but…"

"It clearly didn't work properly."

"Uh…yeah."

Silvana shook her head. "I'm sorry. I won't buy from that alchemist again."

"Oh there's no need—"

"It's fine. I'm not sure I like him anyway, he's too difficult to deal with. And his potions are a little inconsistent with results."

Jason was intrigued. He knew he had decided to focus on Silvana tonight, but now he had to ask. "So…alchemists. Are they like magicians or something?" Silvana frowned at him like he'd just said something dumb. "Oh right. You're not allowed to tell me."

She softened. "Yeah. But I should though. I didn't tell you about physically enhanced immortals, and it nearly killed you. I should tell you about mentally enhanced."

"Just in case I run into a wizard, hey?" Jason smirked.

She did not smirk back. "Don't even joke about that. Wizards are terrifying."

"Oh." Jason wanted to laugh it off. But the look on Silvana's face told him not to. "Hmm. So the guy who made my elixir is a wizard?"

Silvana shook her head. "Alchemists, witches and wizards are three completely different things."

"Oh." He blinked a few times. "So one does potions, and the other two are magicians?"

She offered him a pained smile, and he knew he'd made yet another ignorant statement. He decided to stop trying to guess and just listen.

"First of all, a potion is just the ingredients in the cauldron. Alchemists actually combine potions with magic to create elixirs.

They're extremely difficult to make, very rare and very expensive. That's why no mortal can create elixirs by accident. There's a magical component."

"Right. And the magicians?"

"You probably think all witches are women, and all wizards are men, right?" Jason nodded. "Yep. That's a common mortal mistake. Ever since King Arthur, you've all thought wizards were like Merlin and witches were like Morgan le'Fay. But there's nothing gendered about it. Witches are more like doctors. They use magic to heal and both men and women can be witches." She smiled. "You know, technically I'm a witch."

"You are? A vampire and a witch?"

She laughed. "I'm joking. I haven't studied magical arts because you can't be two types of immortal species. But I've studied mortal medicine. So you could say I'm a witch because I heal." She waved her hand in a self-deprecating way. "Witches don't just heal. They're all about using subtle magic, like curses on a family line or haunted houses. They do all the weird stuff."

"Interesting. So what do the wizards do?"

Silvana grew very still. When she spoke, there was a gravity to her voice. *She sounds genuinely afraid.* "Wizards are also men and women. And they're the best of us. They are the strongest of all immortals. It's the wizards who rule the Immortal Imperium."

Jason realised his hands were nervously tapping the table, so he cupped them together to keep them still. "What makes wizards so powerful?"

"Their magic. It's not subtle like witches, it's direct. Their magic is awesome and terrifying. A wizard is a one-man army. Some of the older wizards could stand against the world's biggest militaries on their own."

"You're joking again."

"I'm not."

"But that's only old militaries, right? Knights and horses. Surely not the modern military?" She just stared at him flatly.

"Really?"

"Yes, Jason. That's why everyone respects the Imperium. The wizards have the power to enforce their rules." She leaned over the table and whispered, "That's why I obey the vampire laws about marriage. The Imperium has a police force of sorts, known as the Vigiles. They are wizard enforcers. No one can challenge a Vigile."

Jason had been considering getting seconds, yet now, he was no longer hungry. He took a long sip of his wine to help calm his nerves. He felt like his mind was struggling to believe this, in the same way he had struggled to believe everything about vampires. To help himself process this information, he went into detective mode.

"So what can wizards actually do with their magic?"

"Honestly, I'm not sure. They don't exactly hand out textbooks on what they can do. I know they can summon things to them, or move objects. A bit like the force, in Star Wars."

"That's concerning."

"Some wizards can change the weather. Others can cause natural disasters like earthquakes and hurricanes."

"That's... very concerning."

"But that's all I know. The wizards guard their teaching materials carefully. No one knows where they get their power from. But we do know that all their power comes from speaking. They cast spells using ancient words. If a wizard had a hand over their mouth, they'd be powerless."

"Well, that's something. But what are these ancient words? Could anyone say them?"

"No. The words only work if a wizard says them. The words themselves don't have power."

"What makes it different when the wizard says them?"

"No idea!" she shrugged helplessly. "That's why they guard their secrets. In all of human history, no one has ever become a wizard on their own. You cannot discover magic. You have to be taught the secrets by an existing wizard."

"Then who taught the first wizard?" Jason said with a laugh.

"God."

He blinked. "Excuse me."

"Well, that's what the mortals call him. Every immortal knows that the first wizard was a man called Zapherahlious Amphearados."

"Zaff…what?"

"Zapherahlious Amphearahdos. The first wizard. He discovered the first magic words, and we believe he then created the other immortal races. Some immortal theologians believe that Zapherahlious became known as God, and the first immortal races were Adam and Eve."

Jason sat back in his chair. "My head hurts."

She laughed at him. "Sorry, that was probably a bit too much information. You just asked about elixirs."

He tried to push his flurry of thoughts aside. "I know. But I got distracted too. I was actually trying to ask about you."

"Oh."

"We got so far as 'you speak French.'"

They laughed, both a little nervously, and some of the tension left the room. Jason got up and closed the window. The sky was dark outside and distant car horns and music played from the street. He realised he was searching the shadows for signs of someone watching.

"I'm sorry," Silvana said as she collected the plates and carried them to the sink. "I guess I'm a little uncomfortable talking about myself. I think I steered the conversation away from me on purpose."

"Why is that?"

She gave an awkward smile as she started washing the dishes by hand. "I don't know. I just prefer to talk about other people. I like to help others."

"I can see that." He pointed to her cleaning, and she blushed. Jason cleared down the table while carefully thinking through his next words. "I think you might be one of those people who spend their whole life helping others and forget to help yourself."

"Oh I'm definitely one of those people!" she said with a laugh.

"I understand. It's just that if we are to, you know… 'fall in love and get married'," he said with quotation marks. Yet she looked back at him with a glimmer of hope in her eye. He realised how serious this was for her. Literally life and death. He spoke gravely. "I need to know the real you."

"Jason. I'll be whatever you need me to be."

"But that's not fair to you. I don't want you to have to wear a mask every day for my benefit." She looked away. It seemed like he was getting through to her, so he kept going. "I believe all parties in a relationship should be equals. They should be a team. They win or lose as a team, not as individuals competing against each other. I would rather you be honest about what you want in life, and not just agree with me on everything."

Silvana looked up at him sharply, a sudden intensity in her eyes. "You don't really want that."

"Yes, I do! Silvana, be honest with me. What do you want in life? What do you want right now, more than anything?"

She's probably going to say 'your blood'.

Silvana stared back, looking hungry. "What do I want?" she asked. Then she leaned across the kitchen counter and whispered.

"I want to fuck."

Chapter 18

Silvana was blushing. Or at least, blushing as much as was possible for a vampire. At the same time, she did not seem to regret what she said.

"If I am being completely honest," she said, "all I want right now is to have sex with you. And I *really* want it."

Jason found himself nodding along, even as his mouth hung open. "Well…um…thank you. I mean, thanks for being honest." He ran his hands through his hair. *Holy crap, that was unexpected.* "Ok then. So um…" he gave a laugh, "tell me why? I mean, why is sex all you want right now? Is that a vampire thing?"

"Of course not," she drawled. "Look, I'm going to be completely honest, since that's what you want."

"Ok…"

"My family gave me some very strict rules when searching for my husband. The first rule was don't talk about my previous husband. It's considered off-putting and bad form. And the second rule was don't sleep with him until the marriage and blood-sharing is official. Otherwise he might not stay."

"I see. So no sex before marriage? You vampires really are traditional."

She rolled her eyes as she turned back to the sink and started washing the cooking instruments Jason had used. He just stood in the kitchen entrance and watched.

"I want to break the second rule. And to explain why, I need to break the first rule too." She paused to think through her words, and Jason gave her space to do it. "Arthur was seventy-two years old when he died."

Jason nodded. *I can see where this is going.*

"He wasn't a very healthy man. He had heart and liver problems for years. By the end, he was basically surviving on elixirs alone. If he'd relied on modern medicine, he would have undergone multiple bypass surgeries." She sighed. "It was horrible. I spent years watching him destroy his health with drinking, smoking, poor living. And he got furious if I ever tried to help."

"I'm sorry."

Silvana tried to smile as she blinked back the faint moisture in her eyes. "All that to say, when we were together, he wasn't exactly… active."

"Oh."

"Yeah. So even though I was only widowed forty days ago, it's been a long time since I've enjoyed, you know, anything physical."

Jason was staring at her back while she faced the sink, and he found himself tracing her curves with his eyes. Her jeans and shirt were tight enough to show the rough shape of her body. He was picturing how he could hold her at the hips, how it would feel to press against her, the taste of her mouth, the scent of her sweat…

"Jason?"

He realised the conversation had stopped. "Sorry. Um…" his mind caught up. "So your husband – Arthur – he only died last month?"

"That's right."

"My god. I guess I knew you needed blood, but I guess I didn't fully comprehend what that meant."

"I know, I must seem so heartless trying to remarry right away. I've always hated this part of vampirism. But I need the blood." She shrugged helplessly, her eyes avoiding Jason's gaze.

"I understand. But Silvana…have you had a chance to grieve?"

"Oh, I've grieved enough. Arthur was dying for nearly two years. He didn't have any quality of life, and he suffered towards the end." She shook her head, but couldn't stop a single tear falling from each eye. "He had multiple cardiac events. This may sound harsh, but honestly, it was kind of a relief when he finally passed."

"Sure, I can understand that. But you must feel some kind of sadness."

"Well, yes. I do feel sadness. And you know how I want to cope with that sadness?" She finally turned to face him and took a single, confident step in his direction. "I want intimacy. I want someone to hold me. I want you to touch me."

Jason felt his heartrate increasing, and his body responded with a flush of heat. She was beautiful. And he wanted that intimacy too. He craved it.

"But it's more than that," Silvana said. "I'm not just pent up and desperate cause it's been a while. It's you, Jason. It's being around you. Looking at you…it drives me crazy. You are…" she shuddered, "…gorgeous."

"What?" Jason was genuinely surprised. He knew he was in good shape, but that was just fitness for his line of work. He never thought of himself as gorgeous.

"You're just so masculine, but not in an over-the-top way. You have good shoulders, you're tall, and you've got a great arse."

Jason stared back. Then blurted, "*You* have a great arse!"

He wanted to take the words back, until he saw the way her face lit up.

"The only question is," Silvana said, "do you want me?"

"Of course! I have eyes, don't I?" She blushed at him. "But I don't want to confuse things for you…"

"Jason, it's alright. Look, don't worry about marriage right now. Don't worry about tomorrow. Just…tonight…I want you. Is that ok?"

They stood motionless, staring at each other as if nothing else in the world mattered in this moment.

He reached up and cupped her face, trying to be gentle. Suddenly she came forward and kissed his mouth.

Her skin was cold to touch. Jason almost forgot to kiss back. Their bodies were still apart, their heads leaned forward so their lips would reach. Then her hands gripped the back of his head. He grabbed her hips and pulled them against his own. Their bodies finally touched. Jason felt himself coming alive in response. He kissed her harder. He stepped back long enough to rip his shirt off.

She leaned back to take in the sight of him. "The bench works for me."

He stuttered, "I have a bed."

"That's the hottest thing you've said all night."

He felt her eyes lingering on him as he took her hand and lead her into his bedroom. Then he saw his police uniform still on the bed. "Sorry, I didn't expect anyone to see this room tonight."

"Oh no, there's clothes all over the room," she said coyly, biting her lip.

She grabbed her shirt at the bottom corners and lifted it over her head, dropping it on the ground. "Oh no, I made it worse," she cried, pausing as if waiting for him to laugh. But Jason was staring fixated at her plain-white bra. "Oops, forgot a piece," she said. A second later the bra came undone and fell to the floor next to her shirt.

Silvana tucked her hands into her jeans pockets, and tilted her hips to the side. She eyed him with expectation.

"You look amazing," he whispered, and she stretched out, arching her back to display herself.

Look how confident she's become. That confidence, more than anything, was driving Jason wild. His pants were already bulging at the crotch.

"Fuck," he muttered.

"You seem surprised?" she said with a laugh, gesturing to his pants. "Were you not expecting…"

"Kinda, yeah!"

She blinked in surprise, her eyes wincing as if hurt. He rushed to explain. "You know how I have to feel comfortable with someone before I'm attracted to them? Usually that takes a while."

She looked down at the front of his jeans. "So, you feel comfortable with me?"

"Apparently," he said. He stepped forward and gestured at her chest. "May I?"

"Oh, such a gentleman," she cooed, then grabbed his hands at the wrist and forcibly pressed them against her breasts. Jason took hold, pressing in his fingertips just slightly. She was round enough that his hands needed to stretch to hold all of her. He caught a nipple between his thumb and forefinger, and gently squeezed.

"Oh hurry up!" she cried and grabbed his belt buckle. He laughed as she undid his jeans. But instead of pulling them down, she shoved her hand down the front and pressed her palm against his cock, lacing her fingers around it and squeezing him hard. His whole body let out a shudder.

"Fuck me," he groaned.

"I'm getting to it," she purred in his ear. Her fingers wrapped further around him and started moving back and forth. He clutched at her shoulders, pressing his head against hers. He panted slowly at first, before an involuntary moan slipped free of his lips.

Silvana leaned up to his neck and gave just the tiniest nip with her teeth. *Oh my god, a vampire just nipped my neck.* And yet, Jason felt no fear at all. He felt totally safe with her. At that moment, Jason felt all semblance of self-control vanish.

He grabbed her at the hips and sat her down on the bed. In one move, he gripped her jeans and underwear at the waist and pulled them all the way off. He knelt before her and parted her knees with his shoulders.

"Jason," she cried, putting a gentle hand on his head to stop him. "You don't have to do this."

"I'd really like to. Is that ok?" he asked. She looked at him a moment, then silently moved her hand out of the way. So he lowered his head down and pressed his lips against her. He ran his tongue along her entrance, then focused on a single spot, stroking with a slow, steady rhythm. She started panting, letting out short gasps and rocking her hips in time with his movement. He sped up, and she grabbed the back of his head and pushed him against her.

He looked up at her from between her legs. She was propped up on her elbows, and from this angle, her breasts were positioned to either side of her face. She look down at him, her mouth open as she gasped for breath. Their eyes met, and Jason thought she looked even more gorgeous when making her pleasure face.

"Get on the fucking bed," she hissed.

She clutched him under the armpits and yanked him up onto the bed like he weighed nothing. He rolled over to face her. A moment later she was straddling him. She clutched his cock as she raised her hips, then started to lower herself down.

"Wait!" he gasped. "Protection?"

"Don't need it," she said and prepared to move.

"Wait, stop," Jason cried. Silvana froze in place. "What do you mean, don't need it?"

"It's a vampire thing," she said impatiently. "You won't get me pregnant."

"What about STIs?" he insisted.

"Don't get them either."

Something didn't feel right. Jason moved back on the bed and propped himself up. She appeared earnest, and maybe it was the truth, but it made him uncomfortable.

"I would still like to use a condom," he said. "Is that ok with you?"

Silvana moved her mouth up and down like she wanted to argue. "Ok, Jason. If it makes you feel comfortable, I don't mind."

"Thank you," he said. He grabbed one out of his drawers and quickly slipped it on, rolling it until it felt comfortable. "Ok, I'm read—"

She slid him inside of her.

She was already moving. Her hands grasped at his chest as she rocked her hips. She began to ride him with more energy and aggression than he had ever expected from such a sweet, timid woman. Almost immediately he felt the urge to explode inside her. He bit his tongue and concentrated. *Jason, don't you dare ruin this for her. LAST, damn it, man!*

He grabbed her hips and forced the rhythm to change slightly, moving the pressure so it wasn't so intense for him. She followed his rhythm for a moment, then took over again. Now he could last.

Silvana began to moan, and Jason could feel the sound of her voice pushing him to breaking point again. He had to help her along faster or he wasn't going to make it. So he pressed his thumb down beneath her waistline, and began to rub in time with her motions. His other hand reached around to grab a firm ass cheek and rock her harder. She began to respond to him.

"Oh yes, keep doing that!" she whispered.

She began to move faster. Sweat glistened on her pale skin. Her breasts were shaking with each motion, and at the sight of their bouncing, Jason was certain he couldn't last any longer.

A loud bang made them stop.

Jason sat up slightly, his heart pounding in sudden fear. The banging came again, three loud knocks on the front door. Jason growled. *If that's Peter, I'm going to fucking murder...*

"Jason Turner!" a male's voice roared loudly. "This is the Plymouth Police Department! Open up!"

"Shit!" Jason hissed. It sounded like Detective Lynch. *What the fuck? Oh God, why now!* He unconsciously tried to hold on to Silvana a moment longer, but she leapt off him in an instant and reached for her clothes.

The thumping came again. They were hitting the front door so hard it sounded like they were trying to break it down. Jason was on his feet, pulling on his jeans. "Hang on, I'll be right there!" he shouted, struggling to force his stiff cock back underneath the zipper.

He looked at Silvana. She was watching him closely, still panting heavily, her chest heaving up and down. He bit his lip in frustration. "Sorry," he said, throwing on a shirt before heading to the front door.

The banging came again. "Hold on, I'm coming!" Jason yelled. He unlocked the bolt and turned the handle.

Detective Lynch barged across the landing and snatched Jason by the shoulder, immediately forcing him up against the wall with enough force to knock the breath out of him.

"Hey!" Jason shouted.

Detective Cole appeared beside him, snatched his wrist, and started putting handcuffs on.

"Jason Turner, you are under arrest for the murder of Alex Bishop, and the murder of Richard Anderson."

"Oh, come on, Lynch. You're obsessed with..." he stopped. "Wait... Richard? Who the hell is Richard? Did someone else..."

"Jason!" a woman's voice snapped. Captain Kader stood in the doorway. Her face was like steel. "Don't say anything, officer."

"But…" he stopped himself. "Yes ma'am." He let himself be handcuffed and didn't ask further questions out loud. Internally, he was screaming.

Someone else must have been murdered. But why do they think it's me? Fuck, Lynch you're such an asshole. Jason knew he had an alibi and it would just be a matter of explaining. This would be ok.

Silvana came into the hallway. "What's going on?" she cried. Everyone was quiet as they looked at her. She was fully clothed. And yet her hair was ruffled and her belt buckle was undone.

"He's under arrest for two accounts of murder," Lynch answered. "We're taking him to the station to process him."

"What?" she cried. "But he didn't murder anyone! I swear it!"

Cole moved to stand before her. "You let us figure that out, girl," she snapped. "Don't interfere. We have jurisdiction here. If you make any attempt to stop us, we'll have to arrest you too."

Silvana scowled, but didn't move.

"It's ok, Silvana," Jason said. "I'll text you in 24 hours, when they let me out because they can't prove anything."

"Turner!" Captain Kader growled. "Shut up!"

Jason bowed his head. He looked back at Silvana for a brief moment, before Lynch and Cole escorted him out of his apartment.

Chapter 19

"Where were you last night, between the hours of midnight and three a.m.?" Cole asked.

"In bed, asleep."

"Can anyone verify your whereabouts?" Lynch asked. "What about your housemate, Erikson?"

"He wasn't home."

"Interesting." Detective Lynch stalked around the dark interrogation room and stood behind Jason. "So it sounds like you have no alibi for the murder of Richard Anderson."

"Ok first of all," Jason growled, "no one who's single ever has an alibi for between midnight and three a.m. And second, I don't even know who that is!"

Detective Cole reached into a duffle bag and pulled out a handgun, wrapped in a plastic evidence case. "Is this your gun, Officer Turner?"

He barely kept his face under control. Seeing his gun in plastic and a label looked pretty damn official, like they were building up to hard evidence. He had to stay calm or it would only look worse for him.

"Yes. A Glock 17, standard issue. So that's why the captain asked me to leave it here, so you could test it. So? What'd you find?"

"Forensics show that your gun has fired three bullets in the last few days. Is that correct?"

Jason hesitated. "Ok, yes, that is true. The first bullet was fired the night Alex Bishop broke into Silvana's house. I escorted him out. When he became belligerent, I fired a warning shot into the woods, injuring no one. And the other two bullets, I fired last night into the air to help dispel the mob at Silvana's house."

"How convenient," Lynch said. He was still somewhere behind Jason, just out of his peripheral vision. Jason knew he was only looming in the shadows behind him to make him feel uneasy, but damn it, it still worked. He felt like a blow was going to hit the back of his head any second.

"You know what I think?" Cole said, leaning back in her chair as if unbothered by the whole proceeding. "I think you got mad that Alex Bishop threatened your girlfriend. So you followed him home and fired exactly one bullet into his head. And the other two bullets, you fired in Richard Anderson's heart and lung."

"I do not know who Richard Anderson is!"

"And I suppose Timothy Harrison was going to take the fall for you."

"What?!"

"That's why you brought him in to the station. Filled out a false report about how Mr Harrison attacked you with a sledgehammer. All to make him look like the violent man."

"That report was the truth!"

"Too bad for you, forensics have traced the bullets back to your gun."

"What are you talking about!?" Jason was shouting now. He was letting Cole rile him up far too easily. If he kept acting emotional, it would only make him look guilty. He lowered his voice, "Can you please just tell me who Richard is? I swear I will answer all your questions and fully cooperate. I just don't understand who you're referring to."

Lynch stalked around the table, his arms crossed tightly over his broad chest. Jason swallowed. Lynch made eye contact with Cole for a moment. Neither of them said anything, or even moved, but Lynch let out a sigh and nodded. Cole reached into her bag, pulled out a manila folder and threw it down on the table before Jason.

"Open it," she drawled when he merely looked at the cover. Jason navigated his handcuffs and managed to flip it open.

A picture of a dead body was inside, bloody and graphic. It was a man in only his undershorts. He lay on his back, with two bullet holes in his chest. And just like Alex Bishop, his body was pasty and white. Completely drained of blood.

"Look familiar?" Cole asked.

Jason picked up the photo. His eyes narrowed in on the man's face. *He does look familiar. Where have I seen this man?* He studied the short stubble on the man's cheeks and the wisp of long hair covering his face. In fact, he had unusually long hair that was only just visible beneath his prone body. It looked like it reached past his shoulders…

The man with the ponytail!

"I've seen this man!" Jason cried.

"We thought so."

"Not like that. He was at the mansion last night," Jason went on. "He had a sledgehammer. He was trying to break down the front door. He gave the weapon to Timothy when I arrived." Jason looked up at the detectives and shrugged. "He ran away when all the others did. I didn't see him after that."

"Well, his landlord did," Lynch sneered. "Found him dead the next morning."

Jason looked up. "So that's what you two were out investigating today." He blinked. "And that's why Captain Kader had me confined to a desk all day. So you could verify my whereabouts at all times."

"Nice job, detective," Cole scoffed. "We shouldn't have let you go home, but forensics took all day to match the bullets to your gun."

"Match the bullets?"

"That's right. The three bullets used to murder our two victims all came from your gun. And we noticed your Glock 17 – named for the 17 bullets it carries – currently only has 14."

Jason scoffed. "That doesn't make any sense. I fired those bullets into the air."

"We have hard evidence, Turner," Lynch growled. "We know where you fired those bullets."

Jason was starting to panic. He'd told them the truth, and they wouldn't believe him. What else was there to say? How had they even got this evidence? None of this made sense.

I'm in deep shit now.

"Look, I don't know what to tell you. I only saw Richard in passing. We never said a word to each other. I don't even know where he lives."

"Then do you care to explain how three bullets from your gun were found in these two dead bodies?"

Jason threw up his hands, his anger bubbling to the surface. "I have no idea! Unless forensics made a mistake."

"That's not possible," Lynch snapped. His nostrils were flaring and his fists were clenched tight. Detective Cole had beads of sweat pooling around her hairline. They were convinced he was guilty, and they were desperate for a confession. But Jason didn't have one.

"I swear to God, I never fired my weapon at Alex Bishop or Richard Anderson."

"So, you think it was magic?" Cole seethed between clenched teeth.

Jason opened his mouth to shoot back a smart-ass retort, but he froze.

Oh my god.

Oh my god!

COULD it be magic?!

Holy fuck...

His mouth dropped open. The possibility of magic changed everything. Three days ago, he would have laughed at Cole even making that suggestion. But now, given what he'd learnt about vampires and skinwalkers and wizards, anything could be possible. Had someone magically stolen his gun both nights and returned it to his possession without his knowledge? Had someone planted his bullets in the bodies? He just didn't know. He was way out of his league here.

The corner of Lynch's lip pulled up into a sneer. "That's got you rattled. Are you scared of magic, Jason? Is this part of your fascination with the supernatural? Why you questioned me about it at Alex Bishops murder scene? Do you believe in fairies?"

"It's not that," Jason said.

"I think you struck a nerve, Lynch," Cole said, smiling for the first time Jason had ever seen. She looked almost sweet, but Jason knew she was dangerous. "Let's talk about your buddies. These 'fairies'. Have you attended any meetings at Timothy Harrison's house?"

"What? No, I haven't attended *meetings.*"

"Really? So you've never heard of the Mohos?"

Jason shrugged. "That's correct."

"But you've been interacting with their members all week."

"What?!" he growled. "I have no idea what you're talking about. Mohos? Is that a cocktail?"

Lynch sighed, and it sounded like he was frustrated by something. "The Mohos are an international movement. More like a cult, if you ask me. They're all...paranormal investigators looking for supernatural signs. Like bigfoot, loch ness, UFOs."

"Ah, the mob from Silvana's house. They're...Mohos? What's the name stand for?"

"Mohos stands for Monster Hunters," Cole added.

Jason smirked. "Hunters doesn't have an O."

"I think you're expecting far too much intelligence from these people," Lynch drawled. "In the last few months, a branch of Mohos has started meeting here in Plymouth. Your pal Timothy Harrison is their organiser. And you know who else has been attending their meetings?"

Jason gave a knowing 'ah' sound. "Alex Bishop, and Richard Anderson."

"Bingo. So now there are two dead members of this cult. How do you think this bunch of whack-jobs are going to react, huh?"

"Geez…"

"But that's exactly what you wanted, isn't it, Jason?" Lynch stood beside him now, his hands on the table. "You want these crazies to go loco."

"No, I don't. I've never heard of this group before now."

"Are you working alone?" Lynch asked. "Or is Mr Erikson helping you? What about Ms Clarke?"

"No one's helping me with anything. I'm not a vigilante. I'm not trying to fight the Mohos because I don't care about them one way or another."

"Oh, I think you do." Lynch bent lower over the table. "You *hate* the Mohos. You know why?" He came down so his face was centimetres away from Jason's own. "Because they remind you of daddy."

Jason inhaled sharply. "Don't, Lynch."

"It's true. Most of the Mohos are middle-aged men, desperate and lonely. They've become so disenchanted with the world that they've joined a cult cause they're looking for an enemy. They want someone to blame for why their own lives have gone to shit."

Jason turned away. He felt his anger burning. *He's trying to get to me. Hold it together.*

"Alex was divorced. Richard was newly separated, and his wife had taken the kids. And Timothy has several domestic violence reports filed against him. You recognise the MO, don't you? Sad, pathetic men who feel powerless. So they turn against those closest to them, those who seem weak, and push them down to make themselves feel better."

"I'm familiar with that behaviour," Jason snapped.

"I bet you are. That's why you hate the Mohos. You want to hurt them. Kill them. So they can't do…what your daddy did."

"This isn't about my father!" Jason snapped. "This has nothing to do with him."

"It has everything to do with him!" Lynch roared back, getting right into Jason's face with open aggression now. "You hate that man. He took everything from you. And now you're going to stop that from happening to the families of Mohos. You're going to stop these violent, dangerous men, and you'll take the law into your own hands to do it."

"That's not true!"

"Isn't it? You've already killed two men. Congratulations Jason, you've become your father after—"

"SHUT UP!" Jason screamed. He stood up and shoved the detective with his shoulder. If he wasn't handcuffed to the table, he would have punched Lynch in the face. "Shut the fuck up! *Shut the fuck up!*"

His cheeks were warm and wet. Jason realised he was crying.

He couldn't speak with the sobs choking off his voice. *Oh god…* Jason turned aside and buried his face in his upper arm. He was gasping for every breath, and no matter how much he tried, he couldn't stop himself from openly weeping in front of the detectives.

Mum…I'm so sorry! I should have stopped him! I should have done something!

He vaguely heard the door open, and Captain Kader stepping into the room. "Think it's time for a break, detectives," she said in a passive-aggressive tone. "It's gonna be a long night. Who's going on the first coffee run?"

"You're not needed here, Aisha," Lynch said coldly. "We're investigating…"

Kader talked over the top of him, "I'm going to pretend you didn't just call your captain by their first name, Detective Lynch." Her voice lowered to a dangerous level. "Now go get me a coffee, like a good little bitch."

Jason finally looked up, wiping his eyes. His breathing was still jagged, though he had mostly calmed down. He saw Captain Kader, staring at Lynch with an air of utter surety. Lynch only glared back at her with a gaze of icy fire. The detective growled under his breath, then growled in a low voice, "Do you have sugar in yours, captain?"

"Two, please and thank you."

He stormed out of the room, with Cole following silently a second later. The door shut with a bang and Jason let out a sigh of relief. The captain moved to sit opposite him.

"You ok?" she asked.

He nodded and wiped the moisture from his face with the back of his sleeve. "I can't believe I reacted like that."

"Lynch and Cole are good detectives. They're experts at getting under your skin."

"But I'm a professional," Jason insisted. "I've had therapy. Hell, I passed my psych test at the academy. I don't understand why I freaked out. All he had to do was mention my father, and I've had a full-blown breakdown." He turned to face the captain. "What's wrong with me?"

She didn't answer. Only stared at him with dark, warm eyes.

"How do you recover?" he asked her. "How do you become normal? I've spent years trying to move beyond this. But just a few words hit every trigger, and I lost all control. Do you see now why I didn't arrest Alex Bishop that night? Cause apparently I'm too emotional to do my job right."

"Ok, that's enough self-pity, officer." Kader sat back in her chair with her arms crossed. "You experienced trauma. That never goes away. Yes, you may carry that scar with you forever, but you don't have to be a victim forever. Your trauma will either make you bitter or make you empathetic. It depends on how you chose to act."

"Yes, I know," Jason sighed. It was the kind of thing he'd heard a few times now. "I know I'll live a good life and make it all worth it."

"No," Kader said, and he looked up sharply. "Nothing you do will ever make all the pain *worth* it. No one can ever deserve to suffer like you did. What you have now is a chance to bring some good out of a bad situation. But it's not your responsibility to justify why the pain had to happen. Because it did not have to happen. And it should not have."

Jason studied her for a moment. "Thanks for believing me."

"Whoa now, I never said I believed you."

"But you're helping me?"

"I'm being nice to you. I'm also waiting until the case is solved before I make any judgements. It's possible you and I will still have to work together after this. It's also possible you'll go to jail. I'm just covering all my bases." Her tone was hard as iron, even as she gave a friendly wink.

"Right…"

She leaned forward and lowered her voice. "Can you honestly tell me how bullets from your gun ended up in our two victims?"

He sighed. "I wish I could. I truly have no idea how that could have happened."

Kader just looked at him for a full minute of long silence. Finally she said, "All right. I'll ask Lynch and Cole not to charge you for the murders yet. I think the forensic evidence of the bullets alone is inconclusive. They need to prove you were at the locations, otherwise it's only your gun that was there."

"Thank you, Captain."

"That said, the detectives can still keep you here for 24 hours. Knowing Lynch, he'll keep you here for the full 24 hours just because he's a stubborn ass. And he'll try to break you. But after that, he'll have to let you go. You just have to last that time."

"I understand. Thank you, captain."

"Don't thank me yet. Let's see if you can survive 24 hours with Lynch."

"Yes ma'am."

"And if more evidence comes forward, showing you did commit these crimes, I will have your head on a goddamn platter."

She stood up and left the room, offering a brief, "Good luck," before she shut the door.

Chapter 20

T he detectives didn't come back after their coffee run and Jason managed to sleep a few rough hours with his head on the table. Lynch was clearly so pissed off that he just went home. But he came back alone early in the morning and started the interrogation all over again. Cole swapped with him around mid-morning. Between the two of them, they kept going for the entire day, asking the same questions over and over, trying to catch Jason in a lie.

They asked about his father again, but this time, Jason was prepared. He kept a stoic lock on his emotions and wore a firm poker face. And that pissed Lynch off even further.

Eventually, five o'clock came around, marking the end of the work day. Both Jason and the detectives were exhausted. Jason knew he still had until around nine o'clock that night before his 24 hours were up. Yet out of nowhere, Lynch slammed a fist on the table and shouted, "Fuck this shit," and left the room in a huff. Cole let out a long sigh and uncuffed Jason at last.

"Get out of my sight," she growled before leaving the room.

Jason finally got out of the interrogation room, stinking of sweat and body odour. His hands felt slimy to the touch, and every inch of his skin was sticky from the humidity of the room. He rolled his shoulders and twisted his back to crack it but only felt partial relief. He'd be sore for days.

The other officers were in the bullpen, preparing to leave work for the day. Everyone stopped and looked up as he entered. Douglas, Martin, and Wilson were silent as he walked towards his desk. Without a word, they all turned around and pretended not to see him.

Captain Kader watched from her office. She gave him a nod but made no move to say anything more.

Jason started to walk out of the precinct when something made him stop. He didn't have his keys, or phone, or wallet. *Damn.* He turned around and walked past his gawking colleagues with his head held high before knocking on the captain's door.

"Sorry to ask, but can I borrow some cash for a taxi?"

She handed him a twenty. "Get an Uber. It's cheaper."

* * *

When Jason finally got home, he half expected everything to be exactly how he left it. Including Silvana, waiting and eager. He sighed. *No chance of that.* The door was unlocked and he stepped in half expecting all his things to be gone.

Instead, he found the apartment in a state of perfect cleanliness. All the plates from the night before had been washed and put away. His bed was made. The whole place smelled like lavender and lemon cleaning products. He took off his shoes and felt the carpet was softer and spongey beneath his feet.

She even cleaned the carpet. Not just vacuumed, but fully soaked and dried.

"My god."

He grabbed his phone off the counter. There were messages waiting, but he swiped them aside and pulled up Silvana's contact to type a message.

"I can't believe you cleaned my whole apartment! It must have taken you hours! You didn't have to do that. I really appreciate it."

He hit send, and immediately added, *"I'm out of police custody, by the way. I have not been charged."*

Peter wasn't home yet again. It seemed he was out more than usual lately. Was he avoiding Jason? He didn't care, just sat on his bed with a beer and shut the bedroom door. A second later, Silvana sent back a massive paragraph of text. *Geez...was she using superhuman speed to type that quickly?*

"Jason! OMG I'm so glad you're ok! I was really worried about you! What happened? It sounded like someone else was murdered. I hope everything's ok. I'm glad you like the apartment! I'm sorry if you felt like I invaded your space. But I was so worried about you, I just had to do something to feel like I was helping. You sure it's ok? Did you want me to come over tonight? We don't have to pick up where we left off or anything."

Jason had to shake his head to clear the numbness from the last twenty-four hours. He snapped to attention at the end there. *Don't have to pick up where we left off? Yeah she definitely wants to.* Yet he felt absolutely exhausted. He hated himself for it, but he texted her back.

"I'm sorry, but I need a quiet night. I just spent nearly twenty-four hours in an interrogation room and I didn't sleep properly. I'd like to see you tomorrow."

He hit send and kept typing, *"Also I really do appreciate the clean apartment. You don't need to apologise. I really like it."*

Jason laid down on the bed, stared up at the roof and took sips from his beer, letting his mind wander over the events of the last few days. Someone had killed two members of this group, 'the monster hunters'.

And it looked like the killer was trying to set up Jason for the crime. Someone had used the bullets from his gun. What possible reason could they have to do it?

Come to think of it, there are a lot of reasons. The Immortal Imperium was probably not happy about a bunch of mortals getting organised with torches and pitchforks and coming after them. Maybe someone from the Imperium was trying to break up their movement.

Or it could be Silvana's family, taking retribution for the attacks on their household. *There's been two attacks at Maristow House, and two murders. Sounds fitting.* They could be collecting the blood for Silvana, since she didn't have any. Although they claimed a vampire never drank blood except when freely given by their spouse. Still, it was possible. And Jason could just be the scapegoat.

The other option was the bikers. *Rion Dankworth the vampire, Kathryn Smith the telepath. And Gerald, last name unknown. The skinwalker.* Jason shuddered. What were those three immortals doing each night while roaming the town on motorbikes? He hoped Captain Kader was at least looking into his report. He knew it was unlikely with him being a major suspect now. The biker gang had probably been unchecked this whole time. But Jason knew they were up to something.

There was a fourth option. Someone at the police department was compromised.

After all, Lynch seemed to especially have it in for him. Everyone avoided Jason now. Only the captain seemed to be on his side, and yet she also gave permission for his gun to be tested. Any one of them could be working for an immortal.

Or even be an immortal themselves.

Silvana said the mentally enhanced immortals could blend in with humans. Was Lynch an alchemist? Or a wizard? There was so much Jason didn't know about the immortal world. There were many physically enhanced species, though Jason only knew of vampires and skin walkers. And there were magic-wielders with powers he knew nothing about. The thought that someone in his workplace could be any number of unknowable creatures…it was terrifying.

Yet somehow, that wasn't the worst option. Jason didn't even want to consider the final option. But he had to. If he was to think like a detective, he had to consider all possibilities.

So he allowed himself to consider if Silvana was the killer.

He hated to admit it, but the idea fit the situation pretty damn well. She was a vampire in need of blood. She could be targeting people who were already a threat to her and her family. Worse, this whole romance could be her way of setting up Jason as a fall-guy. Maybe she had no need for a marriage and it was all a lie to get him interested in her. Most of what he knew about the Immortal world came from her. How much of it was true?

Damn it, Jase. You could be sleeping with the enemy. Yet, just the thought of sleeping with the enemy made him stir with longing for her.

Maybe he wasn't too tired to see her tonight. Especially if she did wanted to 'pick up where they left off…'

Get it together, man. He shook his head. This was all so confusing. Should he be more suspicious of her? Or should he trust her? After all, he knew what it was like to have people suspicious of him for no reason.

But could he even trust his own judgement? Maybe he was under the influence of some vampire magic. Or he could just be too horny to think clearly. *So horny…* He sighed and checked his phone.

There was another text from Silvana. It had come through just after he sent his last one, and had been sitting there for half an hour while he'd been thinking.

"Can I call you? Please."

Chapter 21

Jason sat up on his bed. That text had been sitting there for so long that she probably thought he was ignoring her. So rather than text back, he just hit call. She answered on the first ring.

"Oh Jason! Thanks for calling me. Sorry for being such a nag," she blurted all at once.

But Jason only smiled. "It's good to hear your voice," he said and meant it. Something about the sound seemed to lift stress from his mind.

Careful...

"Aw!" she said. "You're sweet."

Ooh, she's playing me. Right?

"Sorry I didn't reply," he said. "I was about to fall asleep. But I'd love to talk. What's up?"

"Oh...I just thought it would be nice to talk on the phone. I know you're tired and not up for a visit. So we can just talk, if you like."

"I'd love that."

"Good. So...did you want to talk about...your day?"

Jason flinched. Was she hunting for information? "Today sucked. I spent twenty hours handcuffed to a desk. And they asked me the same questions over and over, trying to catch me in a lie."

"Jason, that's awful! They shouldn't be allowed to do that!"

"No, it's perfectly legal. And if I was a murderer, it'd be a pretty effective way to catch me. Just sucks that it was all for nothing."

"I'm sorry. You don't have to talk about it."

"Yeah…I could use a break from it." He trailed off, unsure what else to say. Silvana saved him from the silence.

"Well, last night you asked about me. So tonight, can I ask about you? I don't really know a lot about you."

"Huh… that's true," Jason said. "I guess I've been more preoccupied with you. There was just a lot to learn."

"I bet. So…do you have family?"

Jason went quiet. He realised now he'd been deliberately avoiding this topic with her.

"Hello?"

"Sorry," he said. "I'm here. I just…" he trailed off and forced himself to clear his throat. "I don't have any family."

"No family? None at all?" There was no judgement in her voice, just bewilderment. "I don't understand. What…what happened?"

Jason kept his voice flat and neutral. "My mother died."

"Oh…I'm so sorry."

"It's ok. It was ten years ago now. It's old news. I don't have any siblings. And my father wasn't able to care for me. So I went into the foster system when I was twelve. Changed homes every six to twelve months."

There was silence on the line. Then, "Jason, I didn't know. I'm…"

He scowled, bracing himself for the typical condescending pity everyone always gave him. But Silvana seemed to stop herself. "That must have been difficult," she said.

He nearly sighed in relief. "Yeah. It was."

"I hope you don't mind me asking about it."

"No, it's fine."

"You just had a very different upbringing to me. I've been surrounded by family for nearly ninety years. Almost exclusively. Did you…have anyone that you were close to?"

"Sometimes. Some foster parents were better than others. A lot of them just did it for the welfare and didn't give a shit. Others genuinely wanted to be my parents. I know they tried their best, but that made me uncomfortable. I didn't want parents, you know? The best foster parents were the few that just acted like my friends. I still talk to some of them. But I got out of that as soon as I could. Got a job as a labourer, got my own place. After a few years I decided to put myself through the academy and work towards becoming a detective."

"That's amazing," she said. "You've really overcome a lot."

Jason relaxed slightly. "That's right. I mean, I still have issues. I don't exactly have a lot of friends. All the people I know are from school, the academy, or work. It's why I'm single. I just assume everyone's going to leave in six to twelve months, you know?"

"But you've come so far. A lot of people never recover from their hurts. They pass on their problems to their own kids. You've actually made something of yourself."

Jason felt a surge of pride. "You know what? You're right. I have made something of myself." He chuckled. "It's funny. When I tell people that I grew up without parents, they always assume the same two things. Either that I'm weak and helpless, or I'm a ticking time bomb about to explode. They don't realise the truth. When you go through trauma as a child, you have to become so fucking strong just to survive. It doesn't make you weak or bad-tempered. It makes you so much stronger than most people can even understand."

"Yeah. That's so true."

"It is!" his voice grew louder. "That's why I became a cop. I want to use my strength to protect others. I want to stop what happened to me from ever happening to anyone else!"

He stopped suddenly. "Silvana," he said in a much softer tone,

"Thank you."

"What for?"

"I've…always struggled to talk about my family. I mean, I've talked to therapists. And my mentors at the academy in order to pass my psych evaluation, but I've never enjoyed talking about it. I always felt ashamed. Like it was all my fault, somehow, even though that was clearly not true. But with you…this sounds silly, but…you made me feel safe."

"Good," she said. "I'm glad I could be that for you, Jason. And…can I be honest?"

"Sure."

"I just think you're incredible." He gave a good-natured laugh, but she cut him off. "I mean it, Jason. I thought you were amazing the moment I saw you. But everything I've learnt about you so far has only made you seem even more incredible. I just…I can't believe you're real. Jason…you're a really good person."

He was quiet. He was too choked up to speak, and his eyes stung. Still, a voice in his head said, *she doesn't know the whole truth. Otherwise she wouldn't say that.* But out loud, he just said, "Thank you. And ditto."

They were silent for a little while, but it was a good silence. They rested on the phone together, and it felt right. To Jason, it felt safe. He settled further down into his pillows and let himself relax. Yet, he noticed the faintest scent in his sheets, and his thoughts turned elsewhere.

"Can I ask you something?" he said after their long silence. "Last night, while we were, you know…"

"Ah-huh?" she said, her smile audible in her tone.

"You said we didn't need protection…"

"Oh…" she groaned. "I'm sorry, I should have mentioned that a little earlier, but…" she was silent for a few seconds. "Immortals can't reproduce."

Jason blinked. "Really? That seems…unlikely. How are there still immortals then?"

"We can't produce biologically. But we pass on our power to family members."

"Uh…what family members?"

"Sorry! I'll explain from the top. In every immortal family, we are all born as mortals. Then the immortal power is passed on to the eldest, but only the eldest. So in a vampire family, only the eldest is bitten. And in a wizard family, only the eldest is taught magic."

Jason thought about it. "That seems harsh. So the younger children have mortal lives and die much sooner?"

"Yes, but *their* eldest in turn becomes immortal, through their aunt or uncle. That's how the line continues."

"Huh."

"It's extra important for vampires. We can only be sustained by the blood of mortals. Immortal blood is like acid to us. That's why my aunts and I all have mortal husbands. Or…need one. Anyway, we usually marry the mortals from other immortal families. It forms alliances."

"That makes sense. But it's still weird that they only pass it on to the eldest. Like, shouldn't they get a choice?"

"It's not so bad. The immortal families are usually wealthy and powerful. So even if the mortal members of their families don't get immortality, they still live comfortable lives. You know, in a different age, the mortals in our families used to be royalty."

"Royalty?"

"Yeah. You ever look into the kings of Europe over the last two thousand years? They were all connected to each other by marriage. Well, just about every king or queen was actually the mortal representative for an immortal family."

Jason felt a chill. *The immortals rule the world,* Timothy Harrison had said. Suddenly it didn't seem so crazy. Jason could picture it now. Immortal families, amassing wealth and power over the centuries, and positioning rulers in places of power to keep the mortals in line without their knowing.

But he hid his discomfort from Silvana. All he said was, "Fascinating. But didn't the kings and queens fight all the time? Why would they do that if they were all part of the immortal families?"

"Oh. They just fought for power. Like in Game of Thrones."

"Ah." Something in Silvana's tone was off, like she was worried about something. "Are you ok, Silvana?" he asked gently.

"Not really," she said softly.

"What's bothering you?"

The line was quiet. He wished he could see her expressions.

"Do you understand why I've never had children?" Silvana asked, her voice sober. "Once you're a vampire, your reproductive organs don't work. I can pass on my power through bitting someone, but only to an extended family member, like a niece or cousin, and only with approval from the Imperium." She let out a long breath. "So Jason, what I'm trying to say is…if you marry me, we can't have kids. At least, not naturally."

She went silent.

"Oh!" Jason cried loudly. "I get it now. You're worried this is a big deal to me. That I might leave if I found out."

"Yeah…"

"Silvana, I don't care!"

"Huh?"

He laughed. "Why should I care if we can't have kids naturally? My natural parents didn't raise me! I was raised by people with no blood relation to me. Family is more than just blood. As far as I'm concerned, biology is worth fuck all!" He laughed again. "I mean,

I always dreamed that I would adopt a child one day. Would you consider adopting a child?"

She laughed back, "Of course."

"Then great! Who cares if we have different DNA? That doesn't make you a good parent anyway."

"That's true," She sniffed, and Jason realised she was crying softly and trying to hide it. He let her keep it hidden. "So…you'd want to adopt? Not foster?"

"Oh no, never foster," Jason said.

"But you were a foster child?"

"Yeah, and I know how much it sucks for a child to be constantly changing homes. It's like living with an axe over your neck. I'd much rather take on a kid permanently."

"Oh, Jason, that's beautiful!" her voice trembled, and she sniffed quietly. When she spoke, she couldn't keep her emotions back. "Jason, this is exactly what I mean. Everything I learn about you just proves how amazing you are! I just…" she choked off. "I'm just so lucky to have met you."

"Silvana…you're amazing," he said. He found himself shaking his head. "Look at us. You proposed before we had our first date. And now we're talking about kids!"

"But aren't kids what you're supposed to talk about on the third date?" she said playfully.

"Uh…no. Third date is sex."

"Right. Sex and kids."

Jason just laughed at her. "Well does it still count if we didn't… finish?"

"You were inside me, Jason. It counts." They both laughed.

He smiled. "Huh. I guess this is our third date."

"Yeah."

"It's going well. First time we haven't been interrupted."

He'd just finished saying it when his stomach let out a rumble, and he felt a wave of fatigue cloud his mind. "Oh perfect timing. Silvana, I'm sorry. But I need food, and sleep."

"Oh really? But…I was gonna suggest we have phone sex."

He blinked. "What?"

"You know, phone sex. You describe what you're doing while masturbatin—"

"I know what phone sex is!" Jason said with a laugh. "I just can't believe you suggested it."

"Why?"

"Because we're not teenagers!" he said, unable to stop himself laughing. "And it's so dorky!"

"It's not dorky," she said with mock offense in her voice. "Tell me, were you going to masturbate tonight?"

He stared at the roof in disbelief. "God…Yeah, I guess I was probably going to wank off at some point. I'm still a bit pent up from yesterday, you know."

"Well, just do it now. On the phone to me. So I can listen and do the same."

He couldn't help laughing again. He felt his face going red.

"What's so funny?" she asked.

"Ok first, can I ask a personal question?" She agreed. "You are so quiet and polite around your family. And you talk about being submissive in marriage. But when it comes to sex, you're really forward and confident."

"Oh, I'm sorry. I know I'm a little slutty some-"

"No! No it's not slutty. It's fantastic! It's great seeing you this confident. I'm asking why aren't you this confident all the time?"

"Well…I don't know." She paused to think. "Let me put it this way. I was married to Arthur for fifty seven years. And in all that time…he never once did for me what you did last night."

"Last night? Do…" Jason's mouth dropped open. "You're kidding. He never went down on you? Not once? Not one goddamn time?"

"Never. Even though I did it for him constantly."

"Oh fucking hell!" Jason growled. "I'm sorry, I know he's your late husband and I should be respectful, but that's fucked up!" Silvana laughed. "No, I'm serious. That is just so completely wrong." He bit his tongue. "Sorry. I don't mean to yell. I'm not mad at you, just the situation."

"No, it's alright. My point is, I've spent a long time wanting something more from sex. And with you, I know I can finally have that."

"Ok. But you could have more in *all* areas of your life, you know? You could want more among your family. More independence. And in marriage, you could be an equal. You could be confident and demand what you want all the time." He grinned. "You could demand that your husband eat pussy like he goddamn should!"

She laughed, and it sounded musical. "Alright, Jason. I demand it. Tell me…what would you do to me if we were together right now? Describe it, in detail."

"All right," he said, trying not to giggle like a schoolboy. "Well, the first thing I would do is tear every single piece of your clothes off you. Just *rip* them off cause you look so damn hot naked."

"Really?" she said in a sultry voice, and he arched his neck in pleasure at the sound.

"Utterly perfect. I didn't get a chance to do this last night, but I would bury my face in your chest, sucking on your tits."

"Oh, Jason!" She sounded scandalised. *Holy crap, this is actually working for me!* Silvana purred, "You may be interested to know this, Jason, but right now I've got my hand down the front of my pants, and I've started to…" she gasped, "touch myself."

"Yup. Me too," he said, reaching down to take his cock in hand.

"Well, I want to help you with that," she said. "Right now, I'm squeezing the front of your pants. Just squeezing it so hard."

"Well, I better get those pants out of the way."

"Good idea. That way, I can put my mouth around the tip of your penis."

Jason blinked. *Penis? Did she just call it a penis?* He didn't question it. "Oh yeah? And what are you doing with your mouth?"

"Well," she struggled to speak as she let out another gasp. "I'm running my tongue up and down the length, then flicking the tip. The whole time I'm working on myself with my other hand, cause it turns me on to taste you."

Jason let out a moan. "You are so fucking hot."

"Wait till I push it in deeper," she said. "I can get it all the way to the back of my throat."

"Hoooly fuuuck…"

"Oh yeah." And she spoke as if her mouth were full, "it *tastes so good.*"

That was it. Apparently Jason was much more pent up than he realised, because it was all Jason could take. He let out a moan and exploded into his hand.

"Fuck yes," Silvana moaned along with him. They didn't speak for a few seconds, just listening to the sound of the other person panting heavily.

"Um…well…phone sex was a good idea."

Silvana laughed. "I thought you'd agree."

"Um…can I just have a second to…clean up?"

He put down the phone, and could hear her laughing through the receiver. A minute later, he picked it up again. He cleared his throat.

"That was a bit quicker than I intended."

"No, Jason, don't worry. I'm just glad I could do that with you. I can't wait to do that again, for real."

"Yeah. Uh…did you want to keep going?"

"I'm good, Jason. Thank you."

"Ok. Well…I should probably get some sleep."

"Sure. I can let you go. Can I come see you tomorrow? At your place again? Just, if we came to my place…my family would try to chaperone me."

"Ew. Yeah come to mine. Any time after six."

"Great." She paused for a moment, like she was thinking something over. "Jason, I hate to say this. But I'm getting a bit of pressure from my family. I've been without blood for over forty days. I'm… getting weaker."

Jason nodded. "You want to know if I accept your proposal?"

"I'm sorry. I don't mean to pressure you. But my family will ask me if I've asked you…"

He let out a sigh. "Look, I am really enjoying being around you. It's like you said, everything I learn about you, I like."

"Thank you."

"But I'm just…" he trailed off. He had no idea how to explain what he felt. He was scared of commitment, because everyone in his life had left him. He was scared of hurting her, like his father had hurt his mother. And he was scared that somehow, this was all an elaborate lie, and Silvana was responsible for the recent deaths and would be responsible for more.

Silvana didn't demand an answer. "It's fine. I just…I need an answer soon. Please."

"Ok," Jason said. "I'll give you an answer soon. I promise."

"Ok. Goodnight, Jason."

"Goodnight Silvana."

Chapter 22

Jason woke up slick and itchy with sweat. He hadn't showered when he got home last night and after a day in the interrogation room, everything felt sticky. He stripped and showered in steaming hot water, letting his mind disassociate for a few minutes more before he woke up properly. He towelled dry, dressed in his uniform and came out into the kitchen.

Peter was at the dining table, eating cereal and scrolling through his phone.

"Oh hey man," Jason said. "I didn't hear you come in last night. How's it going?"

Peter gave a tired smile. "Good, mate. Just pissed I have uni so early. It's like, if I wanted a day job, I'd work a day job."

"Ha. Right." Jason poured himself a bowl and sat down opposite his roommate. "How's uni going?"

"Alright. How's work?"

"Great. Got arrested, so that was neat."

Peter's head jerked up. "I'm sorry what?"

Jason chuckled. "It's top secret. But you know that murder victim I found? Turns out they *really* think I did it."

"Damn. But it was just a wrong place at the wrong time kind of thing."

"Yeah."

"That sucks, man," Peter went back to his food and they sat in silence. Jason found himself avoiding eye contact and focusing on eating his breakfast faster than usual.

"Alright!" Peter announced suddenly. "I'll come out and say it. I'm sorry for interrupting the other night."

"Oh."

"Yeah. I feel like an ass. You're my friend and I shouldn't have butted into your date like that."

"Oh. Thanks man."

Peter waved him away. "I just really liked Silvana. I'm annoyed at myself for screwing things up. And I'm annoyed at myself for inviting you along." He grinned. "No offense."

"None taken."

"That's the last time I try to help you socialise."

Jason chuckled as he finished his meal. "I've got to head off. But we should hang out some time. Maybe this weekend?"

"Yeah, man! Name the time and place, I'm there." Peter grinned. "And if you want to invite Silvana, I swear I won't be weird about it. Ok?"

Jason considered telling him things were getting serious with Silvana and asking him to back off. But it was too early for a confrontation. So he just said, "Thanks man. See ya!"

* * *

Jason sat at his desk.

No one had spoken to him that morning. The officers watched him warily from a distance, the detectives glared, but no one approached him. When he sat down, he found an email from the captain, requesting he digitize some old case files.

Great. Data entry. Just why I became a cop.

Pretty soon his brain became mush. For a change of pace, he clicked open the database so he could do more research. But access was denied. He groaned and tried opening other apps on his work computer. Everything was restricted to him now. Except the ability to enter new files. He pinched the bridge of his nose.

This wasn't good. No one was going to investigate the real murderer if they kept watching him. He'd have to do it himself.

Jason pulled out a notebook and a pen, and between typing up reports, he started writing out a chart.

He put a family tree on the top left of the page. Phillip and Emberline, Nicholas 'the third' and Lisbeth. Silvana and Arthur.

One the other side, Gerald, Rion, and Kathryn.

At the bottom left, Alex Bishop, Timothy Harrison, Richard Anderson.

And the bottom right, Captain Kader, Detectives Lynch and Cole, Officers Douglas, Martin and Wilson.

Then he sat back and looked at the chart. His instincts told him he was still missing important information. Something that would tie it all together. But that was no help. There was no way to do any more investigating while tied to a desk. He would have to guess at any clues that were missing and deduce their presence by using the clues already available.

So on a separate page, he started writing down details he knew. He circled the three bikers and wrote 'Immortal'. Then circled the three men and wrote 'Monster Hunters'. Then he added, 'three bullets, taken from two separate instances. Shots were fired at Maristow House. Bullets found in two separate locations.'

What did he know about the immortals? What did he know about magic? He added that.

'Vampires need blood monthly. Slightly faster and stronger than humans at captain America level. Can only use mortal blood.'

'Alchemists make elixirs. Witches are magic doctors. Wizards use magic, including healing, telekinesis, natural disasters level power, and more unknown.'

'Other known immortal races are skinwalker and telepaths. More unknown.' He sighed. That seemed about all he knew.

Glancing up from his notes, he noticed the captain walking towards him. He covered his notes and started typing until she passed, then immediately kept writing on the notebook.

'Immortal Imperium are ruling body, run by wizards. Vigiles are enforcers. Also include immortal families, with mortal family members. Possible connection to police department?'

Jason leaned back and stared at all the facts on the page. He searched through them, reading them slowly out loud. But nothing was clicking. *What else do I know? What else?* So he kept writing.

'Who benefits from the murders? Who benefits from me being framed for it?'

But that was all he could think of. As he looked it over again, he could see nothing. He swore and kept up with the data entry.

Lunchtime came and Jason sat by himself eating two sandwiches and staring at his notebook. He had a text from Silvana. *"Hey Jase. Are you still ok for me to come over to yours tonight?"*

He smiled and texted back. *"Of course! It's the only thing getting me through today."* He added a smiley emoji.

She wrote back. *"Ok good! I had to ask because Uncle Nicholas keeps asking when you're going to visit again. I think he likes you! But I'll tell him we have plans for tonight."*

"Well I like Nicholas too."

A thought occurred to Jason. *Wasn't there a king called Nicholas?*

He got out his phone and searched through google.

Indeed there was.

A second later, he was at his captain's door. "Captain," he said. "I'm not feeling well. Can I go home early?"

Kader glared at him. "Absolutely not, rookie. You're not going to do anything out of the ordinary while you're under investigation."

"But…" he winced, "I spent twenty hours in that cell, yesterday. I think I've caught something."

"Don't you dare," she snapped. "Sit your ass back down at your desk and don't move until your shift ends. Got it? I don't care if your limbs fall off!"

He scowled. "Fine."

Four hours to go. But now he knew. He knew what he had to do. He just had to sit still and wait until he could do it.

The hours dragged by as Jason started tapping the desk in agitation. He sent a message to keep himself busy.

"Hey Silvana…I've been thinking. Would it be ok if I came to your place tonight? I know we had plans. But I just thought it'd be good to spend some time with your family. Get to know them all a bit better. What do you think? You can say no."

He hit send and took a long breath to calm his nerves. *Please don't say no. It would ruin everything.*

A moment later his phone pinged. *"Ok sure. It's nice that you want to get to know my family."*

That was all she wrote. She was definitely disappointed. *God, did I just turn down sex for this?* But it was important.

Then he sent one last text message, before he settled in and waited for work to end.

* * *

A few hours later, Jason arrived at the Maristow House, freshly showered and dressed in jeans and a jacket. He banged the door-knocker on the anvil and waited with his heart in his throat. His hands were jittery with energy.

The door opened. "Jason!" Silvana cried and stepped forward to greet him, her long blue ballgown swishing with her movements. She abruptly stopped short.

"Jason…" she asked.

"Peter's here!" Jason cried.

"Surprise!" Peter said with a wave and a bright smile. "Hi Silvana. Long-time no see, hey?"

Silvana froze in the middle of the door, looking first at Jason, then at Peter, then Jason again. "What's going on?" she asked, a tremble in her voice.

"Well I'm gonna spend some time with your family tonight," Jason said, "and I'm feeling a bit nervous. So I asked Peter to come with me as my chaperone."

"And I was honoured to be considered," Peter said and bowed low.

"Chaperone?" her voice trailed off. She looked at Jason, and her piercing blue eyes seemed to glimmer. "I don't understand," she whispered. "Why do you need a chaperone? Don't you…feel comfortable with me?"

Jason's mouth hung open. *You idiot, you're hurting her. You can't do this.* He pushed the thought aside and shrugged. "Sorry Silvana. It's just for tonight, I swear."

She tried to smile. "Of course," she said, but her voice broke, and suddenly she turned away to cover her face and ran off down the hallway.

Peter elbowed him in the ribs. "Smooth, dude. You should have told her I was coming."

"I didn't think she'd mind."

"Clearly, I just reminded her of what she's missing out on. I'd be upset too." He chuckled and marched through the door. Jason swallowed down his retort and followed.

They walked through the familiar stone hallway and Jason was quick to notice the suits of armour by the door this time. Each had a long two-handed sword resting in their gauntlet. He was vaguely aware of the paintings but didn't take note. He just listened for signs of Silvana.

He reached the main throne room. The whole family was already there. Phillip and Emberline sat side by side on two high-backed silk chairs, while Lisbeth and Nicholas shared a single armchair, snuggled together. They didn't look up when Jason entered, instead focused on Silvana, who was bowing before them and whispering.

"I don't know! I thought it was just him." She cut off when she saw Jason and Peter enter and stood up straight. She wiped a tear from her cheek and Jason felt a stabbing pang of guilt.

"Good evening, everyone," Jason said.

Peter waved dumbly.

"Turner," Emberline said in her cold voice. "And you've brought a guest. Tell me, do you think it polite to invite someone to a house that is not yours?"

Jason checked the archway into the throne room. "Oh look, there are suits of armour here too," he said in a cheerful voice.

He heard Emberline inhale sharply. Nicholas tried to sound polite as he answered, "Yes, Jason. There are a dozen suits all throughout the mansion, so they're always nearby whenever we need them."

"But the sword on this one is different. The others were two handed."

"Jason!" Silvana cried, her mouth open in shock.

Nicholas cleared his throat. "It's a rapier."

"Boy," Phillip growled. "What are you—"

Jason talked over him. "Do you mind if I try?" Without waiting, he took the sword out of the suit's gauntlet and held it up. It had a curved brace and a long, sharp point. It weighed barely three kilos. "It's a good sword," he said.

Then he turned to Peter, and thrust the sword tip up against his friend's throat.

Everyone went quiet. Jason felt them all looking at him. His heart was racing, his chest rising and falling with each breath. Peter looked at him, smiling as if waiting for the punchline.

"Jason," Silvana cried. "What are you doing?"

"My friend Peter here is not what he appears to be," Jason said. He held the sword so it touched the skin. Then he said in a loud voice.

"He's a wizard."

The throne room was silent, making Jason's last word echo around the chamber like a whispering ghost.

Wizard...

Chapter 23

Peter held up his hands and gave a charming grin. "You having a laugh, mate?" He shrugged. "Or perhaps you're trying to tell them I'm good with computers. Cause you know that no one says wizard anymore, right?"

Jason didn't laugh. Nor did he lower the sword.

Peter scowled. "All right dude, this isn't funny. Put the sword…" he slowly reached for the blade, but Jason thrust it forward, the tip piercing Peter's skin. Peter cried out as a cut blossomed under his chin, spilling a single drop of blood. "Geez, have off Jason!" he shouted.

"Check his blood," Jason said. "You said vampires can't consume immortal blood, right? I'm certain this blood is not mortal."

No one moved, instead they just looked between each other with bewildered expressions. Peter laughed, "What are you talking about, mate? We've lived together for three months. Hell, you've known me since the fourth grade! You think you would have noticed something before this."

"Check his blood," Jason demanded.

Silvana moved. She swept across the room, stopping before Peter, and reached out with a finger.

"Silvana, don't!" Emberline snapped. "He is not your husband! You cannot take his blood!"

"I'm not consuming it, Aunty," she said. "I'm only tasting. He can have it back when I'm done."

Peter scowled at her but didn't move. She dabbed the tip of her pinky finger on the sword's edge and moved a drop of blood to the tip of her tongue. It touched...

...and immediately she spat it out with a loud gag. She looked up at Peter in horror.

"He's immortal."

Everyone leapt to their feet. Half a second later, Emberline and Lisbeth were standing next to Peter, their teeth bared with a hiss and nails ready to strike. Their eyes turned a deep shade of red. The two men grabbed their swords from racks by the door and stood shoulder-to-shoulder with their wives. Their blades joined Jason's to surround Peter's throat, giving him no way to escape. Peter held up his hands, his eyes wide with fear, as all six of them were poised within an inch of killing him.

"He's the one behind everything," Jason declared. "He led those men to your house so that they would kill you. Both Alex Bishop and the entire mob. And when they failed, he killed them, to turn us all against each other. He will do whatever it takes so he can have Silvana all to himself." He scowled at his old school friend. "Isn't that right, *dude*?"

Peter looked at Jason, and slowly the fear drained away from his eyes, replaced by...*amusement.* He lowered his hands until they hung limply at his side. His mouth dropped open.

And he started laughing.

At first, his voice was high-pitched, almost squealing in delight before his laugh became full-throated and deep-chested. It boomed across the throne room so it echoed like a chorus of maniacs. Peter's lips twisted into a wide brimming smile. And he laughed right in the face of the vampire's teeth and the knights' blades.

My god...he's not scared of us. Not even a little.

"How dare you!" Emberline roared suddenly, and Peter's laugh faded. "You come into my house, threaten my family! You attempted to court my Silvana, when marrying you would have doomed her to die of thirst! And now you stand here with the audacity to *laugh* at us! I should rip your throat out, pig!"

Peter sneered, "Fuck off, bitch." His voice was flat, emotionless.

He sounds completely different.

Phillip growled, "You watch your tone, cur, or I'll cut your tongue out..."

Peter spoke.

"Haš Edün!"

Something hit Jason in the chest. Hard.

The next thing he knew, he was on the ground. His face was pressed against the dusty carpet. He lifted himself up. The room was spinning around him and he tasted blood in his mouth. He looked up as his vision began to clear.

He was ten metres away from where he had been standing. All the others were on the ground, up against the walls, or blown backwards in a matching circle. And standing in the centre was Peter, hands at his side, with a wide grin on his face.

What the hell was that?

"By what right?" a man's voice roared. It was Nicholas, clutching at his chest in obvious pain, but the fire in his eyes was no less for it. "By whose authority do you come into our house and assault us?"

Peter snapped, "I don't need to explain myself to *inferiors*. Least of all, some dried up old mortal corpse." Peter scanned the room, and his eyes landed on Jason. He grinned again, and slowly stalked across the carpet. Jason scrambled into a seating position up against the wall, but his head was spinning. *They were supposed to stop him! I exposed him, he should have surrendered. How is he so powerful?* Jason couldn't stand. His heart was racing as Peter stopped before him, looking down his nose at him.

"I want to know," Peter said. "How did *you*, a fucking dumbass mortal, figure out my plan? What gave me away?"

Jason was panting for breath. He had seen Peter's face hundreds of times over the years. He'd never been afraid of him before.

But I'm afraid now.

At the same time, he clenched his fist. *I will not cower before a bully. Never again.* And he spoke in a loud, clear voice for the room to hear.

"You used magic in front of me," Jason said. "Twice."

"Bullshit," Peter growled. "I never—"

"You interrupted my date with Silvana because you got a text alert from the fire alarm." Jason pointed a finger in Peter's face. "You were at uni, all the way across town, but you appeared in my door within a minute. You used magic."

Peter scoffed. "But I told you I was already in the area. You believed me."

"At first. The other time you used magic was last Saturday. I arrived home from work and you told me about Silvana for the first time. I said I needed a beer, and you just handed me one." Jason pointed again. "You weren't holding a beer when I entered. You summoned it because you were impatient. You were sloppy."

"Oh fuck off. You didn't even see that!"

"I admit, it took me a while," Jason said. "I only became suspicious when I told the detectives we were roommates. Lynch had the slightest look of surprise. That's when I began to wonder about you. Later, during their investigation of me, they asked about you several times. It was only in passing, they said it like it was nothing. But they asked just one time too many. You're the reason they suspected me in the first place." Jason wanted to stand up to Peter and shove him, but didn't dare it. So he put all the venom he could into his voice.

"You're the one the detectives investigated years ago. You were the one who killed that teenage girl by the docks and travelled fast enough to get away from the crime."

Peter looked confused, until he gave an abrupt, loud laugh. "Oh! The mortal whore from the docks. The bitch who refused to put out. And that detective…that stupid black fucker who tried to catch me. You know, he shouldn't have told you about me. That was very unprofessional of him." Peter rubbed his chin, as if in thought. "Maybe he and I should have a talk."

Oh fuck.

"He told me nothing. I figured it out," he said desperately.

Jason scanned the room to check no one had moved. They all remained where they had fallen, watching him closely. He was hoping one of the vampires would strike while Peter's back was turned, so he kept talking to hold his attention. He avoided mentioning Lynch any further, hoping Peter would forget about him.

"But I admit, I didn't figure out your plans right away." Jason gave a shrug. "You were smart, Peter. You covered your tracks well. I only started to suspect something when Silvana told me that immortal families fought for power all the time. That was the reason for wars between European kings. I figured some immortal must be making a play for power, right here in Plymouth."

"Yes," Peter drawled, like he was talking to an infant, "But what did I do to make you suspect me?"

Jason swallowed. "You kept trying to flirt with Silvana. Therefore, you had the most to gain if I was out of the way."

"Seriously?" Peter waved his hand around and sneered. "What would I gain from this place? A shitty old mansion falling to ruin?"

"No," Jason said. "Legitimacy."

Peter clenched his jaw. The muscles in his cheek twitched with rage. But Jason kept talking and pointed across the room. "It was Nicholas who made me realise the truth. He was the final piece of the puzzle. Nicholas the Third. It got me thinking. Who was the first and second Nicholas? And a simple google search gave me the answer."

Jason turned, and made eye contact with Nicholas across the room. "Tsar Nicholas the Second was the last Emperor of Russia. The last leader of the House of Romanoff. And you, Nicholas, are his relative."

"Zounderkite!" Uncle Phillip shouted across the room at Nicholas. "I told you to stop referring to yourself as the third! You don't see me calling myself the second!"

"Ah…" Jason said, and Phillip whirred to face him. "I thought so. Phillip the Second, just as I suspected. Named after the late Prince Phillip. You are a relation to House Windsor and the British royal family." Jason smirked. "A family older than this country indeed."

Phillip's eyes widened, then he screwed up his face in a harsh grimace. Jason found immense satisfaction in the look on Phillip's face, even amidst the dangerous situation.

"So there it is," Jason said, turning back to Peter. "This family has connections to old royal lines. And you wanted to marry into them to legitimise yourself. That's why you came back to Plymouth three months ago. You knew Arthur was dying, which meant soon a royal title would be within your grasp. At least, a better royal title than the one you have. Now, I'm just guessing here, but as I understand it, the Eriksons haven't had any royal power since the House of Estridsen last ruled Denmark in the 14th century. Does that sound familiar?"

Peter's lip twisted downwards. "You've done a bit of research."

"I was trying to figure out why such a powerful immortal would have gone to public school in Plymouth. I figured either your house was illegitimate, or you were."

Peter's foot lashed out and kicked Jason in the face.

It was abrupt, and completely unexpected, making Jason bite down on his cheek. His vision blurred and he let out a strained moan of pain.

Peter loomed over him, a look of pure fury on his face. Veins stood out in his neck. "You think you're so fucking smart."

"Maybe I am," Jason sneered as he wiped blood from his mouth. "Or maybe, you're just not as smart as you thought."

"You fucking…" Peter growled, and Jason realised his hands were shaking. *Holy shit, I am scared of him.*

He saw Silvana across the room, holding her hand up to her mouth, her eyes wide with fear.

No… Jason's vision went white. *Mum…I should have protected you!*

He found himself shouting.

"Your date with Silvana failed cause you're an arrogant sleazy asshole! So you let Alex Bishop into the house. You paid him for it, didn't you? That's why I saw Detective Lynch going through Alex's bank statements the day after the murder. You paid him to kill everyone except Silvana, so you could marry into the Romanoff line. But I stopped you!"

"All because I relied on a worthless mortal," Peter spat the last word.

"Then you killed Alex, provoking his buddies the Monster Hunters to attack this family. It was a long shot, and unlikely to succeed, but there was no risk to you. Cause you knew I was on a date with Silvana. She was your goal, and she was safe. You just didn't expect us to come back early and intervene again."

"Who gives a fuck anymore?" Peter sneered, but Jason felt his confidence coming back. He scrambled to his feet, his fists clenched at his side and shouted.

"And I was your backup plan, wasn't I?" He pumped his fist against his own chest. "I wasn't just your chaperone. I was your *distraction*. Silvana only had two months at most to find a new husband. If Silvana didn't choose you, she would logically start dating me next because you presented me as an alternative. After all, how many mortal men does she even know? Not many. So I was the backup plan. Because if things didn't work out with me, she'd run out of time and options. She'd *have* to come running back to you. And you knew things wouldn't work out with us if you *framed* me for two murders by using bullets from my gun!"

"It wasn't hard," Peter sneered. "You kept firing those bullets. A simple summoning spell brought them into my hands. They were easy to plant."

"But you didn't expect one thing," Jason said. "Silvana and I started to like each other for real." He looked across the room at her. "She's incredible. I can't stop thinking about her. Every day I can't wait to see her again."

"It's true," Silvana declared, her voice shaking but loud. "I think Jason is amazing." They shared a smile across the room in the face of death itself.

"Fucking children," Peter sneered, though Jason couldn't stop smiling. Even now, he felt butterflies in his stomach.

"You realised this when you interrupted our date," Jason said. "You realised we were falling for each other. So you made sure our date was interrupted again. I don't know how you did it, but you got the police to break us up right in the middle of our date."

"It wouldn't have taken so long," Peter snarled. "Your whole department is so fucking incompetent, I had to slip into the lab and do the forensic report myself just to speed things along."

Jason scanned the room, and still not one of the vampires had moved. *Why aren't they trying to attack? I'm giving them so much time.*

"It was all you, Peter," Jason growled. "You killed that teenage girl, you killed the two monster hunters with my bullets, and you tried to kill Silvana." He shoved a finger in Peter's face, "You fucking bastard!"

There it was. All the truth had been revealed now. Jason expected Peter to slink away, defeated. Instead, Peter's mouth tilted upward.

"You think I killed them with *bullets?*" His voice was chilling, but not as much as the casual way he discussed committing murder.

"Yes. With bullets from my gun," Jason said.

Peter bared his teeth and whispered, "Do you want to know how I really killed those men?" He gave a full smile that seemed almost charming. "I summoned their blood from their bodies." He leaned in closer, so his face was barely a hand's width away. "Do you want to see?"

"Of course not," Jason said. But Peter held out a hand towards Silvana.

"No! Stop!"

"Khàd Nga!"

A sword lifted off the wall behind Silvana and flew across the room. The handle landed straight into Peter's outstretched hand. He clutched it in a tight grip and turned towards Jason.

"Just like that. I summoned their blood straight out of their veins, then I pushed the bullets in after." He shrugged. "I could have shot them first, but it would have been far less painful." He gave a satisfied laugh. "Of course, your mortal detectives would never consider it possible, so they assumed the bullets had done all the work."

Jason tried to put on a brave face, but he couldn't stop imagining Peter suddenly shoving that sword into his throat. Still, none of the vampires had moved. Jason began to give up hope that they would dare challenge a wizard.

Peter hefted the blade. "I shot those bullets with a launching spell. Do you want to see that one too?"

"No!" Jason cried. "There's no need, Peter."

"Oh really? I thought I could spruce up this shit hole. After all, this wall is in a ridiculous location." He held up his hand.

"Pete—"

"Khur Ngīr dü!"

A loud whooshing sound filled the room, and the stone wall behind Jason was blown away. He dropped to the ground and covered his head as a hundred stones crashed around him, filling the hallway with rubble and a cloud of dust.

Jason's mouth hung open. The whole area was covered in debris. *Those stones were huge. And that wall...That would have weighed tons. And he just...*

"Now image all that force," Peter said, "but concentrated to push a single bullet. I was never good at physics, but even I could imagine the kinetic force."

"Bastard!" Emberline shrieked. "Get out of our home!"

"What are you trying to prove?" Jason shouted. "Throwing your power around for thrills? I've already exposed you! There's nothing to gain anymore."

"He's right!" Silvana stood up now, proud and defiant. "I'm never going to marry you, Peter. You will never have my titles. You've lost, wizard!"

"Yeah," Jason added. "And now the Imperium is going to know what you've been—"

"The *Imperium?*" Peter cut in, and his laughter filled the throne room again. "You stupid fucking mortal. What would you know about the Imperium? I'm a *wizard! I rule* the Imperium!" He laughed again.

"You murdered people," Jason shouted. "You've assaulted an immortal family in their home. You tried to kill Silvana by tricking her into marrying you. The Imperium won't stand for it, no matter what you are."

He looked around the room for support, but found none. The immortal family was silent, their eyes downcast. The fire went out of Jason's voice. "Silvana?" he asked. "Surely, the Imperium will punish him?"

She looked back with a sombre expression, and shook her head.

"What?" Jason cried. "But he's a criminal."

"You fucking DOG!" Peter screamed, suddenly roaring as loud as his voice could go. His eyes were wild and feral. "Don't you get it? No one can touch me. I'm not your fucking friend. I'm not a child you went to school with. I'm a fucking *immortal being*. I will live for a thousand years and wield powers you cannot imagine. I am a GOD compared to worthless shits like you."

Jason growled, "You're just an asshole. There's a million more like you."

"I could kill you with a word," Peter growled. "A single fucking word. It's '*Gīl-iŭm*'.Want me to show you?"

Jason felt suddenly powerless. He realised how dangerous this was. Death could occur in a second and be forever irreversible. "Peter," he whispered. "That's enough. There's nothing more to gain here. Please."

"Oh it's no big deal. How about I pick the oldest one here?" He turned to Nicholas. The old man was still clutching his chest. "Oh look how pathetic he is. One little push, and he's practically dead already. At this point, it'd be a mercy."

"Stop it!" Jason shouted. "You've made your point, Peter. I won't do anything to fight you, I swear. Just leave these people alone."

"You do not make demands of me," Peter said. "You have nothing to threaten me with. No power to hold over me. Goddamn it, I should be *ruling* over you all!"

"But murder is one step too far," a voice cried. Everyone looked up to see Lisbeth, standing over her husband, her white face marked with fear even as she stood up to Peter. "You're right, wizard," Lisbeth said. "The Imperium won't interfere with what you've done so far. But if you murder a member of an Immortal family, they will act. As powerful as you are, you are not yet at full strength. The Imperium would crush you if you gave them sufficient cause. You may not have much to fear in this world, but you should fear the Vigiles nonetheless."

"She's right," Emberline hissed. "You've lost, wizard. Go home."

Peter stared at her. His nostrils flared with each breath, and his cheek muscles jerked. "I have lost *nothing*." He turned to the side and lifted a hand towards Silvana.

"No!" Jason roared and launched himself in Peter's direction.

"*Khàd Ngaùri!*"

Silvana's body jerked wildly as she let out a sudden, piercing scream, full-throated and high pitched.

Jason grabbed Peter around the chest, pulled him backwards, and smashed his fist down onto the wizard's nose.

At that same moment, the sword slashed Jason across the face.

Jason roared with pain and collapsed, clutching his cheek as blood filled his hands. The cut went all the way up the right side of his face, from chin to scalp. But with a groan he pushed past the pain and looked up.

Silvana!

She was floating off the ground, arms outstretched as streams of red flowed out of her body. *It's blood. He's summoned her blood!* Jason screamed in panic. *But she doesn't have any blood to spare!* Silvana gave a pained gasp and collapsed to the floor.

A blob of red formed in the air in front of Peter's outstretched hand. It was the size of a single kitchen bowl. He gestured upwards with his hand, and the blood burst outwards in all directions. It splattered across the entire throne room, painting the roof, walls and ground in drops too fine to collect again.

"No!" Emberline and Lisbeth screamed as they moved to Silvana's side. They lifted her up, holding her head tenderly between them.

Silvana was deathly pale. Her face was shrunken and gaunt. She looked like she'd lost so much weight as to be nearly starving to death.

"The Imperium will execute you for this," Emberline growled.

"No chance," Peter sneered. "I haven't killed her. Her *hunger* will. Everyone knows she was unmarried. Now her blood reserves are gone, she will simply die more quickly than expected. Her death will be marked as a natural occurrence. I'd be surprised if she survives twenty-four hours from here."

Peter stalked across the room to stand over Silvana. Her aunts shrieked curses at him, but he didn't care. And Jason could only watch while clutching his slashed face in agony.

"Now you have no choice!" he shouted. "Marry me now, Silvana."

"She can't use your blood, fool!" Emberline roared.

"But now she knows what I could do to her family," Peter said. He held up a warning finger to the aunts. "With a word, I could drain all their blood. Is that what you want, Silvana? Would you rather they all die?"

Silvana could only gasp. Her breathing was rapid and shallow.

"Marry me, Silvana," Peter said. "I don't care what you do afterwards. Suck Jason dry if you want to. Suck the blood of this entire town. But right now, declare your intentions to me. Say your vows or your whole family will suffer the same fate."

"Silvana!" Jason cried as he crawled across the room. Blood pooled in his eyes and he was almost blind from the pain. He clutched the wound in one hand, and crawled with the other. "Silvana! Take my blood."

"Wait your turn, Jason," Peter sneered. "So, Silvana? What's it going to be?"

Silvana coughed as she tried to slow her breathing. She looked Peter in the eye.

"Stupid question," she wheezed. "Of course I'll marry you. To save…" Her voice trailed off, and Jason felt like the ground had dropped beneath him.

"And I'll marry you," Peter said, then held his sword towards Nicholas. "Declare it so."

Nicholas scowled at him. "I won't."

"Do it, you old bastard! Or I kill everyone in this house!"

Nicholas lifted his head high and openly scoffed at him. "Go ahead. Make my day."

Goddamn that man has balls.

Peter growled and raised his hand towards Nicholas. "Fine. You're a waste of a king anyway."

"Nicholas!" Silvana wheezed out, and everyone went still. "Give him what he wants."

"Silvana. If you marry him, by law you won't be allowed to take blood from anyone else. You will die."

"It's me, or all of you. It's no choice at all." Silvana let out a pained rasp and a dry cough. "Please, Uncle Nick. Do it."

Everyone looked to the old man. Nicholas's thin face seemed to wither and age, and twin tear drops ran down his wrinkled cheeks.

"I declare it so," he whispered.

Peter let out a loud sigh. "Thank fuck," he said. "Should have done that in the first place, instead of all these niceties." He shouted, "Fuck this place! Fuck all of you. I have your titles now. I don't need anything you have. Enjoy your shitty, rotting house and your pathetic illusions of power."

He turned back to Jason, his eyes filled with rage. "If I see you again, mortal scum, I will *burn* you. One body part at a time. Starting with your fucking eyes."

Peter stood up straight and uttered the word, *"Śilaŭrudu".* The room seemed to bend and twist around him, warping space itself. When it finished spinning, he was gone.

Chapter 24

Jason was first on his feet. "Is everyone alright?" he asked, even as a glob of blood dripped from his hand. Silvana had collapsed against her aunts, her eyes closed, her chest slowly rising and falling.

"Nicholas?" Lisbeth said softly.

"I'm alright, my love. It's just my chest that's hurting."

"Is it your heart?"

"No, bones. I've probably broken one or two ribs."

Lisbeth turned to Emberline. "We should use an elixir."

Nicholas waved his hand. "Wait, it's not that serious. Give it to Silvana. Or even Jason."

"Don't even say that!" Phillip roared, suddenly appearing among the others. "We are not giving this boy anything. Not after he brought a wizard into our home and let him murder our child!" Phillip stood before Jason with a red face and a vein line in his forehead throbbing with fury. "Get the hell out of my home, you vile beardsplitter!"

"You had no right to do that," Emberline hissed at Jason. "No right to bring that creature into our home. You knew he was a wizard."

"I exposed his plan!" Jason cried.

"He's a wizard, fool!" She snapped back. "You don't fight them. If you knew, you should have slit his throat then and there! Why would you bring him here and announce it?"

"That's enough," Nicholas said in a quiet voice of command. "Look at his face. He took that wound standing up to a wizard. None of us dared to do that."

"But Silvana is dying because of him," Emberline growled.

Nicholas shook his head. "He fought for Silvana, like a true Knight Templar. He physically attacked a wizard, while we cowered in fear. He showed more courage than all of us combined. I will not send him from our home."

"He endangered this family," Phillip said, pointing to the broken stone wall. "He brought an enemy into our home. Look what he did to Silvana."

"I thought…" Jason muttered, "…if I revealed him…the Imperium…"

"Fool!" Phillip shouted. "What does the Imperium care about us? We're former royals. Our power is useless to them now."

Jason looked between them, his hands held up, pleading. "I don't understand," he whispered.

"Of course you don't, rantallion!" Phillip gestured towards the sky. "The Imperium aren't our protectors. They're not here to protect our rights like a *mortal* government. They're enforcers! They protect their own power, and that's all. They don't give a shit what happens to us."

"That can't be true."

"Look at their laws," Emberline said. "The first law of the Imperium: 'An Immortal cannot kill another Immortal, or a member of an Immortal family'. That's why Peter couldn't kill us. But he was within his rights to work through mortals, or claim Silvana died of thirst. Therefore, the Imperium won't act because he didn't commit murder directly."

Jason could only shake his head. "But that's unfair! He exploited a loophole."

"Second law," Emberline went on. "'An Immortal cannot kill a mortal if it will expose Immortal powers.' Do you see the gap? They don't care about mortal murders, as long as the immortal isn't *caught*."

"No…" Jason gasped. He looked at Silvana. "That's why you didn't want me to call the cops when the mob attacked your house. Because it was dangerous to the police officers. Any immortal can kill the police without consequences as long as they don't reveal themselves."

"That's how the Imperium works, Jason," Lisbeth said in a much gentler tone. "They've existed for over two thousand years. Their laws aren't modern like yours."

"So exposing the wizard," Phillip growled, "was never going to fix anything! Maybe if we were rich and powerful, we'd have friends who do us a favour. As it stands, no one will give us justice."

Jason looked around the room. He felt sick to the stomach. "I'm sorry. I'm so sorry. I thought Peter would give up and leave. Or maybe three vampires and their knights could fight one wizard. I never imagined he'd be that powerful. I thought the Vigiles of the Imperium would help."

"No one helps us," Emberline snapped coldly. "We must survive on our own."

"We used to have power," Nicholas said, his voice sober and deep. "Our houses were among those who ruled the world. The royalty made us strong." He sighed, and his eyes seemed ancient. "But the monarchy was abandoned. Too many arrogant rulers who didn't care for their mortals. With the rise of democracy and science, the mortals cast off the old ways. The belief in a ruler's divine right was lost. Some immortal families were able to adapt. But ours wasn't."

He looked up at Jason with mournful eyes, and gestured at the decrepit mansion with gaps in the walls. "Now you see what we are. Ghosts of our former glories. Irrelevant and forgotten. The world has passed us by while we lived in the shadow of the past." The others were quiet at his words, and the dusty mansion stood in silent affirmation.

"And yet, we're the lucky ones," Lisbeth said. "We don't have power, but at least we have a few properties and assets. We have a home here in Plymouth, away from the rest of the world. Many immortals have less than that. They're outcasts from both mortal and immortal societies. Homeless, destitute. Living in fear of mortal persecution."

Like Peter, Jason thought. *Illegitimate. Living as a mortal.*

"Is that why Peter wants your titles?" Jason asked. "Because at least it's more than he has?"

"He's a fool," Emberline spat. "A young immortal, drunk on stories of the glory of monarchy. We still have immortals who think kings and queens will come back to the mortal realm. They seem to think all their problems would be solved if they could just claim a throne. Peter genuinely thinks he'll become king of Russia, now he has the Romanoff title. He doesn't see how useless that title is nowadays."

Jason's mouth was hanging open. "King of Russia? But…there isn't even a throne left."

"Now you see how dangerous Peter really is," Nicholas said. "He's not just a powerful wizard. He has delusions of grandeur that warp his perception of reality."

Silvana coughed again, and gave a pained whimper. Her aunts turned back to her and cooed softly. Jason crossed the room and knelt at her side. His right hand was cupped to his face as a stream of red flowed through his fingers, down his forearm and dripped from his elbow.

"Silvana," he said. "Here. Take my blood."

"It's too late, fool," Emberline hissed. "You should have made the offer when it would have mattered."

Jason froze in horror. "You mean, nothing can save her now?"

Lisbeth shook her head, and a tear fell onto Silvana's withered face. "She's married to an immortal whose blood is useless to her. There's no undoing that marriage. She will starve."

"What!?" Jason shouted. Everyone turned to him, but he kept shouting. "You mean you won't LET her have my blood because she's not married to me?"

"Third law of the Imperium," Emberline declared. "'Vampires can only consume blood from their marital spouse.' What you're describing is an abomination."

"It's just another corrupt Imperium law. They won't even protect us, so who gives a shit what they think? I'm trying to save her fucking life! What do the Imperium care anyway?"

"They will destroy us," Emberline growled, "if we break their laws. There is no challenging a wizard. You think we can break their laws without consequence?"

Lisbeth gave a pained sigh. "It's not just a law. These are our principals. We don't use our power to steal and destroy. This is how we are different to immortals like Peter. Our power is a gift from someone else. Someone we love."

"But this is a gift!" Jason held out his bloody, dripping hand. The gash on his face stung horribly when he took the pressure off, but he kept his hand out. "I'm giving it to her. Because I care about her. I don't need marriage to prove it."

"Get away from her!" Emberline growled and slapped his hand away with enough force to make him stagger and fall to the ground. "You will not corrupt her with your impurity."

Jason felt his anger – his frustration at his powerlessness – come to the surface all at once. He shouted like he hadn't shouted in twelve years.

"You're still stuck in the past!"

His voice carried through the mansion. Everyone went still at his words. It felt good to let it out. So he yelled some more.

"Your family has come to ruin because you wouldn't change! You wouldn't adapt with the times! Now you'll let Silvana die rather than break one of your fucking outdated rules!"

The mansion was still. Phillip and Emberline were glaring daggers at him, but didn't say anything. Meanwhile, Nicholas and Lisbeth wouldn't meet his eyes.

"Jason…"

Silvana's voice was weak. Her eyes were shut as she held up a weak hand, reaching towards him. "Jason…"

Lisbeth moved aside, allowing Jason to kneel next to Silvana to cup her hand between both of his, smearing blood on her palm. "I'm here, Silvana."

She moved one of her fingers slightly to touch him back. That was all she could do. *She's so weak.*

"Jason… listen…" her voice was raspy, barely more than a whisper. "I wouldn't want to be with you…if we weren't married."

"What? Silvana, that's…"

Emberline held up a hand to silence him. Silvana was struggling to speak, so Jason bit his tongue and waited.

"Jason…you deserve someone who is committed to you. If I were married to you…" she smiled weakly, "I would work hard every day to make you happy. I would make your meals, clean every room, wash your clothes…"

"You sound like a slave," Jason said despondently.

"No, a servant. Jason, I would serve you every day of my life. And it would make me so happy…" her lip quivered, and a single tear fell from her eyelid. "You deserve that, Jason. You…you would have made a wonderful husband…"

Oh my god…she's saying goodbye…

"Silvana," Jason cried, "you don't have to do this."

"Yes I do, Jason. Yes I do."

"But marriage doesn't mean anything!"

There were several gasps from the family and a look of pain crossed

Silvana's face. Jason half regretted his words. Her eyes opened again to look at him.

"Jason…I know your parents had a bad marriage, but ours would have been different."

Something snapped inside Jason, and suddenly he found himself determined to speak.

"I didn't tell you the true story," he said. "Silvana, my parents didn't just have bad marriage." A pain that had nothing to do with his wound made him grimace as he struggled to get the words out. "It was abusive in all the worse ways possible. An endless nightmare for my mother…"

He didn't want to tell this story. He hated this story. But if it could save Silvana's life, he would tell her the truth.

"It's one of my earliest memories. I might have been two, or three. I remember my father, standing over my crying mother, screaming at her that he was the husband, she was the wife, and she had to submit to him." He looked up at Silvana's pained expression. "It was like that every day. And you know what the worst part was? *I believed him.*" Jason felt tears sting his eyes. His voice wavered, and he made no effort to hide it.

"I thought she deserved it." He had to swallow to clear his throat. "I know I was just a child, a frightened little boy trying to make sense of a scary world. But I truly believed for a while that my father was right to treat her that way. I even copied him. I became like him. I was horrible to my mum. I treated her so badly."

"But…" Silvana whispered, "…you said, your mother taught you to respect women?"

Jason gave a black laugh. "Yeah. She taught me why I had to."

Silvana managed to squeeze his hand a little. "You said…she died…"

"Yeah."

Jason stared at the ground. He'd told this story a dozen times, to all the therapists, school counsellors, and all the psych evaluators at the academy. But it was still hard every time.

"I was twelve. I came home from school. I found her body…hanging from… the…"

He broke down, gritting his teeth together as his body shook with each wracking sob. Each cry made his chest heave in pain. The room blurred as tears completely obscured his vision. But he looked at Silvana and forced out the words.

"My father blamed her for it. Said she was weak and selfish. That she abandoned me because she didn't love me. *And I believed that too.*"

Someone touched him on his back and he turned to see Lisbeth crouched beside him, patting him on the shoulder with tenderness in her eyes. She had a genuine tear on her cheek in sympathy.

For a moment, Lisbeth felt like his real mum, coming back to give him strength just when he needed it most.

"A few months later, I was seeing a school counsellor because of my bad behaviour. She told me something no one else had the guts to say. That my father was abusive, and my mother was a victim. I yelled at her so much that I was sent home. But the thought stuck in my head. I started looking at my father differently. I questioned him. Then one day, I got it. I remember everything about the exact moment it happened. I had just come home from school, Dad was sitting on the couch and he said to me…I'll always remember his exact words. 'Clean the dishes, Jason. That bitch ain't gonna do it anymore.'" Jason smiled. "And right then, it hit me. *He* had killed her. It was *his* fault. And I just…snapped. I ran at him. I just started screaming and punching the fuck out of him. I kept screaming, 'you killed her' over and over."

"Did you…" Silvana whispered, "…kill…"

"No. My father was a violent man. I only got in a few good hits before he beat the absolute shit out of me. It was so bad that I was removed from his care. That's when I was forced into the foster system. I haven't seen my father in twelve years. Not since that day." He took a long breath and said the hardest truth of his life. "The worst part is knowing my mum died, believing I hated her. When I should have been the one to save her."

"I'm sorry." Silvana gave a knowing look. "That's why you're…a policeman. You want to protect people like her."

"Yeah," he whispered.

"And that's why…you're scared of monsters…"

Jason nodded. He wiped the tears from his eyes, but ended up poking at the wound on his face and crying out in pain. "Do you see why I don't want to get married? I've seen how marriage is used by evil men to dominate women. I could never do that. I would rather die than do that to you."

He held his bloodied hand out to her again. "But I still want to give you this. Do you understand? Marriage is just a word. What matters is who we are, and who we choose. I want you, Silvana. I choose you. Please…just take my blood."

Silvana looked at him with teary eyes. "I'm sorry, Jason. But marriage…it's more than just a word to me. And I would rather die…than live unmarried to you."

She slumped down into Emberline's arms, and her eyes shut.

"Silvana!" Jason cried.

"She's asleep," Emberline said softly. "She doesn't have much time left."

Jason looked around the room at the others. "Will one of you take my blood? Keep it in a vial. You can use it to save her, if she changes…" he trailed off when he saw them all avoiding his gaze.

"She has made her choice," Lisbeth said, still patting his back. "Honour that choice, Jason."

"We'll watch over her," Nicholas said, now standing beside them. "We'll enjoy these final precious hours. You have conducted yourself with honour, Jason. You are welcome to spend those hours at her side."

Emberline lifted Silvana up and started carrying her towards the bedrooms. Phillip followed her without a word.

"I'd be happy to stitch that cut of yours," Lisbeth said. "I have some experience."

Jason just watched Silvana go. He stared after her, and felt like his heart had been ripped clean from his chest.

"Will you stay, Jason?" Nicholas asked.

Jason only clenched his fist. "I would appreciate that stitching, Lisbeth," he said. "But I'm not staying."

Nicholas and Lisbeth glanced at each other. "Why not?" Nicholas asked.

"Because I'm going to go find Peter. And cut his fucking throat."

Chapter 25

" Jason, please," Nicholas said from his armchair in the corner of the bedroom. "Peter is more powerful than you realise. Even his demonstrations here did not truly show what a wizard can do. Attacking him would be suicide."

Jason sat on a leather chair next to a chest of draws. He held his chin up and sat perfectly still while Lisbeth threaded a needle carefully through his cheek. The sword had entered from the right side of his chin, cut up through his cheek, and narrowly missed his right eye to exit beside his temple. She used a numbing injection to remove most of the pain but now part of Jason's speech was affected.

"I don' care," he slurred. "If he's dead...she can mar'... me instea'. Then take blah..."

"Blood?" Nicholas asked. Jason nodded. "Look, you're brave, son. But you have no idea where Peter's gone. What do you think his plan is now? Go conquer Russia and proclaim himself Emperor? Or go home and play arcade games?"

Arcade games? Jesus, Nick...

"You don't know," Nicholas went on. "He could be anywhere in the world by now."

"The worl'?"

"Wizards move quickly, Jason," Lisbeth explained as she continued to weave the needle through Jason's cheek. "You saw him teleport himself out of here. There's no limit to how far they can go. You need to consider that Peter could be anywhere on the planet."

Jason growled in frustration.

"Face it, son," Nicholas said. "You'd be better off spending your time by Silvana's side. She's in her bedroom with her other aunt and uncle. You should be there with her. Treasure your final hours together. It's your last date."

Jason stared at the floor. *Our last date.* The thought was too terrible to even consider. He refused to face the possibility until he had tried everything possible to destroy Peter.

Lisbeth stood up. "You're finished. Go easy on it, sweetie. That'll take two weeks to heal properly." She gracefully swept over to Nicholas's side and took his hand. "We should go."

Nicholas wrapped an arm around her. "Come with us, Jason," he said softly. "Please."

Jason's face was still burning. He thought of Silvana, screaming as her blood was ripped from her body. And Peter, his eyes psychopathic and drunk with power, the look of glee on his face as he threatened Jason.

"If I see you again, mortal, I will burn you. One body part at a time. Starting with your fucking eyes."

He stood up and looked at the old couple. Nicholas and Lisbeth really were lovely people, in their own quirky way. He hated to disappoint them.

"Can I borrow one of your swords?"

Lisbeth gave a pained sigh. Nicholas just studied him.

"You would have made Silvana a wonderful husband," Nicholas said. "You would make a great Knight Templar." He gestured around him. "Take whichever sword you think best, and go with my fullest blessing. Godspeed, Jason."

They left the room hand in hand to go stand vigil by Silvana's deathbed.

* * *

Jason sat in the driver's seat of his car. On the seat next to him sat the same rapier that had sliced his face open. The blade rested on the floor. The handle was within his reach. He gripped the steering wheel with both hands, his knuckles white, and he drove…

…to nowhere in particular.

"Where the hell are you, Peter?" he growled.

Jason tried to think about the wizard's next move and where he could be headed, but his brain was screaming at him to go back to Silvana. She needed blood. Could he force her to take…no, she'd made her choice clear.

Stupid Silvana! You stupid idiot! Damn it, Silvana, you stupid idiot!

But he stopped that line of thought. She wasn't an idiot. She was just like his mother, forced into a choice that seemed inevitable to her. She wasn't to blame. Peter was the one to blame.

Silvana's family loved her. Maybe they were overprotective, but they were all clearly aggrieved by her situation. They weren't responsible for what was happening. She wasn't abused or forced into her choice. She willingly chose not to break the law, knowing it would keep her loved ones safe from the Imperium's retribution.

"Damn it, Silvana. You could have just taken it…"

He looked at the sword. A streak of red still stained the tip. *Get it together, Jason. You must find Peter.*

But how could he do that? Jason was in over his head. He knew nothing of the magic and skills Peter possessed. He truly could be anywhere in the world right now. The question was; why? Why did Peter want the royal title? Was he going to the Imperium to claim his new privileges? Was he going to attack mortals in Russia? Jason had no idea what the title could mean to him, and what doors it would unlock for an already powerful wizard. What was next for Peter?

Jason still had Peter's phone number. *I could call him. Trick him somehow into revealing himself.* Yet he remembered the last thing Peter said. The threat to burn Jason alive. *I don't care what he does to me!*

But it wouldn't help. Calling Peter, or even messaging him, would only show that Jason was still fighting back. At least now, Peter thought he was beaten. Jason knew there was no way he could take Peter in a straight fight, not alone, especially since the wizard had beaten two knights and three vampires with a word.

No. The only way to have a chance against Peter was to take him unawares. Kill him while his attention was elsewhere. A single sword thrust into the chest. *No, the throat! So he can't speak any spells!*

The thought made Jason feel sick. Even if he could find Peter, there was only one way to save Silvana. She would only accept Jason's blood if they were married. She could only marry him if Peter was out of the way.

Jason had to kill him.

Am I even capable of that? He hadn't been able to arrest Alex Bishop. He couldn't stop his father, and he couldn't stop Peter back at Maristow mansion. *I'm afraid of violent men. What if I become like them?*

He tightened his grip on his steering wheel. *No. I must kill him. It's the only possible way to save Silvana.*

Jason sped up and drove to his apartment. If nothing else, he could search through Peter's belongings. Maybe he'd find some clue to his next stage in his plan.

He entered Plymouth town and navigated the dense evening traffic to get to his apartment. Things slowed down even more when all cars had to make way for a fire truck rushing past, but Jason thought nothing of it. It was only when his apartment complex came into view that he understood.

Black smoke was billowing from the top of his building. Flames flickered out the widows, spilling soot and ash onto the pavement below. The first fire truck arrived and half a dozen firemen swarmed from the vehicle, rushing to get their hoses into action.

My God.

Jason pulled over to the side of the road and stared in horror. The whole complex was filled with smoke. *Did Peter just kill everyone in that building because of me?* His stomach churned in revulsion and he put a hand to his mouth.

Yet people were running out from the entrance, safely exiting the building. He realised that not all of the complex was on fire. No, just one set of windows two stories up and on the south side. It was his apartment alone that was up in flames.

The walls were blackened and the widows blown outwards. There was nothing that could have possibly survived. Nothing to salvage. Everything he owned was gone.

"Damn you, Peter!"

Jason rushed over to the firefighters. "Sir, step back please," said a man dressed in a fireman's uniform and helmet.

"I'm a police officer. What can I do to help? Are there people in there?"

The man seemed to take him more seriously. His eyes drifted to the vicious scar on Jason's face and squinted in suspicion. "Just keep a perimeter. Don't let anyone in or near the building under any circumstances. Got it?"

Jason nodded, and the firefighters went to work. Gawkers had begun to arrive at the scene. He recognised some of his neighbours on the opposite street, watching the flames billow up into the sky and blend with the orange sunset. No one tried to get inside the building though, so Jason began a short patrol up and down the footpath. He watched as the hose and ladder went up and his apartment was doused.

It was only then that the truth hit him. He was homeless, and everything he owned was lost.

The only things he had left in the world was his car, a couple hundred pounds in his bank account, and the clothes on his back. Nothing had changed. After all his years working and training, he was still a helpless little child forced out of his home with nowhere to go. But that didn't matter right now. Silvana was still dying. There was nothing he could do to save her now. He had nothing. No leads, no resources, no magic.

The firefighters let out a cheer and announced the flames were out. The watchers on the street applauded. Jason wandered back to his car in a daze, not even bothering to offer more help. He sat in the driver's seat and stared at the roof of his car. Night had fallen. Streetlamps had begun to come on. And his car was getting cold. Jason wrapped himself in a spare jacket and hoped it was enough. He might be spending a few nights in his car in the future.

Jason pulled out his phone on a whim and started a call.

The phone answered, and a woman's voice came through, calm and professional. "Hello, this is Aisha?"

"Captain," Jason said.

"Turner?" her voice was surprised, then instantly became tense and alert. "What are you calling me for? Is everything alright?"

"No. Captain, I…"

"Jason? Where are you?"

"I'm in my car. Just chilling."

A pause. "What are you planning to do?"

Jason let out a short laugh. "Captain, I'm not going to murder anyone. You don't have to talk me down from a ledge or anything, ok?"

"Ok," she said. Her tone was still guarded.

"I'm calling you because…I don't have anyone else." The words were hard to admit. He almost felt the urge to cry. "I know it's probably inappropriate, but can I just talk to you?"

She didn't hesitate for a second. "Of course, Jason. What's on your mind?"

He felt a rush of gratitude for the terse woman and had to steady himself. "You know what happened to my mother. How my father… drove her to it."

"Yes, Jason."

That simple acknowledgement made tears well in the corners of his eyes. For years, he'd listened to people try to justify his father's behaviour. Well-meaning people, even medical experts, had all tried to say it had been her choice, and no one could make you commit suicide. But Jason knew the truth. And just hearing Kader agree with him so easily meant the world to him.

"I swore I'd never be like my father. I'd never hurt anyone. I'd never be violent. It's the whole reason I became a cop, so I could protect people. But now…I wonder if I made a mistake."

"How so, Jason?"

He thought of his father, who walked free after destroying his wife and nearly doing the same to his own son. He thought of the Imperium, who did nothing to help its citizens. And Silvana, dying, while Jason was powerless to bring her killer to justice.

"What do you do when the law fails to help people?"

"Ah," the captain drawled. "Is that all?"

Jason gave a black laugh. "Jason, that's the question every law enforcer has at some point. Do you know why? Because the law will never be perfect. It's always going to have loopholes. Some officers will never realise this and stay blind. Others realise it, and become shitty cops who don't try. But good cops will just keep doing their best."

"But my best isn't good enough," Jason said. "People still get hurt."

"Jason," Kader said gently, "you can't save everyone. No matter how much you want to."

"Then what's the point!" Jason cried. "What good are we, if we can't save everyone?"

She was silent for a few seconds. Then she said in a voice ringing with strength. "Because sometimes, we can save *someone*."

Jason sat up straighter. He relaxed his grip on the phone and let out a long sigh. He finally understood something he'd never realised before.

"I've always been angry," he whispered, "that no one saved my mum. We had extended family. We had neighbours, police, even myself. None of us saved her. We all failed her." His breath was shaking, and his voice cracked. "But someone saved *me*."

His lip trembled so much he couldn't speak, and tears were filling his eyes.

"That's right, Jason. Someone did save you. I know it was hard growing up the way you did, and I can't begin to imagine what you went through. But a lot of people came together to help you. They probably made a lot of mistakes, sure, even though they tried their best. Sometimes, Jason, that's all we can do. We can't save everyone. But we can try to do the right thing. We can do our best. And every so often, that's enough to save one person."

Jason let out a long sigh. "Thank you, Captain. I needed to hear that."

"It's alright. Are you..." she paused. "Is this about you being accused of the murders?"

He smiled to himself. "Sort of."

"I don't suppose you know who is responsible?"

"Oh yes," Jason said in a flat tone. "A wizard did it."

"Very funny, Jason. But if you do want to talk to me about the case, like professionals, you always can."

Jason sighed. It was worth a try. "Thanks, captain. I'll see you tomorrow."

"My pleasure. Take care, Jason."

He hung up and sat back in his car seat. He had to keep going. If only he knew what to do. There were no more leads to explore. Peter was gone, and there was no one who knew where he would be. *Except, that's not exactly true.* He pulled out his phone and started searching.

Do your best. Sometimes it's enough.

He searched for the Monster Hunters.

He went through google, social media sites, and platforms, finding nothing by vague similarities. Until he ended up on Reddit and found a username with 'moho' in the title. He clicked through, and found a picture of Timothy Harrison.

There was a pinned post under his name. "Emergency meeting tonight, Plymouth town hall."

It's a lead. A weak one, but it's something.

Jason entered the address into his phone and started driving.

Chapter 26

Jason stood on the footpath, hands in his jean pockets, and the hood of his jacket drawn over his face. The old town hall stood before him painted in a hideous lime green and built from flimsy wooden panels that looked like they were installed on a tight budget. Grey steps led up to the entrance. The sounds of male voices filtered through the open double doors, though the cars driving past were masking the exact words.

An extra weight pressed against Jason's chest now, after a visit to the police station. He wore a holster concealed under his jacket. And inside, his Glock 17 handgun, the very one that was supposed to be in the evidence locker where Jason was banned from going. But none of that mattered now. He needed it. If Peter appeared, Jason knew what he needed to do. Only this time, he wouldn't hesitate.

"Into the lion's den," he muttered as he stalked up the steps.

Someone was shouting from inside. It sounded like Timothy Harrison, the leader of the Monster Hunters. Jason stepped through the open double doors and into the light.

The hall was mostly empty. Only twenty or so people were there, and all were crowded around the stage at the far end. Two men stood by the door at a checkout desk. They spotted Jason.

"Hey, new guy?" one of them asked. The man was young, Asian, and sounded friendly. Maybe a bit overly friendly. Jason recognised him from the other night, when the angry mob came to Silvana's house. He was the nice one who had tried to deescalate the situation.

Jason kept his voice gruff and low. "Yeah. Wanted to see what all this was."

"You're welcome here, mate," an older man said. "We're the Monster Hunters. We protect the town from vampires, werewolves, yetis, that sort of thing. You ever seen any of them?"

Jason tilted his head to the side and raised his hood slightly. The men jerked back at the sight of the grisly scar up his face. "A monster did this to me," he growled.

"Whoa…so cool," the young guy murmured, leaning forward to get a better look at Jason's patched scar.

"You came to the right place," the older man said, glaring at the youngster next to him. "We'll fuck up the bastards that did this to you. I just need a name and email address to let you in." Jason concealed his face again. He wrote down his real name, but used a fake email. Both men nodded at him. "Welcome, brother."

"Hey, I had a friend who told me about this place," Jason said. "Either of you know a guy called Peter Erikson?"

Both shook their heads. "Someone else must have checked him in," the young guy said, nodding to the larger group of people near the stage. "We change roles a lot."

"s'alright. Thanks."

Jason walked across the hall, each step echoing on the wooden floors. He listened as a man on the stage shouted down to the others. It wasn't hard to recognise the pudgy form of Timothy Harrison. "…two of us they've killed now. You know what this means. We are in a battle to the death between man and monsters. It's them or us! We didn't start this fight, but you can be damn sure we're going to finish it!"

The people below gave an angry shout in agreement. Jason stood at the back of the group and scanned through the faces gathered around Timothy. He recognised a few of the men from the attack on Silvana's house, but couldn't see his old roommate's face amongst them.

Where are you, Peter?

"You saw what happened the other night," Timothy went on. "The police were acting on the monster's orders. They arrested me, just for standing against those foul beasts. Then they locked me up in a cell all night, unprotected. By God's grace, I was spared."

The crowd stared up at the stage, so Jason couldn't see every face from the back. He moved to the left side to get a better view and studied each person from there, one at a time.

"But now is the time to take action. We must attack again. We cannot stop until they're all dead!"

Even from this vantage point, Jason still couldn't see every suspect. He tried moving again and bumped into someone. He mumbled an apology but couldn't help making eye contact.

It was just a stranger. Their eyes widened when they saw Jason's wound.

"Beg your pardon," he muttered again and moved on.

Timothy's voice filtered down from the stage. "If you have firearms, now is the time to collect them. If you don't have any yourself, Brother Aaron has agreed to supply us with some of his personal weapons. Brother Aaron?" Timothy gestured to someone by the edge of the stage.

God, firearms? This is bad.

An old man in a blue flannel jacket moved up to stand next to Timothy. This man looked about seventy years old, though still able-bodied. He held up a hand to acknowledge the crowd. "I'm happy to contribute in this way," he said. "I'm not as strong as I used to be. But together, we can purge our town of evil."

Jason blinked. Something was familiar about him, but Jason couldn't pinpoint what exactly. *Aaron's face? His voice?*

"You might be afraid right now," Aaron continued. "But fear not. You know the bible says God has given us victory, and a spirit of courage and not of fear."

Jason knew that voice. He was certain now.

Aaron declared boldly, "And God said, 'Let him have dominion over the fish of the sea, and over the birds of the air, and over the beasts of the earth.' Do you get it, men? Our dominion over the monsters is a divine right!"

I know that verse. Jason couldn't take it anymore and leapt up on the stage. Every set of eyes glared up at him. Aaron's eyes grew wide in recognition.

"*Gerald!*" Jason screamed and drew his gun.

The crowd screamed as everyone dropped to the ground and covered their heads. Timothy fell back onto the floor.

But the man known as Aaron stood totally still. He held up his hands and his mouth hung open in shock. Yet the corners of his eyes were smiling in amusement.

Jason froze. He suddenly realised he couldn't fire. *What was I thinking?* Gerald had done nothing to attack him. He couldn't murder Gerald in front of all these people. But he couldn't arrest him either. *Damn it, I got spooked.* Jason took a breath and tried to speak in a calm voice to control the situation.

"Listen to me, everyone," he said. "That man is not Aaron. He is a changeling. A skinwalker, and his real name is Gerald. He is one of the monsters you are hunting and he's been lying to you."

No one was saying anything. Gerald just stared at him with the face of a terrified old man. "He's one of them," Jason insisted, thrusting his gun towards Gerald's chest. "He can change his shape. I've seen him do it. He attacked me as a polar bear."

"It's you!" Timothy cried.

Jason looked down to where the group leader lay sprawled on his back, pointing a shaking finger. "It's the cop who arrested me! He's snuck into our meeting!"

"Hey. I didn't sneak in! I signed in at the entrance," Jason said indignantly. "But this man is the real imposter. Gerald, reveal yourself."

"I don't know what you're talking about," Gerald said, acting scared. "I'm human. I've been coming here for weeks."

Jason hesitated, unsure for a moment. *No, it's definitely him. I saw the look of recognition when he saw me.* He studied Gerald.

"What are you even doing here?" Jason asked. "Where's Rion Dankworth? Where's Kathryn Smith?"

Gerald's eyes widened slightly.

"Yeah, I know who they are. I tracked them," Jason cried. "And I'm currently tracking…" he trailed off. "Oh…Oh I get it now. You're working with him, aren't you?" Jason snarled. "You're working with Peter Erikson!"

Gerald recoiled slightly, a look of genuine surprise on his face. "I…I don't know any Peter," he stammered.

"It makes sense now. You three harassed us, the night of Peter's date with Silvana. It was all an act. Peter was meant to fight you off to impress Silvana, except I got there first." He grinned. "No wonder he seemed pissed with me. Then the next day, you three followed me on my date with Silvana, to make sure we stayed away from the mansion during the hunter's attack."

"What are you talking about?"

Jason pressed on, shouting as the realisation hit him. "I bet you're the ones who started the Plymouth branch of the Mohos. You gathered these men together. You've been lying to them, grooming them for your use. You're Peter's servant, which means you're the one who paid Alex Bishop! You transferred him money to kill Silvana's family.

You've manipulated all these people."

"I haven't done anything!" Gerald cried, turning to the others to plead. "I'm just trying to protect this town from the vampires."

"You're working for a wizard." Jason turned to face the room, lowering his gun and gesturing. "You call yourself Monster Hunters. But what you're really looking for is immortals. There are many immortal species. Vampires are just one kind. There are wizards too. And a wizard has been tricking you into attacking his vampire enemies. The vampire family you're attacking are good people."

"That's a lie!" Timothy cried, finally finding his courage and getting on his feet. "This cop has corrupted the law. He arrested me, and his buddies let me go because I'd done nothing wrong. He's a rogue cop!"

"Listen, there's a wizard who's been using you. Don't let yourself be controlled."

Gerald held up his hands. "Holy Moses…" he cried.

Jason talked over the top of him.

"This man who you call Aaron—" Something moved in the corner of his eye and Jason spun on the spot, pointing his gun towards the movement.

A figure had appeared from behind the stage. A man, lean and fit, his hair cut short. He appeared behind Timothy with his fangs bared.

Rion! The vampire!

"NO!" Jason shouted.

Rion sank his teeth into Timothy's neck, and a jet of blood sprayed across the stage.

The hall erupted in screams. Jason blocked it all out. He raised his gun, took careful aim to avoid Timothy. He breathed out to relax. And *pulled the trigger* without hesitation.

The shot hit Rion in the bottom jaw, making his head jerk sideways as he fell back. A clump of white bone flew upwards from the impact.

"RION!" Gerald cried.

The vampire hit the ground with a shriek, clutching at his injured face. Jason glanced at him – *no damage to upper head or neck. Superficial wound only* – and dropped next to Timothy.

The monster hunter was bleeding from the neck. He had two very human bite marks on the skin, yet the place where the incisors bit down had pierced deeply into flesh. Jason ripped off his jacket and pressed it against the wound. Timothy was awake, and fully alert.

"Hang on," Jason said. "You'll be ok. I know it looks bad, but you haven't lost much blood yet. You should survive this."

He looked up. Gerald was right beside him, crouched down over Rion in an identical position to Jason. He had shifted back into his own body again, young and fit with blond hair. His eyes were filled with tears as he clutched his boyfriend.

Then he suddenly looked Jason in the eye.

Oh fuck...

Gerald shrieked and launched himself at Jason, morphing into a lion. A fully grown male lion with a thick mane, massive padded feet with claws, and a jaw that opened shockingly wide.

Jason dived off the stage. He felt searing pain as something cut into his thigh, and sent a tearing sensation right down to his knee. He hit the floor a metre beneath the stage, rolled onto his back, and fired.

Two shots hit the adult lion in the left shoulder. It roared and ducked out of sight. Jason could no longer see it from on the ground. He tried to stand so he could get off another shot but his legs wouldn't work. He looked down.

His left leg was bleeding profusely. He stared at it…and felt nothing. A numbness was sweeping over his whole body. His mind was screaming at him that he was going into shock. There was a lot of blood. *A lot of blood!* The lion's claws must have hit an artery. It was already forming a pool at his feet. Jason watched as the red puddle moved slowly away from him.

Focus!

He had to staunch the flow. He ripped off his belt and tied it around his thigh just below his groin. Something banged on stage. He saw a gorilla, silver-backed and huge, hobbling backstage with a wounded Rion in its thick black arms. The two of them disappeared out back and the sound of a door slamming open marked their escape.

Jason glanced around. The other people were still there, cowering near the entrance and keeping well away. They were all motionless.

"Help me," Jason cried. "I'm bleeding out. Call an ambulance!" No one moved.

"Can someone help Timothy? Please! You need to…"

A woman's shrill voice cried out, "It was a vampire! You all saw it! A vampire attacked us! We need to fight back!"

Jason turned, and he saw her. Kathryn Smith. Young and beautiful, with her long brown hair tied up in a ponytail. She saw Jason watching her, and she smirked in satisfaction.

"We need to arm ourselves now! We know where they live. It's time to *kill the vampires!*" she screamed.

The cry was taken up by all those remaining. "Kill the vampires! Kill the vampires!" Everyone sprang towards the exits. Someone ran onto the stage to carry Timothy away. A few lingered around Jason, looking at him with worried eyes, but none stepped in to help.

"Leave him," Kathryn said from their sides. "You know he came here to spy on us and trick us. He works for the enemy."

"She's lying!" Jason cried. "She's a telepath. She can read your mind. She's playing on your fears!" They all turned to go. "Wait!" Jason cried, but everyone was already running out of the hall.

He felt too dizzy to stand, his mind foggy, and the pain was only coming in sudden stabs. *Oh my god. I'm dying. And I did nothing to help Silvana.*

Someone was near him. "What can I do?" a young voice said. A man was crouched next to Jason. It was the guy who had met him at the entrance, the young Asian man. Up close he had a mop of hair, brown eyes, and he looked petrified.

"I need…" Jason cried.

Someone had stopped to help him, but he didn't even know what to do. He had already lost too much blood. He'd be dead before any ambulance could arrive. It would take a miracle to save him now.

Or magic. But you don't have any of that…

Jason's eyes widened. "Get me to my car!" he cried, shoving his gun back into his holster. The young man stammered, so Jason gave him orders. "Help me stand. Carry me outside. Quickly!"

The man grabbed Jason under an arm and lifted. Together they got him standing. The room swayed, and Jason nearly fainted. But he leaned on his companion and started hobbling.

"What's your name?" he groaned.

"Freddie."

"And why are you helping me, Freddie?"

He struggled to speak through gritted teeth, "Cause we're supposed to help people. That's why I joined…"

They made it to the front doors. Someone had shut them when they left, so Freddie shoved them open with his shoulder and helped Jason through. The night was cold, yet Jason's wound was on fire. His good leg wobbled with each step. His whole body was tingling.

"Which car is yours?" Freddie cried.

"Brown Hyundai."

"I don't see it."

"I parked…around the corner…"

Jason collapsed. He felt exhausted, and he knew it was the blood loss. He was running out of time. "Freddie," he cried, and pulled his keys out. "Go to my glove box. Inside is a glass vial with blue liquid. Get it, and force me to drink it."

"What? What's it gonna do?"

"It's...magic..."

He saw the look of horror on Freddie's face. "I can't do that. I'm a Hunter..."

"Please trust me. It will save my life. It's the only thing that can. Please, Freddie..." Jason felt his head drop down, and his vision went black.

"Please..."

Chapter 27

Something rushed through Jason's body, burning, freezing, and filling him with strength. His awareness came back to him. His eyes opened.

He was on the ground, his cheek pressed to the pavement. Freddie's face was in front of him. And the empty glass vial was on the ground in front of his mouth.

The elixir!

It was working. Jason could feel it running through his body like electricity and targeting the pain from every wound. The burning sensation in his legs began to vanish, and the sheer absence of pain became an ecstasy, making him gasp with relief. He sat up and checked his legs. The wounds were closed, though they still looked bloody and tender. Even as he watched, he saw his flesh…*wriggling*.

"Oh that's unsettling," he murmured.

But as gross as it looked, it felt amazing. His skin shifted into place and formed up again. Soon Jason only had a lot of blood stains to worry about. The wound itself was gone. Something tingled on his face and he reached up to feel the stiches unravelling and sliding out of his skin as his cheek knitted itself together as well.

He looked up, and saw Freddie leaning over him, his face white. "Hey, thanks buddy. You saved my life."

"Uh-huh," Freddie murmured, looking like he wanted to be sick.

"You don't have to throw up. It's ok."

Freddie kept staring at the place Jason's wound used to be. But not in revulsion like Jason first thought. The guy was terrified. His eyes darted to Jason's face. "What have I done?" he gasped.

"Whoa now," Jason said. "I'm a human. Just like you. I'm not a monster. I was just given that healing elixir by a friend." He held out a hand. "My name's Jason Turner. I'm pleased to meet you, Freddie."

The young man seemed to calm down when he saw Jason's extended hand. He offered his own. "Freddie Je." They shook hands. Freddie's grip was weak.

"Je…that's Korean?"

"Yeah."

"Uh…that's great."

Jason tried sitting up. He suddenly felt so light headed he nearly collapsed. The world spun around him and he felt a strange tingling in every limb. "That's not good," he muttered. Freddie helped him into a sitting position. He found himself still on the front steps of the town hall. The street was deserted now. His car was parked directly in front of them. Freddie must have brought it around.

"Your friends," Jason said, while hanging his head between his knees. "Are they really going to attempt to murder the Clarke family?"

He couldn't see Freddie's face but he heard the reluctance. "Yeah man, I think they're gonna try."

Jason nodded. "And what about Gerald's suggestion, to give them all firearms?" A pause. "Aaron. The guy you knew as Aaron. Does he have guns?"

"I saw them," Freddie said. "Miriam was handing them out from Aaron's car just a few minutes ago. You were unconscious."

"Miriam?" Jason murmured. Does he mean Kathryn? It could be another fake name. "Ah!" he cried, suddenly getting it. "Aaron and

Miriam, from the bible. They were the brother and sister of Moses. And Gerald called out 'Holy Moses' just before Rion attacked. It was a signal. They were using codenames."

Then he swore. This whole operation was just too well planned out. He'd thought the motorbike gang were merely a bunch of dumb teenagers with immortal powers. But this meant they could be more dangerous than he feared.

"Freddie, what kind of guns was Miriam handing out?"

"I...I don't know."

Jason sighed. "Were they handguns? Shotguns? Or automatics?"

"Handguns," Freddie cried. "Well, mostly. There were a few big long ones. I don't know what they were. Oh shit, man, what am I doing?" Freddie started jittering in place, holding his hands to his head.

"Stay calm, Freddie."

"But I'm betraying my friends! I just thought they were wrong to leave you when you needed help. I...I don't know if I should stop them now. Maybe I should join them! Help kill all the vampires. You saw what that vampire did to Tim."

"Freddie, you helped me because you're supposed to help people, right?"

"Yeah man. That's why I joined the Hunters. It was supposed to be simple."

"Well it's not simple any more. Your friends are being manipulated. There's a chance that some of them could die. We need to stop them. That's the best way to save them. Are you ok with that?"

Freddie seemed undecided. Then nodded. "Yeah. They don't deserve to die. They're really, really good guys."

The fuck they are.

"Alright. Help me get to my car, so I can radio for help."

"I thought you were healed?"

"I am. But I feel horrible." *I really should have asked Silvana more about this. How long does it take to get me back to normal?*

Freddie helped him to his feet. "Oh man. What could it be? Is this like some magical hangover? Or was there something wrong with the magic drink thing?"

"I nearly died, man. It's probably that."

"Oh yeah."

Together they hobbled down the steps to the car and Jason collapsed in the passenger seat. Freddie stood over him in the open door. Jason's body was still swaying. He was in no condition to do anything. Why had the elixir left him feeling so sore? His stomach hurt the most…

Hunger. He was hungry. That's all. It was such an intense hunger that it felt like nausea.

Jason laughed as he reached into his glovebox and grabbed one of the protein bars he kept there for emergencies. It was gone in three bites. The pain in his stomach lessened, but his body still felt weak. He started working his way through the box of twelve bars as he reached up to the dashboard and grabbed his police radio.

He hesitated.

What if he called for backup and police officers were killed? He could potentially be sending them into a gunfight with armed lunatics, and immortal monsters urging them on. Not to mention any immortal could legally murder the police if they could get away with it, according to Imperium law.

No, it's still my duty. Even if it's risky. The captain said I should have called for backup, so that's what I'm going to do. He swallowed the food in his mouth and cleared his throat.

"Attention all officers," he said, "this is Officer Turner. We have a Code 245. Repeat, a Code 245. Armed suspects heading towards Maristow House. Possibly twenty suspects. A witness claims they have handguns, potentially automatic weapons. Request backup.

Repeat, request backup."

The moment he released the call button, his radio echoed back to him.

"Officer Turner, this is Captain Kader. Is this some sort of prank?" She sounded pissed.

"No prank, captain. The group known as the Monster Hunters, aka Mohos, have been radicalised. Repeat, the Mohos have been radicalised. They have compiled weapons and are preparing to assault Maristow House. It is believed their intent is to murder the occupants."

Captain Kader radioed, *"And how the hell do you know this, Jason?"*

She keeps breaking radio protocal. Am I the only professional around here? He radioed back, "Because I went to one of their meetings tonight. Thought it would be fun."

"Jason, I just heard that your apartment was set on fire. What the fuck are you doing?"

He paused. Would she even believe him if he told her the truth? This wasn't just about wizards and vampires. He'd spent his whole life being ignored. He'd been a child in the foster system where teachers and guardians always thought they knew more than him. The idea of trying to convince his captain made him panicky.

But he had to try. He could convince her, if he just explained it as a crime.

"Captain..." he stammered. "You have to believe me. But my roommate, Peter Erikson, is trying to kill my girlfriend, Silvana, and steal her property. He's using the Monster Hunter cult to do it, and he armed them with weapons. I'm going there now to try to stop them, but I'm expecting a gun fight. I need backup."

The radio paused. Then...

"Copy that, Officer Turner. Tactical is on their way."

He blinked. "Copy that, captain. Thank you."

The line went quiet. Jason frowned. *I didn't know we had tactical.*

He became aware of Freddie standing by the open door. The young man looked helpless and confused. "You think I'm in a cult?" Freddie asked.

"Yeah, obviously."

"Huh…that sucks." Jason chuckled. "Hey, don't laugh at me! How do you even know when you're in a cult?"

"Did they tell you everyone else was wrong and only they could be trusted?"

Freddie scowled at him. "Well by that definition, my parents are a cult."

Jason raised an eyebrow.

"Alright fine, I'm in a cult," Freddie groaned. "So what now? Do you want to go after the other Hunters? Or should I take you to a hospital? Or should I go home?" He said the last part hopefully.

Jason opened his mouth to answer, but ended up shouting, "Damn it! This is all a distraction. I'm supposed to be finding Peter! Unless I k—" he censored himself, "stop him, Silvana will die."

"Peter? Who's Peter? And what about saving the Monster Hunters?"

"God, I don't care about those assholes!"

"Well, I do. And what about the vampires? I thought you wanted to save them?"

Jason gritted his teeth. He wanted to save Silvana's family, but he wanted to save Silvana more. Besides, the police were on their way. They would have a better chance at stopping the Hunters. He would not be very effective against an armed mob. He should be focusing on Peter.

But he still didn't even know where Peter was. He'd come to the meeting hoping to find a clue. He'd found nothing!

That's not true. You found Gerald, Rion, and Kathryn.

Jason nodded to himself. Those three had been manipulating the

Hunters, tricking them into attacking Silvana's family. They had to be working with Peter. But what were they getting out of it? Was it all about allying themselves with a powerful wizard?

The real question was, why were they *still* doing it? Peter already had his marriage. He had his title. So why was the Immortal trio at the meeting tonight, leading an attack? Why had they brought firearms to supply them?

"Jason?" Freddie asked, tapping the hood of the car impatiently. "Where are we going, man?"

"Hold on, I'm still thinking."

Jason's head was swimming from the aftereffects of the elixir. He kept eating the protein bars as he closed his eyes and tried to focus.

Let's assume Peter and the trio are working together. So why would Peter want Silvana and her family dead? Maybe there was some obscure Imperium law that would explain everything. Or maybe he just wanted them all dead out of spite. But if that were true, why wouldn't he kill them all himself? He had the power.

No. Lisbeth said the Imperium would intervene if Peter killed them directly. It was the first law of the Imperium.

Which meant Peter was trying to kill them *indirectly*. That's why he had been using Silvana's thirst against her and acting through the Hunters. But again, why? What else did he have to gain? Was he trying to kill Silvana so he could be free of the marriage ties, and still have the title? No, surely that could only weaken his claim to House Romanoff. There had to be...

Wait. Peter doesn't want to kill Silvana.

That's why he had the Hunters attack the mansion the first time, while Silvana was out on a date. He was trying to kill her family, while sparing her. Was that still true now that they were married? Surely not, since he had removed her blood to kill her. So what possible reason...

And it clicked.

"It's a royal line," Jason murmured. "Peter's part of the family, but he's not the *leader*. Nicholas is the head of the House. Peter is just the heir. That's why he's trying to kill them. He doesn't want to inherit the family crown in a few years when Nicholas passes away. He wants it *now*."

He turned to Freddie, and saw the confusion on his face. Jason nearly shouted in excitement. "Of course! The wizard wants the family dead so he can use their titles immediately. If there's a death in the royal line, the crown passes to the next blood relative. So Peter wants Silvana alive…"

Jason's eyes widened. Freddie stared at him. "What?"

"Get in the driver's seat. I need you to drive."

"Why?"

"NOW!" Jason shouted, and Freddie ran around the car and hopped behind the wheel. "We have to get to Maristow House."

"To stop the Monster Hunters?"

"No," Jason shook his head. "To stop a wizard."

"I don't understand," Freddie asked as he started driving. "What wizard? Is the wizard at the house already?"

"Yes," Jason said. "Peter never really left."

He checked his Glock 17. He'd fired three more shots tonight at Gerald and Rion, plus the three over the course of the week. Eleven shots left. It'd have to do. He spoke his thoughts out loud.

"The wizard wants the family dead, but Silvana alive. That's why on our first night in the mansion, Peter was trying to find her bedroom. Not for sex, but so he could personally guarantee her safety during Alex Bishop's attempt to murder the family. That's why he waited until she was out on a date during his second attempt. Now, on his third attempt," Jason gripped his Glock with white knuckles, "he will personally be at her side. Watching her. Making sure she survives the carnage." He smiled to himself. "On the plus side, it means Peter was never going to let her starve to death. Although, he would probably force-feed her blood from the Hunters to keep her alive. She wouldn't want that."

"I don't understand any of this," Freddie cried. "Why does this wizard want the girl alive?"

"Because he's married to her. If Silvana died, his claim could be weakened and the titles might pass to a cousin or something. But this way, with the others dead and Silvana alive, he will claim the kingship tonight."

"Kingship?"

Jason shook his head. "Don't worry about it. I've been talking to myself. Just get me to the house as soon as possible."

"Right." Freddie hit the accelerator, and Jason mentally prepared himself for combat. He listed off the combatants.

"Twenty armed fanatics," he growled. "Led by a vampire, a skin-walker, and a telepath, and all trying to kill a family of vampires and their knights. Police will be involved. Behind it all is an evil wizard, and a captured princess who needs saving. And here comes a lone cop with his new sidekick, ready to be heroes and save the day."

Jason grinned. "I don't get paid enough for this shit."

Chapter 28

Night had fallen. Candlelight flickered through Silvana's room and filled it with a warm glow, yet even the dim light was blinding, causing searing pain in her head. She found it easier to just keep her eyes shut.

"Can I get you anything, my dear?" Lisbeth asked, sitting on the edge of the bed.

Nothing helps anymore. I just want to die.

"No thank you, Aunty."

"You did the right thing," Emberline said from her other side. "Jason was wrong to offer you blood. His disrespect to Immortal customs has gone far enough."

Silvana was too tired to argue. She knew disrespect had nothing to do with it and that Jason had been willing to save her at any cost. But there was no point trying to convince her aunt now. Her entire body hurt too much to move, or exist for that matter. It only hurt less when she was completely still.

"Where is he?" Silvana asked.

"He left, sweetie. We told you that an hour ago," Lisbeth said.

"Why?"

"I don't know. I begged him to stay at your side, but he said he had things to do."

She knew Jason wouldn't do that. Her aunts were keeping something from her. If not for her weakened state, she would have fought them and demanded the truth.

"Did you hear that?" Emberline said.

"Outside."

"What?" Silvana asked. Her hearing had lost its power. Now she was only able to hear as a mortal.

"It's nothing, dear," Lisbeth said.

"Is it Jason?"

The bedroom door swung open, but Silvana couldn't bare to open her eyes and look. "Jason? Is that you?"

"Not exactly," came Phillip's voice. "We've got trouble. Those village beardsplitters are back. I can't be sure, but I think they have guns this time."

"For God's sake!" Emberline growled. "Can't they give us a moment's peace?"

"Nicolas is arming up. You should get Silvana to the basement."

"Armour won't do much against bullets," Lisbeth said.

"No, I mean he's arming up with his own guns."

"Oh."

"Sister," Emberline said, "get our child to the basement. I will join the knights in defending our home."

"That's not necessary," Phillip said.

"Oh it is. My daughter is dying before my eyes. I require someone to murder."

Silvana felt herself being scooped up in her aunts' arms and nestled against her shoulders. "Rest, daughter. I've got you," Lisbeth whispered.

Silvana sensed herself being moved down the hallway. She heard angry shouting from outside the house and a short burst of loud popping sounds. *Is that gunfire?* Lisbeth increased her speed and the movement jostled Silvana's head and made her brain jolt with a fresh burst of agony. She almost asked her aunt to let her die, just to spare her the pain.

"My heart!"

It was Nicholas's voice and Lisbeth came to a sudden start. "I'm taking Silvana to the basement." Lisbeth said. "I…I must guard her there."

"I know. I only wished to look upon the two most beautiful faces in all of existence, one last time, before I go into battle."

"Oh Nick!" There was the sound of a kiss. Silvana felt a hand stroke her cheek.

"I will join you soon, my dear Silvana," Nicholas said.

Did he mean in the basement, or in death?

"Nicholas," Silvana wheezed.

"Yes, my daughter?"

"Why did Jason leave?"

She heard only silence and wondered what look was passing between her aunt and uncle. They must have disagreed because Nicholas said, "She deserves to know the truth."

"It will only upset her."

"She's already upset with this fight about to take place." The hand stroked her face again. "Silvana, Jason said he was going to kill Peter."

Kill Peter? But that's impossible. Why would he… "Is it revenge?"

"No," Nicholas said sadly. "He's trying to save you. I told him there's no way he can defeat a wizard, but he would not be deterred."

Silvana understood, even as Lisbeth carried her away and more sounds of gunfire rang out. Jason wanted to kill Peter so Silvana would be free to remarry. *Because he wants to marry me. Even though he hates marriage. He'd still choose it for me.*

Arthur never loved me like that.

* * *

"I want to fight!" Freddie cried.

Jason clutched desperately at his passenger door as Freddie took the corner significantly faster than Jason would have liked. The guy drove like a demon. Jason had no idea his crappy cheap car could even drift like that.

"You're not coming with me," Jason insisted, having just eaten his seventh protein bar in a row. It was only now starting to settle his spinning head. "It's too dangerous. I shouldn't bring a civilian into a fight-zone."

Freddie cried, "But I can't stand by and do nothing. I need to help!"

"Look, your courage is awesome. But you don't have any fight training. Unless you know martial arts?"

"Oh, so you just assume the Asian guy knows martial arts? That's racist."

"Ok, but do you?"

"No! That's why you should give me a gun."

"No, that's why I *shouldn't* give you a gun."

"Come on, man! Let me help you."

Freddie reached a straight line of road and floored the car to a hundred and twenty kilometres an hour. Jason chose not to mention that the speed limit was half that.

"Freddie, you would help me by letting me save your life. That way, no matter what else happens tonight, I know at least one person is safe."

Freddie growled. "Then at least give me a job to do. I can keep watch, call out movements to you. Something!"

"All right. Stay by the car and wait for the police. Point them in my direction. That would genuinely help."

Freddie gave a grumble, but agreed.

They reached the woods near Silvana's house and Freddie used the handbrake to spin the car into the parking space, chewing up the forest floor with the tires. Rows of cars were already parked along the line of trees. Jason held his Glock ready in case someone saw him and started shooting. Nothing moved in the area.

"Shit, they're already at the house," Jason yelled.

He took a breath and hopped out. His head swayed a little, but not so much that it would become a problem. He held his Glock in a two-handed grip, aimed at the ground. "Keep an eye out for the police and send them after me. Under no circumstances can you follow. Is that clear?"

"Yes sir," Freddie grumbled.

"Good. And hey, thanks mate. I owe you big time."

"Yeah yeah yeah."

Jason grinned as he closed the door quietly and stalked through the woods.

Leaves crunched under his feet. The skeletal trees were lit only by moonlight. Distant male voices were shouting in tones that might be anger, terror, or agony. Jason felt his heart racing. *God, help me get through this.* He pressed on through the shadows.

A gunshot went off somewhere in the distance. Jason froze. It came from down near the house. Were they shooting at him? There was no way to tell. He couldn't see anything.

He ducked low and kept moving, using the trees for cover wherever possible. *The last time this happened, there were at least lights coming from the mansion. Why is it so dark? Are they all dead inside?* Jason checked the path ahead. Nothing was moving. He took another step.

A loud thump came from nearby.

Jason fell into a shooter's crouch and aimed towards the sound. He waited. Nothing happened. His breathing was so rapid that it made too much noise in the quiet darkness. He took longer breaths to slow down his breathing. The sound didn't happen again, but Jason could feel some primal instinct warning him. Something was off.

Someone was stalking him.

The hairs on his arms were raised and his ears kept picking up the merest echo of noise. A steady hum came from the forest as the leafless trees creaked in the soft wind.

Lions can see in the dark. Most big cats do. His breaths were getting so shallow now that he was near the point of hyperventilating. The woods had become eerily silent. He forced himself to wait with total stillness. His hearing went to highest alert for any sound.

The wind whistled as it moved back and forth, flowing through the woods.

No, not wind. *Breathing.* From something big.

Jason aimed towards the sound, and fired twice. The noise of the gun was nearly deafening. It took precious moments for his ears to adjust. But he didn't hear anything. No sounds of impact or cries of pain.

Instead, he heard a bestial huff, followed by a deep, rumbling growl. *Oh god. That's a grizzly bear.*

Jason swallowed. He suddenly remembered a documentary about a man killed in a grizzly bear attack. It was about the most terrifying thing imaginable. And a horrible, violent death.

Stay strong, Jason. For Silvana.

"Gerald!" he shouted, exposing himself in the dark. "Stop this! We don't have to fight."

He heard a bear's answering roar, somewhere between a growl and a sharp bark. It echoed through the woods and seemed to come from all around him.

"Gerald! I don't want to hurt you."

The skinwalker spoke in a human voice. "Tell that to Rion!" he hissed.

"I'm just trying to stop you murdering people."

The bear's roar filled the woods, and at the same time Gerald screamed, "How dare you oppose us, game!"

A piercing shriek came from behind Jason. He spun around.

Rion leapt out from darkness. Jason saw only a glimpse of a ruined face – with a gaping hole in its bottom jaw – before the vampire was on him.

They hit the ground hard. Rion was shrieking like a beast through his broken mouth. He climbed on top of Jason and pinned both of his wrists back before he lowered his ruined jaw towards Jason's throat.

Jason head-butted him directly in his wounded mouth. Rion howled with pain. He relaxed his grip, and Jason slipped a fist free and punched the wound again. Rion fell backwards with a scream, cupping his jaw. Jason drew both legs up and kicked him in the chest, sending him flying back down the hill.

The grizzly bear roared and thumped the ground repeatedly. *It's charging!* Fear lent Jason wings and he was on his feet a microsecond later.

He rounded a tree, placing the thick trunk between him and the massive creature. Gerald's bear form emerged out of the dark at a run. *Shit that thing is fast!* But it hit the tree and came to a sudden stop. Its black eyes focused on Jason. It moved to the left side, and Jason jumped to the right. *That's the expert advice,* he told himself. *Don't outrun, don't fight. Just keep something between you and...*

Gerald raised himself on his hind legs and fell on the tree. The whole thing snapped off at the truck and fell in his direction.

"Argh!"

Jason sidestepped the falling tree. There was no cover, nothing between him and the grizzly. Desperate, Jason raised his gun and fired rapidly.

The bear was suddenly gone. Just vanished. Jason stared at the empty forest. Was Gerald invisible somehow? Something moved on the ground. Jason looked down. *Is that a mouse?*

The tiny creature swelled in the time it took to blink, and the bear reappeared.

"Gah—!"

The bear paw swiped him across the chest, and Jason was thrown back down the hill by the heavy weight striking his middle. He rolled several times before his face hit something hard. When he finally came to a stop, his chest was burning.

Another roar made him look up the steep slope he'd just fallen down. Gerald's bear form was sprinting down the hill after him. Jason reached for his gun. It was gone. He'd dropped it somewhere in the fall. He pushed himself up, but his chest convulsed in pain. He couldn't move in time.

"Gerald, stop!" he cried.

An explosion of sound ripped through the trees and the bear gave a corresponding shudder. It tripped on its own legs and fell face first in the dirt, skidding a few metres down the steep hill and coming to a stop directly in front of Jason. The bear raised its head, revealing a fresh red wound on its shoulder. *It's been shot!* Jason looked up.

A figure stood in the dark, dressed in full tactical police gear. Every inch of the person was covered in Kevlar armour. They wore a helmet with a screen over their face. A set of tanned hands holding an assault shotgun was the only flesh that showed beneath the uniform. The big gun aimed at the bear. The figure turned its head towards Jason.

"Move it, rookie!" came the commanding voice of Captain Kader.

"Yes ma'am!"

He scrambled back on his hands and feet, his upper body aching with every movement. The bear gave a weak whimper as it struggled back to its feet. Kader held her shotgun to her shoulder and took aim.

"Gerald!" Jason cried. "She will shoot to kill. She doesn't know you're a person. Change form and surrender. You won't be hurt."

"Jason, what the fuck?" Kader yelled.

The bear stood still, watching him with black eyes that glimmered with the moon's reflection. "I mean it, Gerald. This is your last chance."

A partial human face appeared on the bear's muzzle. The fur on the face slowly turned blond, and the eyes became blue.

"I will not cower before mortal scum!"

Kader took a step back. "By Allah…" she whispered.

The bear crouched low. In a single movement, it shifted into a leopard and sprang towards Kader, howling like a great wild cat.

She was quicker.

The gun went off, and the leopard's hind quarters jerked sideways. It fell to the ground with a cry. A second later, Gerald was lying there in human form, moaning in pain.

"Oh no!" Kader screamed. "What…he was a bear! I swear, just a second ago…" She shook her head to clear it and leapt into action, kneeling down next to Gerald, dropping the gun at her side. "Sir, can you hear me?"

Jason was on his feet, feeling disorientated but mostly unharmed. He searched for his gun on the hillside. Where had it fallen?

"Jason!" Kader called. "We need to help this man. Get over here!"

"His companion is still out there," Jason cried.

Kader paused, her hand moving to her shotgun. "Are they armed?"

"Yes," he declared. It was the simplest way to explain the danger. He kept searching for his gun as Kader armed herself again.

"Katie!" The cry came from Gerald, lying on the ground. "Katie! Help!" he cried again.

He's calling to the telepath. Can she hear him like that? Damn it, where is Rion?

Something gleamed on the ground. Jason finally spotted his gun and retrieved it without a problem. Then he moved to his captain's side. Nothing opposed him.

That was too easy. Why didn't Rion come back for more? What is he doing? He checked Gerald. There was a patch of blood on the metamorph's left shoulder, and another on the back of his hips and buttocks. It wasn't deep or bleeding heavily. It looked like the shots hadn't done as much damage while he was in his animal forms, or maybe the shifting process didn't transfer wounds as precisely. Still, even with Gerald down, Rion would be coming for him any second now. Where…

Voices came from down the hill. The creak of opening doors filled the woods and Jason saw movement in the corner of his eye. Men were coming through the trees. They had guns.

"Captain, those men will kill us," Jason shouted.

She nodded and raised a mouthpiece on her jacket. "Team. Deploy canisters."

A voice echoed back through the radio, *"Aye captain."*

She looked to Jason. "You might want to protect your eyes, rookie."

Jason lifted his shirt up over his head just as the popping sound of air rockets echoed over the woods. Several cans landed among the trees and sprayed a thick white gas, so that within moments, an artificial fog filled the entire dark acreage.

Tear gas. Jason tightened the shirt over his face but he could already taste a sour sensation like vinegar coating his tongue. His eyes were burning, and his mouth and nose were filled with a stinging acidic fire. The skin of his arms was exposed and started to feel like someone was flicking droplets of boiling water over them.

Rion still hadn't shown himself. Any second now, he was about to attack. Jason had to keep his eyes open. He lowered the shirt to search, and immediately his eyes filled with tears.

"Come on, rookie," the captain called as she grabbed Gerald by one arm, holding her handcuffs in the other. Jason could barely see but he managed to copy her and grab Gerald's other arm. Kader clapped the cuffs on both hands and Gerald let out a low moan. Together they dragged the wounded metamorph towards the top of the hill.

They reached the end of the gas cloud within seconds, and Rion still hadn't appeared. What was going on? Where *was* he?

Jason was coughing heavily when they reached the summit of the hill. There were five other people waiting for him there. All were dressed in tactical gear like the captain.

Oh that's what Kader meant when she said tactical was on their way. It's just us regulars in armour.

"Hey guys," he said.

Douglas came to the front, looking like a massive Viking in his armour. "Fear not, mate. Calvary's here!"

"Damn, Jason, your eyes look demonic!" Martin said. "Or you've been crying."

"Don't mention crying," Wilson moaned. "My daughter was so upset when I left the house."

Jason couldn't help laughing. It was good to have them all here. *And risky.*

Detectives Lynch and Cole came forward. They were holding the launchers for the tear gas. Lynch seemed taller than ever. "Turner, you need to sit this one out," Lynch said. "I'm not going into battle with you at my back."

"Agreed," Cole said.

Jason looked at the captain as they lowered Gerald down. "You're out of armour too," Kader said. "You'll be safer watching this guy."

"All right, Cap—"

A scream ripped through the night. Jason spun around. But all he could see behind him was the white mist of gas, swirling through the dark woods. Another scream came, crying the word, "Help!" It was definitely the sound of agony.

"Rion," Jason murmured. "He's not hunting us."

Then it occurred to him. There had been two recent murder victims and both had been drained of blood by Peter's spell. And yet, there was no blood left on site.

"Oh my god," Jason cried. "Peter is using the Hunters twice over. He's collecting their blood as a back-up for Rion."

"What are you talking about?" Lynch growled as he grabbed Jason by the wrist. "Get in the car and sit there until this is—"

Jason ripped his arm out of his grip and sprinted into the cloud of white. "Turner!" Lynch roared, but Jason had already entered the tear gas and left him behind.

The mist stung at Jason's eyes, even though it had partially dispersed by now. He could barely see anything between the darkness and the tears in his eyes, but he ran anyway with his gun at the ready. He kept seeing figures in the mist that looked human, yet turned into trees when he approached. His brain was telling him to get out of there. He ignored it and sprinted as fast he could.

Something moved. He held up his gun. It was a man, staggering, his eyes covered by his hand. Jason ignored him and kept moving.

Another scream made his blood turn cold. It was close by. He braced himself and ran straight towards the sound. Figures emerged in the mist. He aimed his gun. The blurry shape became two separate people. One on the ground, twitching, legs kicking. The other leaning over their face.

"Rion! Stand down or I'll shoot!" Jason roared.

The figure spun around. It was Rion. But his face had completely repaired itself. Blood dripped down his snarling mouth and chin. His eyes were dark red. And he was…*glowing.* His skin was luminescent, and an aura of shimmering red light surrounded him.

What the hell?

"Game!" Rion screamed. "Your blood is mine!"

Jason didn't bother responding. He immediately opened fire, hoping to surprise Rion. But the vampire merely frowned like he was concentrating, and the bullets made curling wisps through the white mist as they flew to either side of him.

"Oh…" Jason said with eyes wide. "Super vampire. Right."

He turned and sprinted towards the mansion. *Yeah, definitely the right call. I am NOT fighting that thing.*

A shriek came from behind him. He glanced over his shoulder, and saw Rion floating two metres off the ground and flowing like a wraith through the mist, leaving streaks of white streaming behind him. The tear gas glistened with the reflection of his red aura. His crimson eyes flared brighter and his bloodied teeth were bared in a predator's grin.

Shitshitshitshit!

Jason sprinted. He burst through the border of white cloud and reached the front of the mansion. Half a dozen figures were huddled against the outer walls. They looked broken and defeated, slumped down against the mansion walls as if the gas had completely incapacitated them. Jason ignored them and moved towards the open mansion door.

He stepped inside, and froze.

Ten men stood halfway down the hallway, taking cover in archways and behind furniture. They all looked in Jason's direction as he entered. They all held guns, and two of them had assault rifles.

Jason didn't move. There was no cover in the open doorway. The nearest cover was another hallway, ten metres away, leading to the east wing of the mansion. If he could get to it…

Jason spun, just as Rion came flying through the door behind him.

I'm trapped!

The vampire's aura flickered like a twisted version of the northern lights, lighting up the dark stone walls. His red eyes fell on Jason. "Where is Gerald?!" he hissed.

Jason looked over his shoulder, towards the Hunters, and yelled, "Help me! A vampire is trying to kill me!"

It worked. Several men didn't hesitate to take aim, one with an assault rifle. Jason sprinted to the corner and dived down the adjacent hallway just as the heavy gunfire thundered through the mansion. The burst cut off a second later.

It worked! They aimed at Rion! Jason rolled on to his back.

Rion still floated in mid-air, unaffected by the hail of bullets. His eyes locked on the armed men, and he leered with a look of hunger. The sight was truly terrifying when combined with his bloodied teeth and glowing aura. "Shoot the vampire!" one of the Hunters screamed, and suddenly all ten men were emptying clips at Rion. Bullets started ricocheting around the hallway. Jason covered his head and huddled down.

A second later, all the gunfire cut off. In the silence, another voice howled in terror. Jason looked up. Rion floated in place and held out a hand, as if reaching to grab something. The screaming continued, getting louder.

Then a man suddenly flew straight into Rion's outstretched hand. The helpless victim had been lifted off the ground by an invisible force. Now Rion squeezed the man by the throat. He made choking sounds as his legs kicked frantically. The other Mohos cried out. Rion moved in a blur and buried his face in the man's neck. A streak of blood burst upwards. The man made a horrible, gurgling, choking sound as Rion seemed to grow brighter.

Jason had been watching all of this without even thinking of what to do. Only now as the shock was fading did he remember his gun. He raised it, took careful aim, and fired twice. The gun muzzle flashed bright yellow in the darkness. He could clearly see the shots hit Rion, yet they seemed to bounce off the air surrounding the vampire and zip away. Rion didn't even look in Jason's direction. A second later, the roar of gunfire ripped through the hallway. The unfortunate man in Rion's grip jerked and thrashed as bullets ripped through him. The vampire rocked backwards and fell onto the floor.

The bullets hit him! Jason fired again, but once more his bullets went around without hitting. Rion now had a hand up in defence.

Why did it work before? Was he distracted? Or is he weak while feeding? But there was no time to test it. Rion's eyes locked on Jason. He was clutching his chest in pain, yet only a second later he stood up straight and strong once again. *He healed those bullet wounds already!* His right hand faced the Hunters to deflect bullets, and his left hand reached towards Jason. Clutching...

Jason was on his feet and running down the east wing. Nothing grabbed him and held him in the air. *So Rion missed. Maybe I got out of range too quickly. Or maybe he can't stop bullets and grab me at the same time.* He made a note of it and ran.

This was the hallway where he'd fought Alex Bishop on the night he met Silvana. His previous bedroom was on his right. Should he hide in there? Or keep running? He had no idea if hiding from Rion was even possible while he was in this empowered state. Silvana had mentioned how vampires had a heightened sense of smell. There was no place Jason could hide without Rion sniffing him out.

Unless...

"GAME!" the vampire shrieked, his voice echoing down the east wing.

Jason found the strength within himself to increase his speed. He had no idea where he was going or what the plan was. There was just no way he could fight Rion on his own.

He rounded a corner. There was a grand ballroom before him, a hundred metres long and empty, with a massive, dusty chandelier suspended from the ceiling above. *Jesus that's a big chandelier.* This was an old room for hosting parties. Which meant a kitchen was nearby. A kitchen with foods, and lots of smells that might mask Jason's scent.

"There," he whispered to himself and stepped through a pair of two-way doors. He found an old eighteen century kitchen with wooden bench tops and a few modern ovens. An industrial fridge was standing across the room with a pantry next to it. Jason swung both doors open at once.

There was nothing inside. Just empty racks with dust balls. The fridge wasn't even turned on. This kitchen hadn't been used in decades. *Oh crap.*

Something moved outside. There was nowhere else to go and no time to try another plan. Gritting his teeth, he stepped inside the fridge and shut the door.

And waited.

Chapter 29

Silvana clutched at her head. The sounds of gunfire and screaming were not as loud as the pounding inside her skull. She could feel her consciousness slipping away from her, no matter how hard she tried to hang on to it. She was dying. Yet somehow, she was too weak to even feel a sense of panic.

"Don't fret, my dear," Lisbeth's soothing voice told her. "The others will be ok. They'll be at your side soon."

"Help them," Silvana begged. "Leave me."

"I won't leave you. You are my child."

"I'm…already…dying."

Lisbeth gave a pained gasp. "Don't say that," Lisbeth said. Silvana felt her aunt gripping her hand and shoulder, but she couldn't move an inch to respond. Her entire body felt like it weighed a million pounds.

"How pathetic," a male voice said.

Lisbeth gave a wordless shout. A sudden deafening roar filled the tiny basement like a crack of lightning in close quarters. Silvana's head was ringing. She nearly passed out from the pain of the sudden noise, but somehow she managed to hold her hands up to her ears and wheezed out a pained gasp. Silvana forced her eyes open.

The light was piercing and sharp. Yet it was only the light of a few candles. The basement was nearly pitch black.

Her aunt was gone and another figure emerged from darkness.

"Jason?" she cried.

"You'd like that, you little whore."

Silvana recognised the voice. "Peter!"

The wizard came to stand beside her. He wore a brown cloak and hood that partially covered his handsome face. His gorgeous blue eyes were screwed up in disgust. "Look at you, Silvana," he spat. "You're a disgrace to Immortal kind."

Each breath was a strain. "What did you…do to… my aunt?"

"I broke her," he sneered. "With a mere word from my lips. The mortals will finish her off when they get here. There's only Emberline left now."

"My uncles…will…"

"They are mortal scum! What could they possibly do? They're not even worth considering. I have three immortals working for me, and you have one immortal left on your side. It's already over." He leaned over her, his face so close that his breath fell on her neck. "You will be the last Romanoff. Your throne will belong to me."

Silvana glared back, "I am…minutes from death…"

"Only until I force feed you the blood you need." He grinned. "I will provide for my wife. Just as you will provide the title I need…" he jolted forward and ran his tongue up her neck and jaw, "…and all the pussy I fucking deserve. For an Immortal lifetime. I will fuck you when I want, how I want, or I will rip the blood from you again. How's that sound to you, my dear wife?"

Silvana saw something in Peter's face. For just a moment, he reminded her of Arthur.

He always thought he had the same entitlement to her body. Like she was a piece of meat that existed for his enjoyment and nothing else. Scarlet rage flashed within Silvana, louder than all the screaming pain in her dying body. Finally, she said to Peter what she always wished she'd said to Arthur.

"Go fuck yourself!"

* * *

The kitchen was silent. Distantly, the sounds of rapid gunfire kept going off with unforgiving brutality. Every pop of a fired bullet made Jason sick to the stomach. Any one of those sounds could mark the death of his friends, his colleagues.

A sudden loud noise came from beneath Jason like the crack of a bolt of lightning, followed by an echoing aftershock that had an almost electronic buzzing hum. He glanced at his feet, expecting to see something in the blackness. The reverberations ran through the mansion with deep rumbles that lasted several long seconds. Jason felt the tremors in his feet.

Was that magic? What has Peter done?

Jason clenched his fists in helplessness. Silvana was somewhere in this mansion. Peter was going to ensure every member of her family was killed. And Jason was stuck here hiding in a bloody fridge. He had to fight back.

I can't let her die!

The memory of that day came to mind. He saw her feet, dangling. Her body swaying from the beam on the roof. He remembered the sheer, blinding horror. *I can't let her die! Not again!*

He opened the fridge door, and instantly saw a flicker of red light shining under the kitchen entrance, coming from the ballroom.

And he shut the door again. *Dammit! I still don't know how to fight Rion!*

He sat perfectly still, focused on controlling his breath to limit noise. He waited for the sounds of the kitchen doors to open. His mind started conjuring up images, picturing Rion, sucking the blood out of that Moho's neck. The way he glided through the tear gas like a demon.

He saw his father, standing over his mother, screaming at her, while she lay on the ground sobbing. And Jason watched, doing nothing.

The kitchen doors banged against the wall.

Jason let out a sharp gasp. Then he covered his mouth with his hands. He still had his gun. He checked the gauge that clearly showed the ammo. Five shots left. *What the hell? Where did the rest of them go?* But he clutched it in both hands and aimed it at the fridge door.

"Game?" Rion called, his voice high and drawling. "Quit hiding, you little bitch." His footsteps echoed through the empty room, his hard-soled shoes clipping at each contact with the tiled floor. *Why is he walking? Saving energy?*

"The police are no match for us," Rion said. "They never were. Nothing you mortals have ever done can compare to the might of Immortal kind." His voice was moving towards the fridge. Jason clutched his gun tighter. "I've spent my life surrounded by insects like you. I was forced to live among you. As if you were somehow… my *equal.* I should have been *feasting* on you all along. Because that's what mortals are meant for. Domination!" He barked a laugh. "Like a farmer rules over cattle."

A gunshot went off. It was nearby and staggeringly loud. It went off again a second later; a sharp bang, followed by an echoing roar that lasted several seconds. *Holy hell, that's something heavy. Who the hell's firing that thing?*

Jason waited. A growl came from outside the fridge, and the sounds of the kitchen doors banging came again.

He sighed with relief. *He's gone.* Jason felt his body surging with adrenaline. He knew Rion was distracted. Now was his best chance. Silvana had already waited long enough. This was the time to strike back.

Jason stepped out of the fridge. The kitchen was empty. Slowly, he crept along the workbench towards the door, gun held at the ready. He reminded himself, *Rion can only move one thing at a time. He's weaker when feeding or distracted. I can do this.* He stood at the kitchen door, braced himself, and stepped out.

He saw Rion instantly, striding across the middle of the ballroom, glowing brighter than last time Jason saw him. The vampire's back faced him. Jason held up his gun. And smiled.

"RION!" he screamed.

The vampire spun around in a blur and flung up a hand in self-defence. Then he saw Jason, and relaxed immediately, letting out a laugh that echoed around the empty chamber.

"Oh hello, game," Rion drawled. "What makes you think you can speak to me like that? Don't you know I am your master?"

"You're just a human, Rion. No more or less than me."

"Wrong. You're just a speck of dust, game," Rion said as he raised himself off the ground once more. The glowing haze of red shimmered around his body and threw menacing shadows across the ballroom. "Your life is meaningless. Here today, gone tomorrow. What does it even matter if you die today or not? The course of the world wouldn't change."

"So what?" Jason yelled. "Most people don't change the world. Doesn't mean they don't improve it a little."

Rion began to move forward, gliding across the open floor. "No, you fool. I change the world. Because I'm immortal. I will live for a thousand years. I will outlast civilisations! I will stand upon—"

Jason fired.

Rion held up a hand. Then he frowned. "What the hell was that?

You missed by miles. What were you even aiming—"

A rope snapped with a sharp twang as a thunderous creak came from above. Rion looked up just as the massive chandelier dropped from the ceiling, directly onto him.

The chandelier jolted to a stop with an ear-piercing shriek of grinding metal and jangling crystal ornaments. A cloud of dust ballooned outwards. Jason realised the whole thing had stopped two metres off the ground.

Rion was underneath, his hands reaching towards the chandelier. It floated half a metre above him. He held the whole thing with his mind.

Jesus...

Jason took aim. *He's weak when he's distracted and using his power!* He fired. And Rion gave a pained groan as the bullet hit him in the shoulder.

"Yes!" Jason roared and fired again, hitting him in the stomach.

In the half-second it took to fire a third time, Rion tilted the chandelier sideways to cover himself, then suddenly *launched* the whole thing across the ballroom like it was nothing, flying straight at Jason.

"Oh."

In a split second, Jason dropped to the ground in a ball. But there was no avoiding something that large. The force hit him and drove him back. Pain exploded. Everything blurred around him and went black.

Jason blinked his eyes open. Something was pressing down against him. He could only gasp for breath over and over as a searing pain flared in his chest.

The chandelier. He threw the fucking chandelier at me.

He looked around and found himself underneath several frames of metal. Silver crystals hung from bronze chains and dangled in his face. A metal beam dug into his chest, right where the bruises had been left by Gerald's bear claw.

The chandelier creaked as it rose up and Jason groaned in relief as the pressure eased off his chest. Rion came forward, the aura of red energy reflected in thousands of tiny crystal fragments, casting flowing crimson shadows over his face. He floated forward like a wraith, and with a mental shove, flipped the chandelier backwards.

Jason groaned as he sat up. He knew there was no hope in fighting now. Other Mohos had tried with an assault rifle and failed. *At least I shot him...no...*Rion had already healed the wounds. And Jason only had two bullets left.

There was no way he could fight and win. Maybe…he could stall?

He fell on his hands and knees before Rion, and bowed with his face to the ground.

"Master!" Jason cried. "I am unworthy!"

Rion stopped. His feet floated in front of Jason's face.

"I didn't realise how powerful you are," Jason pleaded. "I was wrong. If you spare me, my lord, I will worship you all the days of my life! Truly, there is none like you!" Jason swallowed all his pride, leaned forward, and kissed the vampire's feet.

"You filthy little liar," Rion scoffed. "You think I'm going to fall for this?"

Jason couldn't think of what to say next. He thought back on his childhood days going to Anglican churches, and the prayers he had to memorize. *My old priest would be horrified at this blasphemy. But if it saves my life...*

"Open my lips, O Lord, and my mouth shall proclaim your praise! Oh Lord, Son of God, have mercy on me!"

He waited. Rion wasn't moving. Gunshots still racked through the mansion. But the ballroom became silent and still. Except for the droplet of blood that rolled down Jason's mouth. The act of bowing was agony but he pushed through the pain and stayed perfectly still.

Rion breathed in sharply. "You dare ask me for mercy?" he hissed. "After you tried to defy your masters?"

"Forgive me…"

"After what you did to Gerald?" Rion growled.

"My lord. Gerald is in police custody. He was just wounded and handcuffed."

Rion sneered, "It's not your fault, you know. Of course you tried to attack me. Because the Imperium have been ruling from the shadows. You only dare oppose us because our elders have us hiding. It's time we step into the light! No mortal will dare lift a hand against us once we rule in the open."

A sudden cold hand clutched at Jason's chin and tilted his head upwards. Jason looked into those red eyes, as the touch became a caress.

"I will be a good master," Rion purred. "There's no need to gorge myself on every mortal. There will be favoured servants in the new world. You would find me to be a caring lord." The hand lowered towards Jason's throat and clutched there much, much tighter than Jason was comfortable with. He felt something lifting him under the armpits, raising him up to face Rion. The vampire sneered at him, yet in his eyes was a glimmer. "I would enjoy your worship, game."

Jason thrust his gun nozzle directly into Rion's chest.

"Dodge this," he whispered…

… and found he couldn't move.

His whole body had gone rigid. His trigger finger seemed stuck in place. The grip of Rion's telekinesis held every inch of him and the vampire's hand on his throat tightened even further. *Oh fuck no!* Jason growled as he thrashed against his bonds. He could wiggle slightly but whatever was holding him was as strong as steel. It was a struggle to breathe. *Just pull the trigger!* He growled and tried to squeeze…

"I knew you were lying," Rion hissed from so close that breath fell upon Jason's face, and it smelt of blood and iron. "All my life I've been hungry. Well, no more." His fangs seemed to lengthen, and he lowered his teeth towards Jason's face. "I will take my vengeance on your body. Would that please you, mortal filth? Is that what you want from your god?"

Jason winced and tried to pull back. But Rion kept the telekinetic pressure on Jason's body and his fingers digging into the flesh of Jason's neck. *Oh God, he's going to tear into me.* He tried begging again. "Lord! Have mercy upon me!" The vampire's teeth pressed into Jason's jaw and cheek, and remained there, waiting, poised ready to pierce the skin. Rion sneered in pleasure from drawing this out as long as possible. "My Lord…" Jason pleaded.

"This is what happens to mortals who rise against their masters," Rion hissed, his lips brushing Jason's face as he spoke. Then he raised Jason higher with the hand at his throat. The pressure was unbearable. Jason heard himself making strangled, gargling sounds as if they came from far away. He couldn't kick. He couldn't raise his gun. Rion's voice raised into a crazed shout.

"The Immortals will rule the world once aga—"

A sword appeared out of the darkness. It swung down and cleaved Rion's arm at the elbow.

Jason fell as the vampire howled in sudden pain. Blood burst from the severed limb and splashed over Jason's face and torso. Emberline appeared, wearing a full-length black gown that made her blend into the shadows. She carried a two-handed sword like a child play-fighting with sticks. She snarled as she swung the sword upwards, cutting Rion from hip to shoulder in a vicious slash. Rion gave a wordless cry as the blade sliced him across the middle.

He was silent before he hit the ground. The red aura disappeared, and his skin returned to its usual pale tone.

Emberline spun around, her dress twirling with her movement. Her dark eyes focused on Jason as she flexed her grip on the sword.

Oh god...she's gonna kill me.

She moved suddenly. Jason flinched back. But she was only holding out a hand.

"Hurry, fool!" she hissed. Jason took her hand, and she yanked him to his feet. "I see you managed to cause still more injury to my home." She shook her head at the broken chandelier.

"If it makes you feel better, it injured me more."

Her lips turned up slightly. "That does make me feel better."

He groaned as he checked Rion's body. The huge gash across the middle had cut to the bone. He was dead and finished.

"Thanks for saving me. Now where's Silvana?"

"In the basement. Lisbeth's with her. She's safe there."

Jason shook his head. He had to raise his voice as more gunfire ripped through the mansion. "Peter will come for her."

Emberline turned sharply, her face a mask of ice except for her eyes that widened with horror. She whispered, "The wizard? Are you certain?"

"Yes. He wants Silvana alive, and everyone else dead."

Emberline's eyes widened with understanding. "So he can use the House title immediately." She hefted the sword up in one hand. "We need to get to Silvana now. Come with me, mortal, and prove your worthiness to stand at Silvana's side."

Jason hefted his gun weakly. There were only two shots left. And he had just had the crap knocked out of him. *But hey, time to impress the future mother-in-law.*

"Lead the way, ma'am. Let's save a princess."

Chapter 30

Jason followed Emberline down a long corridor, leading back to the main wing of the mansion. Her long gown swayed like moving shadows, and her sword glittered with moonlight through the windows. Jason held his gun ready in a two-handed grip. The sounds of gunfire had not slowed at all.

"Where are Phillip and Nicholas?" Jason asked.

"They were trapped in the front parlour room," she said without turning back to look at him. "I was supposed to circle around the intruders and take them out from behind. Then I heard the sounds of my chandelier being destroyed."

"Sorry. Also, which one's the parlour room?"

She turned sharply to glare at him. "The one where your wizard friend blew the wall down."

"Oh, that one. I've been calling it the throne room." She huffed in annoyance. He kept talking before she could start calling him an idiot again. "I'm almost out of ammo. But the police are here in armour. They will help the two knights."

"Far as I'm concerned, the knights and police will have to help themselves. The wizard is the greater threat, and Silvana is helpless to protect herself. Now, who are these other immortals? Friends of the wizard?"

"Yes. A metamorph, a vampire, and a telepath. But my police captain and I took out the Metamorph. Handcuffed him."

"Impressive. He won't be able to shift."

"I thought so. He seemed pretty upset when we handcuffed him. And you took out the vampire. Now there's just the telepath, Kathryn Smith. At least she won't be a big threat. All she can do is read minds. Right?" He was met with silence. "Right, Emberline?"

The vampire looked back, her eyes flat. "Not necessarily. Telepaths can influence minds. They don't just read thoughts. They *plant* thoughts. People can't tell which thoughts are their own."

Jason frowned. "That's why all the Hunters listened to her. She convinced them to attack. Maybe if we stop her, it would convince the Hunters to stop too."

"More likely, she'll fill all the mortals with paranoia and turn them on each other, to cover her tracks."

Jason stopped walking. "Are you kidding me?"

"These immortals are all youths like Peter. Naïve, impressionable, and convinced they can still rule the world as kings and queens like their grandparents did. I doubt the telepath is strong enough to influence minds. They're all too young to have developed their abilities to full maturity. Even Peter is far below a wizard's average strength."

Well that's terrifying. "Still. There is a chance all my friends could die."

"A chance. But your friends can fight back. Silvana cannot, so her need is greater." She held out her hand for silence and started walking through the still hallways towards the distant sounds of gunfire. "Now be quiet. Stealth is our best weapon. The secret entrance to the basement is through the library."

"Secret entrance?" Jason shook his head. "Emberline, wait a second." She looked back at him, impatience written over her face, but Jason held still, thinking. "We need to leave Silvana alone."

"What?"

"It's obvious," he said. "Imperium law says immortals can't kill each other, but they can use mortals to do the deed. That's the whole reason why Peter has led all these gunmen into your house. He needs to use *them* to kill you and your family. But he won't kill anyone himself."

"The wizard is in my home," Emberline growled, "at my daughter's bedside, watching her die of thirst. I will not stand for it."

"But Peter's just guarding her. It's the mortals who are the real threat here, especially if the telepath is influencing them."

"You said the police could deal with them," she snapped.

"Maybe. Or maybe the telepath will turn the police on each other. Listen Emberline, help me stop the mortals first. Then Peter will have no one left to act through."

Emberline hesitated. "No," she said finally. "The wizard may yet grow desperate enough to break Imperium law. If we stop the mortals, it might just make him cross that line. He is still the main threat."

Another huge gunshot went off, sounding close enough to leave Jason's ears ringing. A woman was screaming in terror.

Jason stepped up to Emberline and took her hand. "Help me. Please. We need to save the police. That's the best way to stop Peter."

"I...can't..."

"Emberline! Please!"

But she pulled her hand out of his grip and stepped away. She glanced at Jason with eyes full of pain and sorrow. "I'm sorry, Jason," she whispered. "I will forever be shamed for this. But I cannot lose Silvana."

"Emberline, wait!"

But she moved with abrupt speed and disappeared into the dark depths of the mansion, barely making a sound. Jason stared after her, the cold press of her hand still lingering on his fingertips. He took a step after her, then thought better of it.

Just then a woman's voice rang through the mansion, "Plymouth police department!" *Captain Kader!* Jason gave up on Emberline and moved towards the sound of violence.

His captain's voice was muffled from this distance so he kept moving towards it. The hallway came to an end and split via two doors on either side. He stepped into the left door, the one that led in the direction of the gunfire.

He found himself in the throne room. *Correction, the front parlour room.* The shattered wall still lay in a pile of debris. There was a flicker of movement.

"Hey punk!" a raspy voice shouted from within the darkness. Jason couldn't see anything or recognise the speaker. It had to be a Monster Hunter.

"Don't shoot!" Jason cried.

"I'll give you one chance to surrender," the voice called across the open room. "Otherwise, you'll have to deal with me. And I'm public enemy number one!"

Jason's jaw dropped. That sounded like a quote from Dirty Harry. "Nicholas?"

"Oh, Jason!" Nicholas cried in relief.

Then it clicked. *He must be firing a magnum. That was the big gun I heard earlier. Oh my god, it's probably a .44 magnum. Dirty Harry's gun.* Jason didn't know whether to laugh or slap his forehead.

Phillip's voice cut in, "Get to cover, boy. There's gunmen in the hallway!" Jason ducked low and ran towards the sound of Phillip's voice. "Don't come over here, you zounderkite!"

"I don't know what that means," Jason hissed back as he joined the two old knights. They were crouched down behind a barricade of stacked furniture, facing the blasted hole in the wall and the gunmen beyond.

"It means idiot!" Phillip snapped.

"Then just say idiot. Speak English."

"I *was* speaking English! It's not my fault you don't know the word."

"Is that what you've being saying all this time? Olden day insults? I thought Silvana was joking."

"Gentlemen," Nicholas whispered to interrupt. "We have a situation here." A round of enemy gunfire punctuated his statement and sent them all ducking to the floor. Phillip glared at Jason like it was his fault. The gunfire cut off again, so Nicholas went on in a low whisper.

"There's at least ten insurgents wandering the hallway outside. We have police coming through the front door. We need to act like an anvil to their hammer. But it's possible the insurgents will overrun us if they come this way. We don't have a lot of firepower." He gestured to Phillip, who then held up an old double barrel shotgun. It had dust streaks along the shaft, and brown rust had built up on the nozzle.

"I've only got a few spare shots," Phillip said.

"I've got plenty of ammo," Nicholas said and waved his hand-cannon around proudly. "But my little friend here fires slowly."

"Nicholas, is that the magnum from Dirty Harry?"

"Yes!" Nicholas had a huge grin. "I'm so glad you recognised it! This is a .44 magnum, the most powerful handgun in the world, and would blow your head clean off."

Jason glared at him. "It *was* the most powerful handgun. *Fifty years* ago! And my god man, stop quoting Dirty Harry! It's not even that good a film!"

Nicholas raised an eyebrow. "You gotta ask yourself…"

"Stop."

"…one question."

"Nicholas."

"'Do I feel lucky'?"

"You don't have to do the whole thing…"

"Well do ya? PUNK?!"

Jason gave an exasperated sigh. He also had to hide his smile.

"Leave him alone. It gives him courage in battle," Phillip said, with a friendly nod to his companion.

Nicholas grinned back.

"All right. Do the gunmen know you're here?" Jason asked.

"Yeah," said Phillip. "Rambo over here was a little trigger-happy. I thought we should have ambushed them. Taken out a few, instead of wasting warning shots."

"First of all, it's Harry, not Rambo, and you know how I feel about this," said Nicholas. "Second, I'm trying to avoid killing people. That's how a knight conducts himself."

"A knight protects his family," Phillip snapped back.

"Hey," Jason cut in. "We don't have a lot of time. The wizard is here." Both knights turned sharply to look at him. "Peter's behind this attack. He wants to use these mortals to kill you and your family. He has a telepath here, influencing them. A young girl called Kathryn Smith."

"Dear Lord," Nicholas murmured, wiping his brow with a trembling hand.

"This means they won't stop until we're all dead," said Phillip. "We need to use lethal force."

"Not necessarily," Jason said. "One of those Monster Hunters was a good man who saved my life. I don't think they're all evil. Do you think the telepath is controlling them all at once?"

"No," Phillip said. "Telepaths can only influence one mind at a time. She will focus on one, set them on a goal, then move on to the next. Over time that influence will fade."

"Then there may be a chance to reason with them. I have to try." Jason crawled forward and ignored Phillip's harsh whispers as he moved towards the broken wall leading into the hallway.

"HEY!" Jason shouted. "Monster Hunters in the hallway!" There was silence as all gunfire cut off. "This is Officer Jason Turner. I was at your meeting tonight at the town hall." He waited a moment for that to sink in. "You're being manipulated by a wizard. There's a witch here who's controlling your minds. You need to stand down. Surrender your weapons to the police. You'll be taken into custody. You will not be harmed." He waited.

"I remember you. You were attacked by the lion!" a man shouted back.

"That's right. So the monsters are clearly fighting against me. I'm on your side!"

A pause. Then, "But you were wounded! You should have died. How did you survive?"

"Uh…"

"You must be one of *them!*"

Jason growled, "Ah come on!"

"We'll never surrender! We'll take you all down!"

Nicholas shouted back, "Go ahead! Make my day!" Jason rolled his eyes.

A burst of gunfire made him drop to the floor. Stone fragments were spaying off the archway and walls. Muzzle flashes filled the mansion.

A pop of air came from the front door and a single gas canister flew down the hallway. It started hissing. The Hunters immediately began coughing and shouting in panic as tear gas flooded their hideout.

"Yes!" Jason cried.

The Mohos tried to shoot back. Jason ducked for cover behind the archway again. The flashes of gunfire lit up the hallway and reflected against the white clouds that crept through the house. But all visibility was gone. The men started panicking and shooting wildly. "Cease fire! Friendly fire!" one of them shouted. "We have to move out!"

Jason couldn't see anything in the white cloud but he heard the sounds of footsteps moving further away. The Mohos were fleeing. He covered his mouth and poked his head around the corner. All he could see was a billowing wall of whiteness covering everything. He listened to the sounds of shouting. He heard the Mohos moving far to the right. *They must be going down the west wing, opposite the one I went down before.* This was perfect. Now he could reunite with the police. Best case scenario.

"Move out!" a voice ordered. It sounded like Captain Kader. Jason waited as the sounds of footsteps came down the hallway towards him. He heard sounds of scuffling and movement.

Someone yelled, "Stay down."

Another cried, "…under arrest."

Clearly some of the Mohos had been injured by the tear gas and friendly fire. Jason waited until he heard several handcuffs being used. Then he called out.

"It's Officer Turner. I'm coming towards you from down the hallway. Hold you fire."

He put his gun in his belt and started walking through the tear gas with his hand over most of his face. He held his other hand up high and waved slowly. Through the wafting mist, he saw someone standing tall and straight against the wall. Jason watched them, ready to draw his gun again. But it was just a suit of armour. Jason sighed and relaxed.

A sudden bang rang out and a bullet whistled past Jason's his head.

"Hold your fire!" he shouted and crouched low.

"Cease fire, Jason!" a man's voice roared. It was Lynch. "You're shooting at the police! Throw your gun down and surrender."

Jason blinked. *What?* "I'm not shooting at you. You're shooting at me. Stop it!"

A second bullet whizzed past from the same direction. Jason dropped flat onto his belly. "Stop it, Lynch!" he screamed louder.

"Turner!" Lynch roared. "I repeat, cease firing at me, or I will be forced to shoot you!"

Jason froze in place. And understood. *The telepath!*

"Kathryn," he growled under his breath. Then he yelled louder, "Captain! Tell Lynch to stop shooting at me!" He cringed. He sounded like a child tattling on his sibling.

But it worked. "Lynch, cease fire," Kader shouted from somewhere further down.

A third gunshot went off. Jason was still on the ground, covering his head with his hands. "Turner!" Lynch was screaming. He was panting erratically. Jason could now see Lynch's tall silhouette waving his gun around with jerky motions. "Cease fire, Turner, or I'll be forced to kill you. Do you want to die?"

"Lynch, stop," Kader ordered in a calm voice. "You're the only one shooting right now."

Lynch shouted, "Are you blind? Did you not hear him fire directly at us?"

"No one's firing at us, Lynch," Cole said in her steady voice.

"It's Turner! He's shooting at us right now! Open your fucking eyes!" The shape of Lynch in the mist held up his gun. Jason took out his own gun on instinct. He lay perfectly flat and held his breath.

Lynch fired. Again. And again. "Where are you, Turner? I won't let you kill anyone else! Do you hear me, you bastard? It ends now!"

"Lynch! Stand down!" Kader roared.

Footsteps approached. Lynch's armoured body emerged out of the white cloud of tear gas. He looked like death itself. The big man's plastic helmet pointed down towards the floor, and Jason saw the dark eyes inside focus directly on him.

"There you are," Lynch whispered.

Oh god. No matter what I do, he's going to think I'm trying to kill him.

There was no way out of this.

Unless...I actually do kill him.

He looked up at the giant policeman aiming his gun at Jason's head. Jason needed to live. He was the only cop who knew about the telepath. He had to save Silvana and her family. He had to live. Surely that would justify...

But he relaxed his grip on his gun. *No. I'm not a violent man.* He held his hands out.

"Help me!" he cried instead. "He's going to kill me!"

"Put the gun down!" Lynch screamed. "Final warning!"

"Help!"

A figure emerged out of the mist and crash tackled Lynch around the middle. His gun went off...and the shot went wide.

"Lynch, get it together man!" Cole shouted as she wrestled her larger partner. They banged into the suit of armour, and a metallic clang echoed through the hallway.

"Cole, stop! He's gonna kill us all! *He's gonna kill us!*" He elbowed her in the head, and she fell back onto the floor. Lynch swung around again with his gun.

The twin bolts of a taser hit the skin on the back of Lynch's hand. The detective went rigid as the cracking sounds of electric jolts ran through his body. Then Lynch dropped down, unconscious.

Captain Kader stepped forward, holding her taser. "Everyone alright?" she asked. "Cole? Turner?"

"Fine, captain," Cole said. "Nice shot!"

"Mmyeah..." Jason mumbled, too shocked from his near death experience to speak clearly. "Captain, detective, you two saved me."

Cole just shrugged. Kader stepped forward and held out her hand. "Yes, I did. For the second time, I might add." He took her hand and got on his feet, then gave her hand a soft squeeze before letting go.

Kader looked at him through her visor, and her brown eyes abruptly shone with tears. "Can't save everyone, though," she said.

"On no. Have we lost someone?"

She shook her head. "But I did." She moaned, "By Allah, why did I do that?"

He frowned at her. "Captain?"

"I could have saved him," she murmured. "I *should* have saved him."

"Captain? Lynch is ok…"

She clutched Jason by the shoulders. Her eyes were wide. "What have I done? Oh god…" her voice choked up. Tears filled her eyes, and she blubbered out the words. "What have I done?"

Jason understood at last. "Captain, there's a telepath here. She's influencing your thoughts. It's not real!"

"It is real. I did it. It's my fault," she cried. She stepped back from Jason and pulled off her helmet, letting her hair fall out of place. Tears were running down her cheeks. Cole looked on from Lynch's side, a confused expression on her face.

"Listen to me, captain. Someone is forcing you to think this," Jason cried.

Kader pulled out her handgun.

"Captain, wait," he said and held up his hands in surrender.

Then she put the gun to her own head.

Jason froze. His mind went blank from sheer horror. All thoughts retreated in fear of sudden trauma and pain. *She's going to kill herself. Like my mother…she's going to kill herself.* Jason found himself unable to move and unable to speak.

"I should have tried harder to save him," Kader whispered. "By Allah, I deserve to burn for this. I deserve to die! I need to die!"

"Captain, stop this," Cole called out. "Aisha, please."

"No!" Kader screamed. "You don't know what I've done! If you did, you would kill me yourself. It's what I deserve. Everyone would be better off if I were dead."

Jason noticed his hands were shaking. His mind was locked down, unthinking. He was more scared than he'd ever been in his life. *Do something! She's going to die again. You have to save her! Don't let that murderous bastard kill her again.*

That one raging thought was enough to sweep aside the cloud in his mind. Where was the one responsible? The one making her kill herself? All he could see was Cole, by Lynch's unconscious body, laying at the feet of the suit of armour. The hallway was empty.

"Jason," Kader cried. There was real fear in her eyes. "Help...me..." Her gun was trembling.

Jason lifted his gun. Took aim. And fired.

Into the suit of armour.

A woman's voice gave a shrill scream. The suit dropped to the ground and crumpled, revealing a young woman hiding within.

Kader suddenly jerked the gun away from her head. She dropped the gun outright, fell to the ground, and frantically crawled backwards away from it. "Fuck! What the fuck was I doing?" she cried.

Jason marched to the fallen armour, snatched the girl by the arm, and dragged her out of the plates of metal and into the middle of the hallway. She groaned with pain, clutching at the wound in her middle, her breathing shallow. "Kathryn Smith," he said. "You almost did it."

She looked at him, her beautiful blue eyes burning with icy hatred. "You pig! You disgusting fucking slimebag!" she hissed. She groaned again and folded over her wound. The bullet had hit her in the side of the hip. It wasn't life threatening, but it would hurt like hell. *And possibly limit her mobility, long term. Don't think about that now.*

"You'll be ok," he told her. "Don't try to play anymore tricks."

"Don't tell me what to do, game!" she spat.

A sudden image appeared in Jason's mind.

His father, standing over him, punching him over and over.

Pain all over his body...so helpless...so powerless...

"Oh please," Jason said. "I've done years of therapy. I am *so* past being disturbed by this. Cole, do you have any handcuffs?" The detective threw him a pair, and he cuffed Kathryn's arms behind her back, even as she kept pushing his dark memories to the surface, and he pushed them back down again.

Ok. That's Gerald, Rion, and Kathryn down. Time to face Peter.

The three other officers arrived then, just as Lynch was waking up and Kader was settling down. "Everything alright here?" Douglas asked, his voice cheerful and wildly out of place.

"Yeah, we're good," Kader said in a shaking voice. She rattled off facts like she was reading from a list and her voice steadied. "There's five gunmen left. Down this wing. They're probably low on ammo by now, so we should be able to take them."

"Good," said Wilson. "Cause I want to survive this night. I've got two kids, you know."

"We *know*," Martin drawled, rolling her eyes.

Lynch was back on his feet. His eyes settled on Jason, and they widened.

"Hey," Jason said. "Sorry I ran off before…"

"Oh shit" Lynch cried. "Jason, mate, I'm so sorry!" He shook his head. "What the hell's wrong with me? Why did I do that?"

"It's not your fault," Jason said and pointed to Kathryn. "This one's a telepath. She makes you relive your worst fears." He looked to Kader. "She knows how to get inside your head. It wasn't your decision. That's why I had to run ahead of the team. You guys weren't prepared for this."

All the officers looked between each other. "I'm sorry, did you say telepath?" Douglas said. "What the fuck, man?"

"We'll discuss this later," Kader said. She looked shaken but she gave a brave nod. "Let's move out. Jason, you're still out of armour, so let us handle it from here. Unless there's any more weird shit we should know about?"

"No, that's in the basement. I gotta fight a wizard."

"Jesus Christ," Douglas groaned.

Lynch chuckled and spoke in a soft voice. "Don't do anything stupid." It came out awkward, but it was clearly his attempt at being nice. Jason gave him a friendly smile all the same.

"I'll stand guard over the wounded here," Cole said and took position by the hallway corner.

"Squad," Kader ordered. "Move out."

The police marched down the west wing. Jason didn't stay to watch them. He moved back to the front parlour room where the two knights were waiting.

"Nicholas, Phillip," he called. "I'm coming in."

"How'd it go, cowboy?" Nicholas asked.

Jason stood out in the open. "We got the telepath. The police can handle the other mortals from here."

Phillip stood up and hefted his shotgun up against his shoulder. "Impressive, boy."

"Come on, we need to go stop the wizard."

The two old knights exchanged a glance. "Right," Nicholas said and held up his magnum. "Whoever kills the wizard gets a bottle of my Chateau Lafite Rothschild."

Jason blinked. "Is that…a wine?"

Phillip glared at him. "Zounderkite."

Chapter 31

Jason and the two knights walked in single file, each with their weapon at the ready. The distant pops of gunshots marked the police battle with the Monster Hunters, but they faded into the distance. Jason had to focus on the fight ahead.

"If I'm right," he said, "Peter won't attack us. He wanted the mortals to kill you. He won't directly break Imperium law."

"He might kill you," Phillip said, "since you're not a member of an immortal family." His tone was a little too optimistic for Jason's taste.

"Possibly. But I still need to be here for this. Silvana needs my blood."

"Agreed," Nicholas said. "If we kill Peter, we will tell the Imperium he was trespassing and threatening us. Then you can legally marry Silvana, and she can take your blood and live." Jason grimaced, but the others didn't see. "As far as I'm concerned, the wizard must die."

"Hear, hear," Phillip said.

They entered the library. It was honestly smaller than Jason had expected. There was a row of single bookshelves on both sides of the room, and several reading lounges in the centre. A fireplace with a mantle decorated the feature wall, and two more suits of armour stood guard on either side.

"So, Emberline mentioned a secret entrance?" Jason asked.

Phillip glared at him again. "You know too much, for someone not yet part of the family."

"He's standing next to us in battle. He's family already," Nicholas said.

He gave Jason a simple, curt nod, and Jason found himself blinking rapidly to clear the tears welling in his eyes. *Damn...I really want to be a part of this family. Even if it includes bloody Phillip.*

Nicholas turned towards the bookcase. All the books were stacked on the side so only their spines were visible, yet one large tome was faced outwards. Nicholas opened the cover. Inside was a door handle. He turned it, and the entire shelf swung outwards, revealing a dark tunnel inside. Nicholas held a finger to his lips, and everyone marched forward in silence.

The tunnel held a staircase built of cold stone, leading down into the depths of the mansion. A faint light from below illuminated the path. Phillip pushed his way to the front. Nicholas came last, and Jason found himself in the middle. Each man took a gentle step on their toes, making no sound. Nicholas was going extra slow. The stairs seemed difficult for him to manage. But Jason didn't offer to help. The old knight had his pride.

The basement below was silent. Jason held his breath. How could it be silent? Lisbeth had been here with Silvana the whole time, and Emberline had come down after. Had Peter already killed them all? *Surely he won't kill them, right?* Jason felt overwhelmed with helplessness. He didn't understand Immortal laws well enough. And he had no idea what Peter was capable of. *I'm still in way over my head.*

Phillip held up a fist. They all stood still. A soft voice was murmuring ahead. A woman. *Well, at least one of the vampires is alive.* Jason cringed. *That was a dark thought.*

Phillip crouched low and stalked forward, shotgun at the ready. Jason followed several steps behind.

The basement had several wine racks and large wooden barrels positioned across the floor. The air held a thick layer of dust that threatened to make Jason start coughing with each inhalation. Even the softest footstep would echo easily along the stone floor. Jason stepped extra carefully. The sounds of a voice drifted through the dark, coming from the dim golden light ahead.

"…nothing to gain. The monarchy is dead, you fool. You'll achieve nothing."

"I achieve what you couldn't," came a man's voice. It was unmistakable to Jason, who had heard that voice almost every day for the last few months. *Peter Erikson.* Jason squeezed his hand into a fist.

"Royal titles are wasted on you. They should pass to the deserving. Those with the will to seize power and rule."

"That world is gone, fool," said Emberline, her tone thick with derision. "I'm two hundred and thirty years old, yet kings and queens were already becoming obsolete before I was born. Give it up, wizard."

"The Russian throne will be mine," Peter growled. "The Imperium will bow to my will. And by the time I'm done, you'll be begging to suck my cock to curry favour."

"BASTARD!" Phillip roared.

"No!" Jason hissed, but unheeded.

Phillip shoulder charged the basement door to knock it open and fired his shotgun with a deafening ring. He stepped through the doorway and fired again.

"*Haš Edün!*"

Phillip went flying backwards through the door and crashed into the stone stairway. He let out a groan on impact and went still.

Holy shit! Jason had to hold a hand over his mouth to stop from crying out.

Someone touched Jason's shoulder. Nicholas was at his side, gun up. Clearly, he thought they should attack now rather than check on

Phillip. Jason nodded and followed his lead. Nicholas held up a hand and counted with his fingers. *Three...two...one...*

They rounded the corner at the same time. Jason had half a second to glimpse Peter in the middle of the room with the three vampire women surrounding him. Jason aimed at the wizard...

"Khàd Nga!"

Both guns flew out of their grip. Peter caught the Glock in one hand and the magnum in his other. He grinned.

"Well, that was easy," Peter said. "Jason, please come in. You're just in time."

Jason glanced around the room. Silvana was lying on a makeshift bed which has been set on top of an old wooden table. Her whole body was still pale, shrunken, and gaunt. She was barely moving. Lisbeth was crumpled in a corner and Emberline was floating off the ground with her hands behind her back, restrained by invisible bonds. Blood coated her lips.

Peter Erikson was dressed in a long brown cloak, with a white sash around the middle and long tassels hanging under his arms. His hood was thrown back, and his hair was messy in a way that looked deliberate. He smiled a handsome smile.

"Now you're all here, under my power," Peter said. "As soon as those Monster Hunter fools get here, they'll be able to kill you without a fight."

"Peter," Jason growled. "You should know, you've failed."

"Oh?" Peter quipped.

"Your friends are beaten. Gerald and Kathrine are in police custody. And Rion was just fucking eviscerated by Emberline's sword." Jason couldn't help grinning at the look of shock on Peter's face. "The Plymouth police are rounding up the last of the Hunters now. There's no one left to enact your 'master plan.'"

"You're lying!" Peter snapped. "Rion had unlocked his enhanced vampire state. He was indestructible! He was powerful enough to help me destroy the Imperium! There is no way you could stop him."

Jason frowned at that. "The Imperium? Was that really your plan? A total government overhaul?"

"It'd be easy, too. The old fools running the Imperium are passive, limp-dick assholes. They're weak and ready to be overthrown. Then Rion and I will set up a new generation of kings to rule the mortals in the open. None will challenge us. We will be the new gods."

Jason blinked. "Well you can forget that. Rion's dead. And the Imperium will stop you if you try to kill this family. Admit it. You have lost. Again."

Peter looked around the room, his mouth hanging half open and his face drained of colour. He focused on Emberline and the sword that lay discarded at her feet. There was a thick layer of blood coating the silver blade.

"No…" Peter growled. "You're a mortal, Jason. A fucking mortal! How could you possibly affect my plans? How could you fuck this up so bad?"

"Because you're not as powerful as you think you are!" Jason roared. "You were born with more power than most. But that doesn't make you better than anyone. I was still able to beat you. Me, a simple mortal, not that smart or strong. A mere police rookie. Don't you get it, Peter? You're just as human as the rest of us."

"I'm a wizard!" he roared. "I have the power of Zapherahlious himself! I can shatter mountains with a word!"

"And you were beaten by a mortal!" Jason shouted back. "You think you can bully anyone weaker than you and take what you want. But a single mortal could stop you."

Peter looked at him, and slowly, a smile crept over his face. "Yes. A mortal. You are…mortal."

Jason blinked. "What?"

Peter lifted up Jason's Glock, pointed it at Emberline, and fired.

Blood burst out of the centre of Emberline's chest, splattering against the wall behind her. Lisbeth screamed in horror. A pained expression crossed Emberline's face, then it slackened as she slunk forward. The magic holding her up was released and she crumpled to the ground like a rag doll.

"Aunty!" Silvana cried.

Emberline didn't move. She lay flat on the ground as blood pooled around her. Nearby, Lisbeth was feebly crawling towards her, already sobbing and saying her name over and over as she reached for her sister.

"I need a mortal to kill these people," Peter said, staring at the gun in fascination. "And now I have a mortal's weapon to do it. I don't need the Monster Hunters. I have you, Jason. You're going to be the new killer."

"NO!" Phillip roared and charged back into the room, running directly at Peter. The wizard lifted Jason's gun at the old man and smirked casually as he pulled the trigger.

Nothing happened. The gun was now empty.

Peter had barely registered that fact when Phillip crashed into him and drove the wizard to the ground. A second later Jason and Nicholas had dived on top of him.

"Watch his mouth," Nicholas yelled.

Jason grabbed Peter and clamped his hand over his mouth. Peter's lips were moving. His head jerked, and he mumbled out muffled curses. But no spells took effect. Nicholas dived on Peter's legs. Jason knelt on one of Peter's arms and pressed both hands to Peter's face. And Phillip just punched the wizard over and over again in any area he could reach.

"Make way," a woman's voice commanded.

Jason looked up and saw Lisbeth standing over them all. Her gentle face was now a twisted rictus of cold rage. Her long hair hung over half her face, eyes and down her shoulder. She held Emberline's long sword in a two-handed grip, facing downwards.

Peter let out a muffled howl. Lisbeth stepped over him and raised the sword up. Jason pressed down hard on Peter's mouth. But the wizard jerked wildly and yanked his neck sideways.

And Jason lost his grip.

"Tàb Izī!"

A ball of flame exploded outwards from Peter's chest, and Jason was thrown backwards as a raging heat seared him all across his body.

He landed on his back with a painful thump. Fire was racing all along his clothes. Jason's skin was starting to burn with heat. He frantically swatted at the flames and rolled onto his front to smother them down.

"You scum!" Peter howled. "How dare you touch me!" The wizard started floating off the ground, rising up to the ceiling, his cloak billowing out behind him. "I will crush you like the ants you are!"

A savage scream cut him off as Lisbeth launched herself across the air and swung the sword in a powerful two handed grip. Peter cursed, and a spell blocked the sword. Lisbeth swung again and again, screaming ferociously with each strike. Peter was forced to move backwards and cry out multiple spells just to block her attacks.

Jason tried to rise, but fell backwards. His whole body was in too much pain to stand up. The flesh of his chest and neck had been badly scorched, and the skin on his forearms had already started peeling.

I'm beaten.

He looked up to watch the battle. Peter was being forced across the room by Lisbeth's attacks. Nicholas was picking his magnum off the ground. He seemed mostly unaffected by the blast. And Phillip was huddled by Emberline's side, cradling her. He was holding his wrist to his wife's mouth.

Offering her blood. That's what I should be doing.

Jason crawled along the ground. His legs and core were unburnt, so he moved by kicking with his knees and feet. Each shift forward was excruciating. The sounds of magnum fire rang out through the tiny room with ear-shattering volume. Then the room lit up with the light of flames. A fireball struck the wall above Jason. But he ignored the battle. He kept crawling until he reached Silvana's side. He climbed up the table with the last of his strength, and collapsed next to her.

Her cold hand clutched his. "Jason," she whispered.

He turned his head to look at her. He saw her crystal blue eyes staring back at him. They brimmed with tears. She stared at him with such affection. Even with all his physical pain, he felt his heart lurch in response to her.

"Silvana," he whispered. "Take my blood."

She twisted her lip in a sad smile. "Jason…" she murmured weakly. "I…can't…"

Jason lifted his hand out to her. There was blood already on the skin. "Silvana, Peter will kill us all. I'm sure the Imperium will understand." He lifted his trembling hand towards her lips. "I can't stop Peter. But you can. If you take my blood, you'll be strong enough. You're stronger than you realise. You can beat him."

"I…would need…it all…" she whispered.

He nodded. "I want you to have it all."

"You would die…" she cried.

He nodded as he pressed his bloodied hand against her mouth. "I would rather die than let someone hurt you."

She looked at him with wide eyes. He knew what he had to say. The words felt heavy on his lips. But he forced them out anyway.

"Because I love you, Silvana. I love you."

He thrust his hand against her lips.

Silvana stared at him silently.

Then she bit down.

Chapter 32

The taste of blood sent a powerful sensation rippling through Silvana's body. It was agony and ecstasy in equal measure. It burned like fire and froze like ice. And it seemed to run through every vein and every skin cell.

She could feel her sunken cheeks filling out. Colour returned to her skin and muscles to her limbs. *It's working!* She gave a crazed laugh of exhilaration as her skin kept growing more flushed with colour.

Then she started glowing.

Her skin turned luminescent. An aura of energy exploded out of her. Her vision turned red. And she rose off the table and floated in the air.

What the fuck? What's happening to me?

She saw Jason, lying face down on the bed, his body still.

"No," she breathed. "No, no, no, Jason?" But he didn't move. The skin on his forearms was burnt and shredded. Blood pooled from his wrist from where she'd bit into him.

Her mind went white with rage.

"PETER!" Silvana screamed.

The battle had stopped. Peter was standing over a battered Lisbeth, her sword lying discarded nearby. Nicholas was slumped against the wall, bleeding from his nose. His magnum was clicking as he tried the trigger repeatedly, but he was out of ammo. The wizard had a cocky smirk on his face, but it disappeared fast when he saw Silvana floating in the air.

"What in God's name…" Peter cried.

Silvana felt power surging in her mind and knew on some instinctive level that it would obey her commands. She tilted her head forward and *thought.* Peter was thrown across the room and slammed against the stone wall.

Yes! You're mine now!

She gave a full-throated scream and rushed at the wizard.

Peter came off the wall shouting and hurled a ball of fire. She caught it with her mind and with a mental push she sent it flying back at him, splashing against his robes and burning holes. He roared in fury and she shrieked back at him. She could feel blood in every cell of her body, and somehow it connected her to the world around her.

She floated in the air with just a thought and pushed at the wizard with her will. He threw more fire that bounced off her invisible barriers. She reached out with a thought and picked up discarded stones from around the room and hurled them at him. Peter took dozens of blows within seconds of each other. He started to speak but Silvana reached out a hand towards his face, and Peter's mouth was briefly gagged shut.

Until he snarled his mouth free and spoke, and she was sent flying back.

Silvana let the blood surge into her fists. She floated off the ground and charged him again and again. Their powers clashed with violent cracks of impact. Yet Silvana kept approaching him physically, while he kept trying to force her back where his spells could take more effect.

I'm physically stronger. If I can just get close enough to touch him, I'll rip his fucking head from his neck!

She came within reach and snatched his hair. She yanked out a clump with enough force to pull a chunk of his scalp free. He roared in pain and turned the shout into a curse that threw her back against the wall.

Silvana lifted herself and charged, but she seemed slower this time. Already her aura was less bright. The power was fading. She wanted to scream in frustration. Her power must have been a quick boost. If she didn't kill Peter now, there was no chance.

And Jason would have died for nothing.

With all her power, and all her desperation, she launched herself at Peter one last time. He backed up until he struck the wall behind him. He looked at her with equal parts rage and terror as he shouted a spell that slowed her momentum. She reached out a hand. She slowed down even further. Her nails clawed at the skin on his neck…

But she came to a complete stop.

Silvana let out a scream. Her aura was completely gone. Peter realised it at the same time, and threw all his power into her at once. She was thrown backwards and smashed into the wall behind her.

No! I failed! My family will all die because I failed.

She tried to keep fighting. But she collapsed, exhausted, and Peter stood over her with a burning fireball in his hand.

"Fucking bitch!" he screamed. "I don't care about Imperium law anymore. I'll show you what happens when you challenge a wizard!"

Silvana looked towards Jason one last time.

And saw him sit up.

* * *

The thought occurred to Jason. *Why am I still alive?*

He opened his eyes and looked at his body. His burns had faded. His pain had almost vanished entirely. He felt strength in his limbs. *I'm healed? Wait, am I actually dead?*

Someone was shouting. He sat up.

Peter was standing over Silvana. He had her against the wall now and she struggled to move. The wizard held a fireball in his hand, ready to burn Silvana's face. His back was turned to Jason.

Jason rolled off the table and landed on his feet. His body was stiff, exhausted, but strong enough to move. He was silent as a ghost as he crossed the room to Lisbeth's side. He picked up her sword.

I have to do this. Don't hesitate this time.

"I will put you in your fucking place, my *wife!*" Peter roared.

Jason suddenly felt like he was a child again, listening to his father screaming abuse, and watching his mother whimper in terror. He saw Silvana wiggling in Peter's magical grip as he moved the flame of his hand closer to her face, sneering in joy at her helplessness.

No! I won't let you kill her again!

He was not a child anymore. This time, he would fight back. This time, he would save her.

Jason lifted the sword high in a two-handed grip. Its weight was like holding a car above his head. His arms wobbled.

Peter thrust the flame into Silvana's face.

Jason roared in fury and swung down with all his strength.

And the blade split Peter's skull in half.

The flame in his hand winked out as the sword lodged somewhere in the middle of his face. The wizard immediately crumpled into a heap on the floor, his body limp, blood pooling around his head. The sword handle fell from Jason's trembling hands.

Peter was definitely dead. The blade was wedged halfway down Peter's hairline. Dark red matter had spilled out...

I killed Peter. My school friend. My roommate. I killed him with a sword.

He looked away. He flexed his hands back and forth. The ringing of the impact was still vibrating in his palms from where he'd held the handle. He shut his eyes and breathed deep. Bile was rising in his throat.

"Jason?"

He opened his eyes. Silvana stood before him. Alive, and healthy. *And really fucking beautiful.* Silvana rushed forward and gripped him in a tight hug. He held her just as tight and nestled his head against her, breathing in her scent. She was safe. She was ok. Despite the shock and horror at what he'd done, this felt right.

All too soon she pulled away. "Are you ok?" she asked gently.

He swallowed back the bitterness in his throat and nodded. "I just…I swore I would never be a violent man."

She clutched his hand. "Jason…you saved me," she whispered.

He remembered Captain Kader's words. *"Sometimes, we can save someone."* He looked at Silvana and squeezed her hand back. The nausea in his stomach began to settle, and he breathed easier.

"I saved someone," he whispered. "Yes. I did." He was even able to offer a small smile. "That's good."

Someone groaned nearby. Emberline was sitting up, clutching her chest with one hand, and gripping Phillip with the other. Her eyes were only half open as she scanned the room. Blood still dripped from her canines and her husband had a corresponding bite mark on his wrist. Phillip lay on the ground, cupping the puncture wounds on his wrist.

"Emberline," Jason cried in relief. "I thought you were dead."

"I'm fine," Emberline sighed. "I've healed sufficiently. But I took more blood than usual."

Jason crouched by Phillip and put his hand on both shoulders to help him up. "Will you be alright?"

"Of course, zounderkite," Phillip growled. He sat up with a groan, and fell back against the wall with a grunt. His face was much paler than usual. "I'll just need some rest for a few days. And some… red meat."

"Steak and wine for everyone," Nicholas said, from where he still lay on the floor. "And Mr Turner, I believe there's a bottle of wine with your name on it."

"There's a wine called Jason?" he said and laughed. No one joined him.

Then Silvana snorted and burst out laughing, her voice ringing through the basement. A round of light chuckles came from everyone else as the tension finally lifted. They were all alive and safe again.

Lisbeth weakly crossed the room and knelt by her husband's side. "Oh darling, you were magnificent," she cried. "A true Knight Templar of the finest quality."

Nicholas grinned back at her. "And you were a true queen. It was my honour to fight at your side."

"Oh Nicholas!" Lisbeth said, wiping her eyes before kissing him softly on the lips, and he tenderly cupped both her cheeks between two hands.

Jason felt a brief twinge of discomfort. It looked like a young woman aged thirty, kissing a man in his late eighties. Then he pushed the thought aside. These two were just possibly the cutest couple he'd ever seen.

Silvana silently took his hand. They stood quietly and watched her aunt and uncle hold each other close.

He glanced at the other couple in the room and saw Phillip and Emberline just sitting next to each other, nursing their wounds. They weren't touching. They were just sitting a hands-width apart, but with a certain familiarity between them. Jason couldn't help smile. *There were many forms of love.*

"I've gotta ask," Jason said, turning to Silvana. "You took my blood.

You said you would need all of it and it would probably kill me. But I'm fine. And you became…supergirl."

"I would have said Scarlet Witch, personally," she quipped.

"Fair." He smiled. "Does that happen every time? The first time?"

"No, of course not," she said.

"Then…what happened?"

Silvana could only shrug and look around the room for help.

"I've certainly never heard of it," Emberline said, her voice weak. "Silvana was clearly an enhanced vampire. But it should have required the blood of many victims. I doubt she had more than a litre. And she was in her weakened state to begin with. Your blood should have barely been enough to get her back to normal."

"Maybe it was love," Lisbeth said with an adoring smile. "True love."

"Oh really?" Emberline drawled. "Then why have you or I never experienced something like that?" Lisbeth seemed to bite her tongue.

"Maybe there was something in your blood, Jason," Nicholas said. "Were you smoking marihuana before coming here?"

"Of course not!" Jason said and couldn't help laughing. "I didn't take any performance enhan…" he trailed off as his eyes widened. "Oh my god…I had the elixir."

"What?" Silvana asked. "Oh, you mean the elixir I gave you two days ago? No, Jason, that would have passed through your system already."

"Uh…actually, I only had it an hour ago." She blinked at him. "I'm sorry. But when you gave it to me, I didn't exactly…trust you." He avoided her gaze. "So I just hung on to it. But I was wounded by the metamorph tonight and the elixir saved my life. So, thank you. And it might have still been in my system when you had my blood."

Silvana merely smiled. "Its fine, Jason. I'm not offended. But if the elixir was in your blood, then it still doesn't make sense. It was just a healing tonic."

"It's a question for another day," Emberline said. "The point is, something worked, and Silvana became powerful enough to match a wizard's strength. There is definitely something special about you two. Speaking of which." She pointed at Jason and Silvana. "You're both single now. I suggest you make that marriage official before you go any further."

"What? Right now?" Jason cried with a short laugh.

"You've certainly proved yourself, boy," Emberline said. "You fought like a knight and conducted yourself with honour. You are worthy of this family. In fact, I think it is this family that now needs to prove itself worthy of you." She bowed her head towards him.

"Let's not overstate things," Phillip grumbled, still holding his bleeding wrist. "He did well, I won't deny it. But we don't need to exaggerate."

"He saved all of us," Emberline cut in. "He brought the police and fought alongside us. He even challenged an empowered vampire and a wizard."

"And a grizzly bear," Jason said. All eyes turned to him. "Sorry."

"The point is, Jason is worthy of this family," Emberline said. "I give my blessing."

"As do I," Nicholas said.

"And I," Lisbeth echoed.

"And I," Phillip finished, with only a slight hint of reluctance.

Jason looked at them, and turned to Silvana, cupping both of her hands in his. He felt a wave of relief when he looked at her, knowing she was finally safe. "Silvana, I think…oh." He winced. "Uh…can we not do this in the same room as the body?"

Everyone became aware of a certain smell coming from Peter's split head. They were all too eager to move out.

The family helped each other climb back up the stairs. Everyone bore an injury of some kind. Nicholas was hobbling and letting out grunts of pain, so Jason stood on one side with Lisbeth on the other, and together they lifted him to the top.

Upstairs, the mansion was eerily quiet. All battle sounds had ceased. Now there was only a distant murmuring of voices, speaking in calm tones. Jason sighed with relief. They wouldn't sound so calm if there were severe injuries.

The family moved into the front parlour and settled on their lounge chairs. Emberline whispered in Silvana's ear, prompting her to move to a nearby cabinet that looked hundreds of years old. Silvana opened it, and it made a suction sound of a modern fridge door. Inside were several vials of blood. She gave them to her aunts, who took out the rubber stoppers and began to sip.

"When you're done," Phillip said, "any chance you could whip me up a steak? I'm feeling light-headed."

Jason nearly snapped *'she's not your servant'* at him, but Silvana just said, "You'll have to wait, Phillip. The police are coming." She looked to Jason and gestured towards the outside hall. He nodded and crossed the room, poking his head around the corner.

"Captain?" he called out.

A flashlight was shining through the dark hallway. A second later, Captain Kader and Douglas appeared, escorting a handcuffed man between them. "'Ey Turner! You made it," Douglas called.

"The gunmen?"

"All accounted for," Kader answered. "Idiots ran out of ammo. They still refused to surrender until we gassed the shit out of them."

"Everyone all right?" Jason asked, looking past them for the rest of the team.

The captain shook her head. "Wilson got shot."

"Oh my god!" Jason cried. "Wilson? Is he ok? What…"

"Relax, rookie. He got grazed by a bullet, on the very tip of his shoulder. He's fine." Jason sighed. "But you wouldn't know that to listen to him. The way he tells it, the bullet grazed his brain."

"Yeah," Douglas groaned. "Won't shut up about how his kids were nearly orphaned. We're going to be hearing about this for years." He glared at Jason. "This is your fault, rookie. I hold you responsible for this."

Jason grinned.

"How are the residents?" Kader asked, gesturing to the others.

"No casualties. A few minor injuries."

"We'll need to take statements. But after we get these twenty odd criminals back to the station." She sighed. "This will be an all-nighter. We're ready for you to sub on, Jason, anytime now."

"Oh, great," he drawled.

Lisbeth and Silvana appeared beside him. "Captain," Lisbeth said, "I want to thank you for your assistance in protecting my family tonight."

Jason smiled. Until he realised she was talking to Douglas.

"Uh…" Douglas stammered.

"You're welcome, ma'am," Kader said with a smirk.

"Oh dear!" Lisbeth said. "If I've given offense, I'm …"

Three loud bangs came from the front door knocker. Everyone turned to look down the hallway. The front door was wide open and two shadowed figures stood in the darkness, silhouetted only by the moonlight.

"Oh what now?" Kader groaned.

"Uh, guys?" Jason asked. The vampires were frozen in place, a quiet tension building between them. "Do you know who they are?" he asked as he clutched at his empty holster on impulse.

"Yes, Jason," Silvana whispered. "Those are Vigiles."

Jason looked back at the shadowed figures. "Vigiles? Do you mean…"

"Wizards," Lisbeth whispered. "The police force of the Immortal world. Each one is a highly trained expert in battle magic."

"Oh." Jason's blood turned cold, sending a shiver down his spine. "They're the representatives of the Immortal Imperium."

Chapter 33

"Can someone explain this to me?" Douglas asked, his eyes never straying from the two Vigiles looming in the doorway. "I heard the word 'Immortal'? And 'wizard'? I assume you're about to get to the punchline. Did they walk into a bar or something?" Douglas gave an awkward laugh, but no one answered him.

"What will they do?" Jason asked.

"They will uphold Imperium law," Lisbeth said. "Remember, that law is not about justice. It's about enforcing their power."

"Then what should *we* do?"

"Give your full cooperation. Do exactly what they tell you. Answer every question truthfully. Hold nothing back."

"But Aunty…I was enhanced," Silvana whispered as the fear grew in her eyes. "And I drank the blood of someone not my husband. What will they do to me? And Jason…he struck down an Immortal."

"Oh shit," Jason muttered.

Lisbeth patted Silvana on the shoulder. "We'll explain that the wizard attacked us first. We'll hope, and pray, that it will be sufficient." She glided towards the front door like a queen crossing her throne room.

Kader cleared her throat. "You struck down someone, rookie?"

Jason turned to his captain. "*That's* what you have a problem with?

After all the weird shit we just said?"

Hushed whispers came from the front door, and everyone grew quiet. Lisbeth bowed low. She gestured to welcome the Vigiles into the mansion and they slowly marched down the hallway. Their footfalls barely made a sound and their faces were still shadowed by the moonlight behind them. They stepped into the flashlight.

Both Vigiles were women of a similar height and build. They wore matching black tuxedo suits with black bow ties over white shirts. One Vigile had long locks of curly red hair that reached to her middle back. She had pale white skin, blue eyes, and full pink lips. She also had high cheekbones and a strong jawline. She would have been stunning, if not for the blazing cold intensity in her expression that stood out even more than her beauty.

The other Vigile had long black hair in dozens of braids that reached to her waist. Her pitch-black skin and matching brown eyes made her blend into the night. Her face was smooth and delicate, yet she held her eyes in thin slits. She wore golden beads in her hair. Golden earrings dangled to her chin.

While the red-haired woman appeared to be mid-twenties, the dark-haired woman looked just over forty. Jason figured if they were Immortal, they might have been somewhere between about one hundred and four hundred years old respectively.

"Everyone," said Lisbeth in a tone both formal and grandiose, "This is Vigile Portia." She pointed to the younger woman. "And this is Vigile Desdemona. They're here to—"

"Still thy tongue," Desdemona cut in, her tone flat, lifeless, and chilling.

She cast her dark eyes over the group. No one dared move.

"We are here to deal with this grievous front," Desdemona continued in her thick, deep voice, speaking with crisp, clear diction. Her accent sounded like it had originally been from somewhere in Africa, but had been diluted over time. "The Imperium detected the presence of an empowered vampire," she paused to glare directly at Jason, and spoke slowly, "and the death of a wizard."

Oh shit.

"We are at your service, Vigiles," Lisbeth said with another low bow.

"I should expect so," Portia said, her upper lip twisting upwards. "You know the penalty for killing an Immortal. Anyone who aids the killer is treated the same."

Jason opened his mouth to speak, but Silvana shushed him. That, more than anything, made him realise the danger they were in.

"You," Portia said and pointed at Douglas. "Are you the leader of the local law enforcement?"

"Uh…"

Kader stepped forward, her chin high and her thumbs resting on the edge of her Kevlar armour. "I'm Captain Kader. And I'm running this operation."

The Vigiles looked at her, and somehow their flat expressions seemed slightly more approving. "Thou will be permitted to remove all mortal knaves involved in this incident," Desdemona said. "But the Immortals belong to us. Including the metamorph and telepath already in thy possession."

Jason shuddered. The Vigiles had only just arrived, and yet seemed to know so much that had happened. What kind of powers did they have?

"Metamorph?" Kader asked.

"The shape shifter," Portia drawled.

Kader's eyes widened. "He…so he WAS an animal! I thought so. He wasn't human when I shot him." She looked up sharply. "He assaulted a police officer. He needs to be charged. What authority do you have to claim him?"

"Captain," Jason whispered, taking a step towards Kader.

"Hush, child." Desdemona dismissed him with a wave of the hand. She faced the captain. "The law-breakers will be dealt with judiciously. Not by thy hand, but by ours."

Kader stepped up to the Vigile without a hint of fear. "They broke our laws. I will hold them accountable."

"Challenge me not," Desdemona said. "I would abhor to deal unfavourably with such a merited warrior as thee."

"Are you quoting Shakespeare or something?" Douglas chuckled. Everyone cast furious eyes at him. He cleared his throat, "Sorry."

"By whose authority?" Kader repeated.

"Mine," Desdemona said. The two women stared each other down for several long seconds.

"If I may," Jason said gently. He even bowed low. "Ms Vigile, my captain does not understand that you are a wizard. I'm sure if she understood, she would be willing…"

Desdemona gave the slightest of grins. "*Tab Izī.*"

She said it in the faintest whisper, and yet a sudden, deafening whoosh drowned out all other sounds, and Jason was blinded by light. He blinked rapidly to adjust to the brilliance that lit up the whole world. A constant roaring came from everywhere. He saw red. The walls were swimming in motion. Then his eyes finally adjusted.

Everything was on fire.

Huge pillars of flame filled every empty space throughout the mansion. It wasn't just the walls and building that was burning. It was the air itself, wreathed in flowing columns of red. Someone was screaming.

Desdemona and Portia stood before the wall of flames, calm and still, like demons emerging from the depths of hell. The older wizard lifted her hand, and with a small flick of her hand, the flames shifted into a deep, dark blue, and all sound disappeared entirely. In the empty silence, with the furious motion of the fires behind them, Desdemona whispered.

"I'm a warlock of the Imperium. My authority is my own."

She gestured again, and the blue flames vanished with a wink.

Jason's eyes struggled again to adjust, this time to the sudden shift to darkness. Slowly he made out the shadows of his companions beside him, unharmed. He scanned the mansion, but nothing was burnt. The flames hadn't touched anything, or anyone. He also realised he'd fallen to his knees. *Yeah. If anyone deserved worship, it'd be the wizard who could do the burning bush thing.*

Kader just whispered, "The prisoners are yours."

"Thank you," Desdemona said, over-pronouncing each syllable. "Now, we desire to speak with the Immortal residents and their relatives. The rest of thee can go about as thou wish."

Jason frowned in surprise. They were letting him go?

"Right this way, honoured guests," Lisbeth said and led the Vigiles into the front parlour. Neither bothered to notice Jason as they past. He saw they each wore cufflinks on their wrists and collar. Portia's were both silver, and Desdemona's were gold.

"Wait," Jason said. "I'm free to go? What if I ran away?"

Desdemona ignored him, but Portia spun around, fixing her stunning blue eyes on him. For a moment, they seemed to flicker with the hint of blue flame.

"We would find you," she said simply.

* * *

Jason joined the other officers in moving through the mansion and arresting the Monster Hunters, then walking them out to the road and piling them into police cars. Kader and Douglas said nothing about the wizard's powers. Their eyes were wide and vacant. The other police hadn't seen anything. Apparently, they'd been outside the mansion at the time and hadn't heard a sound.

The clean-up got underway. There were eighteen Hunters arrested in total. Five more had been murdered by Rion. Many of the survivors were suffering the effects of tear gas exposure, such as red eyes, weakened vision and difficulty breathing. The forensic team was called in, despite the midnight hour. They examined the bodies as the detectives started taking statements from the Hunters.

At one point, Lynch approached Jason while avoiding all eye contact.

"We've gotta take about a dozen more statements. Can you do a few for us, rookie?" Jason agreed without any further discussion. It felt good to have Lynch's trust again.

Soon they began ferrying Hunters back to the station for lockup. Jason did a trip himself. He found the young man, Freddie, still outside, totally safe, and furious about not being involved.

"Next time," Jason promised.

"I'm gonna hold you to that," Freddie said, doing his best to look menacing.

It was nearly two in the morning when he got a text from Silvana. *"The Vigiles want to see you now."*

Jason felt his chest constrict. He excused himself from the police and moved back into the mansion's front parlour room. Silvana and her whole family rested on the lounge chairs. The two aunts were sipping from vials, and the two uncles had empty plates of food next to them. The Vigiles stood opposite them, calm and in control as ever.

And behind them crouched Gerald, Rion, and Katherine.

Jason blinked. Rion was awake, alert and looking right at him. *How the hell is he still alive?* He was still missing an arm, and Jason took some satisfaction in that. All three young Immortals looked like they'd taken a beating, and each one glared at him as he entered.

Peter's body was slumped in the corner beside them. Jason looked away from the bloodied remains of his head.

"Ah, so the boyfriend appears."

Portia was smiling at him openly now, her teeth perfectly straight and white, reminding Jason more of a shark than a person. "The one who gave his blood to an unmarried vampire, fired a weapon at three Immortals, and shoved a sword into a wizard's head. Did I miss anything, Mr Jason Turner?"

Jason was silent. He could feel eyes both young and ancient studying him. He took a breath to slow his pounding heartrate, held himself upright and spoke in a level voice.

"You didn't miss anything. That's exactly what I did."

Desdemona twisted her lip. "I dislike thy tone, boy," she growled.

Silvana was staring at him, shaking her head. Jason bowed his head. "I apologise. I am unfamiliar with…Immortal customs."

"Huh," Portia scoffed. "There's an understatement. You attacked several Immortals, killed one, and seemed surprised that we're here to pronounce judgement on you."

Jason blinked. "Judgement?"

"Vigile Desdemona," Nicholas said, his voice more respectful than Jason had ever heard. "This man is courting my daughter. He fought to protect us. I do not think it premature to grant him the rights of the House of Romanoff."

"And Windsor," Phillip echoed. Jason couldn't help smiling at both of them.

"You've already stated your case," Portia said. "Now is time for judgement. You will not intervene. Mistress?" She turned to Desdemona with a nod of reverence and backed away. The elder Vigile glared hard at Jason for a long moment. His hands were sweating.

The Vigile stepped forward. And Jason noticed that Rion was smiling.

Oh no.

"Stand still," she instructed. She stood a half metre shorter than him, yet she made Jason feel small. She reached her hands up towards his head.

"Ma'am?" he asked. But she said nothing. And he forced his muscles to obey her. She placed her hands on either side of his head. Up close, her eyes were even darker than he'd realised.

She whispered, "*Zu Üri Akkesentü!*"

Nothing happened. Jason stood motionless as best he could. Desdemona shut her eyes a second.

Then she jerked back, a look of mild surprise on her stony face. "How art thou alive?" she asked.

"Um…what?"

"Thy injuries are…significant. Thou were cut in a dozen places. Thou should have bled out. Yet still were thou burnt and fed upon." She frowned at him. "There is no doubt. Thou acted in defence. Thou hath stood in battle on behalf of Immortals and faced down opponents far greater than thyself."

"Uh…thank you," he blurted out.

"My judgement is thus." She stood back into the centre of the room. "The mortal known as Jason Turner will be accounted an honorary member of this family until such a time as it becomes official. Thus, the actions of these three individuals were committed against a member of an Immortal family."

"That's bullshit!" Gerald shouted as he thrashed against his hand-cuffs.

"*Kà!*" Desdemona barked, and Gerald's mouth was forced shut by an invisible power. He immediately strained his face, trying to force his lips apart. He went red in the face. *He can't breathe.*

"His slaying of the wizard," she went on, "has been deemed as preventative, and thus appropriate action."

Silvana gave a cry of relief, and her family broke into happy smiles and sighs. Jason was even able to produce a smile himself.

"However," she cut in, "all members of this family will be on probation. Mr Turner is not permitted to give blood to Silvana again until such a time as their relationship is formalised. Any further anomaly in vampiric abilities should be reported immediately to the Imperium. Any use of that power will mean an immediate sentence of death."

Jesus...

Gerald was purple in the face from suffocation. Portia mumbled something, and he gasped loudly as he started breathing again.

"Take them," Desdemona ordered.

Portia mumbled again. Whatever spell she used, she was deliberately masking the words by speaking quietly. The three immortal youths were raised off the ground, levitating, and restrained by invisible bonds. Portia gestured towards herself and they floated to her side. Peter's body joined them, lying flat in the air, his limbs dangling.

"Our time will come," Rion growled. "It is our birthright to rule. The Immortals will claim their place!"

"Silence," Desdemona snapped. She spared one last glance at the room, and her cold eyes lingered on Jason.

I better ask now.

"Vigile Desdemona," Jason cried. "May I ask a question?" She merely continued to look at him, so he assumed that was permission. "Why was Silvana affected by my blood like that?"

Portia glanced between him and her mistress, before letting out a laugh that had a menacing echo. "Oh sweet thing," she cooed. "Did you think it was true love?" She laughed again.

"The magic lingered," Desdemona said. "Wizard magic was used to drain her of blood. That magic remained within her. It had the reverse effect upon her blood's return. It enhanced the blood's power to heal both of you."

Jason frowned. "So it wasn't…us."

"No, boy. It was the young wizard. He was undone by his own action. Thou might even say, his pride slew him." She smiled. "And people say there is no justice in this world."

The two Vigiles stood before their prisoners. Then with a firm word…

"*Śilaŭrudu*"

…the five of them vanished.

Chapter 34

It was four in the morning when the police finally settled every Hunter in a cell. Captain Kader ordered the squad to rest, then return again at ten. Everyone walked to their cars and drove home without another word.

Except Jason, whose apartment had been set on fire. He was considering if he should ask Silvana if he could stay at her place, when he accidently fell asleep in his car, in the parking lot of the police station.

He woke up several hours later with Captain Kader tapping on his window. She had just picked up several trays of coffee and croissants for the team. He helped her carry a tray inside and slowly sipped his coffee as the other officers returned.

"There's a lot of paperwork to get done, today," Kader told the four officers when they'd assembled. "We can only hold these guys for twenty-four hours without charges, so we'll need to process all of these people by tonight. I need to know who we can charge for a crime and who we can let go. But we can't afford to slip up because of time restraints. I don't want any murderers being released today. We've got to get this right."

"Yes ma'am," they chorused, and got to work.

Jason spent the morning taking more statements and writing

reports. He listened to the frantic ramblings of each Monster Hunter and tried his best to remain impartial. It was tedious and frustrating, and he was tired. Though all the officers felt the same. In a way, it was gratifying to be included once more as an officer, not a suspect. The others looked at Jason with respect again. Still, it was a relief when the captain called him into her office.

"Rookie," Kader said in greeting. "Grab a seat."

He did. "Hi captain. I suppose you want to talk about what we saw last night."

"We'll get to that," she said, then paused to shake her head in disbelief. "First, I have a forensics report here. Remember last night, when you did a trip to the station to drop off perps?" he nodded. "Lynch and I used that time to do a report on the basement. We found a body there."

He blinked. "Oh."

"We found a sword in its head. And we found your gun beside it." She opened the manila file on her desk. "The deceased was one Peter Erikson. Friend and roommate of yours. Also a suspect in several incidents of violent crime." She held up a sheet with Peter's face, and a fingerprint image. "We found his fingerprints on your gun. The same gun that was used to kill Alex Bishop and Richard Anderson."

Jason thought he knew where she was going with this. "What do you think that means?"

She eyed him. "Reports seem to suggest that Peter Erikson used your weapon to murder two people, and was preparing to murder a third, when someone killed him with a sword. Does that sound correct to you?"

He stammered for a moment. *There's gaps in that story. Should I tell her the truth?* He didn't hesitate long.

"That's incorrect, ma'am. The truth is the gun was almost out of bullets by the time Peter held it. And Peter only touched the gun last night. The timing doesn't quite line up."

She let out a long breath. "I admire your integrity, officer. Still, I haven't found any evidence to support your claims. Those…women took his body before we could finish the investigation. Therefore, as things stand, the detectives and myself are willing to lay blame for these murders solely on Mr Erikson, and credit you for stopping him before he could murder again. Is that, more or less, the truth?"

He shrugged. "Well, yes. I mean, he didn't use the gun."

"Magic, then?"

He blinked at her. "Captain?"

"I know what I saw, last night. Something supernatural. Paranormal. Whatever you're involved in, rookie, it goes beyond what would be considered in a court of law. I can't report that Mr Erikson murdered someone with magic. But if that's what actually happened, then I'm willing to stretch the details if it means justice is done."

She leaned forward in her desk. "Officially, I'll be writing that Mr Erikson used his connection with you to steal your weapon and commit murder, and that you exonerated yourself by stopping him. I'll even put your name down for a commendation."

He nodded. "And…unofficially?"

"I believe you knew there was something supernatural going on the whole time, and you couldn't tell us. Hence why you were acting suspiciously over the last few days. I believe you did everything you could to follow the law and uphold its principles."

Jason blushed and ran his hand through his hair. "Well…yes. That is the truth. Thank you, captain."

She waved his thanks away. "I want you to write a report that's completely off the record. Include everything, believable or not. Magic, monsters, exactly as they happened. I want the truth. Spare no detail."

"So anything to do with Immortals?" She nodded. "Ok. Though if you don't mind me saying so, you seem pretty accepting of all this."

She shrugged. "I used to believe in supernatural things. Not magic exactly, more religious. But in a weird way, this kind of makes sense to me."

"I understand."

"Now, rookie," she cupped her hands together, and her tone grew sombre. "It looks like you had to use lethal force last night."

Jason went quiet for a while. The captain sat there in silence until he responded. "I had to. He was going to murder us all."

"Then you did the right thing. You know that, right?"

"Objectively, yes. I know. But it still feels wrong." She didn't say anything, letting him process things at his rate. "It's just, I never wanted to be a violent man."

"Hold on," she said. "You're thinking about this the wrong way. You're calling it violence. A better way to describe it is 'action'. You took action. Just like, if you don't mind me saying, your father took action. The difference is his action was evil, and yours was good. In that sense, what you did was completely different. His actions took lives. Your actions saved them."

Jason nodded. "It still feels gross."

"Good. You should only be worried when it stops feeling gross and starts feeling good." She smiled. "I'm proud of you, rookie. You're becoming a better cop."

Jason tried to smile back, but his throat threatened to close up with emotion. He looked away and forced out a cough. "Thank you," he whispered.

"You're welcome."

He had to take a few breaths to settle the wave of feelings. "Captain, can I ask, what happened to you last night? That telepath was making you relive something."

She held up a hand to cut him off. "I'm not talking about that yet."

"Oh. Sorry if I overstepped, captain."

"That's all right. Just so you know, I'm fine. Really. I'm just not talking to *you* about it. I've already got a therapy session booked." She smiled playfully, and he smiled back. "You're dismissed." Jason stood up and turned to leave. "Jason," she said.

He noted the change in formality. "Yes, Aisha?"

She offered him another smile. "I heard a report from the fire department. Your apartment burnt down and they're waiting for us to investigate."

"Yeah. Peter blew it up."

"Do you have somewhere to stay? Do you need anything?"

Jason gave a contented sigh. His captain was looking out for him, and it felt great. "I need to talk with Silvana first. She might have room for me."

"Yes, about that girl. Are you in love with her?"

"Yeah." He startled himself. The answer had come straight out, no hesitation. He meant it too.

"Good. Because you'll have to be," Kader said. "Whatever she's involved in, you can expect more of what we've seen so far. You best be cautious. And keep an open report on everything that happens."

"Off the record?"

"Naturally."

He smiled. "I'll get started on the Immortal investigation right away, captain."

"Good. That said," Kader paused, as if weighing her words. "Good relationships aren't really that common, no matter what Hollywood tells us. People who actually love each other are rare. I would hate to see you throw that away, just because her life is…weird."

Jason considered her words. He needed time to process them, so he just said, "Thank you," and left the office.

Outside, he noticed Douglas sitting at his desk, staring at the screen with vacant eyes. Jason moved to sit next to the older officer. "Hey big guy. You doing alright?"

Douglas just shook his head, eyes still staring ahead blankly. "Man, I have seen some *shit*."

Jason patted him on the arm. "It's ok, buddy. I've seen it too."

"I just…" he groaned and finally looked at Jason. "This all started with us chasing bikers. I liked that. Now any second, things could turn into a gunfight. With fucking magic fire." He shuddered. "Ugh!"

"How's the family?" Jason asked to distract him.

Douglas seemed to relax. "Good. They got a bit of a scare when I left late last night. And when I didn't get home till four in the morning… oh! Hey guess what?" He slapped Jason on the arm and gave his trademark goofy grin. "Good news. My daughter, Tracey. She finally did it."

"Did what?"

"She came out to me! This morning."

Jason was tired and a bit slow to put it together. "Oh, right. That's great!"

"Yeah. Although I buggered it up, just like I knew I would. See, she was scared last night when I left. She thought I was gonna get shot and she'd never get the chance to tell me something so important to her. So first thing when I walk through the door at four in the morning, she tells me. And I was so tired I was basically drunk. She goes, "Dad, I'm…" and I cut her off too soon and started shouting that I accepted her and I loved her very much. She cried and gave me a hug, and I thought that was that. It was only later when I went to sleep that I realised, I didn't actually hear what she was."

"Oh dear."

"Yeah. So when I woke up, I gave her a hug and said, 'there's my favourite gay daughter'."

"Douglas, mate…"

"Yeah. Turns out she's not gay. She's trans."

"Ah."

"And I immediately called her daughter, which was apparently the wrong thing to do."

Jason couldn't help laughing.

"I just really wanted to support her! And it took me five minutes to screw up. I don't even know what trans means!"

"Well for one, you've been calling Tracey 'her' and 'she' this whole time. You might need to use 'they/them'. Or if Tracey is a trans man, use 'he/him'."

"See, I didn't know that." Douglas buried his face in his hands. "I'm such a shit dad. Maybe I should buy her flowers or something." He sat upright. "*Them.* I should buy *them* flowers, oh god."

"Relax, buddy. You're a great dad. Cause you're trying your best." He patted Douglas on the arm. "Besides, I can help you do some research. Did Tracey say what type of trans they are?"

"What? There's different *types*?" Douglas groaned.

The rest of the day passed in a blur of work, coffee, and mental fatigue. He saw Lynch and Cole coming in and out several times, looking just as tired as the rest of them. Each detective offered him a friendly nod when they walked past. Jason knew that was all the catharsis he was likely to get from the detectives. But it was enough.

The Monster Hunters, for the most part, were scared by what they had seen. They were all too eager to dob in their friends and fully cooperate. Jason began to suspect that the Monster Hunter group would cease to exist after this. *At least the Plymouth branch.*

However, their leader, Timothy Harrison, remained outspoken against the police and Silvana's family. "You're protecting the monsters that feed on our children!" Timothy still yelled, even with his neck fully bandaged. "You should have helped us kill them." Unfortunately, a few other Hunters seemed to agree with him. Including the ones who had fought to the last.

"We can't let them go," Douglas pleaded with the captain. "These are the ones who were firing on us."

"We don't have enough evidence," the captain argued. "It was dark, and a lot of bullets were fired. We can't prove they aimed at us. Best we can do is hold them for a few days. At least now, they have a record. It'll make them stand out if they ever offend again."

Douglas wasn't the only one complaining, but the captain was right. At the end of the day, all but four of the Hunters were released. The remaining four would be held up to seventy two hours under suspicion, then be released as well.

Still, Jason wasn't too worried. His squad was alive. And they trusted him again. He joined Martin and Wilson at lunch and had a friendly chat about mundane life. Douglas's mood kept improving over the course of the day. And Jason had his captain's approval. This was the best-case scenario for them.

* * *

Jason drove back out to the mansion later that evening, after using the showers at work and running a few quick errands. He knocked on the front door and a second later, Silvana appeared wearing a wonder woman t-shirt over short shorts. She leapt into his arms and kissed him firm on the mouth, right there in the middle of the doorway.

"Whoa…" he mumbled.

She rested her face against his chest and squeezed him tight. Her body was cold but her touch was warm nonetheless. Jason held her in silence. His tiredness seemed to fade. His body began to respond to hers being pressed against him.

"I've been thinking about you all day," she said. "Driving me crazy, in fact."

"I know what you mean."

Silvana clutched at his shirt and stared him in the eye. "We've got to finish what we started."

"Oh? *OH!*" He checked over her shoulder. No one was there, but he still lowered his voice to a whisper, "Right now?"

"Aunt Lisbeth is serving dinner in thirty minutes. Which means we've got exactly that long until we need to be at the table."

She clutched his hand in hers and dragged him through the front door.

"Hang on," he said as she led him up the staircase to the second floor. "Are you sure about this? Last time, you said your family would get angry if they knew. Immortals don't do sex before marriage."

"Yeah, but those rules suck," she said. "The rules also said you couldn't give me blood and save my life. Thank God you ignored them." She spun around. "That was stupid. I can't believe how stupid that was."

"You were standing up for your beliefs. You showed integrity."

"I was willing to die to avoid breaking a rule!" She snapped, and broke off. Her next words where much softer. "I thought I was honouring my family. But I realised, I'm just doing everything the way someone else expects. I'm living my life entirely to please others. Just this once, I want something for myself." She blushed. "Is that…ok with you?"

He laughed. "I am ok with it. But are…"

"Good," she cut in, a sly grin on her face as she dragged him into the nearest doorway. It was a bedroom, filled with movie posters and bookshelves of comic books. In the centre was a four-poster bed with white sheets strung across the upper frame.

"Is this…your room?"

"What gave it away?"

"The Spiderman poster."

She blushed as she locked the door behind her. "Is that going to be…off-putting?"

"Only if I get distracted looking at Tom Holland."

Silvana gave a bright laugh. She wrapped her arms around his neck and kissed him. Her lips were soft and just a little wet. She tasted like red wine.

Then she was grabbing at his shirt and pulling it over his head. Jason helped her get it off. But it wasn't enough. Immediately she was clutching at his belt buckle. *Oh wow.* From there, Jason lost track of everything except the pressing need to be with her. To touch her, feel her, and be as close to her as possible. And he had to get these bloody clothes out of the way. He pulled off her shirt in the same way and cupped each breast in his hands. His thumbs pressed into her small, pink nipples, and began to squeeze.

"Jason," she breathed.

"Yeah?"

"Can you…um…do that thing with your mouth?"

He couldn't help laughing at her. "You can just say oral. It's fine."

"It's weird to ask! It's so direct."

In answer, he grabbed her ass and lifted her off the ground before laying her in the centre of the bed. He slid her shorts down her legs. Then he began to use his lips. And his tongue.

She stayed perfectly quiet, even as she constantly squirmed underneath him. Her hands grasped the back of his head. Her back arced high and her mouth was wide open. Jason was desperate to move on and feel his own pleasure, but he forced himself to be patient. He kept going for as long as she wanted. At last she pulled him forward, and he was all too happy to oblige. She shuffled further up onto the bed as Jason climbed straight on top of her.

"Do you want to use a condom?" she asked.

He paused to think about it. "No," he said.

"You sure? I don't mind, Jason. I want you to be comfortable."

"I am comfortable with you."

So she guided him forward, and he gently entered her. He waited a few moments for her to adjust. Then he began to move at a steady rhythm.

Jason lay propped up on his elbows, their bodies pressed against each other, moving together. She clutched at his shoulders and gasped into his ear repeatedly. They both wanted the same thing. The nearness of sex, more than the pleasure itself. At least, initially. But soon her gasps were getting louder, and the sounds of her pleasure was driving him wild. *I can't go first.* He sat up slightly and pressed his thumb against her, just above the point of their contact. He stroked her softly in time with each thrust and she let out a full-voiced *moan* that sounded so good that he couldn't help spilling himself inside her in the full ecstasy of release.

But he didn't slow down for a single second. He squeezed his eyes shut and focused on keeping up the rhythm.

"Did you finish?" she asked.

He shook his head. "I want to keep going."

She opened her mouth to say something, and another moan came out instead. He kept moving his hips and rubbing with his thumb, pushing through his own discomfort, gritting his teeth to focus him. *I want her to enjoy this. She deserves to enjoy this.*

And with a gasp, she released too. Her pelvis thrust down, her back arced upwards, and she clutched at the sheets with eyes and mouth opened wide. She held that position for a long time before she slumped back against the bed.

Jason withdrew, and knelt on the bed in front of her, catching his breath, and staring at her slender form. She stared back at him. Neither spoke. Then she reached out her hand, and he clutched it, their fingers entwined. She smiled softly at him. He smiled back.

A bang came from the bedroom door, making them both flinch.

"Silvana?" Emberline's voice called. "Will you be joining us for dinner?"

"Yes, Aunty," she called, her tone implying that was obvious.

"Then come join us. Dinner is ready early, and you don't want to risk being alone together."

Jason's jaw dropped in disbelief. Silvana offered him a helpless shrug. "Ok Aunty. We'll be right there."

They climbed off the bed. Silvana passed Jason some tissues to help clean up, before they slipped back into their pants and shirts, watching each other the whole time and blushing. They each stepped into her ensuite and washed with water from the hand basin, both needing to straighten their mussed hair. Within a minute, they were ready. Silvana opened the bedroom door.

Emberline was standing directly in the doorway, arms crossed, face flat.

"Is that what you're wearing?" she asked.

"Yes, Aunty," Silvana said, standing with her hands on her hips and tilting to accentuate her shorts.

Emberline sneered, "You shouldn't be behind closed doors."

Jason could only stare at her. *Is she serious?*

"We've just been talking," Silvana said in a pleasant tone. Jason could see her clutching her hands into fists.

"You can talk in the dining room with the rest of us," Emberline said.

She eyed Jason a moment, then walked away with the clear expectation that the two would follow.

Chapter 35

Jason had not seen the family dining room before. A long, mahogany table had seats for twenty people. The four members of Silvana's family were sitting and waiting all bunched together on one end. Old golden candlesticks were lit with white wax candles. Silver platters and cutlery lined the table, paired with goblets of bronze. Both of Silvana's aunts wore long formal ballgowns, and they eyed Silvana's shorts with open disapproval.

"Ah, Jason," Nicholas called, sitting at the head of the table. He was wearing tracksuit pants and a cotton jumper. His arm was in a sling underneath. "Glad you could make it. We have something to discuss with you."

Jason squeezed Silvana's hand. She guided him to their chairs, side by side. Everyone was silent as they waited for them to get seated. He couldn't help noticing their positions. Nicholas at the head, Emberline and Phillip on his left, Lisbeth and Silvana on his right. And Jason stuck out just one seat too far.

"Let us begin," Nicholas said, taking Lisbeth and Emberline by the hand. Everyone else linked hands. For a moment, Jason looked across the table to Phillip. *Please don't reach for me. Please...Phillip stayed still. Thank God.*

"Thank you Lord," Nicholas prayed, echoing Jason's thoughts, "for our meal, our home, and for your protection. Thank you most of all for our family, and our new son, Jason. Amen."

Jason's mouth dropped open and stayed there. *Son. He called me son.* Nicholas grinned at him and gave a knowing nod, as if he had used that word very deliberately. Jason smiled back in disbelief. It would take him a while to get used to that thought, being someone's son again.

"Welcome to the family, Jason," Nicholas said.

All Jason could say was, "Thank you."

Phillip started serving food onto his plate, breaking the ice. Jason inspected the dishes. There were loaves of mini bread rolls that gave off hot steam when pulled open, a bowl of salad, and a smoking dish filled with slices of roast beef that smelled of flame and rosemary. *Red meat,* Jason noted. The knights were probably still trying to replace the iron in the blood from the night before. Jason helped himself to a bit of everything.

"So Jason," Lisbeth said in a sweet tone, "how was everything at the police station today?"

"Yeah, very busy. Lots of reports to write up. You'll be happy to hear every single Monster Hunter now has a criminal record. Not many are getting charged, though."

"And your comrades," Nicholas said. "Are you back in their good graces?"

"Oh, yeah. We've sorted it out."

"That's good," Nicholas said, and went silent.

Jason took a mouthful of beef and chewed it with enthusiasm. It was soft and tender, easy to chew probably for Nicholas's benefit, though Jason kept that thought to himself. He noticed a few of them were watching him.

"Oh, thank you for this food. It's really good," he said. No one said anything in reply. Phillip was death-staring him hard. The others were casting furtive glances. "So, uh…is something wrong? You just all seem to be looking at me. Do I have gravy on my chin?"

"The proposal," Phillip snapped. "Beardsplitter, we're all waiting for your answer to the proposal."

"Oh."

"How can you be so blind?" Emberline asked. "Jason, you're a fine warrior and a brave man. But you're undisciplined. I don't know if you've been single too long, or if you just don't know how family's work—"

"All right…"

"But the fact that you have the audacity to come into our house and try to seduce our daughter in her bedroom…"

"Aunty!"

"Good Lord, Emberline."

"…tells me that you're just not interested in commitment." Emberline inhaled sharply, ignoring the look of outrage on Silvana's face. "Well, our daughter's well-being is of paramount importance to us. She doesn't need a boyfriend. She needs a husband."

"Aunty, can you please not—"

"Don't start, Silvana," Phillip cut in. "You've already acted foolishly by going on dates to his home without a chaperone. If you sleep with him prematurely, you'll be lucky if he sticks around for the next week."

"Excuse me," Jason growled.

"Everyone," Nicholas said, and the table went silent at his gentle word. He turned to face Silvana and Jason. "No one is doubting your courage or your character, Jason. But we've already been too lenient with you. If you were from an Immortal family, you might have been married within the same day as *meeting* Silvana. Since you're unfamiliar with our customs, we've tried to be patient. But it's at a point now where this simply cannot go on any longer. We need a definitive answer from you." He shrugged and clasped his hands together. "What shall it be?"

Jason's mind was filled with dozens of thoughts. He felt a rising anger in his chest, and he worried that if he started speaking, he might say something he'd regret. He just hated how they kept talking down to Silvana. He knew they were trying to protect her, but they were coddling her. And he especially didn't like that they were checking up on her sex life.

Yet at the same time, Jason hadn't belonged to a family for over twelve years. He'd only had temporary families. Even before that, living under his father's tyranny was not exactly a normal family either. Maybe this was what a real family looked like. Maybe he had no idea what was normal, and he shouldn't be so critical of them.

He turned to Silvana, and reached into his pocket.

"Silvana," he said as he pulled out the small, velvet blue case he had picked up earlier that afternoon. His hands were shaking as he opened it. Inside was a plain silver ring. No diamonds, or jewels of any kind, just a simple white band. *It's more symbolic anyway.* He pushed his chair back and knelt on one knee before her. His heart was pounding in his chest so hard that it was hard to speak without his voice shaking.

"Will you marry me?"

Silvana's mouth dropped open. "Jason?" she cried. "Are you serious?"

He nodded. "I was wrong. When I said I didn't want to marry. I was just afraid I would turn out like my father. But I realised something last night." He offered her a smile. "I'm never going to be my father. Action can be used for good or evil, just like marriage. It's whatever we make of it. So I'm willing to do everything I can to give you the best husband you could ever ask for. It's what you deserve."

"How romantic," Phillip drawled.

Silvana reached forward and clutched at his hands. "Jason," she whispered. "Are you just doing this because…" she looked askew at her family.

"No. I already had the ring with me when I arrived. I was gonna propose the moment I saw you in the doorway, but…" he smiled, and she blushed. "I'm serious, Silvana. This is my choice. I want this. I want to be with you."

"Wonderful!" Lisbeth cheered, and all four members of the family began to applaud. Lisbeth gave a happy cry and clutched her hands to her chest.

"Thank you, Jason," Nicholas said. "You don't know what a relief that is to us."

"Well done, boy," Phillip said, a genuine smile on his face.

Even Emberline had a quiet look of satisfaction.

"And you know what this means?" Nicholas said, now looking like an excited teenager. "We can begin our apprenticeship! Your training will begin at once."

"Training?" Jason asked, looking between the old man and Silvana.

"Of course. To become a Knight Templar," Nicholas said, puffing his chest out proudly. "I will train you myself. You'll learn swordplay, chivalry, and all the court customs that comes with being an Immortal family member. This is a real honour. You'll be able to claim rights within the Imperium."

"Oh…" Jason stammered.

"But you'll have to call me master," Nicholas said with a sombre expression. "And I'll push you hard to perform. After all, if you're going to inherit my title…" he raised his eyebrows.

"Oh…" Jason said again.

"We'll worry about that tomorrow," Emberline said. "Right now, we can officiate the…"

Jason ignored them for a moment and looked to Silvana, who had a strange expression on her face. She was decidedly not as happy as

Jason had expected. He leaned closer to her and whispered. "Silvana? Are you ok?"

Her eyes darted up to meet his, and something dawned in her features.

"I don't want to get married," she whispered.

Lisbeth gave a laugh. "What was that, my dear?"

Silvana stood up suddenly, banging the table and knocking her chair to the ground. The sudden noise made everyone fall silent. She looked at her family, then declared in a loud voice, "I don't want to get married!"

The room fell silent for only second. Then everyone spoke at once.

"Don't be ridiculous, child," Emberline said, waving her hand in casual dismissal. "It's the law. You cannot have blood until you are married."

"The Vigiles are already watching us," Phillip said. "If you break another law, they can seize our property."

"You already proposed to him twice!" Lisbeth cried.

Jason was silent. A faint smile was growing across his face. Silvana was holding her shoulders up near her ears with tension. But her fists were clenched, and her nostrils flaring.

"Listen, child," Phillip growled, standing up from the table to stare down Silvana. "You've already endangered this family enough. You need to do your duty. Accept the ring and don't be so stubborn—"

"Shut up, Phillip!" Silvana screamed, the sudden increase in volume making everyone jump. "I am thirty-five years older than you. Do NOT speak to me like I'm a child!"

Jason couldn't help it. He started laughing.

Emberline stood up from the table. "How dare you speak to him like that," she hissed. "He is my husband, and you will not be so disrespectful in our home."

"I have done everything you've ever asked of me," Silvana snapped.

"All I've ever done has been for this family. And it has made me miserable." She pointed at Emberline. "You pressured me to marry Arthur. He was a spoilt teenage boy at the time, and I was still distraught over losing Henry. But I made a major life decision before I was ready, just to make you happy. Then I spent fifty-seven years married to a man who treated me like a maid-servant."

Jason blinked. *Henry?*

Then it occurred to him. Silvana was ninety-one. She'd been married to Arthur for fifty-seven years. So of course there was a husband before that. *She probably married Arthur within a week of losing her first husband. My god...*

"Do you know how awful Arthur was? He used to slap me in the face all the time, often for no reason."

"Silvana," Emberline said, "you were three times his strength. It couldn't have done any damage."

Jason nearly screamed at her, but Silvana got there first. "It was *humiliating!* It was degrading! And if I wasn't a vampire with three times his strength, I know he would have beaten me much worse than that."

"Silvy!" Lisbeth cried. "Honey, we didn't know."

"Yes, you did!" Silvana snapped and pointed a stern finger all around the table at each of them. "You all knew I was miserable with Arthur. All of you knew. That's why you kept Arthur away from me whenever you could. You distracted him and ran interference. But you wouldn't let me divorce him. No matter how much I wanted to."

"Divorce is dangerous!" Emberline growled. "It splits up titles and lands, and makes enemies..."

"I don't care! You were all willing to turn a blind eye to my abuse. And now you think you can tell me what to do and who to marry. Well you know what? You all forfeited that right." She pointed at Jason. "Jason has always treated me with respect. He speaks to me like I'm his equal. He encourages me and compliments me. And you know what?" She stood up even straighter. "We just had sex!"

"What?!" Emberline roared.

Silvana snarled, "And it was better than anything Arthur managed in half a century!"

"Oh my god," Phillip groaned, burying his face in his hands.

Jason couldn't help it. He laughed again.

"So no. I don't want to get married. Because I want to make my own decisions." She held her head high. "I hope you can respect me enough to accept that."

"What about the blood?" Lisbeth asked. "Honey, you're not thinking straight. You still need marriage to get blood."

"Jason was willing to give me blood even before we were married. Is that still true?"

"Absolutely!" Jason said, still grinning.

"Then I accept."

Emberline cried, "You'd be breaking Imperium law."

"They won't know," Silvana said.

Phillip threw up his hands and shouted, "You need marriage! It is how you show that you're committed to each other and to this family."

"Jason's already shown his commitment," Silvana said. "He fought for all of us. He was willing to die for me. And he just proved that he's ready to marry. He looks committed to me. And as for myself, well, I spent fifty-seven years in a miserable marriage, sharing my bed and my body with a man who had no respect for me. I've proven my devotion to this family a thousand times over. I owe you nothing more."

Emberline growled, "You don't know what you're doing. If the Imperium finds out you're accepting blood without marriage, they could execute you."

"Fine. I'd rather die free than live in chains."

The table went silent. Silvana took Jason by the hand and pulled him into a firm hug. He gave her a fierce squeeze. "I am so proud of you," he whispered.

"I don't give my approval to this," Phillip said.

"Me neither," Emberline echoed. But no one else chimed in. "Nicholas?" Emberline cried. "Surely you condemn this. If you remain silent, you condone their breaking of Imperium law."

Nicholas was scratching the stubble on his wrinkled chin. "Jason," he whispered, "are you still willing to become a Knight Templar?"

Jason shrugged. "Sure."

"Well," Nicholas grinned, "I see no other problem." Jason burst out laughing again.

Meanwhile, Phillip banged the table with his fist as he stood up and left the room without a word. Emberline silently followed him, her skirts sliding across the carpet with sharp swishing noises. Jason remembered how fast she had moved the previous night during the fight and how ruthlessly she had sliced Rion's arm off. *It's no victory when I've angered her. I need to be careful.*

Silvana picked her chair off the floor and slumped back down in it with a sigh. She looked exhausted after standing up to her family. Jason sat down next to her and held her hand.

"I didn't realise you'd been married twice," he blurted out. "I should have figured it out though."

Silvana nodded. "I should have told you. It's just…" she went quiet for a few moments. "Henry and I were married for eighteen years. He was a good man. Just…a little too formal. Not very romantic." She gave a sad smile. "He died of a heart attack. It was very sudden and I was completely unprepared. But I had to put on a brave face. Get remarried within a matter of days. And Arthur…he had no time for my emotions. It was always about my behaviour, with him, making sure I acted the way he wanted. So I put on a mask to hide my grief, and just never took it off again." She squeezed her eyes shut, and a single tear fell from each eye. "I never grieved for Henry. I never got the chance."

"Honey, I'm sorry," Lisbeth said, taking Silvana's hand in her own. "We shouldn't have pressured you, all those years ago. We were just so worried. We thought you would be safe if you were married again."

Nicholas spoke in a grave voice. "We were all shocked by Henry's death. We all acted rashly, from the grief. I'm sorry, Silvana. I was only a young man then, but it was still my duty as a Knight to protect you. I was blind…" he covered his face with his hands.

"It's ok," Silvana said softly. "I'm not angry. I just don't want to go through that again. I'm going to take some time to…just be myself."

"You take all the time you need, sweetie," Lisbeth said.

"The Imperium won't find out," Nicholas added. "We'll protect you properly this time. I promise."

"Silvana," Jason whispered as he leaned on her armrest and came in close. "Are you sure this is what you want? You're not just doing this for me?"

She nodded. "I'm sure. It still means a lot to me that you proposed. I know how much trust that took for you." She took one of his hands and squeezed. "I still want to marry you. Really. Just not yet. Is that ok?"

"You bet it is," he said.

She kissed him right on the mouth. She turned to her aunt and uncle, and announced, "Jason's going to be staying the night. And many other nights too. Is that going to be a problem?"

Nicholas and Lisbeth exchanged a glance, trapped between their discomfort and trying to show support. At last they shrugged. "As long as you're happy," Lisbeth said with obvious reluctance. Nicholas gave a grimace but said nothing.

Silvana looked at Jason, a glimmer in her eye.

"This is the happiest I've ever been," she whispered.

Jason picked up the case with the engagement ring. He closed the lid and put it back in his pocket.

"Me too," he said.

Epilogue

The Vigile Desdemona stood in the cell doorway, dressed in her black tuxedo. Inside, a formerly empowered vampire was now a grovelling mess, like a worthless piece of meat that was already rotting. She held the door wide open beside her, as if daring the prisoner to try escaping.

"I don't know anything else," cried Rion Danksworth from where he lay slunk in the corner. "Please, I need blood!"

"Thou hast devoured blood sufficient already," she answered. "Thou hath drained seven mortals of all the blood they had. It should have sufficed for the next two years of thy rations."

Rion was weeping. "I'm sorry. Please! Just let me see Gerald!"

"Beg me once more, and thou shalt experience the limit of my patience." The boy fell silent.

"Mistress," Portia whispered in her ear from out in the hallway. "He doesn't know anything. Let's leave him and get back to our investigation."

"He knows," Desdemona said calmly. "Of course he knows. But foolishly, he thinks he should fear his conspirators more than he fears us." She tucked a long strand of braided hair back behind her ear. "Perhaps we should show him how wrong that is and inflict the..." she trailed off and let a slow smile creep over her face, "...necessary motivation."

"Do whatever you want to me! I've already told you everything."

"Not to thee," she answer. "To thy love."

Rion's eyes widened. "Please. Don't hurt Gerald. Oh God, we just went along with Peter's plan!" He was screaming now. "Peter was the one who knew everything. He had the contacts!"

"How unfortunate for thy friend," Desdemona said, turning around to leave. "With such a want for information, we shall be forced to question the metamorph."

"No! I…I…"

"Farewell, vampire-"

"*Yamato!*" he screamed. "I heard the name Yamato."

Desdemona paused in the hallway, just past the door. "Is that it? We already knew of Yamato's connection…"

"Al Khalifa," the vampire said, his voice now a whimper. "And Glücksburg. That's everything. I just heard those three names. I don't know…what else Peter was planning."

Desdemona turned to Portia and couldn't resist gloating. "What was thou saying? He doesn't know anything?"

"I bow to your wisdom," Portia drawled. Then added a respectful, "Mistress." Desdemona couldn't help smirking.

"What about Gerald?" Rion cried. "I told you everything. You'll leave him alone, right? You won't hurt him?"

Desdemona glanced at the vampire. Then she sent out a mental push and slammed the door shut without answering. She had no need to hurt the metamorph now. But why share that information?

"That's five houses now," Portia said, her voice echoing through the prison hallway as they walked away from the cell door. "You see the pattern, don't you?"

"Old houses, with diminished strength, and youthful fanatics with dreams of reclaiming that strength of old." Desdemona nodded to herself. "The Royalists are planning a takeover. I can feel it."

"I feel it too, my love," Portia said. "Where to next?"

Desdemona clenched her fists. She gathered her mental fortitude and began to shape the fabric of the universe around her will.

"I want to investigate the vampire. Silvana. And her new husband, the mortal. Jason Turner. I want to find out what house they each came from originally."

"You suspect something?"

Desdemona nodded. "One of them is connected to this conspiracy, somehow. One of them is planning something. I intend to find out which one, and why."

"Of course, Mistress."

She clutched Portia's hand, uttered the ancient words, and vanished.

* * *

The story continues in Book Two: The Mortal Knight

Acknowledgements

This book began life as a short story in 2015. It grew into a full drafted novel in 2021, and was 40% rewritten in 2024. As such, the acknowledgements are weird.

Thanks to my wife, Kit, who spent over six years telling me to turn the short story into a romantic comedy novel. You were half right.

To Sam, Nick, Peter, Anna, Nix, and Kit (again) for reading the messy 2021 version and giving damn good suggestions. Each one of you shaped the story in a positive way.

To Kirsty Inic, my brilliant editor, who had a LOT to fix with this book and challenged me to step up my writing game. If it looks professional now, that was largely her doing.

To Wouter K, a patron supporter and good friend, who voluntarily read an early version of this book and caught more typos than I care to admit. He was then roped into proofreading all future books. You know what they say about no good deed. My deepest thanks.

To Michael R Miller, author of Songs of Chaos, for invaluable advice and coaching on Indie publishing, and for his genuine friendship.

To every member of the YouTube community who supported my

channel, The Book Guy, and supported the Kickstarter launch. Special thanks to Elliot Brooks, John from Talking Story, and Daniel Greene. You know what you did.

Finally, to Kit (again, again). For managing so many behind the scenes jobs, such as the cover design, the entire Kickstarter process, book formatting, website design, setting up multiple author accounts, and probably more that I'm forgetting. But most of all, thank you for reminding me to write the acknowledgements.

About the Author

Michael Cronk is an independent author from Brisbane, Australia.

He has a special love for fantasy stories and can often be found trying to convince random strangers to read The Wheel of Time. Or Discworld. Or anything by Robin Hobb. Or… well, you get the idea.

Michael is passionate about encouraging others to read on his popular YouTube Channel, The Book Guy. He firmly believes that reading has the power to change our lives - and the world - for the better. With that in mind, this debut series is written to be easy and enjoyable for both voracious readers and those who haven't read in a while.

When he's not reading or writing (or having nightmares about endless editing), Michael enjoys playing all sorts of music from heavy metal to classical on his many instruments. Much to the delight of his cats and neighbours.

You can connect with me on:
- https://michaelcronk.com
- https://www.youtube.com/@cronkthebookguy

Also by Michael Cronk

The Immortal Investigations is an urban fantasy series full of magic, monsters, and mystery. With thrilling action, romance, and twists, this book is a must-read for urban fantasy lovers.

The Mortal Knight (Immortal Investigations #2)

Silvana's family has been invited to a gala for the rich and powerful Immortal Houses that rule from the shadows. Silvana knows this is her chance to make allies and save her dying House from fading into ruin. But the Immortal world is a ruthless, cutthroat society that preys on the naïve and gullible. Her family is weak, and the vampires smell blood in the water...

A King In Waiting (Immortal Investigations #3)

In the middle of the night, a hooded stranger arrives on Jason's doorstep begging for help, with a terrifying assassin close on their heels. The stranger is a witch named Leslie Toussaint, and they need Jason's detective skills to find out *who* sent the assassin...